KT-381-456

KCola

This item is to be returned or renewed before the latest date above. It may be borrowed for a further period if not in demand. **To renew your books:**

- **Phone the 24/7 Renewal Line 01926 499273 or**
- **Visit www.warwickshire.gov.uk/libraries**

Discover • Imagine • Learn • *with libraries*

Warwickshire
County Council

Working for Warwickshire

CHASING RACHEL

An urgent call brings Rachel Falconer, naturalist and TV presenter, to manage Kestrel House, her father's botanical research institute on Dartmoor. There she meets Michael, her old rival and now a respected archaeologist; the hostile Daniel, once her colleague and lover; the truculent forester Colin; and Leo, computer wizard and Don Juan.

As Rachel puts Kestrel House back on its feet, her past returns to haunt her. One phone call, made years ago in Brazil, has set off a devastating chain of events. On Dartmoor an unknown enemy is closing in – skilled in deceit and with an intimate knowledge of fire.

CHASING RACHEL

CHASING RACHEL

by

Lindsay Townsend

Magna Large Print Books
Long Preston, North Yorkshire,
BD23 4ND, England.

British Library Cataloguing in Publication Data.

Townsend, Lindsay
    Chasing Rachel.

    A catalogue record of this book is
    available from the British Library

    ISBN   0-7505-1619-4

First published in Great Britain by Robert Hale Ltd., 1999

Published in Large Print 2001 by arrangement with Robert Hale Ltd.

Magna Large Print is an imprint of Library Magna Books Ltd.

Printed and bound in Great Britain by
T.J. (International) Ltd., Cornwall, PL28 8RW

To my father, Gordon

Prologue

March, Helmsley, North Yorkshire

Legs drawn beneath her, Rachel relaxed into the sofa and reached for a chocolate mint.

The phone rang, displaying the number for Falconer Laboratories. Dad, calling from the research institute in Devon known more often by its older name, Kestrel House. She listened, smoothing a hand firmly over her hair. 'Have you talked to the police yet?' she asked finally.

'The police think I'm paranoid. No obvious damage. No sign of breached security. No witnesses. The incidents are occasional, but they're always enough to delay, to spoil. I'm convinced it's sabotage.'

Rachel stared at the South American flute pinned to the stone wall of her rented cottage. A fire fluttered in the grate. The sound she could hear in the dark outside was the swirl of snow. Yet her unease stung sharp.

'When did this start, Dad? Was it around the time Daniel Mason arrived to replace Dr Stamper? I did warn you against taking him on.'

'Much later: only in the last month or so. I know you don't care for him now, Rachel, but Daniel's not an obvious suspect. Our work is in different fields. I might add that the man has always been very civil to me.'

'Why not leave, let somebody else run the place?'

'I'm not going to be driven away. I'd like help. When you were in Brazil you fought this sort of thing and won.'

She had not won.

'You really got after them.'

Rachel rose from the sofa and touched the Indian flute hanging above the bare mantelpiece. The Amazonian woman who had given her this instrument had been murdered. Aoira had been killed in Rio.

Guilt, anger, painful memories. No change there. Rachel coldly laid into her father's enthusiasm. 'Circumstances were different. Certainly the cost was high. I'm not sure that, given a second chance, I'd do it again.'

'Not for the chance of running Kestrel House? I need a sabbatical.'

Rachel thought of the tors and stunted woods of Dartmoor, the cold streams, heather and rugged ponies. She knew what she could make of the post in her fight to preserve wild places. 'You don't have to step aside, Dad. Not for me to help.'

'With you as acting director, I'll be able to concentrate on my real work. I'll always be in the lab and greenhouse. Maybe then there'll be no more "accidents". Say you'll come, Rachel. I can't cope alone here for much longer.'

'Oh, I'll most definitely come. If someone is causing you trouble, I want to find out who and why.'

Rachel frowned. Her father was working on a

life-saving cure: a fully effective malaria vaccine derived from his work on plant genetics. Working as an ethnobotanist, she'd seen more than one life wrecked with malaria in the rain-forests of Brazil. Dad was right – if he uprooted himself now he would lose time. More would die.

'You be careful.' Rachel tapped the phone receiver. 'Very careful.'

'Naturally.' Paul suddenly became sanguine, as though he'd already deposited his worries onto his capable daughter's shoulders. 'Don't worry.'

'How can I not be worried?' Any successful vaccine for malaria could be worth millions in hard cash in a ruthless business.

'Think about being in charge, Rachel. Monarch of all you survey.'

Rachel laughed but, as she and her father said their goodbyes, she was thinking of Daniel. Her ex. Soon, if only for a year, she would be his boss.

This time round.

Chapter 1

After working out her notice at the North York Moors National Park, Rachel drove to Devon. Resigning for a year, Paul Falconer had told colleagues that the management of Kestrel House in addition to his research was too much. His daughter knew that was not the full story.

Powering her diesel estate along the M5, Rachel felt her persistent anxiety drop away. She was here. She could fight whatever – whoever – was plaguing her father. Born in Exeter, she had come home.

And Dad was in Parma, addressing a scientific conference.

Chuckling at his timing, she slackened speed. Why hurry? Kestrel House was closed for the weekend. It was a mellow April evening. She could revisit one of her favourite places. A walk there would clear her mind.

Rachel cruised the drumming road to Cullompton, leaving the motorway for the market town and an older highway. Passing Toad Hall hotel, she swung past hedgerows studded with primroses, slowing to watch a buzzard slide across the lemon sky. No snow here and the hawthorn out, dazzling fresh green. A day's journey and such a difference. Even the place names were lusher: '–clyst' endings everywhere, reminding Rachel of tryst. Secretive, like the spot she was looking for.

She remembered the steep, high-banked lane, turning as the low sun flared on a white road sign. Third gear dropped to second as she coaxed the diesel up a twisting tunnel of hedges, scenting ploughed earth and smoke through her open window. Soil, red as her hair, spilled down a sheer ditch near hunched thatched houses and then she was amongst trees.

Rachel turned off the single track road by a signpost for Hele and parked in a dirt clearing. Switching off, she opened the boot to change from shoes into wellingtons.

Roaring from the turning to Caddihoe, a motor-bike shot past, slowed and skidded round. Rachel hefted out the car toolbox as the biker buzzed by again; a teenager practising wheelies. She was looking for her botanical file. A cardboard box containing her cutlery had ruptured. The notebook was buried under a mound of domestic clutter.

Rachel grinned. 'I'll be picking teaspoons out of there for hours.' She thrust head and arms lower into the boot. The woods of Ashclyst, softly darkening, beckoned.

Silence warned, plus a sudden feeling of uncertainty she knew wasn't hers. Rachel was reminded of an incident that had taken place years before, off a wooded track in Brazil. Then common sense kicked in.

Picking up her notebook, she whirled about. 'I'm really not interested.'

She was diverted to find herself staring at a broad torso. It was unusual to find a man so

13

much taller than she was.

'Fine by me. I only stopped because of the toolbox. I thought you might have a flat.' Tension strained the faint Devonshire accent. 'Now unless you're going to lay into me simply for trying to help, I'll be on my way.'

Irritated by this masculine assumption of female helplessness in all things mechanical, Rachel examined the speaker's face – what little she could see under the blue helmet. 'Don't try to guilt me into gratitude. It's obvious from the way I'm parked that my car works.' Recovering her laid-back temper, Rachel couldn't resist a tease. 'If you wanted a different reception, why didn't you say something? Announce your presence?'

'Sorry! Shall I cough now?'

The funny side of their encounter tweaked Rachel's mouth but she said nothing to make it easier. This one was big enough to look after himself.

'I was about to introduce myself,' the biker continued, keeping body and hands absolutely still. 'I didn't mean to creep up behind, but I did want to approach downwind.'

Rachel automatically inhaled. The ripe smell gagged her throat, a reaction the stranger acknowledged by a wrinkling of his nose. At least, that was what he looked to be doing under the helmet.

'Work near drainage ditches can be an unsavoury business.' His head flicked downwards slightly. 'Look here, we've plainly set off on the wrong foot. Let's start again. I'll take off my helmet and–'

'No need. You're leaving.'

Faced with such sanguine indifference, the biker had no choice. He took a long step into the road, marking her with frowning, curious eyes, turned on his heel and strode away.

Rachel glanced at her watch and dropped the notebook back into the car. Too late now for Ashclyst. Regretfully, she returned to her driver's seat.

Before gunning out of the trees, the thought struck her that the stranger had spun his Norton round in the lane before she'd lifted out the toolbox. Something about her had caught his attention. Rachel shook her head. 'Men!' she said softly.

Chapter 2

Rumbling over a cattle grid and cresting a rise, Rachel gave a silent cheer. She was on the edge of moorland, overlooking whitewashed farms, woods and fields, with a view across higher moors. Seeing this sweeping landscape, she felt the shackles of her journey burst open.

Filled with enthusiasm, she thought of her father. Now on Dartmoor, should she keep on going to Kestrel House? She could grab another look at the institute, memorize its layout.

Torn between weariness and concern, Rachel hesitated. Time decided her. She'd settle in her new place tonight and leave Kestrel House for the morning, when she was always at her best.

Rachel floored the accelerator. If those trees ahead were what she thought they were, and where she thought they were...

When she'd rented the farmstead, no one had mentioned trees. Closing on the isolated granite cottage and its small orchard, Rachel could scarcely believe her luck. 'Oh, my word!'

Of all trees, she loved the pear's elegance, white blossom, many-varied fruits. She spun off the road into the grassy short drive. Using the biggest key from the padded envelope sent by her landlord, she dumped the diesel in the outhouse-turned-garage. Leaving the garage door hanging, Rachel ran into the orchard through a blue gate.

Surrounded by a mossy wall, the pears were protected from the prevailing wind by three huge beeches. Clambering over a fallen branch, Rachel traced a hand down the squared-off bark.

'Tree-hugger,' scoffed a voice in her mind: she remembered it from the past as Daniel's. Dismissing him, Rachel wove through tall grass and roses to examine the farmhouse. Two storeys, small windows, slate roof. She sidled down the dandelion and pebble path to the door with its wolfs-head knocker.

Inside she smelt damp, heard the hum of the fridge in the kitchen/sitting-room. On top of the dark wood table under a dingy jam-pan was a scrap of paper explaining the hot water system. Checking lights, then taps at the back-breakingly low porcelain sink, Rachel returned to the car.

Four staggering trips brought her stuff inside:

16

bright rugs and sofa throws, TV, radio, books, clothes from 'Long Tall Sally', carefully packed plants and botanical equipment, crammed-in pots, tissue-wrapped snippets of cloth for her quilting. And the pipes given to her by Aoira. The colourful healing-flute and a smaller, deadlier hunting-pipe she always kept hidden.

Keeping her head tucked, Rachel heaved pale blue bedding up the twisting narrow stairs into the master bedroom. Pastel wallpaper, sprigged with roses, new double bed and fresh-smelling oyster carpet – her landlord, Mr Collard, had done his best. Rachel sausaged her duvet on the bed then knelt at the dusty window to open the sash.

She ignored its reflection of her strong features, the warm, intelligent eyes mysteriously at odds with a faintly down-turned mouth – the natural expression of a sphinx, Rachel thought scornfully, when she considered it at all. She was concerned with useful matters.

Sturdy houses like these were never meant to lie idle. The place would most definitely do: cheap, near to her work, close to the moors and with that lovely pear orchard.

Him again. She drew back behind the veil of hanging folds. How on earth had he found her? What the blazes did he want? Recalling that she'd shut the garage and locked the front door, Rachel watched him coast and park the softly idling grey bike by the roadside. Swinging a rucksack off his back, cradling it over the garden gate, he stalked inside, long, stealing movements a blur against the blue-black sky.

Taller in the evening shadows, the stranger ranged up to the farmstead and clattered the knocker.

'Anybody there?'

Rachel heard his voice through the opened letter-box and frowned as the door rattled but held fast.

'Thought she'd be here by now.'

Who was he?

Someone who'd changed. As he backed up a step to lean under the lintel and peer in at the kitchen window, Rachel caught the tumble of an Arran sweater. Tan trousers covered the rest – nothing dark, nothing threatening.

When she'd visited Kestrel House last month, several of its members had been absent. Including a youthful rival she'd not seen since they were fourteen, when she and Mike Horton had been joint firsts in the same grammar-school class.

Staring down at the stranger crowding her doorstep, Rachel recalled that he'd been working near drainage ditches. Michael Horton at Kestrel House was an environmental archaeologist. Even so, was it possible?

Had that irritating, opinionated scruffbag grown so much?

Astonished at the idea, Rachel's lips formed his name without sound. Amused – if this was Mike, he'd failed to recognize her, too – she made a decision. Whoever he was, she needed to find out how this man knew her, why he'd called the day she'd moved down to Devon. What was so urgent? She banged her palms under the frame and the window shrieked open, whistling cold air into the room.

The stranger lifted his head.

He'd taken off his helmet, revealing a face she did not know. No sign of Mike's guileless, impudent, mobile features: only the bold colouring and a certain gleam of curiosity in those heavy-lidded eyes. If there'd ever been youthful waves in that collar-length light brown hair they were gone now.

Twilight revealed no freckles under the cheekbones, only shadows. Long forehead, thick, steeply arched brows, sensual mouth. An arresting face. An actor's – or an assassin's, with narrowed eyes the colour of gunmetal.

Rachel thrust her head out of the window. 'Well? Obviously you didn't follow me from Ashclyst and I'm afraid you just won't pass as part of my call-out service, so who are you? Explain yourself or I'm calling the police.'

'Oh, for God's sake–' The man's protest turned into a muttered curse as a pager went off in his hip pocket. Fumbling off the bleeper, he glanced up again at her then reached into the rucksack.

Rachel scrambled to her feet, striking the bulky tallboy with her shoulder on her way up. Running downstairs and outside, she heard the Norton rumble away and found a winebottle left on the path.

Under the bottle a note: *'Sorry about today. There's no reason you should remember. Don't worry, I won't embarrass you. The best, Michael.'*

Chapter 3

When his bleeper went off, Michael knew there wouldn't be time for explanations. He couldn't wait for the adult Rachel to decide he wasn't related to the Beast of Bodmin. He had to go. Michael sprinted to his bike, strapped on his helmet, revved up and streaked off.

Swaying round bends as he dropped into Darcombe, Michael wondered what was waiting ahead. Prepared for the worst, his feelings tumbled back into a tight inner space. He was aware only of the rushing wind, the energy of the moment. And Rachel.

Their first meeting had been a disaster. He knew he shouldn't have stopped in the lane, shouldn't have used the lame excuse of chivalry, but would the truth have been better? The glimpse of her, those long legs shapely even in trousers, had produced a startling response, like some inner pager being hit. Michael had known he must go back. He wasn't a sad lonely type: women liked him and he them. But not to snatch another look when he was consumed with curiosity... Was the face as sexy? Would she maybe look at him? A swift rush past, a glance. It was the whole marvellous wonder of chase and partnership, condensed into a second's encounter.

He hadn't planned to stop: one, because he

could appreciate that a lone woman might be alarmed and two, because he stank. After a day's rescue archaeology in a drainage ditch beside a slurry pit he was fruitier than a chunk of warm Stilton.

Then he'd spotted the toolbox. A deserted lane, evening coming on, a woman in trouble. Thinking back, Michael swore. Never mind that he smelt like a pig, he'd acted like one.

And she'd confronted him. He still wasn't sure whether to laugh or curl up in embarrassment. 'I'm not interested.' Straight to the root of things, as ever, Rachel, except he hadn't realized then who she was. Stupid, considering the hair, but during those few minutes he'd been too busy taking in everything else.

Inconsequential details were the most confounding. The top of her head was level with his nose and, in the instant before she raised her face to his, Michael caught a delicious scent of rosemary. Purposeful hands - he sensed the urgency of her limber fingers clutching that notebook. Yet the hip slotted just beneath his curved with the elegance of a Roman arch, foundation for the long ribcage. Her left breast brushed across him, a jolt that left his upper body feeling naked. There was a strawberry mole by her left temple.

He couldn't rightly remember her face, except that it was beautiful without being pretty or handsome. Were her eyes blue or green? What was their natural expression? How did she hold herself when she wasn't stressed? How did she move?

21

These were questions Michael couldn't answer, but he intended to find out. He'd just have to make certain that this time he didn't let his need to know stir up more trouble than that knowledge was worth. Sometimes the best thing to do was to leave alone – something he'd never been good at.

Michael frowned and, accelerating into the Darcombe fire station carpark less than one minute after his bleeper had gone off, slammed on the brakes, dumped the bike and raced to join the gathering crew.

Chapter 4

Parking at the back of Kestrel House on a Monday morning in April, Rachel walked round to the front to approach along the gravel drive. She had things to do today, people to see, but now she slowed, allowing herself to enjoy the view. No wonder Dad didn't want to leave.

The house was of classical design, standing on drained moorland close to Statts Bridge, in sight of Soussons and Fernworthy forests and surrounded by heather moor. Its walls were white, the sloping slate roof and tall chimneys grey. There were two storeys pierced with Georgian windows, and two wings extending from a central block with a colonnaded portico. Rachel strolled towards the entrance steps, catching the faint scent from a late-flowering winter jasmine grown against the colonnades, the yellow streamers of blossom arching in welcome above the double doors.

She smiled at a visiting Zambian researcher as he slipped out to amble in the institute's arboretum. With fifty acres of tree, flower and heather gardens, Kestrel House had many enticing spots. Inside as well as out, Rachel thought, glancing over the pale green marble hall.

She paused but heard no murmur in the nearby common room, nor footsteps in the teaching rooms. She was hoping to catch the caretaker-cum-security-guard soon, but apart from the Zambian had seen no one. The permanent staff must be in their ground-floor labs at the back of the house. Or were they already waiting for her in the formal meeting-room upstairs?

Rachel shrugged off that idea – she wasn't even officially due in for another thirty minutes. She continued her sightseeing tour. On her various visits to Dad during the last ten years, she'd been inside this place only twice.

Fifteen minutes later, after hearing her staff begin to move upstairs, Rachel was standing by the largest of the upper south-facing windows in the portico, gazing out at a vast blue sky.

She felt panic. Her name and title – 'Rachel Falconer, Director' – shone on the tag pinned to her olive-green suit. From the tip of her russet hair to the toe of her polished court shoes she sparkled. But was she ready? Ambition and concern had brought her so far, now she'd no idea what she was doing. In three minutes, she would be chairing her first staff meeting. She'd be the only woman except for the secretary, Angwen Parkes. The other permanent female member of staff, Professor Edie Fleming, had been on maternity leave since February and was staying with her family in Nigeria.

No, recollected Rachel, Angwen was with Dad in Parma. Michael would be at the meeting, and Daniel. Old adversary and ex-lover. She had prepared, but had she done enough?

'I won't let them put me off.' Rachel checked her fingernails were clean. She hated briefcases and had memorized what she needed but, waiting to go into the staffroom, she wanted something to hold. A note-pad. No – they'd try to make her take the minutes. She needed to be free.

You don't need a cigarette. She'd stopped smoking in the new year but at times – especially just before her period, as now – she found the habit jagging at her nerves.

A thin, horse-faced woman emerged from the office across the landing – her office – and began to mop the stairs.

'Warm today,' said Rachel.

'It is.' The cleaner glanced up, pausing to push metal-framed spectacles back along her bony nose. Looking at Rachel for the first time, she gave a smile that transformed her face. 'You're very much like your dad, he always speaks to me. I'm Mrs Lees, by the way – Lorna.'

Mrs Lorna Lees, married to Stephen Lees, the retired policeman turned caretaker and security guard at Kestrel House. Rachel wanted to speak to Mr Lees as a matter of some urgency.

'Pleased to meet you.' Rachel put out her hand but Lorna shook her head, holding up a plastic-gloved fist.

'These are a beggar to take off and on. What do you think of the place? Grand, isn't it?'

Rachel agreed, then asked, 'Is Mr Lees about?' She knew the security guard worked a split day: early mornings and evenings. Had she not had a doctor's appointment in Darcombe at 8.30 a.m. for a smear test, she would have arrived earlier at Kestrel House. Mum had died of ovarian cancer and she needed these checks more than most.

Rachel stuffed the fear back into the farthest corner of her mind and continued briskly, 'I didn't see him near the entrance gate when I drove in after nine.' There'd been a long wait at the surgery.

Lorna resumed mopping. 'Oh, he'd be off fishing by then: Stephen loves his angling. If you want him, he's on his usual late shift this evening and coming back here around four. Moll! You bad girl - stop that and wait.' This to a black Alsatian whining and pawing at the closed double doors in the entrance hall below them. 'Stephen brings her in with him on his rounds. She's not used to being shut out.'

Rachel nimbly stepped over the bucket balanced on the top step. 'Shall I fetch her in?'

'Goodness, you're as soft as he is. I'll be done in a minute.'

'Go on,' teased Rachel, who liked dogs. She started down the steps but stopped again as the staffroom door opened.

A man's head appeared. 'Are you coming?'

'I'll let everyone get seated,' Rachel told him, ignoring, from within the room, a muttered 'Wants to make an entrance.' Daniel's voice. After skipping breakfast, because of pre-smear-test nerves, she felt her stomach rumble but hadn't time to slip into her office for a chocolate mint.

She blew on her scrubbed fingers. Through the window and beyond the narrow road bridge she could see a herd of grazing ponies, fluffy coats patchy and shedding in the spring moult. Kestrel House was within the Dartmoor National Park, part of the shrinking world's wilderness, like Brazil's diminishing forests. A wilderness she had vowed to protect.

Confidence, spiked with the added anger that had haunted Rachel since Aoira's murder in Rio, surged back. Grinning at Lorna's 'Good luck in there', she launched herself at the meeting.

Chapter 5

Rachel greeted the four men, shook their hands, then settled into an empty chair alongside the marble-topped table. White walls, white marble cornices and fireplaces, white coats or pale tweed jackets, white faces.

She regretted the absence of the cosmopolitan members of staff. Carter MacDonald and Dr Mohammad Khan had been absent since the new year. Carter had been visiting his parents in Antigua and gone from there on a six-month field trip to Chile. Dr Khan was spending a year in Bhutan.

The only good thing from this was that they and Edie Fleming had to be in the clear so far as sabotage of her father's work was concerned. For the men round this table, it was different.

After a weekend poring over their files, Rachel felt she should know them. Michael Horton, Dr Colin Benwick, Leo Cartwright, Daniel Mason – the names, if not all the faces, were certainly familiar to her. In her two previous visits to Kestrel House, she'd spent her time in Paul's lab, seeing no one but Dad and his live-wire secretary, Angwen Parkes. On her last visit, Daniel had joined the permanent staff, but she'd avoided him.

The man sitting farthest away from her glanced up from his agenda. The photograph she'd never been sent to complete Michael Horton's c.v. couldn't have captured that face. He smiled at her for the first time since Ashclyst. No hurry, suggested the mouth, but the level eyes absorbed their own answers – all in the instant that Rachel looked at him and Michael acknowledged he was looking at her.

'Just to say good luck to you,' he said. 'And remind everyone I've a class in two hours.' Based at Kestrel House, Michael lectured for half the week at Exeter University. His teaching included field-work and for this he often, as today, brought students onto Dartmoor.

'Thank you, Michael,' said Rachel, fingers

rising slightly from the table. She too could wait, the gesture indicated. She too had questions.

Neither was fooled by her conventional response nor her use of his name, but no one else had noticed. A dark, slim young man in a spectacularly grubby lab-coat spoke up. 'Welcome to Kestrel House.'

'Thanks, Leo.' She'd been sent his picture and profile. Leo Cartwright, the junior member of the staff. His skills were with computers and in geographic information systems. By now she also knew that he was practising to be Dartmoor's Don Juan. The instant she'd entered the room, his eyes had locked onto her with the fervour of a heat-seeking missile, whilst his handshake had been a flirtation. Yet she felt his goodwill, knew the sight of her had turned him from doubting employee to interested party. Rachel smiled, more at herself than at Leo. It was an advantage sometimes to be a red-head, though was it fair to make the most of it? But Leo obviously flashed that sumptuous just-showing-my-teeth smile without compunction, as Daniel had always used his looks.

Was using his looks, Rachel amended. Daniel at forty was in his prime: athletic figure, lightly bronzed skin, extravagantly handsome and with golden hair. Tipping back in his heavy seat, displaying the aggressive concentration of a stalking animal, Daniel played for attention and got it.

'Where's the logo?' he demanded.

Michael spoke before Rachel. 'Clearly, this time the agenda simply isn't printed on standard Kestrel House stationery.'

'Why not?'

'Daniel, is this a major issue?'

'Not for some of us, obviously.'

'Gentlemen, please address your remarks to the Chair. To answer your question, Daniel, I chose not to use the in-house stationery because I considered the new logo too similar to that used by J.C. Fultons.'

Hoping no one would hear her faintly growling stomach, Rachel paused, watching reactions closely. Profound uninterest blinkered Leo's sensitive face, but beside him Daniel's blond cool had slipped. The anger hardening in his wide blue eyes was mirrored in the slash of Dr Colin Benwick's mouth.

'Yes, Dr Benwick?' She addressed the stocky, black-bearded man who had earlier put his head round the door. Colin Benwick was in charge of the arboretum at Kestrel House. Shaggy as a Dartmoor pony, the doctor was respected in forestry circles for his work in tree survival strategy, yet Rachel found she couldn't warm to him. Her initial impression was confirmed as Dr Benwick leaned back in his chair and fired off a salvo about ethnobotany.

'You've trained as an ethnobotanist, so perhaps you'd like to tell me what one is. In my day, people were just botanists.'

At thirty-two, Dr Benwick was most definitely young enough to have heard of ethnobotany, even if the beard and the pipe-smoking made him seem older, Rachel thought. Aware of Daniel's smirking face farther down the table, she was more than happy to explain the difference. Daniel, too, had once been part of this new science.

'The difference between a botanist and ethno-botanist is time – ethnobotany is the study of plants and plant uses within cultures, not simply raping a plant and then ignoring the beliefs and customs of the natives who showed you where to find it. The aim always is to learn from indigenous peoples and to give back to them in a two-way exchange.'

'And do you believe you'll get much chance to practise that kind of thing here?'

'You already grow elder and mountain ash in the arboretum for biomedical study. So, clearly, some Dartmoor tales are worth pursuing.'

As the sallow Colin Benwick glanced at Daniel, Rachel knew she'd found her first faction. *Poor Dad. No wonder you wanted to escape.*

'I'd welcome any more of your observations, Colin. You obviously have something else on your mind.'

'Some graphics female, one of those media types, designed us a logo. Cost the institute an arm and a leg and we finish with a piece of three-coloured whimsy we can't photocopy without losing half the design. Daniel took it over and gave us something workable at a fraction of the price. If–'

'If this topic is going to develop,' Rachel broke in, 'perhaps we should leave it until "Any Other Business". We have several big items to get through. Leo, since Angwen Parkes is not here, could you take the minutes? Thank you. Now, our first item.'

She hassled them through the agenda like sheep through dip, finishing within the hour, then left first and slipped across the landing to the stairs. Before she settled into her new office, Rachel wanted to take another look at her father's lab.

Chapter 6

Punching in the new access code on the laboratory door, Rachel let herself into the ordered, silent world of her father's research space. Skimming over the cream vinyl, she walked the length of the room and tapped the numbers in the second door pad to unlock her father's small hothouse and seed bank. She checked both over before re-entering the lab. Rachel brushed a fingertip along the glass-sided cabinets bolted to the floor along the centre of the room. From one of these tiny petri dishes, from out of the complex molecules of a plant –perhaps a rare orchid, perhaps a tiny, overlooked lichen – might emerge the answer to a mass killer.

The same could have been true of Aoira's healing-tree, but Aoira was dead and half the lands of her people mined out. Rachel knew how desperate it was because she sometimes received letters from the Gapo: words scribbled on gun-cartridge paper or newsprint, smuggled from Brazil.

'Stop it.' Rachel smudged fingermarks on the

limpid surfaces of the glass as she unconsciously pressed against the side of the cabinet. She didn't need to remind herself that time was short for the Gapo and their rain-forest, nor of what might have been had the Rio branch of Fultons Pharmaceuticals not lost the seed sample from Aoira's special tree. As it was, the tree had been cut down.

'Do what you can, not what you can't.' Over the years, this glib little speech had become her motto, Rachel thought, heading for her father's computer. Yet, after Rio, she had to believe in something or she would have gone mad. Dad had asked for her help: she must do what she could.

From what he'd told her, his research had been affected each time at a crucial stage when samples were in culture, by critical fluctuations in temperature or moisture. Since no one had been spotted in the lab or in the institute buildings or grounds when this happened, Paul was unsure if it was the result of malice or of faults in the power supply. Even with its own generator and safeguards, such interruptions were possible at Kestrel House.

Or they could have been programmed in, thought Rachel, booting up her father's computer. Dad knew very little about systems. She knew more. Enough, she hoped, to recognize if a virus had been introduced into his computer. A hacker could be working anywhere in the world, including Rio.

Rachel leaned over the humming terminal and began checking the system details of each of her father's computer programmes against the instructions on his back-up discs.

Thirty minutes later, straightening and stretching her cracking neck and shoulders, Rachel froze. 'Got you!' She snatched for the wall phone.

Halfway through dialling the number to Daniel and Leo's lab, Rachel put the phone down. The inconsistency she'd spotted was no longer there.

Ten minutes later, Leo Cartwright ambled in. 'I'd love to be able to help, but computer programming isn't exactly my field.'

He smiled, long-lashed eyes melting in their eager-to-please seriousness. Rachel stuck him with a slow smile of her own. 'I'd really appreciate it if you could check for me.' She moved to stand behind him, beckoning towards the computer.

After a sideways tilt of his head to check she was watching, Leo tapped a careful series of commands. His deliberate method made Rachel seethe with impatience but convinced her of one thing. Whatever his skills in G.I.S., Leo was no computer whiz. Otherwise that dark narrow head would have been bobbing from the screen to her face as he showed off. Instead there was methodical tapping.

Twenty minutes later, Leo rubbed one black eyebrow with a tight fist. 'I can't see anything that shouldn't be here.'

Standing behind him, Rachel folded her arms. 'Neither can I.'

'Your dad needn't worry then. He didn't make a mistake in setting the temperature controls before he went off to Parma.'

Rachel nodded. 'So it would seem,' going along

with her own fib. So far as she knew, her father had never made a mistake in setting up his botanical experiments. Yet she and Leo had found no trace of any tampering or any inserted programme. The mystery remained.

She touched Leo on the shoulder. 'Thanks.'

Leo glowed. 'My pleasure, chuck. Anytime.'

Rachel stepped back before he leaned closer. 'That's the first time I've heard Yorkshire in your voice.'

Leo was diverted by her deliberate mistake. 'Wrong, chuck. Manchester.'

'Sorry.' By now she'd opened the lab door. 'Would you indulge me in a spot of women's lib, Leo, and go first? I need to reset the security door.'

Walking into her corner office, Rachel sighed. The house's classical designs had been abandoned here in favour of 'medieval' Gothic: beams and mullioned windows. A granite fireplace decorated with a pair of ponderous stone kestrels dominated the room, whilst a stag's head ornamented the otherwise bare stone walls.

The coffee-maker and china she had brought in with her that morning were dwarfed by the bench they were set on. Rachel tipped off her courts and strolled across the faded Indian carpet to fix herself a drink.

Tucked against the wall were a modern office desk and swivel chair. Balanced on the black seat was her despised briefcase, silver-grey in the dim electric light. Passing the desk and its computer, Rachel noticed an envelope threaded through the handle of the briefcase. Plucking it free and ripping it open, she found another apology.

Saying sorry to you seems to be becoming a habit, but I apologize for not returning your call this weekend. I was on watch at Darcombe and spent most of Saturday and Sunday nights responding to the bells. Maybe this week we can get together for the reunion I tried to fix last Friday? That call-out was false, wouldn't you know. The best, Michael.

Rachel had tried and failed to contact Mike that weekend. He was a volunteer fire-officer on certain nights and weekends – that information, like his phone number, had been on his c.v. So why had it slipped her mind last Friday when his bleeper sounded in front of her cottage? A reunion of senior-schoolfriends: what could be more innocently corny?

But she and Michael had never been 'pals' – not as she remembered it. He was trying too hard. Animal attraction wasn't the answer. He was interested in her, but not in the lusty manner of Leo Cartwright.

Rachel tugged open a drawer, removed a chocolate mint from the box in her desk and popped it into her mouth. Perhaps to Michael she was another goad to irritate Daniel with, she thought, sucking on her sweet. The two men made no effort to conceal their mutual dislike, unless that in itself was a clever disguise. But for what purpose?

Locating the half-full wastebin by her desk – Lorna must have missed it when she had cleaned the office – Rachel tossed Michael's letter into it, wishing she could dispose of her thoughts as effectively. Five years ago, at twenty-three, she'd not been so suspicious. Of course, she'd been going out with Daniel then and not yet made that final, fatal visit to Rio.

Fighting regrets, Rachel stalked past her laden in-tray to the coffee-maker, poured herself a mug and took it back to the desk. Unlocking the briefcase, she drew out the urgent papers, spreading them over the blotter next to the computer.

Quite apart from her father's suspicions, Kestrel House was teetering on the brink of financial trouble. Anticipated government and European grants hadn't been quite enough, lottery money hadn't been forthcoming and the institute was split between those who wanted to tout for business sponsorship and those who insisted on somehow remaining independent. Daniel was the undeclared leader of the pro-business faction and, so far as Rachel could tell, he had with him Dr Benwick. Leo wasn't interested. The other permanent members of staff couldn't be contacted and, except for his clear dislike of Daniel, Michael's view remained as much of an enigma as was his motive for seeking her out.

Rachel jotted down Kestrel House's immediate needs, then added her own priorities. Extra security: fixed video cameras, old alarms and one caretaker plus dog – soon to retire – were inadequate. Even without the possibility that her father's research might have been tampered with, security was a headache. It was a pity she couldn't speak to Stephen Lees, but another morning wouldn't make much difference.

Extra fire precautions: Michael had raised this point at the meeting and Rachel had totally agreed.

But where could she raise the money?

Tapping her front teeth with her pen, Rachel found an irrelevant yet persistent thought recurring. Why had Angwen Parkes gone to Parma? She knew Angwen was a dedicated secretary, committed to her father's work, but Paul had never taken Angwen with him to any other conferences.

Rachel grinned. Maybe Angwen was the reason Dad had been keen to off-load the day-to-day running of Kestrel House onto her for a year.

'My word,' she murmured. 'I really hope so.' Bubbly Angwen was certainly no shadow but, even as she hoped, Rachel had the sinking premonition that her father's motives weren't that simple. He'd founded Kestrel House. Even for his daughter, even for a possible lover, he wouldn't lightly let it go – unless it was interfering with his search for a vaccine.

Rachel left aside the delightful puzzle of Angwen and her own sinister doubts. Tomorrow her father would be back from Italy: she'd talk to him then.

She juggled sums. The money was only just enough. Nothing remained to upgrade the fire or security systems. Perhaps it wasn't surprising that Dr Colin Benwick resented her appointment. In the long term, permanent jobs would be

obvious casualties. Except that she disliked the
obvious – particularly when presented by Daniel.

He'd been blatant at the meeting. 'I've a con-
sultancy with J.C. Fultons. I've never made a
secret of any links with my old firm. Unlike
some, I don't regard a major pharmaceutical
company as an anathema. Fultons would be
happy to give K.H. full financial backing.'

'But only for the price of my father's vaccine,'
Rachel had suggested. Now, fast-forwarding in
her mind the uproar that suggestion had
provoked, she wondered yet again why Daniel
had been allowed to join the institute.

'A brilliant chemist and microbiologist,' her
father had said, as if that was the end of the
matter. Paul had known of Daniel's continuing
involvement with Fultons but had dismissed it –
to him Daniel's splendid track record in
botanical research was much more significant.
He'd brushed aside her warnings and pointed
instead to the lump sum of capital investment
Daniel was bringing with him to Kestrel House.
It was substantial enough to silence even her,
except now Rachel wondered if Paul was
regretting his decision. Certainly he'd entered it
open-eyed, aware of Daniel's connections and of
Rachel's former relationship with him.

Surely, Rachel reflected, even Dad had noticed
that Daniel was still bitter over their parting?

Take his aside during 'Any Other Business',
'I'm surprised with your artistic talents and net-
working ability, Rachel, that you can't get the
press and TV interested.'

'The media types?' Rachel and Michael had

replied simultaneously. Refusing to be distracted, Rachel kept her eyes on Daniel.

'That programme you were in last Friday, for instance. Undeniably popular. Isn't it likely that the TV people might come sniffing round for more?'

Rachel smiled at him. *'The High Country* was one of a series, made throughout last year, and I was only one of several experts. Don't you think it more feasible that for any follow-up, Dr Smiels or Professor Yater would be approached first?'

And if you admit that I'm an equal authority to those then you're a better man than I thought you were, Daniel.

'So, since television isn't going to be stampeding to Dartmoor,' Daniel had persisted, 'what are you going to do, Boadicea?'

The old nickname, once used fondly, had been a punch below the belt. Holding his sky-bright eyes, Rachel had answered steadily, 'Not go rushing into the arms of my old firm.' She'd had the satisfaction of seeing Daniel's fashionably tanned face fill up with subtle colour.

Her cup was empty. Putting it aside, Rachel remembered the first day of her first job for J.C. Fultons, when she had met Daniel and the two others who had once been her work colleagues and whom she had later betrayed.

'After what happened in Rio there was no other choice,' she told herself, but the past did not forgive. The memory of a dead friend's gentle, laughing face brought renewed guilt amidst long-standing grief.

Rachel licked her lips and reached again for her

briefcase. Inside, tucked into a corner, was a new packet of cigarettes. She felt the lighter in her skirt-pocket. Why had she brought it? She couldn't recall slipping the thing into her clothes.

The cigarettes, fresh in their cellophane, mocked Rachel's resolve. Angry, intending to rip them apart, she tore into the packet. The scent of rolled tobacco was as nostalgic as meeting an old friend.

She'd lost a friend – and betrayed old allies.

Defiantly, to test herself, Rachel lit a cigarette. The glowing tip blossomed. She watched, mesmerized, then, disgusted, hurled it down into the wastebin beside her desk.

A soft crackling. As Rachel turned her head, feeling a rush of hot air, the wastebin exploded into flames.

Chapter 7

As I stroll through to the drawing-room of Castle Drogo, the National Trust guides greet me as a regular visitor. They allow me a quiet, harmless joke about the dummy board figures – resplendent in fifteenth-century Spanish royal dress – holding court before the fire in the entrance hall. They nod as I praise the Venetian chandeliers.

This place was built by Lutyens for a business man, Julius Drew, but his name for it reminds me of Tolkien. Castle Drogo, built of granite from Staple Tors in Merrivale. I share my insight with a guide, who smiles. 'See you next week.' They think they know me here, but they don't.

They know me no better than Rachel Falconer does. I am delighted to observe that my long-term career plan for Rachel is working. Paul Falconer has reacted exactly as I anticipated and appealed for his daughter's help.

Neither Rachel nor Paul suspect anything yet. No one does. Nobody will, until the final trap is sprung. Life really is a joy just now.

Chapter 8

It had been one heck of a day, Rachel thought, switching off the computer and blowing on her fingers. The wastebin fire had only been the start, and her briefcase would never be the same.

Spotting no handy extinguisher – another shortfall – Rachel had up-ended her case and used it to cover the bin and smother the flames. By the time Daniel, followed by Leo, had lunged into the office, the alarm was belting out but the panic was over.

'Where's Mike?' Leo's question bounced against her eardrum as the Kestrel House alarm continued to ring.

'Cleared off the grounds altogether,' Daniel answered. 'Gone bog-trotting somewhere with his Year Ones from Exeter.'

Rachel was more interested in why the alarm was ringing: it was only a small fire, scarcely any smoke. 'Can't we shut that bell off?' she called.

'Not really – I broke the glass on the landing alarm.' Daniel tilted his head. 'Here comes the fire-brigade.' The slow whoop of a siren could be heard along the road over the moor. 'Too bad they have to turn out.'

'You're enjoying this!' Rachel spat above the din. Accident or not, she would look like someone who couldn't cope from day one.

'Don't be bloody ridiculous. It could have been very dangerous in here. Did you want me to risk fire spreading to the labs and glasshouse by not raising the alarm?'

'The emergency services will need to know how it started.' Leo put himself between Rachel and his boss.

Perhaps he was afraid one or other might use the computer monitor as a weapon, thought Rachel. Leo's presence reminded her to keep a grip. She made herself break eye contact with Daniel. 'You're right, of course, Leo.'

Then she flicked him another glance. With his looks, it was easy to pretend she was apologizing to a statue: 'Man with Jutting Lower Lip'.

'Sorry, Daniel. That was uncalled for.' Rachel sashayed to the door, opened it widely, smiling her gratitude. 'Thanks. There's no need for either of you to wait.'

Blue eyes stabbing her, Daniel marched past. 'I'll tell you how it started,' he was grumbling as he attacked the main staircase. 'Cleaner not stubbing out her morning cigarette properly.'

Lorna had already gone home and so couldn't be questioned, Rachel recalled, guiltily relieved.

She didn't want to admit to Daniel that it was her rejected cigarette that had caused this.

'I won't touch anything till they come,' she reassured Leo as he left. She was struck by how young he was, the bloom of twenty-two years shining on the taut, even features. Concerned by the shadows under his eyes, she touched his arm. 'Would you like coffee before you go?'

For answer Leo looked to the stairs, down which Daniel's leonine head and stiff back were fast disappearing. 'I'd better go after him.'

'A few moments alone will allow him to cool off. And I'd like to have a quick word with you about security.'

Leo's even features seemed to sag slightly. 'With me?'

'You're our computer expert, Leo.' Rachel smiled. 'I was wondering if some of our computer network could be used to improve existing security. Also–' A conspicuous cough from the stairs.

'He's waiting. I really will have to go.'

Aware of how wretched Daniel could make those under him, Rachel was still determined to find out one more thing before Leo fluttered off. He might not be a skilled programmer, but his work would surely give him some insight. Right now any knowledge, however slight, would be useful.

'Leo.' She made the young man look at her. 'I forgot to ask earlier, but do you have any ideas about how someone could break in and tamper with our video cameras? A hypothetical case.'

Dad had said the video records from his labs

showed no one in his work areas. Although she thought it unlikely that Leo had tampered with the security – what motive could he have? – Rachel had decided that even his limited computer experience might be useful. It paid to check everything and everyone. She'd learned that lesson the hard way, in Rio.

Leo laughed. 'Tampering here, at Kestrel House? What for?' He subsided as Rachel, keenly aware of the lurking presence on the stairs, motioned for him to keep his voice down. 'Sorry. To be seriously hypothetical, it would take lots of gizmos and gadgets. James Bond stuff.'

Right in front of her, Leo's flirting instincts kicked in again. Lowering his voice quite unnecessarily, he stepped closer, his smile intimate. 'My background simply doesn't extend to those kinds of areas.'

'Have you taken root?' Sharp steps as Daniel began to climb the stairs. 'I need those maps from you this morning.'

Leo glanced at Rachel, who nodded. She'd heard enough for the moment. 'Make him strong tea when you're back there.' Remembering Daniel's preferences gave Rachel a bitter poignancy. 'And for yourself, too.'

She closed the door, though not before she heard Daniel complaining and Leo turning the subject in that way of his: 'I saw that programme Rachel was in. I don't think the camera quite did her justice. She's very attractive.'

Rachel's wastebin conflagration had started as the result of a carelessly extinguished cigarette-stub igniting paper soaked in highly volatile VDU screen cleaner in the bottom of the bin. Unnoticed by Rachel and hidden by paper waste, the fluid had leaked out of a cracked container.

It had been an accident ready to happen.

Deeply ashamed, Rachel had apologized to the firemen and reassured them of the strict no-smoking policy in the labs – a policy she would extend to the rest of the institute.

Her next priority was to speak to Stephen Lees on the gate, ask if he'd seen or heard anything suspicious around Kestrel House over the last two months. Then Stephen himself called on his mobile. He was missing his evening shift and going off sick with the flu. And, yes, in answer to her next query, it had been a lousy morning's fishing.

Rachel worked in her office through lunch. Despite Angwen's gentle badgering, Dad had left a mess of paperwork – he'd known she was coming in as administrative director and mistress of PR. Mistress of the Unanswered Letter, more like. Downstairs through the open doors she could hear Dr Benwick and the researcher from Zambia as they lunched together in the common room. Listening to the African and Englishman laughing as they tucked in to sandwiches, spicy samosas and lashings of tea – a fragrant mix of lapsang souchong and orange pekoe – Rachel ploughed through stacks of correspondence with increasing resentment.

Several tedious hours later she was very glad to have made a few inroads into her massive in-tray. The phone calls had started. Regional newspaper and magazine feature writers, wanting to interview the new 'star' director of Kestrel House, were eager to make contact.

After several conversations with strangers about her work, personal goals, appearing on television and when she'd be available for photographs, Rachel found herself drained. She knew it was feeble to feel so whacked, and wondered how media professionals coped.

Again the phone buzzed. Ignoring the bubble of nerves and thwarted stomach juices, Rachel answered, but now she knew who it would be. It was, after all, a minute after seven.

'Lovely to hear from you, Helen. How are you?'

'Getting there. How come you always know it's me?'

Rachel laughed, refreshed by the mellow American voice. Helen at the end of a long day, was a treat. 'I'll let you into a secret, Ellie.' She curled up on her swivel chair with the phone. 'I called you first thing this morning and left a message. You always listen to your answer-phone at 7 p.m.'

'Not this time, Madame Zaza. Besides, your line's been hot all afternoon: I could have been someone else.'

'Nobody but Helen Warne calls me with the BBC World Service droning on in the background.'

'Fabulous station. You should listen sometime. But to move right along to my reason for calling. You had any feedback yet over *The High Country*?'

Helen had been the independent producer-director of that programme. They'd met the previous spring, when Rachel had been engaged by research as an academic advisor but Helen insisted she be in front of the camera. Persuasive and forceful by turns, Helen was a temperamental perfectionist. Rachel had liked her at once – the more so because she was so rewarding to tease. This time, though, Rachel was serious.

'It's not botanical advice you want, is it? You're sounding me out for some other project? If so, I'm interested.'

'Glad to hear that, Rachel. The ratings are through the roof for *The High Country*. You're the darling of the dinner-party set. Party animals all over are rushing to kit out in cute boots like yours. Quite simply, you're the Natural History face for the nineties, and I want more.

More. Usually a word she detested as much as 'cute', thought Rachel. Right now she loved it. 'Another wilderness programme would be perfect. There's so much I didn't get a chance to explain.'

'One programme: three aspects. You're a woman newly appointed to a fairly unusual job. Then there's Dartmoor, always popular with overseas buyers. Finally, Kestrel House – I'd like to come up soon to recce the institute. I know these English manorial piles are usually rather special.'

Rachel was aware of her jawbone slackening and flicked her cheek with a thumb. Television paid generous location fees. 'There's a breathtaking collection of rare plants here and a ravishing arboretum.' She talked up the place.

47

'The grounds hold a magnificent collection of heathers, and the house is very photogenic and easy to film in.'

'Loving it already. Shall we say we'll meet in the arboretum next Monday and you give me a guided tour? Then, if I like it, maybe we can talk money. No firm figures, just a general idea.'

After they had said their goodbyes, Rachel punched the air in celebration. Money, television coverage to promote wilderness, the chance to see Helen again–

'Christmas begins today!'

'Is this a private celebration, or can anyone join in?'

Rachel stopped her spinning chair and grinned at Michael standing in the doorway. 'Helen Warne, who produced *High Country* is visiting next week. She'll probably want to film here.'

Michael whistled softly, then chuckled. 'Congratulations. That should attract more independent funds to the place.' He fired a searching look over one shoulder. 'I presume the business lobby haven't heard?'

'You're the first person I've told.'

'Why not keep it that way for tonight? Let me take you to dinner.'

Rachel had seen his dark eyes studying the burnt-out wastebin, her scorched briefcase. The problem was, she found, that tonight she didn't feel like being circumspect. She wanted invigorating company to share the pleasure with. Still, the thought of local Devonshire cooking, even if she wasn't one of the West Country's night-owls...

She looked at Michael, recalling her youthful rival. At fourteen she and Mike had been intellectually aware of each other but otherwise uninterested. It would be fascinating to catch up on the intervening years. 'Sizing up the boss?'

Michael's smile prickled the back of her neck. 'No, just celebrating that early Christmas,' he said. 'I'll fetch my coat.'

Chapter 9

The White Hart at Moretonhampstead sat at the crossroads in the narrow centre of the little market town. When Rachel strolled into the green-washed lounge, Michael was waiting for her at a table close to the fire – squire in residence, she thought pertly.

She was grateful for the sensation of entering his territory. However much she felt like toasting Helen's timely interest, she needed to be careful tonight. Michael was an unknown. To look out for her father, to protect research that could save millions of lives, to keep Kestrel House from being sucked into some corporate maw, charm was only one of many weapons she must be prepared to use. Scruples were luxuries she dared not indulge.

Freshly shaved, fawn hair water-slicked off his slightly tanned forehead, Michael rose and stepped round the low table to greet her.

'Rachel, what would you like to drink? The

house wine isn't bad. If you're a real-ale enthusiast like me, that's pretty good too.'

His eyes swept over her. Approval or calculation, it was impossible to say. Her teenage rival
had been simple to read, she thought, perversely
satisfied that the man was not.

'You look sensational,' Michael said quietly.

Rachel smiled. 'I'll have a dry vermouth over
ice,' she responded, tongue teasing on the word
"dry". 'I'm delighted your new sweater doesn't
clash with this outfit.' Michael looked rather
good in fact, in pristine heavy green cords, his
navy-and-emerald jumper shining like a
mallard's plumage. 'Hold still.' She stepped
closer and ripped a price tag off one dark blue
sleeve.

Michael watched her do it, but did not move.
This stillness seemed to be characteristic, yet not
a passive thing. Not with those amused eyes.

'Thanks. I missed that one. After you?'

They walked side by side to the lounge table
and glowing fire. Rachel sat on a plush sofa,
whilst Michael bought her a vermouth at the bar.
Bringing it and two menus back with him, he
recovered his half of Poodle Bitter and pulled up
a green carver chair opposite her. 'I used to work
here every summer as a student, so I can vouch
for the food.'

'Whilst you were studying at Exeter?' Rachel
confirmed. 'You didn't fancy a northern
university?' At fourteen, Michael had moved with
his parents to the Lake District and she had gone
with her father to Geneva, then they'd lost touch.
No, Rachel reminded herself, she and Michael

had never been friends, more rivals.

'I prefer Rugby Union to League. Drink okay?'

'Lovely and cold.'

'I asked the barman to use lots of ice. I suppose you don't chew ice cubes anymore?'

'Not in public. What an extraordinary thing to remember.'

'Bits and bobs are my trade: the telling detail.' Michael looked at her over his menu cover. 'Look, before we order and go in – about Ashclyst.'

Rachel tapped her menu with a finger. 'I was wondering when you would get round to that again.'

'This isn't another apology. I honestly thought you might need help. But that isn't it. What I mean to say is, what I saw first – what I really noticed–' He stopped, then finished. 'You have great legs, you know.'

'Michael, I was in trousers, so how could you tell? And why did you want to see me before my first day at Kestrel House? Don't say as a get-together. We haven't seen each other since senior school and we were never close then.'

'Funny, I remember us as friends. But you're right, it wasn't only as a reunion. Now can we order something? I will try to explain through the evening if you promise not to rampage out of the restaurant before I finish.'

'Leaving trampled corpses in my wake?' Rachel asked, amused by his turn of phrase. So much for subtlety. 'I think it's my turn to apologize. Put it down to delayed reaction after this morning's office fire.' She blushed.

Michael's nod of acknowledgement satisfied Rachel that the crisis had passed, although she sensed that he was not entirely convinced. It wouldn't do any harm to tell him more later, she decided, pretending to study the menu. Swapping confidences should help to create an illusion of growing closeness that would help her to find out more about what her companion was really after.

Amused by her own plotting, Rachel realized that she was also looking forward to sharing a more recent part of her past with Michael. The emotion startled her, making her more wary.

Distraction was the wrong word, thought Michael, aware of a delicately swinging high heel inches away from his right foot. Rachel was incendiary.

But he'd already been singed tonight, deservedly so. His frank admiration had been a student shambles: he and Rachel were twenty-nine. He hadn't planned to speak, but blundered recklessly in anyway. When would he ever learn? Another victory for caveman over new man. Michael flicked another glance at his companion. No, it was hardly just the legs, was it?

They were in the main dining-room in the hotel, silent as a waiter served them with vegetables. Rachel had spotted Leo Cartwright in the place a few tables down from them, dark head leaning over the table towards a blonde, doll-faced girl who gazed back in open adoration.

'Who's she?' Rachel asked as the waiter left.

'Bethany, Leo's latest.'

'Pretty girl.'

'She'll probably last all of two weeks.'

'Don't be cynical,' Rachel laughed.

Michael liked to hear her laugh. Soon he'd have to introduce unpleasant topics, already deferred. For now he enjoyed, imagination smouldering. Female fashion was not usually a thing he noticed, but Rachel's midnight-blue, knee-length sheath dress and black high heels were different, because of the woman wearing them. She was no doubt what some would call a 'big girl', yet there was a slenderness about her height, not thin but honed. Her stomach was flat, her hips delectable. He knew now that she moved with the suppleness of someone not tied to a desk job, the long, graceful motion of a dancer. He'd have liked to have taken her dancing in Spain, where tomorrow he was the guest of Madrid University.

Swiftly, before his face gave him away, Michael ran his eyes upwards to her long auburn hair. Tonight she wore the lightly waving mass up, with little smoky tendrils flicked across her forehead and by her unpierced ears. Light chestnut that would bleach hotter in summer – witch hair, his granny had called it. He wondered if Rachel ever grew tired of the stares.

As she reached for her wine-class he caught a whiff of her scent: her own clean, warm perfume, faintly salty. He hoped he smelt as good, no lingering of slurry pit. 'Do you remember that time in Exeter when you and your girlfriends were trying on perfumes at Dingles?'

Disconcertingly Rachel recalled a different aspect of the occasion, one he'd utterly forgotten.

53

'How they all smelt like wet dogs on my skin, you mean? Oh yes, that taught me that we red-heads have to be careful what we splash on as well as what we wear.' Her eyes, neither blue nor green, were fixed on his. 'Rather an ungallant memory, Michael.'

Michael felt himself blushing. He'd assumed he had lost the habit, but he'd thought before tonight that he was reasonably sophisticated. Two holes-in-one so far. At this rate he was glad to be flying out of the country tomorrow.

'I was thinking about how you stood up to that sales assistant for me. The busty woman with the purple hair.'

'Oh, my word, yes – the blue-rinsed perm who said you were loitering with intent by the underwear. You wanted to buy your gran a birthday present, knew she wanted stockings but were too shy to pick a colour.' Rachel's slight Devonshire accent had grown warmer, her pattern of speech slower. 'I must have known – you must have told me – because I steered you away from fish-nets.' She shook her head. 'I'd completely forgotten.'

'No need to fret. I've kept off black fish-nets ever since.' They laughed, the tension between them slackening.

For the rest of the meal they talked about botany, ancient and modern, the ecology of moors, bullfighter cafés in Madrid. Spain led to conversation about other countries, Rachel filling the gap in Michael's knowledge of her between the ages of fourteen and twenty-nine.

'Dad wanted to move right away from Devon after Mum died. He cast about and when the chance came of a research post at the World Health Organisation in Geneva, he took it.' Rachel smiled slightly. 'That was in the winter after you'd moved north with your family. I remember at the time thinking how lucky you were, Michael, to have got away first.'

There was a great deal of grief in that simple explanation, Michael thought. Sensitive to it, he did not admit that his parents' move had been a wrench to him, an unwilling undertaking. At fourteen he'd had no choice.

'What did you think of Geneva?'

His diversion worked and Rachel's smile deepened. 'Dad loved the challenge, I loved the place. Every day meeting new people from all over the world. I studied at one of the international language schools. My best friend was Juana Menendez, daughter of the Spanish Ambassador. We sat next to each other in classes. I spent every summer at Juana's family villa in Leon – Dad was always away on field trips and happy to let me go.'

Rachel chuckled. 'Juana was supposed to be learning English from me but she hated it. We spoke Spanish together always, even when we were back in Geneva. And when the daughter of the Portuguese Consul entered the school and joined us, we spoke a mixture of Spanish and Portuguese. By then I'd heard of a course in Brazil and decided to include it in time out between senior school and university.'

'Language school?' Michael forked a honey-glazed carrot.

Rachel took another sip of wine. 'Yes, but this

55

combined the study of Portuguese with cruises to the Amazon. One boat trip into the rain-forest and I was hooked.'

She rattled on about the wonders of the jungle. Listening, Michael began to worry about how to steer the conversation back to Kestrel House. They were already on to the sweet, and now that Rachel was easier with him at last, he was reluctant to shatter the mood.

Michael stabbed his spoon deep into the Dartmoor apple-cake. It was no wonder, he thought, that Daniel Mason had pounced on her – the scumbag. Reflecting on his rival at Kestrel House, Michael wished there'd been no witnesses to their latest run-in. Otherwise, there'd have been a different outcome.

'I should have known better.'

The phrase jerked Michael back fully to their conversation. Scanning Rachel's nervous rubbing of her fingertips with her thumb – a new gesture acquired since their schooldays – he felt a strangely protective rush of warmth towards her. He was intensely curious, too, about what was coming.

'Yes, but when you're working it's difficult to keep track of time or people,' he remarked, a subtle prompt.

'It wasn't work.' Rachel shook her head. 'Scrub what I've been saying. I really need to start from the beginning.'

'We've plenty of time.'

Chapter 10

Rachel pushed aside her ice, licked a fleck of chocolate from her lip. 'Seven years ago I joined a research team in northern Brazil. We were looking for medicinal plants, life-savers, and were very committed. What excited me was that we were working with the indigenous peoples. Every day I spent with the Gapo I saw new things, heard of new cures.'

'Daniel ran your team, didn't he?'

'Yes! I've already told you. We were contracted to work for Fultons Pharmaceuticals, but that isn't what I'm talking about.'

Would she be any more willing to talk about Fultons or Daniel later? thought Michael, but Rachel had moved on.

'We were in the Roraima region, an ecological reserve a few hours away by car or boat from Boa Vista. Outside the reserve it was terrible: burnt forest, gun-toting prospectors, starving, ragged groups of Indians driven off their lands by the miners, or the military, or the cocaine growers. We always travelled in pairs, using the same river boats or taxis.

'When I didn't venture outside the reserve with Daniel,' – hesitation as she said his name – 'I moved with Jenny. She was an American ecologist, a few years older than me. Our taxi-driver in the dry season was Placido, a safe, greying sixty:

definitely no groper. He was kind – as time went on Placido introduced us to his wife Rosana. Jenny and I were invited into his home. We were safe there, we could relax. I let my guard down.'

Michael noted the change from 'we' to 'I', the shouldering of the problem. He guessed that Rachel had his difficulty, that because of her height people depended on her. Rewarding but tiring.

'It was our third year with the Gapo, just at the start of the rainy season in May. There was a festival, and Placido wanted Jenny and me to come to his house, join in a big family party. He came to collect us at the reserve's pick-up point. We set out along a dirt road already churned into great tracks of red mud. I remember watching the sun rise over the flat savannah teeming with birds, rainbows and storm clouds beyond.

'We were bouncing past a stand of cashew-trees when Placido was flagged by another taxi. The driver was running low on fuel and had a passenger with him who wouldn't take kindly to walking: some local gold-dealer. I got out to help – Daniel once showed me how to siphon as a joke.'

Again hesitation as she said Daniel's name.

'Jenny said she needed to slip into the bushes. I was scrabbling for hose in Placido's boot, and didn't think to watch out for her. We usually did for each other, but I wasn't paying attention. Then I heard her scream.

'I grabbed the hose and ran, Placido ran. I was faster but not nearly enough. In the undergrowth the dealer had beaten Jenny to the ground,

58

ripped her shirt and was clawing at her trousers. He was yelling, "American whore, you like this?" It was frenzied.

'I slashed him in the face with the hose then kept hitting him with anything I could reach. I knocked him out. He'd bitten her shoulder. That turned bad and Jenny had to fly to Rio for treatment. Took a month to heal, and she never came back. The experience shook her so badly Jenny returned to the States.'

Michael hoped the scumbag was scarred for life. Ashamed of his own masculinity, he could think of no way to respond. 'And you left Brazil and your medical research with Fultons soon after?' he asked lamely, after a silence.

'Not because of that. Why don't we talk about something cheerful? Tell me about Madrid.'

Michael talked until their coffee arrived, finishing on a teasing question: 'Why not take a few days off to see for yourself? Come with me to Madrid, tomorrow. Compare it with Leon.'

A foolish pleasantry, no sooner spoken than regretted. Following Rachel's Brazilian story at best tactless, at worst grotesque. Yet, thrown in as a joke, Michael discovered that he meant it – Rachel would be stimulating company. Maybe after a few days together she'd like him. 'Be my guest, no obligation.'

'Thanks, but can't. I need to find my feet at Kestrel House. Besides, my father's due in from Parma.'

'You'll want to see him. Soon as possible.'

Rachel eyed Michael as she bit into an after-dinner mint. He wasn't being sarcastic. The frown lines she'd registered whilst explaining about poor Jenny were back across his forehead. Despite that astonishing offer of Madrid – which surely had to be a tease, however flattering – he probably faintly despised her. She certainly despised herself. Failing Jenny was not the half of it. Yet if she was ever to rebuild, make something of the things she started, she had to leave the past alone. Kestrel House. Her father. The mystery of his spoiled experiments. These were here and now. Michael still hadn't accounted for his visit to her cottage. Despite this pleasant evening, she still dared not trust him.

'Why as soon as possible?'

Michael poured cream in his coffee. 'I presume Paul's been in touch?'

'Stop hedging. If you know something, spit it out.'

'And be damned? You really don't like me very much, do you? Okay, business it shall be. Paul asked me to look after you at Kestrel House. He hasn't been happy for a while now with Daniel's connection with Fultons – we both think the man's a mole for the company.'

This was news to Rachel. Dad had been adamant that Daniel was above suspicion. 'If that's so, I'm surprised my father hasn't encouraged Daniel to leave Kestrel House at the earliest opportunity.'

'Paul thought it better to be sure first. Daniel has some hefty personal connections, starting with half the local gentry and MPs in Devon. The man could create a serious scandal for Kestrel

House if he were pushed out and there was nothing proven against him. We might lose more than our good name – a lot more government funds could suddenly dry up.'

Michael's scorn made Rachel's hackles rise. This was condemnation without trial. 'Daniel's research is in poisons.'

'Appropriate, too, I'd say.'

Refusing to smile, although she'd had the same thought, Rachel quelled Michael with a glance. 'The biomedical possibilities of various European and Asian poisonous plants. Dad is into tropical botany and medicine, but their two research areas are hugely different.'

'Except that Daniel is also a botanist who worked in the Amazon, and he makes no secret of his links with Fultons.'

'Rather obvious for a spy.'

'I agree. Except now it appears to have gone past spying.'

There was a small silence. Both sipped their coffees. 'Big pharmaceutical companies can fight rough, especially when a new cure's involved,' Rachel remarked. 'Plant-hunting's cheap for them, but the profit for the lucky company can run into billions.'

'Something like that.'

'Go on.' Rachel wasn't about to admit any part of her father's suspicions – the bulk of what Michael had told her about Daniel could be a lie. It could be he who worked for Fultons. Unlikely, but his cover would be perfect.

'Paul thinks someone at the institute is sabotaging his work – you know this already, surely? He came to me. I suggested he take a sabbatical to spend more time in his lab – stop any further tampering – and bring in a high-profile outsider as acting director, someone who could attract the independent funds we need. Though I never expected–'

'That Dad would turn to me?'

'Rachel, I don't mean this patronizingly but you need to be careful – that's why I came to your house. We need to work out a strategy to prove your father's suspicions.'

'Maybe the police have frightened off your man.'

Michael shook his head. 'Paul was deliberately low-key where the police were involved. Joe Penoyre, a former crime prevention officer and an old friend of your father's, came to check the place unofficially.'

'*Crime prevention?* And what was the extent of Penoyre's investigation?'

'He looked, listened to Paul, but asked nothing that would arouse suspicion elsewhere.'

'I see. So what do the other researchers think?'

'Everyone else at Kestrel House thinks Inspector Penoyre was called in as a personal favour, for a simple check-up on current security and so on.'

Rachel smiled. 'Including Daniel?'

'Especially Daniel.'

The menace was unmistakable. Again, Rachel was forced to confront the bad vibes between Michael and Daniel, just as earlier that same evening she'd been an unwilling spectator to a showdown.

The place: the narrow, walled-in staff carpark at

the back of Kestrel House. The time: 7.30 p.m. Reversing his Mazda in this cramped area, trying to avoid cars and a stone trough, Daniel had clipped the tail-light of Michael's Norton. Strolling round from the front of the house, Michael and Rachel had seen the whole thing – including the fact that neither vehicle was damaged. To Rachel that was all that mattered but Michael had set off like a hell-hound.

What was eerie was that he didn't shout. Daniel had stopped and was coolly drawing on his wheel when Michael speared himself forward, thundering past the other crammed-in cars. Reaching the white Mazda as Daniel revved the engine, Michael's hand closed around the metal mounting of the passenger wing-mirror.

Rachel missed the verbal content of their tense exchange. All she could see was a broad, hunched figure that suddenly straightened, moved off sideways and brought the Norton out ahead of the Mazda. Mounting the bike, making a point by slowly strapping on his helmet, her dinner-date for the evening went blistering off. Daniel rolled up the electric window, completed his manoeuvres in the cobbled yard and left through a hovering blue cloud of the Norton's exhaust fumes.

As an exhibition of simian chest-beating Rachel had given this display full marks, but Michael's bad manners had disturbed as well as entertained her. She recalled his baiting of Daniel during the staff meeting. Was it just a bad personality clash, or was there something she should know about?

Trying to glean answers, she was provocative. 'Michael, why can't you and Daniel rub along? You go out of your way to annoy him.'

'One day at the institute and you automatically take his part. Haven't you been listening? Obviously not – but how do types like him manage it?'

'I don't think that deserves an answer.' Rachel glanced up the long dining-room to where Leo and his lady were now standing, preparing to leave. Leo was winding a shiny black scarf around his companion's throat, arranging the tasselled ends between her breasts. The implied intimacy of the act made Rachel embarrassed for having seen it. Swiftly, she turned back to Michael. 'And this evening, in the carpark?'

'I lost my temper.'

'Why, Michael?'

'It won't happen again. I'll apologize to the man if you insist.'

'I'd prefer that you did it for yourself, and meant it.'

'That's not possible.'

'Being a fireman makes you perfect? Consider yourself better than everybody else?'

Michael breathed out slowly through his nose and changed the subject. 'Look here, about the fire systems. I don't like this morning's development.'

Rachel felt herself becoming hot. She'd thrown the damn cigarettes away, but they still haunted her. 'I hardly think a wastebin fire qualifies as arson.'

Michael sighed. In some exasperation, it

seemed to Rachel, but then, considering her father again, she was also annoyed, and hurt. If Dad had turned to Michael first, then so much for the 'I can't cope alone' claim he'd given her over the phone. Michael, ahead of her. Why?

'Talk to Paul tomorrow.'

She rose and reached for her coat. 'Don't worry, Michael. I intend to.'

Chapter 11

Next day Michael flew off alone to his lecture trip in Spain. Rachel went in early to work. She finished early and by mid-afternoon was driving down from Dartmoor to her father's cottage at Topsham on the Exe estuary. She was eagerly anxious, anticipating a difficult reunion.

Her first shock came when Angwen opened the door of the square pink cottage. After Angwen had gone with her father to Italy, Rachel had expected to see her at Dad's and was delighted she was there. The shock was the look on Angwen's tanned little face. She was radiant.

'Rachel! Oh, I'm so glad!' Angwen launched herself off the doorstep.

Reacting quickly, Rachel enfolded the smaller woman. Startled by the warmth of welcome, she heard Angwen calling, 'Paul, the champagne!'

The pop of a cork from the study, Angwen kissing her then pulling away, dragging Rachel along the narrow whitewashed hall.

'Here she is!' Angwen skipped into the book-lined room.

'Happy homecoming, Dad.' Rachel crossed to embrace her father, feeling as they touched that he'd put some weight on, that there was a glow about him, too. 'You pair! You look like a couple of teenagers! Who's going to tell me, then?'

Her father handed her a large champagne-glass, the new ring shining above the old one on his third finger. 'May I present Mrs Parkes-Falconer? We were married this weekend in Parma.'

'Wonderful!' Rachel kissed him and leaned down to kiss Angwen. 'Did you get matching rings?'

'Yes – careful there, Paul. Only a small glass for me.'

'I haven't forgotten from the first time.' Paul nodded to his daughter.

A second, bigger shock. Rachel gulped her champagne, feeling her congratulations fall back into her throat. Angwen and her father were having a baby. At twenty-nine she would have a new brother or sister.

'Due next November. Angwen's thirty-seven, we couldn't wait too long.'

Rachel bit down on the answer that it was obvious they hadn't waited at all. Why should she be prissy? She broadened her smile. 'Congratulations.'

Paul sat down in his favourite leather armchair, tugging Angwen onto his lap, chuckling at their near collision with the champagne bottle. 'Here.' He handed his wife a half-filled glass from the study table, stretched and took up his own drink. 'Health, wealth and happiness to my family.'

Rachel repeated the phrase and drank, feeling like a spectator, Not only were her father and Angwen cavorting like teenagers, they were dressed in jeans and trainers, their skins brown and warm. November. Sometime in March, when he'd phoned claiming he was alone and asking for her help, Dad had made love to Angwen. Probably here in this cosy study, before the fire, in the big leather armchair. Rachel blushed, wishing she could stop these thoughts, wishing she didn't have to see her father so far off his usual dignity. Dad and Angwen had known she would be glad for them – which she was. She just needed a little time to adjust.

'Any wedding pictures?' she asked brightly.

'I'll fetch them.' Angwen shot off Paul and Rachel heard her thumping upstairs. The Angwen she knew was a bubbly little body, but not so noisily confident. Rachel was amazed at the transformation.

'What have you done to her? Marriage has brought her out more than ever.'

'I know.' He sounded satisfied. Walking to the nearest bookcase to inspect Dad's books, Rachel couldn't resist giving his shoulder a squeeze.

'Look after her. Once you're back in the lab amongst your plants–'

'No more midnight sessions. I've already promised.'

Rachel drained her champagne, poured herself and her father another glass. The cottage was quiet. Angwen was keeping out of the way to allow Paul and his daughter a moment together.

After waiting to speak to him, Rachel found herself tongue-tied. Her initial anger and resentment following Michael's news of last night had simmered down: besides which, she was aware that Michael might have his own reasons for encouraging a rift between herself and her father. Waiting for Paul to introduce the topic of Daniel's possible spying for Fultons, Rachel found herself wondering about Michael. Why should he help Paul? Honest goodness? Playing the Fireman Sam? There again, why should Michael cause trouble at the institute?

Questions about malaria research and sabotage just seemed wrong to ask a man newly returned from his honeymoon. With a pregnant wife. Still faintly shell-shocked, Rachel found what she hoped was a safe topic. 'How was the conference?'

'Not very informative, I'm afraid. But there was something. I saw Charles Elsham outside Parma Cathedral – remember him? He took Angwen and me for a coffee. Seems to be doing well for himself: own cosmetics firm, glossy Italian wife. Asked after you. Seemed pleased you'd joined me at Kestrel House.'

'I'm glad he's all right.' Rachel could think of nothing else to say.

'Yes. Everything worked out for the best in the end.' Paul cleared his throat, green eyes frowning. 'You don't mind?' He raised thick pepper-and-salt eyebrows to the central ceiling rose.

'Don't be silly, Dad, I'm delighted. Angwen has cared about you for a very long time.'

'How I wish you'd mentioned that sooner. I naturally assumed that at fifty-five, more grey than brown and with a laboratory stoop, I was too old for her.'

Marvelling at this revelation, Rachel said, 'No sign of a stoop now. So how did you two finally realize?'

'The day I admitted to you on the phone about the experiments going wrong. Apparently I looked so miserable coming out of the lab that Angwen asked me if anything was the matter. We began to talk. It started that simply.'

'Angwen knows?'

'Only the basics. Details are irrelevant to anyone who isn't a botanist.'

'Does that basic awareness include anyone else?' Still waiting for her father to reveal his real attitude to Daniel, Rachel decided to ask about a couple of people neither Paul nor Michael seemed to be considering. 'What about Stephen Lees or his wife?'

'Stephen's a good enough fellow at keeping out trespassers but I prefer to rely on my own initiative.'

'You don't trust him?' With Lees only just recovered from the flu, Rachel hadn't yet had occasion to talk closely to the man and hadn't wanted to alert any misgivings by asking for a formal interview. If Stephen Lees didn't know he was under suspicion, so much the better.

'Don't run away with the idea he's any kind of industrial spy. Stephen doesn't have the contacts and doesn't understand the first thing of what I'm doing here. If my work was tampered with, it was by an expert.'

'Which leaves Daniel, Colin Benwick, Leo the serial Romeo, Michael, or an outsider?'

Her father looked at her sideways. 'Naturally, I took Michael Horton into my confidence. He's shrewd enough, decent. I thought he should know something because of his fire-fighting. Firemen often have useful police contacts. Both he and Angwen are discreet.'

Rachel felt strangely relieved. One less Kestrel House suspect was what she told herself, as she felt the breath expanding in her breast. And the 'useful police contacts' must be the reason why her father had turned to Mike ahead of herself. 'I had dinner with Michael last night. He claimed you'd asked his advice.'

'Well, I did. It was Michael who gave me the idea of bringing you in, when he suggested that someone more "high profile" might take over as acting director. Your television work is most diverting, by the way. Angwen set the video to run whilst we were in Parma and we watched your wilderness programme this lunch-time. Superficial but entertaining.'

'You're as snobbish as Daniel,' snapped Rachel, her temper giving way at last. 'He's an idiot, but you should be more open-minded. And whilst we're on the subject of openness, what's your honest opinion of Daniel? Do you trust him or not?'

Paul squirmed in his leather armchair. 'What's Michael been saying?'

'You tell me, Dad.' The last of her champagne tasted like vinegar. 'But do you remember what you said about Daniel to me on the phone last month? How he wasn't a threat?'

Paul stared at the slow golden bubbles in his glass. 'Michael is rather obsessed about Daniel.'

'Is Daniel the number one suspect or not? Or are you so afraid of Daniel's social contacts that you can't even say anything in your own home?'

'No!' Paul was shaking his head. 'You and Michael: you're both so extreme.' He took another sip of champagne and resumed his study of the glass, folding one long leg over the other. 'Daniel may be in touch with Fultons over the principles of my research, but that's all. I'm not even certain about that, but it seems a likely probability and frankly one I'm not concerned about – we're all part of the scientific community. He'll have no details.'

Paul glanced at her over the top of his champagne-flute. 'What neither you nor Michael seem to appreciate is Daniel's talent for attracting funds. By now you must have studied the finances.'

Rachel knew that Daniel inspired confidence. Hadn't she fallen for it herself? 'Okay, so Daniel's no problem as a mole, and great at securing cash. What about the rest, Dad?'

Paul pursed his lips. 'As for the saboteur hypothesis... It no longer seems as attractive as it once did.'

'Yet you still ask Mike Horton to look out for me? Don't you think I can take care of myself? No – don't insult me by attempting an answer, just admit this. There haven't been any more incidents, have there?' Except for her office fire,

71

nothing untoward had happened at Kestrel House for the last month.

'No. I called in at my lab this morning. Everything's fine.'

He hadn't called in to see her, Rachel noted, but let that pass. 'How far are you away from a vaccine?'

'I can't define it in crude terms, Rachel, but preliminary trials could be in less than four months.'

In work that could take years, this was almost immediate. So why wasn't her father more excited? Marriage and impending new fatherhood must have taken the edge off his drive to research, Rachel thought.

She watched her father's free hand absently smoothing the polished leather of his chair. The casual gesture enraged her. This was no worried man. Shamefaced, most definitely, but no longer anxious. Her mind flashed back to her office, the groaning pile of letters in the in-tray.

'It seems I've come down here under false pretences,' she observed sharply. 'I thought you needed help to fight a real threat, not my skills as an administrative assistant whilst you take a sabbatical to rediscover the joys of parenting. Now it appears you haven't even properly informed the police!'

'Joseph Penoyre came, as a favour. He's very experienced.'

'I bet he advised you to make it official.'

'And that would have been pointless!' Finally, Paul was showing some fire. 'Unless the police had camped twenty-four hours a day at the institute, all I would have done with a formal call-out would be to alert the saboteur.'

'If he or she exists. And I suppose Parma was merely part of an elaborate scheme to tempt the person into trying again, and not academic gadding about?'

Under her angry gaze, Paul shrugged. 'In all this uncertainty what else could I have done but call on those I trust? What else would you want me to do, Rachel?'

He had her there. But in the end uncertainty was all it was. There was no one tampering with Paul's work. Her instincts had let her down and she had given up a job she loved for much ado about nothing.

Rachel turned her back on her father, looking through the study window towards the estuary. Upstairs she could hear Angwen moving again. If she wanted to speak to Paul in private about Michael's gloomy warnings about this morning's fire, she would have to be quick.

Why say anything? Don't spoil their home-coming. Leave it.

Chapter 12

'Stone kestrels on the roof, neat. A pity that down here, it's watch out for the pony drop-pings... Wow!' Helen Warne paused on the drive. 'Some kind of magnolia, Rachel? But those blossoms are *huge*.'

'*Magnolia campbellii*. Our specimen isn't as big as the one at Inverewe, but on this slope next to our evergreens it's sheltered. We're lucky to have it.'

'I'll say!'

They strolled off the gravel towards the thirty-foot tree, Helen brisk, Rachel taking the rising, grass-covered avenue in her stride. As she'd hoped, the grey clouds heightened the impact of the flamingo magnolia flowers. They glowed against the tree's fret-work of branches and a background of pines.

Accustomed to pines in the States, Helen was glancing left and right from the main avenue. Bustling ahead, she spoke rapidly into a small cassette recorder. 'Cherry and azalea avenue that'll be great in May. Behind them a maple glade that should be a jewel in the fall. English limes opposite – July for them.' She broke off to confirm with Rachel. 'That right?'

'If you want the flowers.' Allowing Helen to absorb the atmosphere, Rachel kept her commentary to a minimum. There were documents and plans she'd copied for Helen to take away.

She continued to guide her companion through the arboretum, past delicate rowans that would come into their own in September with scarlet berries, past a terraced gallery of ferns and rhododendrons as they attacked a steeper slope. Year-round filming possibilities were what she'd promised: as Helen murmured into her recorder, Rachel was relieved that so far Kestrel House had delivered. Luckily Dr Benwick had taken a sudden day off. If Colin was sulking over Helen's arrival, Rachel reflected mischievously, he'd done so on his own time.

Helen was still due to meet the permanent staff at Kestrel House, including Michael, whom Rachel herself had scarcely seen – much less spoken to – since his return from Spain. What would he and Helen make of each other? And how would Daniel react? Engagingly petite, chic in black tasselled boots and emerald carcoat Helen commanded notice.

Lowering her bluebell eyes from the bare tulip-tree, the brunette turned to look back down the avenue. Spread out below her, as Rachel had intended she should see them, were the grounds of Kestrel House, visible through the treetops.

'Right on prompt, the sun.' Helen pointed to the flash on the big Victorian glasshouse roof. 'How many things you got growing in there?'

'Around five thousand different plants. More with the labs.'

Helen wrinkled her tip-tilted nose. 'Essence of Bunsen burner. Failed high school experiments. And that stuff that stinks – hydrogen sulphide.'

'Not here,' laughed Rachel, thinking again of her father's spoiled research in March, a conspiracy that in the end had come to nothing. 'The main glasshouse is also a lab – with hydrangeas growing round the doors and an indoor vine to cover the brickwork.'

'Pretty or not, a lab is a lab – but don't sweat, Rachel. I'll be enthusiastic when I talk to the boys in there. Can we grab an eyeful of the glass-house next?' Helen raised a neat pair of binoculars. 'Hey, you didn't say it had its own

75

wrought-iron kestrel...'

Rachel, whose sight was excellent, could see the elegant metalwork gracing the apex of the portico entrance to the glasshouse. Much of the structure was hidden by the main house, but enough was visible to show the excellence of its design. It reminded her of a spun-sugar bridal decoration.

'Good girl!' Helen had switched her binoculars from the glasshouse to Jocasta, her research assistant. Exploring the collection of heathers running off from the drive and gated entrance, Jocasta was weaving along meandering paths, trailing a hand over the tops of the springy mass.

'Who's that with her?' demanded Helen.

Shading her eyes, Rachel glanced at the elderly couple pottering behind Jocasta and smiled. 'The first of our weekly visitors. The arboretum, grounds and house are open to the public every weekday except Mondays.'

Another bone of contention, she thought, grimly recalling Daniel's complaint at the first staff meeting about 'grotty Joe Public tramping through Kestrel House, getting in the way'.

She'd been coldly furious. 'The policy of open access to the gardens and arboretum, plus supervised visits to the labs, will continue. People have the right to see what we do here – science is for everyone, not just an élite.'

'Admit it, Daniel. You don't get that many people tapping at your door.' Michael leaned back in his chair. 'Paul's lab's usually the most popular.'

Rachel found herself wondering how many

76

visitors had tapped on the security door of her father's lab back in March. Yet Dad had insisted that his work had been tampered with by an expert. And what chance would an escorted member of the public have for sabotage?

Her attention drifted back to Jocasta and the elderly couple, to their simple pleasure in the living heathers. The best show was yet to come, when the collection blazed in August – in scarlets, crimsons and yellows as well as the royal native purple – but there were already some flowers to enjoy.

She explained the origins of the collection to Helen. 'George Tracey, the man who had Kestrel House built up here, was a heather enthusiast ... and that, before you ask, is Michael Horton, our environmental archaeologist. He can tell you what these moorlands must have looked like when Kestrel House had dinosaurs dropping in to graze on cycads, as well as several million years later, when Bronze Age farmers were clearing Dartmoor of its forest just up the road at Grims-pound.'

Helen's binoculars were raking in the scene unfolding on the drive. Surrounded by chattering young people, Michael was marshalling another group of his Exeter students for a field session in moorland archaeology.

'A camera would love him.'

'Wondering whether he's that big all over?'

'Rachel!'

'I know how your mind works.'

Lowering her binoculars, Helen observed, 'I was considering whether Mike – you did say

Michael? – whether Mike would be useful as an advisor on a new archaeological series that's just in the pipeline. So can you tell me?'

Rachel grinned. 'He seems pretty much in proportion to me.'

Helen looked back at the fair Englishman, a head taller than the milling crowd. 'Well, if he talks as fine as he looks, this should be something. Too many exotic hats and bushy grey beards about in this business. I could do with a fresh young face.'

'You'd like to be introduced.'

'Hold on a minute.'

Catching Michael frowning, Rachel said, 'It's all right, Helen. I realize he can appear a bit forbidding at times.'

'Who cares? That's not it. What I mean is – well, maybe I'm being a bit previous here, but I really don't want to butt in. Is he yours, Rachel?'

Michael, hers? She wanted no entanglements, least of all to anyone at Kestrel House. Rachel shook her head, staring at the tall, blue-jeaned figure as he addressed the group and they took notes. 'We knew each other quite well once, but that was a long time ago.' Had they been friends then, as Michael claimed? Lately, memories had begun to surface in Rachel, times where Mike had been less an irritating rival, more of an ally. Yet their past had no bearing on the present.

'No,' she said. 'He's not mine.'

Chapter 13

Michael saw Rachel wave, asked his students to wait and went to meet her. Since leaving a message on his answering machine – *'Dad was wrong. We don't need a plan'* – she'd scarcely spoken to him. Family commitments on her side, fire-watching on his, work on both, had seen to that.

He was wary, too. He'd spoken to Lorna, who'd confirmed that she'd never smoked. Who'd put the smouldering cigarette into Rachel's wastebin? Had it and the inflammable screen cleaner really come together by accident?

Michael frowned. None of the other firemen or the full-time fire investigator were pursuing this. It was probably that old infernal itch of curiosity that had already cost him and those close to him so much. He dismissed the subject.

For now it was a pleasure to watch Rachel come to him, challenge in her bright eyes. Mystery played about her mouth. To dance with her – that would be something. But first she had to trust him.

Helen Warne was with her and the contrast between the two couldn't have been greater. When introduced, Michael was amused and impressed by how many archaeological luminaries she managed to allude to in under a minute. It was flattering that she was setting out to charm him.

It wasn't difficult to be charmed. What Helen

was proposing – his involvement in a series exploring twentieth-century archaeology – was intriguing. Michael regretted having to cut her off.

'I'm sorry, it's an excellent idea but perhaps we could leave it until this afternoon. My students are going to riot if I keep them waiting much longer.'

'A very genteel riot if I know you Brits. But I've a better idea. We can continue our discussion at dinner tonight – unless Rachel needs you?'

Rachel shook her head. 'I've other plans.' She smiled. 'You two have a good time.'

Michael couldn't resist making Rachel respond to him. 'Where are you taking Helen now?'

'The main conservatory. Our very own Crystal Palace.'

'Remember to tell her about the ghost.'

'Hey, what's this? Rachel, you've been holding out on me. You never mentioned any stately home ghosts.'

Michael grinned. 'Nothing aristocratic about our ghost. Polly Brewer was a Victorian kitchen-maid who was seduced, then jilted by the head gardener.' His voice grew gentle. 'Polly hanged herself in his new glasshouse. On stormy nights she's said to walk through the conservatory, knocking off the budding flower-heads.'

'Wow, a jealous ghost. Ever seen it, Mike?'

'I doubt he'll admit it.' Rachel gave him a wicked look. 'You can't carbon-date ectoplasm.'

Michael didn't let that go. 'Local legend has it that Polly only shows herself to desperate young women.'

Rachel chuckled but her eyes were solemn. Helen looked smug. 'No point me looking then. Lead on, Rachel.'

Helen wrinkled her nose. 'Reminds me of a birdcage.' She pointed with her cassette recorder. 'That the vine you were telling me about?'

'The same.' Rachel smiled at the thick ropes of creeper. Even at this early time of year, the long heavy tendrils completely obscured the brick foundations of the glasshouse. Disappearing through a gap cut specially into a second, modern glass door, the vine wound round the bend of the first octagonal side, vanishing into the heart of the conservatory.

'Nice,' said Helen. Rachel laughed.

'You're ready for more.' She closed the door behind them, opened the second, newer, door immediately inside and stepped into a green silence.

The scents of undergrowth and earth, the densely packed cascade of plants, the explosion of humid heat, took Rachel back. This pale shadow of a rain-forest: why did it still affect her? Returned in spirit to Brazil, she felt the ache of Aoira's murder flower into sharper pain.

'You know, you could try to make it look a bit less obvious when you're not listening to me, Rachel.'

'Sorry, Helen. Would you mind repeating the question?'

'I didn't ask any.' Helen dropped the cassette into her coat pocket and swept along the slightly raised concrete path, the heels of her tasselled boots fluttering like the silky wing-beats of a comma butterfly. 'Right, I've one for you now. Are all these overblown monsters tropical plants?'

'Grown from seed from the rain-forests round the world. Dad and most of the other researchers have their own small glasshouses to nurture specific plants, but they also use this larger conservatory.'

Aware she was losing Helen's attention, Rachel concluded, 'It's a cheerful, colourful mess. Species from Australia growing alongside flora from Columbia. Yet for all our cramming we've less than one per cent–'

Helen tossed up her hands. 'Spare me the lecture. When your eyes glow that way I feel I'm in the presence of a crackpot.'

'Rasputin of the camellias? Okay, Helen, I'll let you off but only if you look at this.' Rachel lifted back a fern to reveal the delicate mat of blossoms.

'Flowers from the Amazonian rain-forests. Don't you think they're exquisite? The Gapo call them skyflowers and thread them into joy garlands. When someone is sad you give them these.'

Helen's forward lunge made Rachel chuckle. 'I'm convinced you're impressed, Ellie. You don't need to drop to your knees.'

'You collected the seeds for these flowers.'

Rachel nodded.

'You miss it, don't you? Ethno-whatever you were in. Ever hear from those people in Brazil? The Gapo?'

'Now and then.' In case she sounded too wistful, she added trenchantly, 'But conservation's important everywhere. What's more British than a bluebell wood? Or a heather moor? Yet drought, arson, the chainsaw boys and the roads brigade are wasting hundreds of acres each year.'

'Arson. That's firebugs, right?' Helen instantly homed in on the most spectacular, personal threat. 'But you won't have that kind of problem at Kestrel House. Everyone's on the same side.'

'That's right,' said Rachel, thinking of Daniel.

Lunch was a semi-formal affair, arranged by Rachel with the usual caterers. Today there were not only Helen and Jocasta lunching at the institute but also five Nigerian scientists, who'd spent the morning with Daniel in one of the lecture rooms, discussing plant poisons.

Escorting Helen into the downstairs staff common room, Rachel heard her murmured, 'No Mike yet,' then an appreciative whistle. 'Well, look at you.'

Stepping alongside, Rachel said, 'Yes, that's Professor Okosun sitting in the window-seat. We're fortunate in our international visitors.'

'Actually, I meant the tapestries. That shepherdess in Arcadia hung on the back wall – wonderful great-house stuff. And this carpet.' Helen paused to caress a boot-toe over the thick pink pile. 'My camera crew will have fun with these geometric designs.' She glanced up. 'Gold leaf on the chandelier?'

'Paint, I believe.' Glancing round to check that

Jocasta was still with them, Rachel guided them through the clusters of comfortable chairs and sofas towards the buffet table. Sensing someone watching, she turned her head and saw Daniel sprawled on a sofa beside Professor Okosun's window-seat, blond colouring shown off by the pale blue walls. Daniel was pointing at her and now he leaned forward and said something to the Nigerian. Professor Okosun nodded to her, then had his attention reclaimed by Daniel.

Damn him, thought Rachel, aware that this little power-and-influence display had been put on for her benefit.

After lunch, Rachel left Jocasta browsing in the library and took Helen to view Daniel's lab. Professor Okosun and his colleagues had left Kestrel House to go on to a conference at Exeter University and Daniel appeared delighted to see the acting director and her visitor. He was pleased to tell Rachel that her father had locked himself into his lab for the afternoon.

'So unless you can remember our new access codes you won't be able to get in without disturbing the poor man.'

'You've changed all the numbers?' Helen glanced back at the glowing pad beside the steel door.

'Our new acting director's first act. Although the trick surely was to have devised an intelligent code to begin with.' He smiled at Helen. 'You do know that Dartmoor Prison is only a couple of hours' scramble over the moors?'

'Really?' Helen was checking her recorder to

ensure it was running.

Rachel wanted to throw a few petri dishes at Daniel's head. 'There's nothing sinister about this. I arranged for the door security codes to be altered as a minor precaution.'

'By the way, Rachel, do I congratulate you on the agreement for filming at Kestrel House? Or am I a little premature?'

'That's okay, Daniel. You always were.'

Helen cleared her throat. 'Actually I've already decided. Our lawyers will talk tomorrow and contracts should be on your boss's desk by Thursday.'

She smiled engagingly at both Rachel and Daniel but it was Leo who came from behind a work-bench strewn with bits of plants, dishes and test-tubes. 'I'm really glad to hear that.' He kissed Helen's hand. 'Welcome to the team.'

'Put her down, Leo.' Daniel shot a look at Rachel and, astonishingly, winked. Before she could react he returned his attention to Helen. 'I imagine Mike Horton will be glad you're going to be part of our "gene pool"... It is rather warm in here, isn't it, Rachel?'

'Afraid I'll faint?' Why should it upset her that Daniel had made the lucky guess that Helen and Michael would hit it off? And why should she be relieved that Daniel knew nothing of Helen's dinner-date tonight? Helen was going to talk business. It was none of her affair, anyway.

Instead, whilst Leo was charming Helen over afternoon tea in the common room, Rachel strolled out to the entry gate.

The disgruntled caretaker might be an obvious

suspect in crimes where there were no signs of forced entry, but Stephen Lees did not come across as unhappy in his work. Fit, tanned, direct and fully recovered from flu, Stephen struck Rachel as being extremely good at his job. He'd pulled out the videotape records of the institute for the previous day – after one day, he explained, tapes were re-used. 'Joe Penoyre's had these over with the forensics boys to make sure they're fully functional and haven't been tampered with. Personally I think your dad went a bit paranoid on that one.'

'Thank you.' Rachel was glad for the additional detail about Penoyre. It confirmed what Leo had told her about how video cameras might be set to run with a continuous loop recording. Since the police had found nothing it seemed everyone at Kestrel House – including G.I.S. expert Leo – was still in the clear so far as sabotage was concerned.

'Do you check these every day?' She tapped the videotapes.

'It's a fairly low-key operation here.' Stephen cleared his throat. 'Unless I found signs of a break-in, there'd be no need for me to watch the tapes.'

'Of course,' Rachel said quickly. Yet, according to her father, some of his key experiments had started to go wrong after two or three days – when the videotape record for those days would have been erased. That was something Kestrel House staff would know, but it also made an outsider's task easier. If a thief or spy had forced his way into the building and his activities not

86

been discovered for several days... 'Has anyone ever tried to steal anything from here?'

'Not since my time. What would they be after, petri dishes?'

Rachel wondered why she was even bothering to check up on Dad's fanciful story but justified the visit to herself by her desire to meet all her staff in person. She justified not giving in to the temptation to ask Stephen about the enmity between Michael and Daniel by reflecting that gossiping about them with the caretaker was inappropriate.

Visiting Stephen also meant meeting his dog: the beautiful black-coated, prick-eared Alsatian, Moll.

'Isn't she wonderful!' This close, Rachel fell instantly for the loping Moll, crouching to scratch her behind the ears.

'You like dogs, then?' asked Stephen, warming to this tall, rather intimidating female whom Lorna had said she liked.

'Oh, my word, yes!'

The answer pleased him. Usually he didn't care for red-heads, but he might make an exception for this one. 'Moll goes with me on my rounds. I patrol the grounds and check the house four times on each shift. Really, I ought to be doing it right now.'

Rachel looked up from petting the dog. With her hair plaited down her back, she looked rather like his granddaughter, thought Stephen, realizing with a shock how young she was.

'I'll walk back with you for part of the way,' she said.

'You're the boss.'

On the way down the drive they passed Leo leaning out of his red Audi, punching in the security code to release the automatic barrier set across the entrance to Kestrel House. The barrier lifted and the Audi streaked up the hill, stopping along the road to pick up a slender, black-haired young woman.

Stephen remarked, 'That's Mary, Leo's latest. Met her at the Warren House Inn over the hill. He always flexis off early to meet a new date.'

A dry afternoon turned into a damp evening. Jocasta was whisked away in a taxi. Daniel disappeared soon after Leo. Michael and Helen left together. Only Rachel and her father remained.

Rachel caught up on paperwork until after nine then walked down to Paul's lab. For politeness, she knocked on his double-glazed glass door. He let her into the long, high-ceilinged room.

'I thought you weren't going to camp in your lab any more,' she teased. Then, as the light struck her father face-on, 'Can I help?'

Paul shook his head, pinching the top of his nose with finger and thumb. 'No, no, everything's fine. It's just–'

The telephone interrupted whatever Paul was going to say. Whilst he answered it, Rachel slipped into the small glasshouse annexed to the back of the lab. Her father's voice made her jump and look round.

'You've done what?'

She started back to him.

'I'm coming home. No, you're not inadequate,

you did exactly the right thing. I'm going to set off straightaway.'

He slammed the receiver and pivoted. 'I'll have to go, Angwen needs me at home. She's called the police.'

'What's happened? Is Angwen all right?'

'Some sod's been telephoning her all today then hanging up. Angwen tried 1471 but each time it was a withheld number.' Paul snatched his jacket off a high-legged stool. 'Her new mountain-bike was stolen from outside the cottage sometime this afternoon. He was that close. The last phone call she got just now, the bastard strummed the spokes of the wheels next to the phone and asked, "Where's your bike now, Angwen?"'

'Sick boy.'

'Lock up, would you, Rachel?'

Chapter 14

Rachel locked Paul's lab, checked the rest and dashed along the connecting corridor to the main block, rattling doors and windows. How had the man known Angwen's name? Rachel kept moving, doing, to shake off the clammy feeling of revulsion. The thought of her pregnant stepmother being pestered by someone who'd learned her name – or worse, who already knew her – was gross.

Rachel quickened, wanting to finish and be

down the road to Topsham. She wouldn't stay, but until she saw Angwen she couldn't be easy.

Why Angwen? What had she done to anyone?

Rachel burst through the double doors at the end of the corridor. Stephen would have already patrolled here; she'd sprint upstairs, retrieve her battered briefcase and leave via the glasshouse, making sure all was secure there.

On the landing a grey wraith, smoke crawling from beneath her office door. From inside a gargled cough, the wicked crackle of fire. The chatter of Stephen's two-way radio, tuned to the police frequency.

Slamming her hand against the door, Rachel felt heat. 'Stephen! Mr Lees!'

Why wasn't the alarm ringing?

Chapter 15

Retiring from the homely Darcombe restaurant to the ordinary hotel close to the church, Helen wondered not when but if Mike was going to make a move. Oh, the big guy was interested, only he seemed to be fighting something within himself.

Trying to do the decent thing? Not flit from one lover to another? Fine – I like loyalty. Only let's make sure it's directed towards the right woman. Rachel may be an old flame, but she's history.

'The moor looks really impressive from up here.' Staring through the window so that

Michael could admire her profile, Helen was glad she'd booked in. Only 10 p.m. and they were alone. Endless possibilities. 'How's my whiskey and ginger coming along?' She'd suggested a nightcap.

A chuckle escaped the crouching shadow by the mini-bar fridge. 'Single malt and ginger – would you do that to a good bourbon?'

'Shut your eyes and pour, Mike. I'm perishing for a glass.' Helen heard the fridge door close and turned to watch her companion cross the room.

'Just how tall are you?' Helen couldn't resist asking, taking her drink.

'Six-five. Not so big these days.'

'It's a good thirteen inches higher than me, and too much to crane up at after a long day. Grab a chair, Mike, please.'

'Sorry – after you.' Michael indicated two cottage chairs and her bed. Waiting for Helen to choose, he retrieved his glass from the fridge top. 'Cheers.'

Helen sipped. 'Not bad.' She draped herself into an easy-chair. 'Can you fix cocktails?'

Michael's mouth twitched. 'Bikes are the only things I fix.' He settled into the second chair. 'Are cocktails part of the television scene?'

'I could probably rustle you up an Adonis.'

'Thanks, but I'll pass.'

'You're right. Don't need any Adonis tonight.'

Michael delighted her by laughing out loud. 'Adonis was skewered by a boar so I'm relieved to hear it. But I'm glad you've enjoyed this evening. So have I.'

'That sounds like a goodbye.' She watched a frown-line score across Michael's forehead.

'Look here, I'm really sorry, but as I explained I'm on standby tonight for the fire station.'

'I know – that's why we had dinner in Darcombe instead of Exeter. But surely so long as you can hear your bleeper?' Helen shrugged. 'Listen,' she said, into the small pause her suggestion had provoked. 'It's started to rain.'

The softly drumming downpour filled the silence. Helen felt the whiskey warming her stomach and the comfort of the armchair, broad as a man's arms. She leaned back. 'I've always loved the sound of rain, especially at night, when I'm curled up in bed, hearing...' She broke off. 'Agh!'

Michael reached her as she clutched at her leg.

'Where is it – here?' He massaged the knotted calf muscle. Helen yelped but relaxed slightly, managing to put down her glass. His fingers gently kneaded as he talked. 'Cramp always happens to me when I'm halfway up a ladder. All I want to do is tear the boot off, stretch the tendons.' He laughed. 'Let's get you more comfortable and out of those lethal heels. Even Rachel's the same - I don't know how you women walk in them.'

Before Helen had time to protest or feel resentment at his mention of Rachel, she was securely gathered up and floated onto the bed. Closing her eyes, giddy at the speed, astonished and delighted by Michael's casual strength, she was aware of a fumble with the strap of her right shoe, then the thing was off.

Supporting her, Michael sat on the edge of the bed. He could feel the tension running through the rigid muscles of Helen's foot as he began to work on her toes and instep. Suddenly her face coloured. She opened her eyes.

'Thanks.' She seemed on the verge of tears. 'It comes on me like that sometimes, don't know why. Maybe jet lag, I don't know.' She sighed, allowing her narrow back to settle against the curve of his arm. 'So much for the sophisticated media type.'

She opened her eyes again, her voice more mocking. 'Takes practice not to snag a woman's stockings. You done this for Rachel?' If Helen was concerned to recover her sang-froid, Michael was trying to stem more primitive responses. His first move had been protective, but now he was acutely aware of Helen's body in his arms. Mention of Rachel strangely heightened his feelings. Unconsciously he tightened his grip.

'Did you?'

'Umm?' Michael looked into the inquiring blue eyes and was drawn in deeper. Only the repeated 'Rachel' made him stop as he leaned closer.

'We didn't have that kind of relationship. We were seniors at school.'

'I see.' Understanding and relief made Helen admit something she'd been fighting all day. 'The way you two looked at each other – I figured you and Rachel must have lived together. Maybe before she and Daniel hooked up. Rachel would never say.'

Michael felt a fire-alarm had gone off in his head. He'd known about Rachel and Daniel being lovers, but not this. 'She actually lived with him?'

'For about a year, I believe. Doesn't talk about it, but I think Rachel must have been pretty devastated when they split.' Staring up at the flushed, still face, reading the brooding grey eyes, Helen couldn't resist adding, 'I think it's put her off men - ow! Watch your fingernails.'

'Sorry.' Michael ran his thumb over the delicate toes, vividly aware just how attractive she was.

Helen raised her head and pouted. 'Kiss me.'

He hesitated, reluctant to take advantage of her obvious attraction to him.

'Don't you like me, Mike? Was this evening only about what publicity you might get out of my shows?'

'No!' Horrified, Michael realized there was only one way to show Helen. He brought his lips gently down on hers.

'Call that a kiss? I don't want you to be kind. You want to say no? Then say it, straight out. I'll understand.' Her blue eyes told a different story.

Michael groaned. This was a moment when he was damned if he did and damned if he didn't. This wasn't only female interest and curiosity: he'd shared enough of that kind of cheerfully earthy liaison to know. He couldn't reject Helen's honest and frankly sexy advances – her moulding tight against him was more than getting him going – without hurting her. And why should he? It wasn't as though he was involved with anyone, least of all Rachel. Yet should he allow this to continue – was it fair?

Helen squirmed delectably, lunging upwards

and poaching his mouth, her thrusting tongue demanding a response.

The Darcombe fire station alarm hacked into their intimate moment, pealing above the gentle sighing of the rain. Then his bleeper went off.

Unable to stop himself, Michael kissed Helen again before reluctantly releasing her. 'I have to go.'

'I'm coming too.'

'That's impossible, Helen. I can't allow it—'

'Don't worry, I'll follow in my car. I need that anyway, it's got the video camera and mike in the trunk. Beat the news crews at their own game – go on!' She gave him a push.

They sprinted out of the hotel.

Chapter 16

Rachel touched the warm door-handle. Dare she open it? The air from the landing would rush in. What if the furnishings were alight? Carpet, curtains, heavy bench-table, old files she'd cleared out and piled by her desk – to be taken away for incineration. If she opened the door whilst that lot was smouldering, what chance then for Stephen and Moll?

'Hold on, I'm getting help!' Shouting to try to keep Stephen conscious, Rachel set off down the corridor, elbowing in an alarm panel on the way. The glass shattered but there was no responding bell. She pelted across the landing and through the open door of the formal meeting-room, lunging for the phone on the white marble table and dialling 999.

She could smell the stench of roasting carpet, hear a sudden spit of burning timber. Out on the landing smoke gushed through the bottom of her office door.

'Stephen, can you hear me?' Rachel thumped the door as she passed. 'Hang on – help's coming!'

In the gloomy corridor she unclipped the heavy cloth fire hose, dragging to reel it from the metal spool. She was shaking it all along the landing, demanding water. 'Come on, bastard.'

The hose spurted in her hands. Cold fluid spattered down her thighs, becoming a pumping puddle over her feet. Fighting, she directed the jet at the base of the door. If she could only get some water through into the room, keep the heat down in there. Hadn't she heard somewhere that after reaching a certain temperature smoke itself caught fire? Bracing herself against a landing pillar she splashed water up and down the door. It hit the wood and slammed back in a whipping drench, almost unbalancing her. She clamped her legs wider apart.

Outside, the din of a fire-engine tanking along the road. 'They're here!' Rachel shouted. 'Just a few more minutes–'

'Rachel!' Michael roared up the stair with hose. Knowing Kestrel House, he was at the head of the crew.

Rachel lashed round. 'A man's trapped in there!'

Five strides and Michael was up to her. 'Go on, now - Jeff will take you down. Go with him.' He motioned to the watch-member immediately behind him and began blasting the office door with the pulsing water.

She was in the way. Not waiting for Jeff, Rachel ran down the marble stairs, nimbly avoiding the fire crew.

'Let her go!' Michael shouldered open the door now the civilian was clear.

By the time Michael reached him, Stephen was unconscious but Moll was dead. Michael laid her body in the wet corridor before returning to damp down the fire.

Chapter 17

I dislike blood, though not as much as I hate dogs: filthy, snooping beasts, whining after their own excrement. It's been a pleasure to dispose of the Alsatian – the creature will certainly be dead by now. Rachel's love of the bitch sealed its fate.

I wonder if the old man will survive? Tomorrow is soon enough to find out. Only professional arsonists loiter at a fire. Fools.

Secrecy is a long-time habit of mine, but I know how intimate love should be, how private.

Rather like revenge.

Chapter 18

Next day, after the police, fire investigation officer and local press had left, Rachel called a staff meeting.

Also questioned by the police, Helen had insisted that she remain. Failing to break through the security cordon and film the previous night's fire-fighting, she was passionate. 'It's part of your job, Rachel. You can't say no now – I've brought a team up specially from London!'

'Letting people see what we do here – isn't that the point?' asked Michael.

Daniel rapped the heavy marble top of the table with a paperweight. 'A media circus is precisely what we should avoid.' He glared at Helen. 'We all know what the police had to say. I think Rachel's been through quite enough, without any additional threat.'

'And just how are my cameras a threat, Mr Mason?'

'Isn't that obvious?' Dr Benwick entered the argument. Suddenly everyone was talking.

Rachel was frozen in her seat. She couldn't stop thinking about Stephen Lees, working towards a calm retirement. He'd been rushed into hospital suffering from smoke inhalation. Lorna was at his bedside. The acrid scent of burnt timber drifted from the cordoned-off office. Someone had done this. Maybe someone in this room.

Michael and Helen, Colin Benwick, Daniel. Leo, ignoring the increasingly noisy debate, leaning forward and asking Angwen if she wanted a glass of water. Angwen, drab in a navy trouser-suit, distressed after the nuisance calls and theft of her mountain-bike. The police had no leads on who was behind those incidents, or why. What was happening? thought Rachel. Had Dad been right? Was this part of a campaign to derail his research? Strike at the place he worked, strike at his wife...

Glancing at her father, Rachel knew that his earlier fear of sabotage had been re-ignited. But that must wait.

'It would be as well if everyone remembered that Stephen Lees is still in hospital.' She shamed the group into silence. She looked at Helen, flushed and stiff in her chair, gold jacket tossing off sparkles of sunlight. 'Personally, I've no objection to you or your crew being present. So long as I have your word that no footage will be transmitted in any form until the entire pro-gramme is filmed, edited and complete.'

'Done!' Helen jumped to her feet to admit her people.

'We should have a proposal, take a vote on this,' Rachel continued.

'I'm happy with that,' said Michael.

'Helen's agreed to film his best side,' dropped in Leo. He returned Rachel's nod of acknow-ledgement. 'I'll propose it.'

'Seconded,' said Michael. The vote went ahead and only Colin Benwick abstained. Everyone else agreed to have the meeting filmed.

Whilst the cameras were brought in and technical paraphernalia set up, Daniel walked round the table to where Rachel was sitting.

'I was sorry to hear about Moll.'

Rachel, who'd been gazing out of one of the long windows, wishing she could hike across the heather, was astonished. 'You don't like dogs.'

'Not as a rule. But I got used to seeing her loping along beside Stephen. And Moll was very obedient.'

'That of course would recommend her to you.'

Daniel laughed. 'You don't have to fight me, Rachel.'

He returned to his seat. Rachel sensed someone watching, and without turning knew it was Michael. What right had he to watch? She jerked her head towards him, catching the coldness in his face, a look almost of dislike, before he twisted sideways in his seat to talk to Paul.

The meeting started at 2.15 p.m. Safety was the first item.

Rachel began by giving an explanation, one that did not entirely convince, but the alternative was horrifying. 'As we know, the police and fire investigation officer have determined why the alarm didn't go off last night. Rats, several of them, had chewed through the connecting cables.'

'Isn't Michael supposed to check that sort of thing regularly?'

'He does. If I may continue, Daniel.' Rachel held his blue eyes a second longer before resuming, 'Rats, of course, have constantly growing teeth which they need to reduce by gnawing. In this case they went for the alarm wiring.'

'But don't we have traps? And how did a group of them – you did say several, Rachel – get into the building?'

'Imagine if they'd broken into the labs,' Colin added unnecessarily.

Leo, smiling, shook his head. 'Impossible.'

Paul gave him a look. 'Is it?'

Aware of the turning cameras, Rachel cleared her throat. 'They pushed through a rusty air-vent in the boiler-room and climbed up an old chimney flue to my office.' She'd been shown the charred furry bodies that had been recovered from the flue.

'Probably smelt the mints in your desk.' Daniel again.

'Whatever,' she responded. 'The important fact remains that the rats didn't get into any of our research labs. This is an old house, and the administrative offices are in the least modernized part.'

Michael spoke for the first time. 'I did warn you of the need for sprinkler systems up here.'

'And I promised that they'd be installed as soon as possible.' Rachel was aggrieved by his 'I told you so' attitude – especially now, caught on camera. 'New fire-protection equipment is already on order.'

Michael regarded her steadily with unblinking grey eyes, fair head tilted to one side. 'As I recall, the issue of extra security was also raised at our last meeting. Any progress?'

'We know from Joe Penoyre that our labs are

quite well protected. The house itself is a low priority, and finances remain a problem.'

Craving a cigarette, Rachel raised her chin, conscious of a dryness in her throat. She didn't want to invite suggestions of how to raise that money. That would allow Daniel and Colin Benwick to bring up Fultons again, an intolerable solution now that her father was so close to a breakthrough. Fultons had ignored malaria for years as a Third World problem. She knew. She'd seen how Fultons had behaved in Brazil. Only now, when malaria was reaching the southern states of North America and westerners were succumbing to infection–

'Never mind the institute!'

The urgency in Michael's voice shattered Rachel's bitter reverie. Blinking, she focused on him. 'What do you mean?'

'You're the one who needs protection.'

Chapter 19

All hell broke loose, as Michael had known it would.

'You can't believe that ridiculous theory!' Daniel attacked first, followed by his sidekick, the shaggy Colin Benwick.

'Totally crazy idea!'

'The police didn't think so,' argued Michael.

'Them!' Daniel snorted. 'West Country plods–'

Michael shot forward in his chair. 'The alternative is that someone here started a second fire in Rachel's office. Perhaps you prefer that theory.'

Daniel twitched, handsome features turning sullen. 'Don't be absurd.'

Michael followed Daniel's look, heart hammering as he saw Rachel's face. When she went white like that, it was time to duck for cover.

'This bickering has to stop.' Blue-green eyes hard as malachite swept the room's occupants. 'A man almost died yesterday – here, Michael!' Again, she looked directly at him. 'Not at my cottage. Not anywhere close to me, except by chance. Kestrel House is what needs protection. The work we do here is what matters.' She turned away, glancing at Daniel.

Of course, Michael thought, her ex-lover. The scumbag she'd lived with for a year. A jealous wave of heat rushed his body. For an instant he forgot everything but the pain that Rachel should dislike him so, that the spark between them was for her only physical.

'This was the second fire, you said.' Leo's enquiry was a godsend, recalling Michael to essentials. Here was a chance to convince Rachel that the police were right. He mustn't blow it.

'The wastebin fire in Rachel's office wasn't started by Lorna Lees and Rachel herself doesn't smoke.'

'But she used to.' Daniel recovered his composure. 'Didn't she tell you?'

This was a shock, but Michael didn't want to pursue his suspicions about the two fires. Not when his own personal suspects were round the table. Watching Daniel and Dr Benwick, waiting for any relaxation or tensing in their bodies, he said, 'Allowing that the first fire and the non-functioning alarm were accidents, the second fire most certainly was not.'

He allowed that to sink in, then continued, repeating what the fire investigation officer had confirmed to him. 'The cause of the fire was hidden behind the stag's head. A complex chemical device, triggered by a timer.'

At the rim of his vision he saw Rachel flinch, knew she was imagining the flaming stag's head.

'The fumes would have overcome Stephen and Moll immediately – as they were designed to, so that no alarm would be raised.' Michael looked at Rachel, driving his message home. 'Had you not been working late–'

Over the minutes she was taking, Angwen stifled a cry. The rest of the room was tense. Rachel was silent, glancing through the window as though drawing strength from the tough, wild landscape outside.

Michael felt himself starting to sweat under the camera lights. Despite his belief that Helen was entitled to film this meeting, there were things which had been said here which many would consider better left untaped, unminuted. He was not one of those people. Secrecy was dangerous, and whatever the risks of exposure, Michael believed Rachel would be better protected by the fullest possible record. Yet if he was wrong, there was no time for regret. Rachel had to realize what danger she was in.

She turned towards him. 'You're saying the device was meant to start a fire, gas the occupants, and that it was set for the caretaker.'

Michael shook his head. 'For whoever entered the room first.'

'And where chemicals are involved, we're all knowledgeable enough,' Leo put into words what no one else wanted to say.

'Except for Mike and Angwen,' Paul picked up on Leo's aside.

'That's not funny,' said Angwen, frowning at the fluffy sound-mike suspended directly above her husband.

'It's not supposed to be.' Hunched over his agenda, Paul held up a hand against his wife's protest and addressed Michael. 'The police also said that not all the components were available here at Kestrel House.'

'True.'

'So this was probably an outside job?'

Under cover of the table, Michael pressed his right foot down over Paul's left. They mustn't be side-tracked into a discussion of industrial espionage or dirty tricks. If such things were going on, it was better to say nothing publicly. None of that mattered now. Rachel needed to accept that she was at risk.

'We also know what else the police said. That because of her recent television appearance and other publicity, Rachel might be a target.'

Still Rachel was refusing to believe it. 'A stalker with a chemistry degree?'

'Stalkers can and do go to extraordinary lengths.'

'There's no proof whatsoever of anyone following me.'

'Have you been looking?'

He heard Rachel catch her breath. Dislike me if you must but believe it, he thought. He wanted to order her to get out now, before the stalker tried again, but knew that was hopeless. She wouldn't run. Besides, would running help?

Suddenly Michael felt cold. A stalker. Rachel under threat from a stalker. The police were warning that the stalker theory was one of several lines of inquiry and that it could be almost any-one at all. Someone who'd watched the film she'd appeared in and become a relentless fan. Someone, maybe, who'd spotted Rachel casually, just in passing.

Or someone from her past.

Chapter 20

Filming was over. Rachel closed the meeting and relaxed into her chair. At last the cameras were no longer prying, recording every flicker in her face. At last people were no longer looking to her for guidance but drifting off in small chatty groups. Dr Benwick was asking Daniel something. Paul and Leo were deep in conversation. Angwen was talking to the sound recordist.

Michael stood by one of the windows, alone, but not for long. Helen emerged from behind the lighting cables and thrusting lenses to claim him.

Longing to escape, Rachel made herself wait for everyone to go.

Even though he knew he'd no right to interfere in Rachel's life – worse, that he'd perhaps even less right than Daniel, whom he was sure was a definite threat – Michael started towards her.

Helen blocked his way. For an instant Michael felt an urge to push her aside. Horrified, he fought it down. 'Helen, you were right to insist on staying. That meeting was pretty dramatic.' He brought his hand up, as though to chop through the knots of people. 'I'm sorry, I need to go and have a word–'

'So do I. Go, I mean.'

The answer made him realize, with a further jab of shame, that he wasn't the only one with things on his mind. Helen was taking time out of her hectic working life to speak to him – something Rachel never seemed willing to do. Rachel clearly didn't want his help and probably didn't need it, either, being so blessedly competent.

Michael tore his attention away from the tall red-head. 'Where?'

'London calls, I'm afraid. The crew and I.'

She looked wistful, and Michael felt even more of a scumbag. Helen deserved more than just polite courtesy. Despising himself, Michael asked, 'How long will you be away?'

'Day or so.' Helen ducked and Michael swayed back as equipment was hauled past them. It was impossible for any kind of close parting.

'You've got my number?' Helen was saying. He nodded.

'Well...' She hesitated. Alongside them, a technician was hovering. 'Helen, about these lights...'

With a breathy 'Another time', Helen disengaged herself and resumed her responsibilities.

There was nothing worth staying for. Daniel headed for the door. Only Colin Benwick responded to his clipped 'Good afternoon.' No one else noticed he was leaving. Certainly not Rachel, busy with farewells to the film crew. Daniel exited down the sooty staircase, stepping over the smeared residue of a puddle by the bottom step. Intending to pick up his coat, he turned from the lobby towards the modest corridor leading to the labs.

A soft rapping at the main doors had him spinning round, blond eyebrows raised in surprise.

'Mr Mason!' Squinting through the square glass panels let into the centre of the oak doors, the postman knocked again.

Daniel strode across the lobby and opened the right-hand door. 'We do have several bells, Frank.' He indicated the shiny metal plate set into the stone wall beside the entrance.

'Sorry, Mr Mason, I happened to spot you there and wanted to be sure you'd heard me.' Frank held out a small package. 'There's a parcel here for Miss Falconer.'

Daniel saw the Brazilian stamps. 'I'll take that. Rachel's in a meeting and can't be disturbed. Don't worry, I'll see that she gets it.'

'Thanks, Mr Mason.'

Closing the door, Daniel flicked his head round. A babble of voices filtered down from upstairs on a waft of smoky air. He was still alone.

Walking smartly to his lab, Daniel turned the

brown paper parcel in his hands. He justified what he was about to do by the most selfless of motives. If Rachel was in danger, it was only sensible that someone else, someone close to her, should open her mail.

Especially when it came from the Gapo in Brazil.

Standing by the window where Michael had stood, Rachel waved goodbye to Helen. Finally she was free.

She had to get out. Away from the ash-and-water stink. Away from the searing television lights. Away from 'inside'. She needed space and a chance to think. Kestrel House felt like a morgue.

Rachel pounded lightly down the broad marble staircase. No one followed as she drove her old green diesel out of the carpark.

It wasn't until she was over the hump-backed road bridge and through the tiny hamlet of Postbridge, driving to avoid tourists from the nearby clapper bridge over the river, that Rachel realized she'd taken Michael's warnings too much to heart. If she wasn't convinced she was being stalked, why was she bothering to check her rear-view mirror so frequently?

Irritated by her paranoia, Rachel deftly swerved to avoid a ewe browsing a tiny patch of grass in the middle of the road. She accelerated, not troubling to check her rear-view mirror again until she reached the junction by the Two Bridges Hotel. Taking the turn towards Tavistock, she pulled into a rough area serving as a carpark and switched off the engine.

Once out of the car, silk trousers tucked into her boots, Rachel began to relax. Hanging binoculars round her neck, hands deep into the pockets of her olive Barbour, she fixed her eyes on the grey tors and the blue May sky.

Striding along a sandy path beside a granite boulder wall, she passed the farmhouse at the end of the track. Nodding to a walker coming off the path, Rachel climbed away from the shadow of the buttermilk-yellow house and out onto the moor. For the first time since fleeing Kestrel House Rachel paused, drinking in the distance.

Silence, punctuated by the low buzz of bees, the harsh call of a stonechat. She could hear wind in the fir plantation across the valley, playing the trees with the sound of sea waves. Yellow tormentil was at her feet and mats of lichens, stonecrop and whortleberries carpeted the tops of boulders in luxuriant, unclipped growth.

Rachel moved off again, refreshed by the moor's tough, living beauty, the bustle beneath the seeming stillness, the crystal air she could taste.

The moor restored her perspective. Balancing over rough stones, smiling at the sight of a ewe sunning herself on a huge flat boulder, Rachel found her attention entranced by the array of plants. Fresh gorse, mosses, lichens, clover, re-emerging ferns. Boulders submerged in grasses growing up in green stars through the withered brown of the old.

A mournful, spiralling cry, rising from a long, narrow wood a few brisk strides away.

'Walking the dog, Baskerville?' Rachel made a joke of it, although the afternoon suddenly lost some of its open blue promise. For the wood was Wistman's: 'wisht' meaning eerie in the old Devon dialect. Said to be haunted by the devil's dogs, the Wisht Hounds had inspired Conan Doyle to create the most famous supernatural beast of all.

'Except that it wasn't real, even in his book,' Rachel told herself, ashamed that her pace had slowed. What was wrong with her?

Another walker swung into view along the meandering path bordering this wood of fantastically stunted oak trees. He was playing 'Waltzing Matilda' on his harmonica, a Labrador accompanying the tune, or objecting to it, with a series of melancholy howls. Her mood lightening, Rachel smiled as she moved off the path to let man and dog pass. She began weaving round the boulders and gorse, climbing over rough grass towards a higher track.

Reaching it and turning sideways, she glanced back. Just coming into view on top of the stile she'd crossed not twenty minutes before was a small figure. Instinct prompted Rachel to train her binoculars on it. Focusing, she revealed a tall golden-haired man, his colouring adored by the bright, clear afternoon light.

Whether or not Daniel had felt the same need to come to Wistman's Wood, he certainly had the same right to privacy. Intent on crossing the high stile he'd not seen her. She could remain unseen.

It was not fear or prudence which made her retrace her steps to the lower woodside path,

111

putting a litter of boulders and the curve of the hill between them. A sense rather of 'not now' or, more precisely, 'not yet' made her reluctant to deal with Daniel. He'd told her that she didn't have to fight him, and had seemed concerned with what she'd been through. Thinking back, Rachel still wasn't sure if Daniel had been referring then to the office fire or if he, like Michael, believed in the existence of a stalker.

Anger scalded her as she thought of Michael. It was time she tackled him about his attitude towards Daniel. Kestrel House was a research institute, not a kindergarten. And this stalking obsession was absurd. He'd had no business to introduce it into this afternoon's meeting. As they were being filmed, for goodness' sake! Whenever that footage went out, it would hardly do her credibility as a botanist any good. And did Michael think she was a victim, unable to take care of herself? It was Angwen who'd been pestered.

Thoughts of Angwen made Rachel feel guilty. Angwen was rapidly becoming the second pregnant woman she'd failed. She'd dismissed her father's conspiracy theories as rubbish – and by so doing, hadn't done enough to protect her family. The police said they didn't think that the arson and Angwen's missing mountain-bike were connected, but Rachel wasn't sure.

For now, there was Daniel. Should she meet him? Rachel hadn't yet decided if her ex was sincere. Better to give them both time to reflect, privately and quietly. It was only good manners. Besides which, she'd had enough of Kestrel

House for one day.

Slipping under a cradle of branches blushed over with tender sprouting leaves and delicate catkins, Rachel clambered down into Wistman's Wood. Carefully negotiating the masses of moss-covered boulders, she made for a huge vertical slab carrying a chiselled inscription, intent on reading it again to refresh her memory. In a few moments, she would continue her soothing, solitary ramble.

Above, out of sight, she could hear Daniel coming.

Chapter 21

Waving Helen off from the car park, Michael saw Rachel leave Kestrel House, hurry to her car and drive out onto the Tavistock road.

'You think maybe she and Daniel will get back together?'

'To be honest, Angwen, I neither know nor care.' Even as he stepped round her, Michael saw the white Mazda turning west after the diesel. 'Excuse me.' He was keen not to let Daniel out of his sight.

'Michael, please—' He felt a hand on his arm. Tearing hot eyes from the rapidly diminishing Mazda, Michael glanced down.

Angwen was shaking an indigestion tablet out of a small packet. Her face had a pinched look and her straight black hair, normally sleek, hung lankly across her hunched shoulders.

She was like a withered peg doll, thought Michael. At once he was sorry for having been annoyed. What women had to put up with because of their reproductive systems was no odds to anyone. 'Want some water for that?' he asked gently.

'No need.' Angwen flipped back her head, swallowed and then wiped her mouth. 'Doctors don't tell you that morning sickness lasts all day. I can't wait to get to the craving stage.'

Michael nodded, wishing he could do something practical for her. 'What is it?'

Angwen stared down at the gravel.

'Fancy a stroll in the arboretum?'

'No! That's where Paul and Colin have gone.' She gnawed her bottom lip. 'I suppose we could follow... Paul and I are meant to be meeting Joe Penoyre at the Warren House in half an hour.' She shrugged. 'I told Paul I'd wait in the car.'

Michael's throat tightened at the mention of Benwick but he said easily enough, 'I'll go fetch him, shall I? Remind him you're waiting.'

A tugging of his sleeve prevented this. 'Paul's fine – I know it's not Colin! We need to talk. I think I know where Rachel's gone. It's not far.'

Michael tossed her a shrewd look from his grey eyes. 'Would you like to come for a ride, get some fresh air?'

'Only if you give it some juice. Paul always drives too slow for me.'

Both of them were anxious, reflected Michael, yet neither wanted to admit it. 'Come on, then. My spare crash-hat's in the bike seat.'

114

Angwen deftly buckled on her helmet and swung herself over the rear seat, feet on the correct footrests and hands gripping the bar behind her. Michael raised an eyebrow.

'You never told me you were a biker.'

'Oh, that was years ago, in Wales. But, see, I'm not such a crumbly. Flaky, maybe.' Angwen puffed out her cheeks at him, reminding Michael achingly of Rachel, who as a teenager had used the same gesture. Nowadays, sadly, she was far too sophisticated in her demeanour and in her choice of men.

'Where to?' Michael asked gruffly. Time was passing. Each second took Rachel and Daniel farther away.

'Wistman's – that's where I think she's gone. She loves the place. We can look in the carpark near the Two Bridges Hotel. If I'm right, you can drop me off at the hotel and I'll phone Paul on the mobile to pick me up there.'

Michael fastened his jacket, checked with Angwen that her navy trousers and short brown car-coat were warm enough, then straddled the Norton. As he started the engine he caught her hoarse, low voice close to his armpit. 'Paul thinks everything revolves around his research. I don't.'

'Hold on,' Michael said. Pebbles sprayed over the heather as they set off, roaring for the road.

Angwen tightened her numbing fingers around the back-grip on the Norton, revelling in the thrusting acceleration, the thrumming din, the sensation of flying over the moor. They flashed into Postbridge, the contents of her stomach lunging uncomfortably towards her throat as

Michael swooped the bike over the humpback bridge.

'Sorry about that back there!' he shouted , as Angwen sagged in her seat, 'Oncoming Range Rover – had to move it!'

'It's okay!' She'd asked for speed, but as Michael accelerated on the straight road alongside Bellever forest she felt waves of nausea washing through her. Throat sticky and hot, Angwen closed her eyes, reopening them as the sensation of sickness grew worse. She'd always thought she would be an earth-mother type – just as she'd assumed she would be able to deal witheringly with nuisance callers and other creeps. Instead she felt inadequate and, in a darker way, betrayed. Paul simply did not see past the idea that she was being threatened because of his research. At a stroke, he'd reduced her from partner to wife: part of himself. The smaller Russian doll inside the bigger.

Not that she was going to admit any of this to Michael. Mike's role as everyone's big brother might be long established, but she hadn't asked to talk to him because of his reassuring size. Apart from herself, only Michael seemed to think that Rachel might be in serious trouble.

They pulled off the road opposite the Two Bridges Hotel, spotting Rachel's and Daniel's cars. Hearing Michael curse, Angwen said sharply, 'Before you go chasing after those two there's something you need to know.'

Tugging off her helmet, she told him about the threatening phone calls, the theft of her mountain-bike.

'Paul, and I think Rachel, believe it's all connected to his malaria research, but I'm not convinced.' Angwen was almost breathless in her haste. 'For a start, when the man spoke I couldn't recognize his voice – it sounded artificial, like something out of a computer game – but I did hear something in the background. I mentioned it as a "something" to the police, but it wasn't until this afternoon that I worked out what it was.'

'That's good, Angwen, you were right to give yourself time. Would you like to tell me what you heard?'

The patient voice was all persuasion. Angwen was reminded that Michael was used to dealing with people under stress. She found herself answering quite calmly, responding to those even tones.

'It was Rachel. Rachel talking on the television. The sound was low, but I know it was her.'

Chapter 22

Rachel yanked her hood over her head to keep out the freshening breeze, tucking bunched fists into her pockets. Down in a pocket she found her penknife – the one she'd taken to Brazil – but nothing else.

It was strange not to find her cigarettes. Her lungs congested on a rasp. Holding it in, embarrassed by a smoker's cough, Rachel listened as the pattern of footsteps drummed past. The dry, bare path above her rang hollowly, the sound fading into the larger sighing of the trees. Striding towards the fragmented bulk of Longaford Tor, Daniel was most definitely gone.

After a few moments, still facing the same way, Rachel herself moved. Left ear tickled by wisps of beard lichen hanging from one low branch, she began the few steps that would take her out of the wood's edge and return her to the lower path.

'Rachel – ah, I see Daniel's no longer with you.'

'He wasn't with me at all.' Rachel ducked under the budding crown of trees and emerged from Wistman's. Daniel's crunching footfalls had obscured this man's quieter approach. 'So you were following.'

Oddly enough she felt no tension or surprise. His face was nakedly concerned, freckles staring out in bold relief. They were familiar to her, like the tiny scar close to his lips.

'I see the wart never grew back,' Rachel added, as he was silent, smiling as Michael twitched, automatically bringing a finger up to his mouth. She'd thrown him by her unexpected response: no irritation, no demand why he was following her. Amused, Rachel found herself teasing him. 'Had you forgotten?'

'No, but I assumed you had.' The glint of curiosity in his eyes softened in remembrance. 'Still do it?'

'Not any more.' Rachel threw back her hood and motioned towards the carpark. Her walk interrupted, she might as well return to Kestrel House, steal a march on the never-ending paperwork. Tomorrow she wanted time to call on Stephen Lees, see how he and Lorna were coping.

Meanwhile, for the first time since she'd met the adult Michael, Rachel felt completely at ease with him. Relaxed by this unusual state of affairs, she spoke freely.

'The last time I charmed warts was five years ago, in Brazil. Placido had a big pink wart on his cheek he was very touchy about. One day, out of the blue, he asked if I'd any magic.'

'So you showed him.' Michael moved ahead at the wide stile to cross first and offer a helping hand. 'I still see John Drees: he's a full-time fireman. We called him Warthog at grammar school till you got your paws on him.'

They'd reached the stile. Playfully batting Michael's outstretched arm away – 'My legs are long enough, thank you' – Rachel slipped expertly over the fence. Looking up, catching Michael's look of speculation, she grinned.

'Considering whether your granny was right?'

When Rachel was fourteen, she'd embarked on a brief yet highly successful career in smoothing away other teenagers' skin blemishes because of an idle remark by Mavis Horton that red-heads were often wart-charmers. As a joke, Rachel had rubbed the blisters on John Drees' hands for about fifteen seconds. A week later John's fingers were clear and Rachel's reputation as a budding witch established.

'You cured that pimple or whatever it was at the

corner of my mouth. I think any self-respecting witch-finder would have had you and my gran dunked in the Dart to see if you floated.' Michael's smile faded. 'Lovely evening,' he said quickly.

They were walking side by side along the path, staring at hills and fields lit by the pinky-orange sun. Below them the rapid sparkle of the West Dart River flashed as it meandered along the valley floor. There was a sharpness in the air and the clouds high above them were pewter-grey.

Rachel glanced at Michael, staring resolutely ahead. She knew why he'd stopped talking about witches. Witches were burned.

Thoughts rattled through her mind. Placido, who gave her a bottle of *cachaca*, the intoxicating sugar-cane drink, when the wart disappeared. Herself at fourteen, learning that her mother was ill, knowing then, with an instinct she did not question, that Mum would die within the year. After that, she'd stopped using whatever 'charm' was in her fingers until she reached Brazil and Placido asked for help.

Recalling that Daniel had been there when Placido showed off his newly smooth cheek, Rachel cleared a muddy section of track ahead of Michael and moved to keep ahead, ignoring the chuckle of a startled grouse. Since Mum had gone, she'd deliberately chosen science over mystery. What she was considering was so improbable as to be crazy.

'I'm not the victim here,' she said aloud, aggrieved at Michael for stirring up these doubts and grief. As the path dropped towards the buttermilk-yellow house, she stopped him. 'What is it you want from me, Michael? What won't keep until work on Monday?'

Her irritation touched off a similar response. Michael's face tightened, his body stiffening. 'Why didn't you tell me you smoked?'

'I don't any more, not that it's any concern of yours. That wastebin fire was just an accident.'

About to walk on, Rachel found Michael's hand around her wrist. Below the straggling fawn hair his eyes were shadowed.

'No – I don't believe that, not any more. It was too deliberate. Lorna had already cleaned the place. She told me that she can't remember if she emptied the wastebin or not: she's sometimes missed it in the past. You know what I think?'

'You're going to tell me, so why bother asking?'

'I think Lorna did empty the wastebin that morning. Which means someone else came into your office and just happened to drop a highly volatile and conveniently leaking bottle of screen cleaner into your newly emptied bin. And that bottle was quite coincidentally covered with a bundle of thin, dry papers. As the fluid leaked out and soaked the paper, any spark would have done. All the arsonist was waiting for was a trigger.'

Rachel glared, exasperated beyond measure that she couldn't wring her arm from his grip. 'I was in my office most of the day, except for the staff meeting, and then I locked it.'

'Pass keys are easily made. Or whoever it was might have slipped in when you paid a visit to the Ladies.' Reddening as he realized he was still holding her, Michael released Rachel and took a swift sideways step. 'It would only take a moment.'

To his dismay, Rachel's naturally solemn mouth twitched. 'You seriously believe someone at Kestrel House was watching my office that closely? Anyone lingering by my office might have been spotted by Lorna, or another researcher – or even me. I'm not entirely un-observant.'

'It would only take a moment,' Michael repeated. 'You may have disturbed him: that may be why the trigger hadn't been set.'

'Until I supplied it myself. You don't have to rub that point in, Michael, I know.' Rachel began to walk away.

'It could have been worse if you hadn't. If he'd supplied a small explosive device with the in-cendiary mechanism...'

Michael had already caught up with her. Rachel had only to tilt her head to look at his face. 'You keep saying "him".'

'Ninety per cent of arsonists are male.'

'And most are between fifteen and twenty. No one that young works at Kestrel House. The fact, is, I didn't see anyone loitering on the landing, and neither did Lorna. Otherwise by now you'd be sure to have told me.'

She was striding now and he was still with her, not scrambling but lithe as a dancer. Even as she wondered if Michael ever danced, Rachel said smartly, 'If you want to follow up suspects at the institute, why don't you keep your promise to my father and look out near his lab? He and Angwen have been directly threatened, not me.'

'I know. Angwen told me this afternoon. But I'm still convinced it's you the stalker is after. Angwen remembers hearing your TV broadcast running in the background when she was telephoned after her bike was stolen.'

'But that caller can't be anyone from Kestrel House, or she'd have recognized him – or her,' Rachel added quickly, wanting to keep a clear mind. 'Of course, the caller might have easily–'

Michael's interruption confirmed her un-completed analysis. 'Angwen said the voice was disguised.'

'Then surely Angwen was the target, not me. So where does that leave your insider's wastebin fire in my office? And what about our second blaze at Kestrel House? Are you going to suggest the rats are in league with this stalker of yours?'

Michael's rumble of laughter showed that her shaft had gone home, but he hadn't given up yet. 'Daniel mentioned that the rats might have been attracted by mints in your desk. Maybe that idea is good for a laugh, but certainly it's not im-possible that the alarm wires might have been baited.' He looked at her closely. 'Are you going to deny the second fire was arson?'

'Of course not!' Stones clattered as Rachel skidded down the track. Two startled lambs broke cover, running to their mother.

'Any suspects, Rachel?'

'Animal rights protesters might have assumed we carry out animal experiments. They often know a few things about firebombs.'

'Yes. I noticed when you spoke to the local

press how you stressed we don't use animals. Not even Daniel,' he added. 'But if the institute was targeted by protesters, why go after your office? Why not the labs?'

'It's much harder to break into the labs. Firing the director's inner sanctum makes a nice political statement.'

'By the same logic, if you assume that J.C. Fultons are behind it, they would scarcely damage any part of Paul's work. Striking at you, however, might persuade Paul to share his findings more readily.'

'Exactly.' Stop watching me! Rachel wanted to say. Yet at least his penetrating gaze was not angry, as it had been earlier in the afternoon when Daniel had spoken to her.

It was almost as if he had read part of her mind. 'Do you believe Daniel might have told someone at Fultons about Paul Falconer's new wife?'

The thought had already occurred to Rachel, but she was reluctant to admit it. 'The police seem satisfied with Daniel's alibi for last night.'

'And I'd say that his long drinking session with Colin Benwick in the Warren House is a bit too convenient – a place far enough away from Kestrel House to be safe but still close enough to watch the fire-engines turn out.'

'Just why do you suspect them?'

'If the two arson attacks were inside jobs then I'd say those two are the obvious candidates. Both are strongly pro-Fultons and both of them know that so long as you're in the director's chair, even as the acting director, any business relationship simply won't happen.'

'If that's true, why didn't they make a formal protest to Paul about my appointment?'

'To get you here to put pressure on Paul. Fultons will want that malaria vaccine. If it means threatening a man's daughter and wife–'

'I know Daniel's no angel,' Rachel broke in, 'but I don't see him as the kind who would agree to bullying a pregnant woman.'

'Well, you'd know, of course.'

That stopped her dead on the path. 'What's that supposed to mean?'

'Isn't it time you had a good hard look at Wonderboy before you get involved with him again? Wasn't once enough?'

Rachel stared, then began to laugh. 'You really think, Michael–'

'You lived with him a year.'

Sobering down quickly, Rachel said, 'Eight months, actually. In Brazil. We were together until–' she paused, then rushed on. 'Until the Rio incident.'

'What was that?'

A spasm crossed Rachel's face. 'You don't want to know. It's nothing to do with what's happening here.'

'Isn't it?' Michael asked softly. 'Are you sure?'

Rachel took a deep breath. 'Maybe I should tell you, if only to get you to stop thinking of me and Daniel as an item.' She shuddered. 'After Rio it was impossible. I couldn't go on with him, or Fultons.'

Michael settled on a flat-topped boulder, stretching his long legs in the direction of the descending sun. 'Well, I'm listening.'

Chapter 23

Early 1990s, Amazonia

Rachel ducked under the entrance to the communal hut, gripping firewood under one arm. In her other hand she carried a basket filled with manioc roots that would have to be peeled, ground and rinsed by repeated washing to break down their poison. Only then would she be able to dry and toast the woody chippings, turning them into food, *farinha.*

A woman called out from one of the hammocks hanging under the lowest roof-eaves. Crossing the hut, flicking away flies with casual patience, she saw Aoira's mischievous face peeping up at her.

'Not tired?' Aoira asked, as Rachel stacked the firewood and put the manioc where she would find it easily in the twilight of the hut.

'Not at all.' Two years ago, when she'd come to the Amazon, the heat, humidity and physical work had beaten her to her knees. It had taken her a season to master basic phrases of Gapo language and two seasons for her to manage to work in the tribe's garden for as long as Aoira. Since then, Rachel's stamina had increased. Because of her capacity and willingness to work, Aoira and the other Gapo tribeswomen accepted her.

Fresh from college, Rachel was proud and excited to be part of a new branch of science, ethnobotany, that recognized the value of tribal beliefs. In this smoky thatched hut, Aoira was the teacher, she the apprentice.

Aoira glanced up from her bead work. She was heavily pregnant and pleased that this tall, pale girl had turned into so useful a helper. Her sister-in-law frequently complained of Charles Elsham. He was happy enough to copy the habits and skills of her brother Carlos, but was as selfish as a jaguar. Glimpsing a long white leg lolling from a hammock, Aoira thought again that Carlos was too good natured. Charles Elsham did not even help gather the ebene seeds that formed the basis of the hallucinogenic snuff the Gapo men took every day when communing with the spirits. Also, at the beginning of their stay, Rachel had given machetes to the people – Elsham had given fish-hooks. It was a poor exchange.

Resting the yellow and scarlet beads on her bulging stomach, Aoira thought of another westerner, no longer with them. 'Jenny will be home in San Francisco?'

'Yes, she'll be with her family.'

'Why do you blame yourself? Jenny was not hurt by you but by the *garimpeiro*, the gold prospector who attacked her.'

Beneath the comforting spit of the family fires and the murmuring of conversation, Aoira heard a slow breath, like the sighing of the treetops before rain.

'We had promised to watch out for each other. I failed.'

Aoira felt that Rachel took too much obligation upon herself but did not comment. Choosing a practical solution, she allowed the strings of beads to slip into the shadows of her hammock.

'Since you are not tired, we should go out before this afternoon's big rain. Paulina has a weeping rash which does not heal and the medicine she needs is deep in the forest.'

Lifting her rucksack off a peg, Rachel carefully shook her hammock for insects before retrieving her notebook, tape recorder, penknife, tiny flower-press and sample bags. 'May I take my things?' She always asked, and so far Aoira had always answered, as she did now, 'Of course – and I will bring my bow and your hunting blow-pipe. You cannot catch armadillo with paper.'

Rachel laughed at the old joke and stood back for Aoira to lead.

Stepping after the Gapo medicine woman into the green wall of the forest, on a trail only Aoira could see clearly, Rachel felt a familiar disorientation. Knowing that ninety-nine per cent of the Amazon was composed of plants was one thing, experiencing it was quite another. Encrusted with trailing lianas, strangler fig and hanging bromeliads, tall, buttress-rooted trees thrust for the jewel-like facets of daylight. Green leaves and stems in every possible contour – spear, fern, dinner plate, twisted, hooped, serrated – bulged down over her eyes in a cloying mass. She was like a wine connoisseur faced by a half-lit cellar stuffed with millions of vintages, displayed in no set order: an exhilarating and ultimately sobering thought. Especially since this vintage was being smashed and burned at the other end of the cellar by thousands of oil miners, gold prospectors, drug dealers and destitute farmers.

Despite this urgent threat, the oozing scent of decaying vegetation, the muffled cries of toucans and monkeys, the slatted criss-cross of shadows and light, were hypnotic, although Rachel was always too enthralled by the possibilities of the place to relax into torpor. And there were more prosaic reasons to stay alert: the chance of spearing something tasty for supper, the hasty avoidance of plant spines, a quick press of her lighted cigarette against a leech sucking at Aoira's calf.

'Too busy to notice a passenger?' teased Rachel, as the leech fell off.

Obsidian eyes winked back at her. 'Remember the grubs I dug out of your legs on the first day you came to us?'

Without waiting for Rachel to reply, Aoira scurried forward, bare feet silent on the dank forest floor. Inside the communal hut Aoira often chose to be naked, but outside she wore clothes as a protection against burrs and insects. Today she had on a pair of Rachel's cotton shorts, cut down and altered to fit, and an old loose T-shirt through which the lines of her pregnancy could just be made out.

Not for the first time Rachel was astonished that 17-year-old Aoira should be so confident and knowledgeable. Although into the eighth month of her pregnancy, the fragile-looking Gapo woman moved over fallen branches and slid between hanging lianas with an elasticity that

129

Rachel could only envy. Leaving her apprentice to wrestle springy vine into her collecting basket, Aoira would glide on in this chlorophyll twilight, sometimes doubling back and gesturing. Then Rachel would blow the smoke from her lighted cigarette into the earnest little face to discourage flies.

After she had finished her cigarette, Rachel was soon feeling hungry: a common state since all food in the communal hut was shared, and the rains had made hunting and foraging difficult. A few metres ahead, faded pink tee-shirt blending into a greater mass of reddish-brown tree trunks, Aoira had found a colony of honey ants and was gorging, scooping the luscious, distended bodies into her mouth.

Leaving Aoira to enjoy her find, Rachel dug into a top pocket – first making sure no stinging livestock had drifted or crawled in there – and found a coca leaf to chew on. The juice merely took the edge off her appetite, but that was enough to inspire her to work. Daydreaming of chocolate torte and mints, Rachel dropped to her knees to examine and record plants.

As she worked, Rachel wished that she could run time back two weeks and have Jenny with them, safe and confident, glad to share the magic of the forest with a fellow student of Aoira's. It had been Jenny who set up the solar-powered re-frigerator supplied by Fultons, full of medicines and vaccines used by the Gapo against western diseases. She and Rachel had inoculated the tribe against measles, chickenpox, TB, malaria and flu, becoming friends in the process. Guilty over what had happened to Jenny, Rachel also found that she missed her – far more than she missed Daniel.

Of course she would be seeing Daniel again. He and Tim Stevens were due to return tonight from their latest plant-hunting foray.

'It's going to rain!' Aoira shouted.

Rain in the Amazon meant tropical storms, crashing thunder, rending lightning. Raising her head, eyes spinning at the green for an instant, Rachel heard the contented snuffling of wild pigs somewhere in the undergrowth being replaced by a restless grunting. Above, a flotilla of huge, bright-winged butterflies tumbled from one heart-shaped leaf to another, seeking shelter. A flurry of birdsong accompanied a drumming of rain high in the canopy. By the time the water dripped to the forest floor, she and Aoira were moving.

Suddenly the tribeswoman launched herself over a trickling stream, laughing at the mud flying up her thighs, and pointed with her knife. 'There!'

The tree was unknown to Rachel, although she recognised it as being part of the *Myristicaceae* family, known for its complex chemistry and as a potential source of cardiovascular drugs. Peering through the sticky semi-darkness and warm trickles of rain, Rachel traced the tree's fight for the canopy, heart bumping with anticipation. If this shiny-leaved, small-flowered tree became one of Fulton's 'staples', raw materials for medicine, then this part of the Amazon would be saved. With life-saving plants fetching prices in thousands of dollars, persuading Brazilians that their rain-forest was worth more growing than grubbed out became easier.

As Aoira nicked the trunk and allowed the sweet, pinky-coloured sap to drain into a metal bowl, Rachel fervently hoped that this healing tree would be powerful enough to stop the bull-dozing, drilling and fires farther downstream.

'The brother of this tree is holy to us,' Aoira was saying. 'My brother Carlos uses it in his spirit-journeys to fight the demons of sickness.'

Rachel nodded, remembering, with a pang of envy, that for the Gapo illness came in three forms. New whitemen's diseases were cured with pills and needles, but the daily aches and pains of toothache, cuts, bruises, rashes, and headaches, together with the entire gamut of 'women's troubles', were the preserve of the medicine woman. Aoira treated these complaints with plants from the forest, traditional lore and common sense, but without the mind-warping drugs used by her brother. As shaman, the living bridge between everyday life and the spirit world, Carlos treated the more serious kinds of illness, fevers and such, which were seen always as forms of spirit attacks and magic. Rachel, a woman, was barred from studying with Carlos.

That honour had fallen to Charles Elsham, who, Rachel grudgingly admitted, was the more experienced botanist. Throughout this trip, seeing Charles sitting on a low stool, chomping tapioca and chatting with the men whilst she left the round house to begin several hours' hard work in the tribe's garden with the women,

132

Rachel had wanted to be Charles. Or Daniel, or Tim Stevens: whitemen trekking in uncharted jungle, going on adventures, searching for new and mysterious plant forms.

Aoira handed her a second brimming bowl. Finishing her own collection of seeds and pressing of the medicine tree's leaves and flowers, Rachel took the bowl of sap and continued to bundle more samples into her rucksack.

'Your husband returns from the forest today?' Aoira asked.

'He does.' Because she and Daniel slept together they were known as husband and wife, yet Rachel found herself increasingly unsure.

Two years ago, at the start of their first season with the Gapo, Rachel had been dazzled by Daniel's knowledge, flattered by his treatment of her as an equal – although the youngest in the team by ten years. As the seasons passed, she became more and more bewitched by his energetic idealism. Living with Daniel became the next inevitable step and eight months ago, she would have predicted that they'd become perfect companions.

Now she was annoyingly aware of having been equally infatuated by Daniel's looks and class. Daniel did not use his full name, Plewes-Mason, but he'd joked of it to her. She could see how deftly he'd manipulated her.

Shamed and alarmed by the shift in her feelings, Rachel hoped that this time would be different, that with this latest reunion she and Daniel would be as they had been. At twenty-three, 'apprenticed' to a woman six years her

133

junior, Rachel didn't want to admit that she had needed to grow up a little.

'You'll be with him and the others, tonight,' said Aoira, the tips of her broad nostrils quivering slightly, 'in the no-man hut.'

That was what the Gapo called the tin-roofed shelter which she and Jenny had erected, with the tribe's permission, to serve as their lab and sleeping quarters. It was also the place where the vaccines were stored. The men in the team preferred to sleep there. Rachel felt safer with the tribe.

'I'll be wherever Daniel wants us to be,' said Rachel, wondering if he would be tired, not sure whether she would be disappointed or relieved if he were. She knew already that Charles and Tim would stay late in the communal hut tonight, to give Daniel and herself some privacy.

Rain had begun to streak their clothes. Aoira glanced up at the rustling canopy. 'Hurry!'

She slipped past Rachel to lead, black head down to renegotiate the stream. They were almost running. Rain weighted down the coiled vine stems Rachel was carrying and drummed against her bowl, splashing into the sap. She tried covering the bowl with her hand, but found it made no difference – presumably that didn't matter, since Aoira plainly wasn't concerned.

They slithered on between the branches, trunks and endless leaves. Suddenly Rachel smelt roasting meat. She heard Aoira laughing because they would eat well tonight. They were at the settlement and, a few slippery steps later, out of the rain.

Chapter 24

Tim Stevens looked up from a work-bench squadroned with test tubes. His severe face habitually melded itself into an expression of faint disappointment, but tonight two spots of colour in his tanned cheeks revealed suppressed excitement. 'She's got something here, Dan. There's some interesting compounds in these samples.'

'Anything useful?' Plump, sunburnt Charles Elsham, tousle-haired and pushy as a small boy, leaned over the taller man's shoulder. He peered at the shadowed stone mortar and pestle used to grind up the tree samples Rachel had collected.

Finally, Tim cracked a smile, nodding his thinning dark head. 'Yes, there's some good stuff. Very useful indeed.'

Next evening, whilst Aoira was resting in her hammock, Rachel came to tell her what Tim had found. The sacred tree Aoira used to treat wounds had many anti-fungal agents within its seeds, sap and leaves – chemicals that could be vital in treating the fungus infections of AIDS patients.

'Our sponsor company, J.C. Fultons, will most definitely be interested, and since it's a traditional Gapo medicine, your people will have a right to part of Fultons' profits if the company develops a new anti-AIDS drug.'

'How large a part?'

Frowning, Rachel studied a big hairy spider spinning its web over Aoira's head. 'You know, I've no idea. Perhaps Daniel–'

'Perhaps Daniel what?'

Rachel started. Sheathed in smoke from the fires, she hadn't seen him moving in the shadows, couldn't see his face now. Yet she could tell from his voice that Daniel wasn't happy.

She opened her mouth to explain, but Daniel got in first. 'A word, if you please. In the lab hut. You're needed there.'

Side by side, not touching, not speaking, she and Daniel crossed the settlement clearing and entered the smaller hut.

Inside, to Rachel's surprise, Tim was already snoring in his hammock, haggard features glowing under the hissing lantern. A bird fluttered somewhere in the darkness close to the tin roof, wingbeats rapid as her own breathing.

Daniel remained standing, squinting at her by the light as he rolled the handle of his machete over and over on the work-bench. 'That was stupid.'

'Telling Aoira about her wonder-drug? Why, Daniel? It's her cure, she has a right to know.'

Daniel's face creased as violently as crumpled paper. 'No! I mean mentioning the contract. Money, Rachel! These people have no concept of cash. All you'll do is raise false expectations.'

A film of smoke seemed to swim briefly before Rachel's eyes and then she could see clearly. 'Fultons intend to take the profits and run. Your company.'

'Never mine.' Daniel shook his golden head. 'I'm right behind you and the Gapo, Rachel,' he added, no longer irritable but sincere. 'That's why we need to go to Rio as soon as possible, to clarify the situation with Fultons there.'

He reached out with his free hand, carefully touching her shoulder where her rucksack had caused a friction burn. Raising an eyebrow at the snorting Tim, he remarked softly, in the gentlest of invitations, 'Elsham's in the main hut, Boadicea.'

The plaintive tilt of his head moved Rachel more than his nickname. In the fan of yellow light she saw a gash down his right arm, whip-back from hacking through jungle. 'You're hurt!'

'It's been treated.' Daniel motioned towards the slumbering Tim.

Smiling, Rachel nodded and took the machete from Daniel's fist, putting it on top of the solar-powered refrigerator.

As Daniel caught her against him, intertwining his right hand with hers, Rachel thought of Rio. She could treat their forthcoming trip as a bit of a holiday, take time off to enjoy the city. Aoira had said once that she was curious to see the ocean, and the statue of Christ. Perhaps Aoira could go with them. Then one of the Gapo people would be a witness to whatever deal Fultons offered for the 'discovery' of her new drug.

Chapter 25

The director of the Rio branch of J.C. Fultons was Lena Clares. She saw Daniel, the leader of the expedition which Fultons had paid for, but refused to see Aoira. The Gapo woman was at first puzzled, then angry.

'Am I a baby?' Aoira demanded on their third morning in Rio. 'Why does this Lena Clares not meet with me?'

Rachel tried to reassure her. 'She hasn't invited me up to her office, either.'

'But I am here to speak for my people!'

Rachel had no answer. She was annoyed and disquieted at how Aoira had been treated. If the company behaved in this shoddy way, what value was their contract with the Gapo?

Rio also shocked her. In the jungle, she'd forgotten the city's extremes of total poverty and indulgent excess, the *favelas,* cardboard slums built against shining apartments. Seeing these again charged Rachel with a furious despair. May in Rio marked the beginning of hot, dry summer, and more time spent at Copacabana beach. The mood of the city, from the paternalistic statue of Christ to the beautiful people flocking on the white beaches, was of acceptance, a form of cheerful and relentless apathy. Nothing could be done for the starving, thieving, drug-crazed children who lived out short, vicious lives on the streets. Nothing would change the stinking, waterless shacks of Rio's *favelas*, except the bulldozer. This was the way things were, so why not enjoy yourself?

Back at the hotel, Daniel said the same thing. 'Look at Tim and Charles, crashed out by the pool, drinking beer and considering which steakhouse to visit tonight. Join them.'

'What about Aoira?' Rachel demanded. 'She loathes the racket and lights down-town.'

Daniel shrugged, new blue blazer draped over one tanned shoulder: he was going out to lunch with Lena Clares. Later he and 'the botanical boys' as Lena called them, were booked to play a round of golf, guests of Lena's husband at the fashionable Gavea Golf Course in São Conrado. Indifferent to what Rachel thought, Daniel merely answered, 'You suggested she came,' and sauntered off into the brilliant sunshine.

'Say nothing. Leave him,' said Aoira, coming in from her balcony where she'd overheard.

Rachel shook her head, remembering how patient Daniel had been with her at the start of the expedition. True, he'd been intent on seducing her, but she felt that the eight months of their subsequent intimacy deserved a proper ending.

However difficult that moment would be, thought Rachel, she had no right to inflict her depression on Aoira – pregnant with her first child and on the trip of a lifetime.

Thinking of the lush, copper-skinned beauty of Lena Clares, Rachel scowled. She'd seen Lena, blonde hair, flashing teeth and jewellery, draping herself like a strangler fig around Daniel and experienced no jealousy, only annoyance at being excluded from their conversation. This afternoon she wasn't interested in a round of golf, but did wonder what plots might be hatched on the beach-front course. Prepared for the worst, she'd worked out her own stratagem.

'Ready to brave the world outside the air-conditioning?' she asked Aoira, jerking her chin towards the neon-dressed people strolling along the baking pavements.

'Are you ready to brave the world outside Daniel?'

'Soon – very soon.'

Aoira nodded, flicking her long bead earrings over her shoulders in a sign of satisfaction. Looking back towards the balcony, she gazed down at the gaudy mob, curiosity and belligerence showing in her delicate features, nostrils opened wide as she absorbed the scents of the city.

'We arranged to meet Antonio before midday,' Rachel reminded her. 'Your lawyer won't like to be kept waiting.'

Resigned, Aoira sighed and wandered to the door. 'Will you buy me a *batida de coco,* when we're finished talking?'

Aoira hated the shoving, groping clamour of Rio but she had taken as passionately as a local *carioca* to the sweet coconut milk and *cachaca* drink. Because of the sugar-cane alcohol, potent and heavy as rum, Rachel tried to ration her, but she was always happy to see Aoira sucking lustily on her treat with the open delight of a child.

'I will – and one for myself,' Rachel answered,

leading the way out and promising Aoira her *batida* in a café with a view of Guanabara Bay and Sugar Loaf Mountain.

Their meeting with Antonio was secret, arranged by Rachel in a series of late-night telephone calls from the hotel lobby. With a string of victories in the courts, where he'd secured major rights and concessions for the native Brazilian Indians, Antonio Olinda was the logical choice for her to approach. She'd faxed him the copy of Fultons' contract with the Gapo: Antonio had been ready with an opinion on that when she'd first telephoned him, whilst Daniel, Tim and Charles were drinking in the hotel.

'It sounds fair but means nothing,' Antonio had stated baldly. 'Without firm figures or percentages, this contract is worthless. Fultons could argue that they've already paid the Gapo by supplying the tribe with free drugs.'

'So what happens now?'

She heard Antonio grunt into the receiver. 'I would like to meet Aoira, of course – see if she would be happy for my firm to represent her.'

'The Gapo cannot pay–'

'No need to be alarmed, *Doña* Rachel. I will take my fee from the sum we shall win from Fultons. And if this new medicine does not come off and no money arrives – "no win, no fee", as they say in the United States. Do not worry on that score.'

Because of what was at stake – huge profits for Fultons if Aoira's healing tree could be converted into a vital First World cure – the hotel had been

141

ruled out as a meeting-place. Rachel was sharing a room with Daniel and the public lounge was too exposed. Even if they talked in Aoira's room, Rachel couldn't guarantee secrecy. She and the lawyer had agreed it was safer and less conspicuous if they met at Antonio's high-rise office.

Conscious of the stares that she and the diminutive, heavily pregnant Aoira provoked, Rachel helped Aoira out of the taxi, across tramlines and quickly towards the marble steps of the black-windowed building.

As Rachel clamped Aoira closer to her side to batter through the persistent street hawkers and beggars crouched under the shade of the office block's concrete portico, a gap opened amongst the grabbing hands and arms. Two men in the steel-grey uniforms of the military police forced their way through this unhappy mob. Something in the way they hugged the pistols on their belts made Rachel uneasy. Softly and urgently, she drew Aoira along, stepping in front of the Gapo woman to shield her.

Calmly, without removing his dark glasses, one of the gum-chewing policemen took out his gun and shot Rachel in the leg.

Screaming, toppling, Rachel heard another shot and felt Aoira fall on top of her.

Chapter 26

May, Dartmoor, England

Rachel took a deep breath. 'We were taken to the nearest hospital, where Aoira and her baby were pronounced dead on arrival. I was treated for gunshot and shock and later released – well, actually I discharged myself. I wanted to get back to the Gapo as soon as possible, tell them what had happened to Aoira, warn them. I knew it was a contract killing. In Brazil there are hundreds of them, mostly unsolved.'

On a warm May evening in England, Michael felt chilled, sickened by Aoira's casual murder. He thought of Rachel being shot. Anger flooded him. He crouched by the granite boulder she was sat on, carefully resting his fists on the stone on either side of her body. 'I know it's hard to say,' he began, assuming who would be behind this piece of butchery. But he was wrong.

'It wasn't Daniel.'

Both of them flinched as a low jet shrieked overhead into the final bleeding rays of sunlight. Michael tugged off his leather jacket and cast it round Rachel's shoulders, on top of her Barbour. It was growing icy out on the moor.

This time, recognizing his need to do something, Rachel accepted his help and nodded her thanks. 'I returned to the hotel when no one was

143

expecting me. Daniel had been forced to leave my bedside to put in another report at the military police's headquarters – he was shocked, I think, and wanted to see justice done.

'Tim and Charles had just visited, Tim looking even more cadaverous than usual. He really seemed quite ill, although at the time Charles made more of an impression. He threw up when he saw me. Knew how to compliment a girl.'

She tried a smile but couldn't hold it. Her hands wound out of Michael's leather jacket and clutched the lapels.

'Do you want to stop?' Michael saw the glints of fire in Rachel's hair as she shook her head.

'I made Charles take his grapes away to eat on the tram. I'm afraid I wasn't very good company – all I could talk of was Aoira – so they did their duty and left. Can't say I blamed them, really. Not then.'

Her thumb rubbed against the fingers of her right hand. 'After Tim and Charles had gone I couldn't stand it any more. I ignored the doctors, ordered a taxi and hobbled out. I had to get back to the Gapo as soon as possible – Aoira needed to be given the Gapo death rites.

'Antonio Olinda had come to see me in the hospital to say that the police never traced any of their own killers. He assumed that Fultons had discovered that Aoira and I were about to engage a lawyer sympathetic to the native Indians – finding that out would have been easy in Rio, Antonio said, where virtually anyone can be bribed. He thought it most likely that my telephone conversations at the hotel had been taped

144

on behalf of "interested parties". He was only sorry and rather surprised we'd been found out. We'd taken care – I'd always telephoned late from my room, when the hotel staff would have been busy with incoming late revellers. But as Antonio pointed out to me, my looks, especially this' – Rachel flicked angrily at her hair – 'meant that I attracted notice. Hoping to listen in on the *gringa*'s conversations with her numerous lovers – it would be assumed that as an unusual, un-attached female, I'd have several – one of the porters, waiters, bell-boys must have overheard what I was actually arranging with Antonio.

'Antonio was certain that Rio Fultons had engineered the assassination, but said that would never be proved. His main concern was over the legal rights of the entire tribe.

'I wanted to help him. I knew I had to help him – Aoira had gone to Rio at my suggestion.'

'Taking the blame for everything even then, were you?'

Rachel ignored Michael's question. She drew her knees up to her chin and tucked the long jacket sleeves into the tops of her wellington boots, staring ahead at the rising evening star.

'At the hotel I went straight to my room to pack. I left Daniel a note saying I'd see him back at the reserve. I'd put off talking to him and couldn't face it just then. He'd been good to me whilst I was in hospital, visiting every day, spending hours at the British Consulate and with the police, keeping the press away.'

'Probably worried about the adverse publicity Fultons would have got.'

Rachel shushed him, saying crisply, without heat: 'That's mean of you.'

'Yes, it is.' Michael leaned forward slightly on his braced arms. 'But I don't see you complaining.'

A silence, rippled at its edges by a sobbing lapwing, then Rachel again. 'I suggested to him that Rio Fultons could have been involved – Lena Clares could have organized it easily. He said I was still in shock, not thinking straight. Daniel wanted to know what Aoira and I had been doing, out in the streets. When I admitted that I'd set up a meeting with Antonio Olinda, he stared at me.

'"But our company's been good to the Gapo!" he said. "Fultons are the only thing that's stopping their forest from being overrun with oil barons and gold prospectors."

'I couldn't budge him from that idea and didn't try: I wasn't entirely convinced that Fultons had been behind Aoira's murder, either – it seemed too extreme. I assumed Antonio was a victim of lawyer's paranoia.'

Rachel paused, taking another deep breath. 'But then I left the hospital and went back to the hotel – and heard Tim and Charles talking in the corridor.'

She frowned, the naturally down-turned corners of her mouth dipping lower. 'Shouting I suppose would be a more accurate description: I could hear them all the way through the walls. A man was with them, demanding money. Charles was refusing to pay: he was raging about a "cock-up". At that point, I limped to the wardrobe and dug out my cassette recorder.

'I started the thing recording when I heard Tim burst out, "The arrangement was just to move them on. Only for a day or so, for Christ's sake! We didn't ask for a fucking blood-bath!"

'Tim's outburst had me scrambling closer to the wall to catch everything. I'd never heard him swear before, ever. He was desperate. He was someone whose world had caved in.'

Michael took her cold fingers in his. Rachel glanced down at her cuddled hands as though they were not part of her at all and then raised her face to his. 'You understand, don't you?'

Seeing her unable to continue for the moment, Michael said steadily, 'There was a mistake. Tim and Charles promised those policemen cash if they could keep you and Aoira away from any lawyers whilst you were in Rio. The police misinterpreted them.'

Rachel nodded, her cheeks sunken. She was now as pale as her grey silk trousers. '"What's one dead Gapo?" I heard that said – the policeman admitted it freely, in a hotel corridor. It was then I finally realised that nothing would be done in Rio. That afternoon, I contacted Fultons in London.

'I told them that if anything happened to me, videotapes of the expedition plus copies of what they were going to hear would be released to the British and American press by Antonio Olinda and my English solicitor. That was a huge lie, but I gambled that Fultons wouldn't dare call my bluff. Tim, Charles, Daniel and I had all been supplied with camcorders, and had used them independently of each other throughout our stay with the Gapo. Even Daniel wouldn't be sure of everything I'd filmed, or whether I'd kept any material back. Then I hit Fultons with the only real weapon I had. I played them the tape.'

Rachel's mouth twitched. 'The company had my picture on file – they'd have to know that in a full-colour newspaper spread with jungle footage, it would make an attractive package. Fultons wouldn't be sure either that I hadn't supplied video recordings of Aoira and myself. the dusky native beauty and English rose. If I'd big boobs that would have been even better for the tabloids.'

Teeth chattering despite her Barbour and Michael's jacket, she huddled tighter on her boulder.

'We were recalled to Britain. My visa to Brazil was revoked by the Brazilian authorities – I was banned from entering the country – Daniel and the others never went back, either: British Fultons didn't renew Charles' and Tim's contracts. Fultons appeared shocked by what had happened. In meeting after meeting, higher management staff and various psychologists kept asking me about Charles' and Tim's states of mind. Had I noticed any unusual behaviour on their part? Did they exhibit any peculiar signs of stress? British Fultons' innocence seemed very convincing, although they suddenly lost interest in the Gapo expedition, pulled funds and never offered me another assignment. So after all the carnage, Aoira's tribe was no better off. In fact they were worse off, because between them, Rio Fultons and Tim Stevens lost the sample of

Aoira's healing tree. So the Gapo had nothing to bargain with when two months later one of the oil companies moved in and decided – with Rio Fultons – that the tribe could manage quite well thank you on half their homelands. The oil company grabbed the rest and paid Rio Fultons "compensation". Now the same company wants more land and the Gapo are losing out again.

'I protested at the agreement then and have kept protesting ever since, but Fultons and the oil barons took even less notice of that. Word leaked out to the other pharmaceutical firms, too. I was a whistle-blower, a bad risk. I found I couldn't get on any research trips.

'After six months of casual fruit- and veg-picking jobs, no botanical work and feeling like a pariah, I decided to change direction. In this country, wild places and rare plants are disappearing at about the same rate or even faster than in the Amazon. I retrained to work in Britain, in the first landscape I'd learned to love: moorland.

'Daniel went off to work in Canada – he'd had enough of Brazil. He asked me to go with him but I refused: I'd had enough of him. He thought I was wrong to phone the company in London – he'd have preferred to have "sorted something out" as he put it, in Rio. Daniel never said the word Judas, but he made me feel it.'

'And you believed him?' asked Michael incredulously.

'Only after Tim Stevens' death,' replied Rachel sadly. 'A month after we returned from Rio, Tim committed suicide.'

Chapter 27

Michael fought the need to touch Rachel, show her somehow that Aoira's murder and Tim Stevens' death were not her fault.

'The thing I still don't understand is why he and Charles hired those thugs,' Rachel was saying, rubbing her fingers hard against her thumbs. 'I never spoke to them alone again. When Fultons recalled us to Britain, the company warned me to say nothing to anyone until I'd made a report to the board. Charles and Tim didn't know what was going on until Fultons had them in for "debriefing".' She spat the word.

'Presumably you didn't tell Daniel anything.'

'No, I wasn't sure how far he was involved. I'm still not sure.'

Her tone warned Michael not to continue, but he couldn't resist. 'Did he offer any explanations?'

'Fultons wanted results from our jungle trips. Daniel said that as senior members of our team he, Tim and Charles bore the brunt of that pressure. He also talked about patenting: Charles and Tim might have been considering taking out a lucrative patent on the drug derived from Aoira's tree.'

'Could they have gone behind Fultons' back in that way, though?' asked Michael. 'Patent a cure?'

'Possibly. It would depend on the terms of their working contracts, which I never saw.' Rachel shrugged. 'I can't see Tim being that ruthless simply for a bigger share of the cash. Charles, maybe: he liked a lavish life style away from the jungle. But Tim was only ambitious academically.'

'Tim didn't want to admit that a Gapo woman had discovered the tree first?' Michael suggested.

'It's what Daniel thought. And I must admit it ties in with what happened later. You know, Tim dying after Aoira was murdered. The only thing I'm sure of is that no one benefited from Aoira's magic salve. After Tim and Rio Fultons lost the only sample I'd given them, the part of the forest where Aoira's healing tree was found was cut down. It's gone forever.'

Uncomfortable at having anything in common with Daniel even in thought, Michael rose. 'Coming?' He held out his hand.

Rachel nodded, shrugging Michael's jacket from her back. 'I do already have a coat.' She tweaked a lapel of her Barbour.

'Keep it. At least till we get back.'

'Thanks.' Black leather snug about her shoulders, Rachel set off, Michael following.

Above them the twilight sky bristled with stars. An early moth fluttered against his eye. Slightly ahead, Rachel stepped quietly over pebbles, shadowy and secretive as a deer.

Michael frowned, matching his steps so that he could watch her face. He didn't trust Rachel to tell him everything. Tall people are expected to be independent, to be relied upon. Learning about Aoira, Michael could better appreciate Rachel's concern over the expectant Angwen. And if he were wrong about the stalker's true target, or if Angwen's stolen bike was an unrelated crime, then Rachel was right to be worried. Stalking was not usually this complex.

'Did Tim Stevens have any family?' he asked as they reached the kissing gate to the carpark.

'Tim left no close relatives to come after me, if that's your next question.' Rachel slipped through the gate.

'What about friends?'

'Only Charles and Daniel – Tim was always a loner. I suppose Charles was his closest friend.' Rachel shrugged the jacket off her shoulders. 'Before I forget,' she said, holding it out.

'Thanks.' Hauling on his coat, Michael didn't want to let her go yet. 'Maybe we should continue this discussion in the Warren House – that's where Paul's meeting Inspector Penoyre.'

Rachel decided that paperwork would keep. 'Good idea'. She glanced round the area of rough ground. 'Daniel's Mazda's still here. I think we should go before he gets back or he'll want to come along too and we can't very well exclude him.'

Her car. Petrol. Oil. Inflammable. 'Wait!' Michael ran to her car and dropped to his knees, peering under the chassis and wheel-arches.

A rattle of pebbles as Rachel caught up. 'I really think you've gone far enough, Mike. This is too much.'

'You only call me Mike when you're really annoyed.' Concern was tipping into craziness.

Michael knew it but was unable to stop. He'd seen too many burnt-out cars, handled too many car-fires and accidents.

'Tell me what to look for and then let's go.' Rachel's urgency returned Michael to himself. Moving at a crouch, he homed in on the final wheel, watching out for wires, for any small lumps of potential explosive.

'My torch, in the bike seat.'

Seconds later, Rachel was pressing the cold torch into his free fist. 'Even if we assume you're right and I'm being targeted, who's doing it?'

Michael swept the torch beam over the door seals and windows, finding nothing. 'The more I think about this, the more I think Paul's wrong. Maybe it's nothing to do with Fultons.'

'Why not?' Copying what he was doing, Rachel was also searching her car. Head bent close enough to mist the paintwork, she was within inches of accidentally skimming her fingers over the rear doors and windows.

'Please be careful.'

'Oh, my word, Mike, of course I'm leaving fingerprints everywhere.'

Michael sighed. 'Unless you've been trained, you could destroy vital evidence. End of lesson.'

'Right, Mr Perfect. What was that about Fultons?'

'Kestrel House's security isn't that sensational. It's possible a firm the size of Fultons could have breached it already, and neither Paul nor anyone else would have been any the wiser–'

'Until Dad's vaccine was pinched.'

'Precisely.' Michael checked Rachel's side and

moved on to the engine, lifting the bonnet. Rachel came alongside, took the torch from him, shone it where he directed.

'So, without Fultons, where does that leave your distrust of Daniel and Colin Benwick?' she challenged.

'I don't know – the whole thing's only a suggestion. Maybe I just don't want to trust them.'

'Well, your latest idea is rather a big – and sudden – change of heart.' Rachel laughed at Michael's startled expression. 'You still think someone is stalking me, but for what possible reason? For gain? I'm not rich, nor likely to be. In some kind of vendetta? The only people I ever actively fell out with were Daniel, Tim and Charles. It's true that because of me, Tim and Charles were no longer employed, but that hasn't prevented Charles from being a success. Dad met him recently in Parma. He's head of a cosmetics firm now, and a successful, happily married man.'

'Perhaps seeing your father brought it all back to him – these incidents have occurred "recently".' Michael repeated the word in order to make Rachel smile, but also in an attempt to persuade her to consider the idea.

'I don't know, Michael. It seems very tenuous. I'm sure Charles would be delighted I considered him such a mastermind, but frankly I can't see the botanist I knew having the contacts to operate such a long-distance hate campaign. And even if, for argument's sake, he has, why should he bother after so long?'

'You think Charles Elsham has no motive.'

'I think it's time to start looking closer to home, if only to discount people.' Rachel's voice sharpened. 'It isn't good for Kestrel House, having the staff wondering about each other. We can start by asking Angwen how she knows it wasn't Dr Benwick who phoned her.'

Glad of the 'we', Michael let down the bonnet of Rachel's car. 'To the Warren House, then.'

Chapter 28

'Before we go, Michael, there's something I'd like to know.' Rachel paused, wanting to be sure she had his attention. Wary, too, of asking.

The gesture still strange to her, she raised her head to those gunmetal eyes. 'I know I've asked you this before, but why do you dislike Daniel?'

She heard Michael mutter something – it sounded like 'scumbag' – before her car-phone shrilled.

'Damn the thing.' Yanking open the door, lunging for the receiver, she heard Michael's bleeper go off, saw him sprint for the Norton. It wasn't Mike's night on fire-watch–

'No more bad news, please,' Rachel murmured. 'Yes?'

She heard a faint click, then: *'Guess what this is, Rachel.'*

A shrieking blast on a whistle followed the flat, metallic whisper, its note so high and piercing that Rachel flung the phone away, onto the

passenger seat. Even as she started at her in-
stinctive reaction and went for the phone again,
another shriek blew down the line.

'*Got it yet, Rachel? Whistle-blower?*'

'The police are monitoring this line.'The lie felt
clumsy in her mouth but anything was better
than the feeble: Who are you? The arsonist-
stalker operating at Kestrel House and Angwen's
mystery caller, now her own.

'They're coming for you very soon.' Rachel
smoothly delivered the threat, despising the
obvious, semi-pleading, What do you want? What
else but her father's vaccine? What else but
malicious mischief? Let the caller sweat too, she
thought, glad that Michael had his back to her.
Come to think of it, had Michael not been
telephoned himself, seconds before, would she
have considered him a suspect? Should she still?

Crazy, thought Rachel, and spoke. 'You're
crazy.'

'See you soon.'

The recorded voice had gone, the line hummed
vacantly. How had the caller got her mobile
number? The reply came to her with depressing
simplicity: from the message on one of her
answerphones.

'I'm going to have to leave you.'

Rachel flicked up her head, seeing Michael
with the Norton, close enough to touch, his face
hovering above her in the dark beyond the inner
light of her car. 'Sorry?' She wasn't sure why she
was apologizing, perhaps because she hadn't yet
collected the wit to contact the police.

A hand solidified out of the starry shadows,

156

gently squeezing her shoulder. 'Rachel?'

'Of course you have to go.' She forced a smile. 'Good luck.'

'You'll be all right?'

'Of course!' *Let him go thinking you're fine, that everything's fine.* She moistened her cactus-dry mouth with her tongue.

'That was Dad, inviting me for a drink at the Warren.' Impulsively, Rachel unfurled herself from the car seat and planted a swift kiss on Michael's cheek. 'Be careful.'

Michael blushed then snapped back from teenager into adulthood. He wagged a finger at her. 'We still need to talk.'

'I know. You owe me an explanation about Daniel. And about why you feel compelled to come roaring after me.'

Michael threw her a narrowed look. 'Will you lock your car doors, Rachel? Do it if only to make me feel easy.'

Anything to make him leave, thought Rachel. He had his emergency, she her very first nuisance caller. 'I will.'

Before the roar of his Norton had ebbed away, she'd locked herself in the car. Then she phoned the police.

Chapter 29

Sergeant Moss, grumbling and with peppermint on his breath, checked the area, made notes and left Rachel dissatisfied and feeling like a decoy. She finally got away and raced, fuming, to the Warren House, only to find her father, Angwen and the elusive Joe Penoyre long gone.

At home, there was good news waiting on the answer-phone: Lorna Lees had called to let her know that Stephen was at home and doing well.

The next day was Saturday. As usual, the dawn chorus woke Rachel and she tossed back the duvet, scrambling off the bed with her customary morning energy. Eager for time to pass so that she could speed down into Topsham to visit her new stepmother, Rachel decided to go straight out into the pear orchard. The brambles there were as thick as a man's fingers and needed scything. It would be refreshing not to be bound to a desk.

Brushing her hair, Rachel left it loose, a home-grown neckshader. She dressed in the red-and-black checked trousers that she nicknamed her 'Rupert Bears', and a cotton jade sweatshirt pulled back to her elbows. Plucking her penknife and tough Amazonian 'gardening' gloves from the tallboy, Rachel ducked downstairs. Closing the outer door behind her and leaning against it, she eased the lightweight black walking-boots that Helen called 'cute' onto her blue-socked feet, slipped a small plastic bottle of mineral water into a pocket and stepped out into the morning.

Her first thought was of paradise. In the orchard, the pears had burst into blossom. To the tips of the slenderest twigs, the trees sparkled with the perfection of snow crystals, bright and crisp still in May.

Rachel breathed in deeply. Already heat rose from the drying earth and the sun rose yellow in a cloudless sky. Despite a promise of rain last night, none had fallen and the dew was burned off. Mosses growing on the gravel path crunched under her heel as she made for the tin-roofed garage. Dragging back the door, she squirmed past her car to retrieve the gardening tools stacked or hanging on pegs at the rear of the building. Hoe, spade, pruners, fork and scythe, all thick with protective grease. Mr Collard had done well by her here. She had her machete, too, tacked to the kitchen/sitting-room wall, close to the healing-pipe Aoira had given her.

Sighing as she thought of Aoira and Tim, Rachel grabbed the tools she needed, plus cleaning rag, and edged sideways back to the path. Past the shadow of the garage and the sheltering beeches, light poured into the orchard in a brimming flame. Above, out of sight even of her keen eyes, a lark climbed and trilled a fiery song of territory and sweetness. A small grey lizard basked on a granite wall.

After a cold, damp start, the weather had turned unseasonably dry and warm. If this pattern continued and there was no rain, plants and animals would suffer. And there would be an even greater danger of moorland fires.

Everywhere I go, fires follow, thought Rachel, climbing the path to the end of the orchard. I'm being stalked by fire.

Above, the lark's song was suddenly cut short as the bird plummeted to earth and Rachel set to her task, driving the scythe in low sweeping arcs through the brambles and tangled dead grasses which grew waist-high around her. The crackle of trampled vegetation reminded her of the spit and pop of fire. Out of the smoke of memory, two heads coalesced against the bleached cut grass: the narrow, laughing face of Aoira, smooth as a beechnut, and Tim's cadaverous, solemn. Dragging away writhing brambles with the curved tip of her scythe, she could hear Tim whispering, *'I've paid my price, have you?'*

Rachel cut faster, working from tree-trunk to tree-trunk, bending her back in shade and sun, stabbing and lashing at intransigent blackberry stems. She laboured to forget, to block out, but even on this spring morning, in an orchard bowered with blossom, death was with her.

She was remembering a sullen, airless noonday in Yorkshire, in the village churchyard of Almondbury, at the edge of the woollen town of Huddersfield. Tim's pale coffin, curiously small for a tall man, being carried out of the fifteenth-century church by six red-cheeked pallbearers. She and Charles Elsham followed, with a black-suited woman from Fultons' personnel department who was snuffling with hay fever. Stepping

160

on the confetti of June weddings, Rachel heard her low heels tapping on the paving slabs. There was no one behind her. A few casual acquaintances and neighbours were expected to put in an appearance at the crematorium on Fixby Road, but otherwise she, Charles and their pink-eyed companion were Tim Stevens' chief mourners. Daniel was working in Canada. There were no relatives.

Instead of a suicide note, Tim had left detailed instructions about his funeral. A service in the church where he had once been a choirboy. Cremation. Donations to be sent to Survival, the charity dedicated to the support of tribal peoples – Rachel had sent a donation, as had Charles and Daniel. No flowers, by request.

A botanist with no flowers. It had been the bleakest funeral she'd attended, and the loneliest. To think of it even five years later made her break out in a cold sweat. To have no second cousins, distant aunts or occasional nephews who would care enough, if only for appearance's sake, to walk behind the coffin. Then, at the crematorium, to have only a half-dozen more mourners.

Resting the scythe against a tree trunk, Rachel drew her penknife out of a trouser pocket and cut a budding flower from the shrub rose scrambling over the orchard wall, its branches and flower-buds mingling with the pear branches. After Tim's funeral she'd wandered in the rose gardens of the crematorium, in search of consolation and hope, but had been depressed by their colourful massed ranks, scentless as waxworks. Not like the straggly-stemmed, gloriously untidy flower now

161

in her hand – she would have to tame this rose-bush a little when it had finished blooming, thought Rachel, digging in her pocket to retrieve the bottle of mineral water.

Taking a drink, she heard the baffled snarl of a motor-bike, its engine note changing as the rider changed gear to attack the steep single track-road that ran past her cottage. Her spirits flew at the anticipated challenge. Nicking the rose stem, she plunged it into the mineral water and, bloom and bottle in hand, crossed the orchard to the blue gate.

The grey bike and its blue-helmeted rider topped the final hill and curve. Michael switched off when he saw her.

'You look like a siren, enticing all comers.' He coasted down to the blue gate. 'I guessed you might be up – you always did like mornings. What are you doing with that rose, casting a spell?'

Rachel grinned, noting the grey bloom under Michael's eyes. When he took off his helmet she saw a peach-coloured stubble, a long face drawn longer by tiredness. 'You look terrible.'

Stripping off his gloves and stuffing them in the helmet, Michael stretched his eyes heavenwards. 'It was a big shout, an area-round call-up for all of us. A garage on the A30 had just gone up.'

Rachel opened the gate for him. 'Any casualties?' She exhaled slowly as Michael shook his head, relieved that he'd not had to deal with death as well as fire. He and others had fought through the night whilst she was in bed.

Examining Michael with sympathetic eyes,

162

Rachel noted how morning and exhaustion had given him a mangy magnificence. From the fawn hair, streaked in drying tangles across his forehead, to the dusty black jacket, faded jeans and muddied heavy shoes. There was a smear of ash across the lobe of his left ear, missed in a hasty shower, and his shoulders were sprinkled with fallen pearblossom.

'Come in, Cinders, and have breakfast with me.' She reached out to brush the smut off his ear. As he strode through the gateway, she handed him the mineral bottle. 'The first off the bush. For you.'

Suddenly Michael was pinker than the rose, but he took the plastic bottle from her neatly enough, with only a small grumble. 'Don't know how you expect me to get this home in one piece.' Cupping the fat bud, he gunned her one of his curious stares, obviously winding himself up to ask something.

A sharp horn-blast hammered the morning. In a brilliant dazzle of car door, Daniel emerged from his newly parked Mazda.

Michael's keen, searching glance was replaced by an angry stare. Not only did he dislike this intrusion, thought Rachel, he clearly resented the older man's style. Compared to himself, Daniel this morning was a model straight from *Gentleman's Quarterly* – lean and tanned in white needlecords, blue-checked Gucci short-sleeved shirt and navy shades.

'Beware of geeks bearing gifts,' Michael muttered at Rachel, who bit her lip against a laugh. Daniel was certainly carrying something in two large brown-paper bags.

'Hello! I thought you'd be about on a lovely day like this. I've brought a small something – something I think you'll agree will be most useful.' Ignoring Michael, Daniel pushed past the taller man and set the larger of the brown-paper bags down on the gravel path in front of Rachel. 'Look inside.'

Rachel pocketed her gardening gloves, knelt on the small round pebbles and unfolded the bag top. 'Oh, my word!' She plunged both hands into the bag. In another instant a small furry black body was in the crook of her arm, a short black tail whirling against her red hair. 'She's lovely!'

Daniel chuckled at Rachel's enthusiasm for the Alsatian puppy, pleasure spilling out from behind his cool blue sunshades. 'A replacement Moll, agreed to by Lorna. We drove to Statts farm last night to pick the beast from Moll's mother's latest litter. Lorna and I both thought that, as acting director of Kestrel House, you should present the new dog to Stephen personally when you visit him at home.'

Rachel found her eyes filling with silly tears at the thoughtfulness of Daniel's gift. And his foresight in realizing she would be going to see the Leeses today. Gently she let the puppy down on the path, where the Alsatian blundered unsteadily towards Michael and urinated on his shoes.

'A dog with taste,' Daniel remarked, giving Rachel a conspiratorial smile. Rachel missed the smile; she was watching the pup, and Michael.

'Steady on, pixie.' Michael deposited his helmet and gloves on an old tree-stump. He crouched to pat the butting, yapping little body. 'No – you don't want to eat the rose, it'll do you no good at all.'

'She's probably thirsty,' said Daniel. 'Maybe hungry, too.'

'What do puppies eat?' asked Rachel.

Daniel frowned, impatience beginning to show through the relaxed façade. 'It's only for a few more hours – Lorna will be able to see to it.'

'Bland things, the same as babies,' put in Michael. 'Tinned rice pudding, for instance, or cornflakes and gravy.'

Daniel grimaced, but Rachel smiled gratefully at Michael. He was clearly a man of many talents. Rising in one movement, she turned to the cottage. 'Bring her inside. We'll all have a drink and cornflakes – with or without gravy.' She chuckled at the idea.

'Ah, yes, well, I'm afraid that's impossible.' Daniel barred the path in front of Michael. 'I've only brought enough hot chocolate and croissants for two.' He held up the second paper bag. 'And your real present, Rachel.' He tapped the breast pocket of his check shirt then glared at Michael, voice hardening. 'Shouldn't you be getting along? You're as foul as a kipper.'

Michael gave a slow, wicked grin. 'I was invited first.'

'But Rachel and I have things to discuss. Personal matters.'

'You can talk about anything in front of me and pixie – can't he, nipper?' Michael scooped up the puppy in one large hand and clambered to his feet.

165

Swiftly, Rachel put herself between the two men. She loathed going back on her word, but she had to grab this chance to draw Daniel out whilst her ex was being so unusually co-operative. And she knew he wouldn't thaw or talk whilst Michael was there. 'I'll take her, please, Michael.' She held out her hands.

'You want me to leave you alone with him?'

'Of course I do.' Couldn't Michael understand that she had to see Daniel alone, that the man would be more likely to reveal things, perhaps important clues or leads, if they were left alone? 'Just go, can't you?' she burst out, caught between irritation and a fear she couldn't define.

Stiffly, Michael jerked out his hand and pressed the small black Alsatian onto Rachel's shoulder. 'Here, give her this.' He plucked the rose coolly from the bottle of mineral water, tossed it aside and placed the bottle next to Rachel on top of the nearest granite boulder. 'Enjoy your breakfast.'

He closed the blue gate with exaggerated care and was gone.

Chapter 30

Daniel gave Rachel a 'good riddance' smile. 'Now we're alone, I've a few suggestions.'

Aware of the fast beat of the puppy's heart in her hand, Rachel picked up the water bottle, desolate on top of its grey stone. Stepping by the ruined rose, she murmured, 'wait', and continued walking to the cottage.

She emerged, carrying the pup in a large cardboard box lined with an old towel. 'It's such a lovely day, I thought we might have a picnic breakfast.' She laid the box under the pear-trees on the scythed grass. 'Two ticks, and I'll bring glasses and plates.'

First, Rachel opened a tin of rice pudding, piling it onto an old plate. She retrieved a shallow metal meat-tin from the oven and filled it full of water.

Out in her box under the trees, the puppy gulped from the meat-tin, then fell upon the pudding, burying her snout in the cold, creamy mass.

'One satisfied customer.' Daniel leaned over the box with his flask of hot chocolate and bagful of goodies. He rattled the bag at Rachel, who disappeared inside and returned with cups, knives, plates, butter and honey, carrying all in her plastic wash-basket.

Sprawled on the soft mound of grass-clippings she'd been raking together, Daniel was opening the flask. Stepping off the path, Rachel passed the discarded rose – she wished Michael hadn't done that.

After regret, anger rushed in, fanned by suspicion. Michael and Daniel both expected her to follow their 'suggestions'. But how far could she trust either man? She sensed she could rely on Michael, but what if her instincts were wrong? She'd been wrong in the past, starting with Daniel.

The spell of his looks worked on her even now,

especially when he was so cheerful and winning. Pouring chocolate, splitting and buttering a roll for her, gesturing that she sit whilst he spread their feast about her. Bread, nectarines, grapes, chocolate-filled croissants. At one point Rachel laughed, playfully snatching at the second paper-bag Daniel had brought along.

'I think you must have a miniature black hole in that bag, the amount of stuff you keep pulling out of it.'

'Organization, that's the key.' Holding the bag out of her reach, Daniel balanced a grape between his nose and upper lip.

'You're a nerd sometimes, Daniel.'

Rolling the grape into his mouth, Daniel observed, 'You haven't called me anything that friendly for years.' He lifted his cup, toasted her, and drank. 'Sorry.' His foot had accidentally brushed hers.

'What's the sugar level of this stuff? Half a flask of this and I'll be running round the ceiling by lunchtime.'

'Eat your bread, then.' Daniel was all sunshine, the breeze ruffling the tops of his well-arranged curls, smile platinum in a golden face. The smile became caressing as Rachel set down her cup and anxiously stretched over to the cardboard dog-pen. 'Don't tell me you've never heard a dog snore.'

'Not a puppy.' Rachel watched the twitching jaws of the small Alsatian. 'It really is good of you, taking trouble for Lorna and Stephen.'

'I did it for you.' Daniel smiled as Rachel narrowed her blue-green eyes at him. 'Is it wrong, admitting to a self-interested kindness?'

'That depends on who you're talking to.' Her own motives in returning to Devon were a similar blend of ambition and concern, although of late concern had been uppermost. Recalling what the police had said last night, Rachel felt herself turning pale with anger – an anger she had no right to direct at Daniel. Except in one careful question.

'Statts Farm – that's a hard place to reach in the dark. Yesterday, you must have returned from your walk over by Wistman's Wood soon after I did.'

'How did you know I'd followed you? I never caught up.'

'Your car was in the carpark when I returned.' Rachel took a bite of roll, another sip of hot chocolate. She was glad they were eating out of doors – it was such a glorious, sunny place, and the cut grass smelt so sweet. 'Moll's replacement – was that an impulse decision?'

'In a way, I suppose.' Daniel spoke between bites of nectarine. 'When I didn't find you on the moor yesterday, I went on a bit of a walkabout – I wanted to think about everything that had happened at K.H. over the last few days. The idea about the Lees' dog struck me whilst I was walking. When I got back to my car, I phoned Lorna at home. She was all for it – it was perfect timing. Steve was down in the dumps about his Alsatian and her cousin – Peter Paston of Statts Farm – had just phoned to tell her the news about the new litter. Lorna didn't fancy driving to the farm in the dark, so when I offered to take

169

her she was delighted. She liked my suggestion of your giving the pup to her man, too.'

Rachel glanced at the still-sleeping puppy. She'd the answer to her question. Daniel had carried no mobile last evening. He couldn't have phoned her in the car park just before 8 p.m. because he was still out on the moor.

Daniel threw the nectarine stone into the uncut grass, wiped his hands and mouth on a napkin. 'Aren't you going to ask about your present?'

'It's not polite.'

Daniel drained his cup, poured himself another, refilled Rachel's, popped another grape into his mouth. Prolonging the suspense.

Rachel meanwhile was sending up a rapid prayer that the gift wouldn't be so extravagant as to be embarrassing, or, worse, put her under any obligation. These thoughts made her guilty and uncomfortable but, going on past form, when Daniel looked this delectable it was time to beware. He knew the power of his charm and how susceptible she'd been.

Looking at him, relaxed and sweet-natured in her garden, Rachel was struck by the disturbing discovery that she was not yet immune. After five years and the Rio incident, Daniel could still move her in a basic way, with the easiest and most casual of smiles.

'Here.' Daniel's eyes were a piercing blue. 'This is for you.'

He handed her a small, slim, yellow case, the size of an antique silver matchbox. Its heaviness revealed its value: the case was of pure gold. Stunned, Rachel traced the design of the stylized tree on its lid.

'Open it.' Daniel commanded in an intense, eager whisper.

Half-dreading what she would find, Rachel gently sprang up the lid, took out the twisted slip of paper and carefully untied it. She sat still for a moment, staring at the dried hard seeds.

After what she'd told Michael about no one, not even Fultons, benefiting from her final jungle trip, Rachel was shocked. Surprise made her tone flat. 'They weren't lost? They were never sent to Rio Fultons' labs?'

Daniel cleared his throat. 'No.'

The negative sent a shudder through her.

Daniel reached out, taking her free, nerveless hand in both of his. 'Rachel, look at me.'

His voice and even more his warm, graceful hands, were hypnotic in their ghastly self-satisfaction. She raised her head.

'You know what these are, don't you?'

She nodded. 'The seeds from Aoira's medicine tree. I'd always assumed that Tim had sent them on to Fultons.'

Daniel laughed and she started, instinctively recoiling. His fingers followed her, refusing to let go.

'I told Fultons we couldn't find the tree again in the jungle, that we'd lost all the seeds and specimen material.' His white teeth gleamed in his grinning face. 'In truth, I removed these from Tim's sample packs – by the time he and Charles discovered they were missing, we were in Rio. Fultons have never seen these seeds.'

'Nor anything else?'

171

'Nothing. I promise. Aoira's medicine tree was yours, Rachel. It belonged to you and the Gapo, not Fultons, Tim, or Charles. Or me.'

Rachel lowered her head. The man's stupidity at this point was mind-blowing. 'Aoira's tree was used by her and the Gapo. It wasn't and can't be owned by anyone.'

'Whatever.' With a spurt of impatience, Daniel released her hand. 'Nit-picking doesn't alter the fact that I never sold you out.'

Rachel was grateful for his easily kindled sense of grievance. It helped her to control her own temper and released her from any sense of gratitude, although she knew that was the reason behind Daniel's gift: to convince her what a fine fellow he was. Instead, by this action, Daniel had utterly destroyed any of her final, faint regrets. She wanted nothing more to do with him.

'So, Daniel, after I say "thank you", what do you want in return?' she asked, closing seeds and paper in the case.

Daniel caught a strand of her hair. 'I'd like another chance. Ever since I saw you again I've thought about it. Now I'm sure. We were good for each other. You kept me on the straight and narrow. I – well, you always seemed to like what I could do for you.'

Rachel backed up rapidly and jumped to her feet. Turning her crimsoning face away from Daniel, she skimmed over the bare orchard floor to where she'd left her scythe. Taking the rough, warm handle of the tool in her hand steadied her.

'I'm sorry, Daniel.' Aware that he didn't deserve it, she still tried to be gentle. 'I don't really think it would work.'

'You need someone to look after you, Rachel. After what's been happening round you lately I've been worried sick.'

Looking round, Rachel saw Michael's haggard, angry face superimpose itself for a moment on top of Daniel's. Michael was the one who was worried sick. Daniel had brought her breakfast and a replacement Moll and the 'gift' of Aoira's medicine tree, but...

Meeting his eager eyes, Rachel's pulse went into overdrive. The glare of sun on the metal scythe pierced under her eyelids, making them smart.

'You expect me to be grateful, Daniel, after you've admitted to holding back a vital sample that quite probably would have saved the Gapo's lands for them? If you did have those seeds five years ago and if you'd acted properly then, and sent them on to Rio Fultons, they might have been enough to stop Fultons selling out the tribe to that oil-mining company! That healing tree was the only recognized thing with "value" in the Gapo territory – maybe even enough to stop the bulldozers. So should I be happy that you didn't do your job?'

Daniel was on his feet. 'It wasn't like that–'

'You don't give up!' Rachel pointed a stiff finger at him. 'But you're right, Daniel – for once you and I totally agree. Just as well for you, or I'd be taking you to court for negligence in the face of illegal seizing of tribal lands, resulting in mass evictions and murder. No doubt the charge wouldn't have stuck, but the publicity would have finished your career. As it is, I realize exactly

173

what happened.'

'You do?'

'You were always ambitious. Nothing on earth, most definitely not me, would have stopped you from shipping a likely anti-AIDS cure out of the jungle. You, holding onto a potential million-dollar medicine for five years? I don't think so. If that gold-mine weren't sufficient inducement, there was still the academic kudos. Daniel Plewes-Mason, discoverer of the new wonder-drug.'

Her voice grew drier still, each word like broken glass. 'All of which means that Rio Fultons did receive a sample and lost the only seeds so far recovered from Aoira's healing-tree.'

Rachel's fingers closed tightly around the gold box. 'These are fresh seeds, Daniel. I'm no environmental archaeologist, but even I can tell artificial ageing. Pop them in the oven last night for a quick toasting? Did you really expect me to be taken in by that cheap trick?'

She lunged at him. 'Where did you get these, Daniel? You owe the Gapo that – these seeds are from a living tree...'

Daniel jutted his lower lip. 'Ask your jungle pals. I've finished here.'

Rachel's eyes widened. She caught hold of Daniel's arm as he twisted round to leave. 'You opened my mail. That's low, Daniel, even for you–'

She got no further. The glass of the downstairs window shattered. Through it came the lightning flash of a flaming spear. Shouting, Rachel threw down the scythe and ran, although she already knew what it was.

Spitting on the gravel, surrounded by glass splinters, were the burning remains of the healing-flute given to her by Aoira.

Chapter 31

Again the police arrived, not Sergeant Moss this time but three different officers. In his forties, with a keen expression and a receding hair-line, the scene-of-crime officer retrieved the charred remains of the wooden flute and bagged a large smooth stone, thrown to shatter the window glass. A couple of constables searched the cottage and grounds for signs of entry. How had the assailant entered and fled unseen from a cottage with one entrance?

Hearing the police joking about Stephen's puppy not being much use except for guarding chewed slippers, Rachel felt her temper cooling into disgust. Certainly Daniel's replacement wouldn't be able to take over as a guard-dog, but that wasn't the point. Moll had been a companion as well as a work-mate. She understood, why didn't they?

'Have you any more relevant questions?' she demanded. 'I've to go to Topsham this morning, so I'd appreciate some speed.'

Before she could move anywhere, she had to find out from Daniel if there were any more seed and plant samples that could be sent to Kew for analysis. Kew Gardens had the expertise and more importantly the power and independence that would guarantee the Gapo's rights if Tim's initial findings on Aoira's healing-tree were proved correct.

'We're being as fast as we can be, love,' said the blonder of the two pink and angular young constables. 'Now why don't you go in and make a pot of tea?'

'Who for? You've work to do and I'm not thirsty.'

'I could do with a cup, Rachel,' Daniel said. 'Unless you want me to leave immediately?'

He was counting on her not asking any more questions whilst the police were there. Rachel decided to disappoint him. 'You can go, Daniel, so long as you tell me what you did with the rest of my Brazilian mail.'

'You've had it all, Rachel. Believe me. Now, is that drink still on offer?'

As Daniel raised a friendly hand to wave at a passing local, Rachel added quietly, 'Please, Daniel, don't delay sending those extra seeds you've kept back on to Fultons. The Gapo need a good result more than we do.'

Daniel stiffened, a red flush sweeping through his fashionable tan. 'Just what kind of monster do you take me for? Do you really think I've changed so much?'

Thrown off balance by the question, Rachel found she had no answer to give him. She felt the policemen watching with an air of long-suffering resignation. Their sympathies would be with Daniel.

'Strong with a dash of milk, no sugar.' He seized the advantage.

Why didn't he go? Rachel thought, leaving Daniel joking with the police whilst she strode back indoors with the remains of their interrupted breakfast piled into the wash-basket. She dumped the lot on the stone floor, tore the jug-kettle off its stand and wrenched on the cold-tap. Water spurted over her hand. Cursing, Rachel heard her name.

She twisted round and saw Michael hunched on the threshold. A freshly showered and changed Michael. 'What the hell are you doing back?' she snapped, oppressed by the appearance of yet another male.

'He'll have come up through there. If the S.O.C.O. goes down first, you should get some decent forensics.' Michael's answer was directed not at her but to the shadowy stranger standing behind him.

Michael pointed to a bare, wallpapered section of the stairwell. The figure carefully went ahead and pushed gently against the wall. The 'wall' swung inwards, admitting a gush of cold air and revealing a narrow series of descending steps.

Rachel shut off the gushing cold-tap and rushed forward to the top of the steps. The stranger turned to meet her.

'Detective Inspector Penoyre. Sorry about my delay in coming here, Miss Falconer. I've only just been assigned this case after Sergeant Moss was taken into hospital this morning.'

Another unwelcome piece of news. 'Will he be all right?' Rachel asked.

177

'Now they've whipped out his appendix, the doctors expect he'll be back on his feet pretty quickly. If you'll excuse me, my officers ought to know about this cellar.' The inspector hurried outside.

Rachel for now was more interested in the dark passageway than in finally meeting Joe Penoyre. 'I never knew that was there – it was just a wall.' She stared at Michael, silently admitting that she was glad he'd come back. 'What is it?'

'The entrance to a keeping-cellar that runs all the way under the back of the house. At one time, the garage and this cottage were all one single longhouse and the cellar ran under both. A very unusual arrangement.'

Walking where Inspector Penoyre had done, Michael came indoors and crossed to the stair-well. He pushed on the wall-doorway with a pen. 'It comes out at the back of the garage, on the blind side of the house. A soil-covered trapdoor, untouched for years.'

'That's why I didn't spot it. How did you know about it?'

'I walked along the orchard wall by the beeches and noticed newly disturbed earth. Different soil colours are a real give away in my job.'

'You did say the orchard wall by the beeches?'

Michael smiled grimly. 'It's good cover there, especially now the trees are sprouting. I assumed your arsonist must have approached from the same angle. You wouldn't have seen anything even from the orchard.'

'So people can get in and out of here without ever passing the door.' Uncomfortable at the idea, Rachel turned and watched the dapper Penoyre talking animatedly to the S.O.C.O. 'Poor old Moss. Him and his indigestion tablets. They weren't enough this time.' Sergeant Moss had talked to her at Kestrel House, and at her car last night. She'd sensed he was as disturbed by recent events as she was.

'Yes, but a new keen face on your case—'

'That explains why he's here, but not you.'

'I passed Joe on the road coming up here and thought it better to arrive with him. I heard it on the police radio at home: suspected break-in and arson, minor damage, owner unhurt. It pays sometimes to listen in.'

'Quite apart from that being illegal, that's the how answered, not the why.' Especially after this morning, when she'd ordered him to leave. Rachel thought of apologizing, thought of the cigarette she wished she could smoke before she apologized. She wondered if Michael had managed to grab some breakfast and felt even more ashamed. 'People who hang around crime scenes usually turn into suspects, so why, Michael?'

'Don't ask daft questions.'

His promise to her father flashed through Rachel's mind but she didn't want to think he was here because of that. For the moment she hadn't time to convince Michael she didn't dislike him – that even at senior school she hadn't really disliked him. More urgent was this most recent attack. Who was it really directed at: her, Dad or Angwen? And the police: would they be any further forward once they'd scoured the cottage and this newly revealed cellar?

Looking at the wall-door, she saw that a long piece of string had been attached inside the cellar door, an entrance she'd missed although she passed the stairwell every day. Staring down the cellar steps she asked, 'If cellars like this are unusual, would my landlord have known about it?'

'I imagine that's something the police will ask him.'

'I hope so.' Rachel had telephoned Mr Collard after calling the police. He was coming over later, perhaps while Penoyre was still at the cottage, to board up the shattered window.

'You're right,' Michael said. 'The police don't seem to be moving out there with any kind of purpose. I'm hoping Joe will stir them up a bit.'

Reminded of the request for tea, Rachel remarked acidly, 'Well, so far they haven't been taking it seriously at all. Do you know what they said to me last night? – I mean today,' Rachel hastily lied. Frustration and irritation had almost made her forget that so far Michael knew nothing about her own nuisance phone call. Less easy to dismiss was the resigned, weary Sergeant Moss, who last night had leaned his heavy frame against the door of her car to explain about staff shortages and the best use of police time.

'I was told that most minor nuisance incidents weren't worth investigating in any depth, because such cases never reach court. Also, in my particular case, the police have had to reconsider their stalker theory. Most stalkers, you see, bombard their victims with letters, flowers, and phone calls. Most stalkers endlessly follow and pester their victims, making their

180

lives a total misery.'

Rachel deposited the jug-kettle on the kitchen table and stared at the half-finished flask of hot chocolate tilting slowly amidst the napkins, rolls and crockery in the wash-basket. 'Thousands of women have to endure all that, sometimes for years, yet stalking's still not regarded as a serious crime.'

Sergeant Moss had grimaced when he'd told her that, slipping a hand into his breast pocket for the inevitable antacid tablet. He'd wanted to supply her with a panic button, but since Rachel already had a mobile phone...

'I'm sorry, my dear,' he'd concluded, hangdog jowls grey with the sharp night air. Last night, watching him clutching his side and limping slowly back to his car, Rachel had been sorrier for Sergeant Moss than herself.

She straightened the slipping flask, then strode to the kitchen door. 'Will you show me where you think the arsonist came in from outside, Mike? Where exactly?' She wanted to see for herself, if only to ensure the spot was blocked off.

'Sure.' Michael passed her without a glance. This new cool manner, without even the fire of sarcasm, was strange to Rachel and she didn't like it. Troubled, she fell into step behind him.

As they left the cottage, Inspector Penoyre stopped them on the path. 'Until my officers have combed round the beeches and cellar, you should stay here: otherwise you might contaminate any clues there are. Sorry, Mr Horton, you know how it is. Thanks for the tip, though. It certainly came through.'

Inspector Penoyre held up a hand to Rachel. 'Shall we go back inside, Miss Falconer, and talk about this?' He motioned to the bare patch of path where the charred flute had lain.

'I've already given a statement.' Rachel was reluctant to move away from Michael, not from any sense of protection but because she felt that he at least was completely impartial.

Joe Penoyre wasn't what she'd expected. Dad had implied someone older, steadier, altogether a more comfortable and experienced man. Taking in Penoyre's clipped black curls, crisp blue suit, green braces, thirty-something slim figure, sleek cheeks and hard little eyes, she was uneasy. A local man, with the broad vowels of her own speech, the detective struck her as being not only competent but ambitious. Not the kind to be intimidated by Daniel's county connections, but shrewd enough to use them if it suited him.

He smiled at her. 'If you could just run through this morning again, it would be very helpful. Let's start with the cellar. Are you certain you didn't know it was there?'

'Not until this morning when Michael pointed to it.'

'So you're sure you wouldn't have told anyone about it. And nothing was stolen this morning? The only thing damaged was an ornament?'

'Yes, but it wasn't just an ornament. The medicine flute was special. It was given to me by a friend in South America.'

'You're suggesting the flute was deliberately burned because it was of sentimental value?'

'Yes – or maybe, as a warning. Part of the

182

whistle-blower warning.' Quickly Rachel glanced at Michael, who had the sense to keep quiet. She could fill him in later, if he was interested.

Michael's expression remained remote, but Joe Penoyre looked puzzled. 'You believe the alleged telephone call from last night is connected with this incident, Miss Falconer? You appear to have had a very unfortunate time since moving down here.'

'Returning, Inspector. I was born in Exeter.'

'And do you think it likely that a young woman like yourself would have enemies waiting for when you came back? Why did you come back, Miss Falconer? I've heard it was because Kestrel House is in rather a sticky patch financially. And then the fires started...' Joe Penoyre paused. 'I think you'd best tell me about that first office fire.'

'Why? Am I under suspicion?'

Inspector Penoyre raised an eyebrow at Rachel's accusations but did not respond, which exasperated her more. She knew she probably looked guilty, but indignation took over. It was ridiculous.

'I presume you think I want or need the publicity, that I'm hoping there'll be lots of media attention about Kestrel House and its glamorous new acting director who's being subjected to repeated arson attacks, mysterious telephone calls and police uninterest. Is that why I was asked to stay in the carpark last night, because the police don't really think I was in danger? And Charles Elsham – have you checked on him yet, or has that been ruled a waste of time?'

'Do you think it likely that Rachel would harass members of her family?' Michael joined in, his steady voice giving her time to rein in her anger and disgust. It might be a legitimate line of inquiry for the police to suspect her, but she could blow a few holes in that theory.

'You implied I might have an accomplice for this morning – hence those questions about my telling someone else about the keeping-cellar – but who? My father and his wife will be still in bed. Stephen Lees has only just come out of hospital. My landlord scarcely knows me. I presume you'll be questioning the other staff of Kestrel House to check their alibis?'

'We'll be questioning a wide range of people,' Joe Penoyre answered stiffly, 'including everyone presently working at the institute.' His eyes fixed on a point beyond Rachel's shoulder. 'We'd better drop the subject for now. I must have a word with Mr Mason.'

He stalked off, his questions about the first fire still unanswered. Rachel breathed a sigh of relief and glanced at Michael. Disconcertingly, he wasn't asking her about the whistle-blower phone call. Wasn't he curious? Or did he already know? A shiver crawled down her back.

'I'm glad you found that entrance,' she said.

Michael nodded. He was still watching Inspector Penoyre and Daniel. 'The police must be wondering if you could have put the cleaning fluid and cigarette together, but if they really believe you had anything to do with that second fire-bomb, they're nuts.'

'I wouldn't have the brains, Mike?'

He didn't laugh, or contradict her. Cold as winter rain, his grey eyes searched her face. 'What's this about a phone call? I thought it was Angwen who had those.'

Rachel explained briefly about the previous night and the strange caller who'd blown a whistle down the receiver. 'You were rushing off on an emergency so I didn't say anything then. Didn't want to hold you up.'

'Or involve me, maybe?'

'Aren't you on a dig?' Rachel asked quickly.

Michael nodded, glancing at his watch. 'We're due to start at 9.30 when the JCB arrives.'

He lapsed into silence. Normally, Michael would be telling her about the location of the dig, what they hoped to achieve by it, what he and his team had already found, thought Rachel. She hadn't realized how much she would miss his enthusiasm.

'Are you on fire-watch this weekend and next week?' she asked, making conversation.

'No, and I'm due in London tonight.' He didn't say what for, or for how long. Or whether he would be seeing Helen again.

'Right.' Rachel folded her arms across herself. Looking away from Michael into the orchard, she saw Inspector Penoyre kneeling by the cardboard box, playing with the yapping puppy whilst deep in conversation with Daniel. The two uniformed constables roamed the road and moor outside whilst she heard the S.O.C.O. moving under her feet in the cellar. She seemed superfluous, only the victim.

The metal of his green braces picked out by the

warm sunshine, Inspector Penoyre left Daniel and the pup and approached her at a smart turn of speed.

'I'd like you to come with me to the station, Miss Falconer.'

Before Rachel could respond, Michael said, 'I'll come too.'

'I don't think that'll be necessary. Mr Mason has said he'll see Miss Falconer safely home again.'

'I don't need anyone to see me anywhere,' snapped Rachel, but the damage had been done. She sensed Michael withdrawing into himself, felt him step away.

'You're right. I ought to be going before the JCB gets there first.' With a terse, 'the best', he left, waving to the police and giving a curt nod to Daniel.

Keen to explain the true situation between Daniel and herself, Rachel moved to catch up with him but found Joe Penoyre in her way.

'Shall we go?' the inspector asked.

'I presume I can fetch my handbag and drive my own car?'

'Of course, and you don't have to worry about locking up. My officers will clear away your gardening tools and wait until Mr Collard and the joiner arrive. That should give everyone time to have a good look round for more evidence.' Penoyre smiled, letting her know he knew he was pushing his luck.

Rachel shrugged. 'They'll tell Mr Collard about blocking off the cellar?'

'Of course.'

Only slightly reassured by that promise, Rachel decided to push Penoyre a little in return. 'Can we make a detour and drop the puppy off at Stephen Lees'? She's a "welcome home" gift.'

'Of course,' the inspector said again. He studied Rachel a moment, then dipped a hand into his suit pocket for a pair of sunglasses. 'I assumed you'd want Mr Mason to drive you down.'

'I prefer to be independent. Can I talk to Daniel before we go?'

'I'll come with you and collect the puppy.'

'And listen to me passing coded messages to my accomplice?'

That earned her a sharp look.

'After you,' said Joe Penoyre and stepped off the path to let her pass.

Chapter 32

Stephen Lees was delighted at the black Alsatian pup, his mouth trembling as Rachel entered his thatched cottage with the dog in her arms. Lorna briskly set about offering coffee, but Inspector Penoyre intervened, explaining that he and Rachel needed to get on.

Rachel spent the rest of the morning at Darcombe police station. First her fingerprints were taken 'for elimination purposes', then she gave samples of her hair, blood and clothing fibre. Next, she gave an account of the two fires at Kestrel House and, prompted by the Inspector, talked about Fultons and the Amazon expedition which had ended so tragically in Rio.

'I did tell Sergeant Moss all this,' Rachel remarked, disappointed when Joe Penoyre didn't make the obvious link with the burning of Aoira's flute. 'And you already know about my father's fear of sabotage at Kestrel House.'

'Hearing it from another source is always useful.'

'Have you any idea who might be behind this? Apart from myself.'

Unsmiling, Inspector Penoyre asked if he might smoke.

'Go ahead.' They were in his office, staring at each other across the desk. She was tired of studying the faint grey stripe in his blue suit-jacket.

Her mouth actually watered as Joe Penoyre lifted an enamel mug from a filing cabinet, lit a slim black cigarette and inhaled. She tried to bat the smoke away, ignored the tap of glowing ash into the mug, listening instead to the shouts of traders from the town's open market by the stone cross and the lowing of cattle as a dairy herd passed down the main street.

Opposite, Joe Penoyre relaxed on his chair and folded his arms on the desk, studying the grain of its wood. Behind him were rows of filing cabinets and on top of those a swamp of files, computer discs, papers and pencils.

'One thing, Miss Falconer.'

Rachel tried not to inhale the sweet scent of tobacco. 'Yes?'

'I think we're dealing with someone who's very smart. Clever enough not to be seen lingering at the scene. Controlled enough to pace events. Diverse in his methods – perhaps I should say their methods, since it could be a conspiracy.'

'I'm glad I'm no longer under suspicion.'

Joe Penoyre allowed a smile to filter through the clouds of smoke. 'Let's say I'm keeping an open mind. Our enquiries so far have confirmed that your affairs and the financial accounts at Kestrel House are completely above board.'

'Which removes the insurance cash as a motive for arson.'

The inspector inclined his head. 'Extortion and blackmail remain possibilities, particularly given these small fires, but you are co-operating with the police.' Smile broadening, he reached behind himself to the top of the filing cabinets, found a bulky folder of pictures by touch and handed it across.

'I'll leave you with these, Miss Falconer. Our local nuisance callers, prowlers and arsonists. If you've seen any of these beauties since coming onto Dartmoor, please say.'

Joe Penoyre stubbed out his cigarette, replaced the unwashed enamel mug in its filing cabinet and wandered off down a corridor. Rachel spent an hour staring at the photographs he'd left. She drew a blank.

'That's it.' She flicked the final photograph away on the desk in a gesture of frustration. 'Now the police will most definitely lose interest.'

So far, the only high point of the morning was the discovery of a second rain-forest healing-tree, a second chance for the Gapo to hold onto what was left of their shrinking territory. She'd have these samples shipped off to Kew by the midday post, before finally driving to Topsham.

Rachel touched the small gold box in the pocket of her trousers. In their stiff parting, Daniel had insisted she take it. Now it felt cold, with sharp edges. A good analogy for herself. Instead of gratitude, she felt obligation. Obligation towards the Gapo and strangely towards Daniel, who after all could have simply stolen the seeds and sample after walking off with her mail. Now she was calmer, Rachel was ashamed she'd condemned Daniel's ambition so swiftly – was she not also ambitious?

More disconcerting was that instead of being relieved that Michael was out of the way, leaving her free to pursue her suspicions her own way, she felt thwarted. Michael was going to London.

Come to think of it, she owed Helen a call to find out when the film crew was coming back to Dartmoor. The azaleas were coming into full bloom in the arboretum and would make a wonderful picture. And maybe by Helen's return this whole mess of the arsonist-stalker-spy would be sorted out.

A welcome voice broke into her thoughts.

'Would you like me to buy you a coffee from the machine here or lunch in the French café in Exeter?'

Raising her head, Rachel asked, 'What happened to the JCB?'

'Flat tyre. And the dig's had to be stopped. We found a body – a modern one. The police think it's a farming suicide, but until it's moved, my team can't work. That's the rest of today out, so far as archaeology's concerned.'

He inhaled, the lines on his forehead etched deeper than tree-rings. Standing in the corridor, Michael looked sad, aggrieved and tired. 'What?' He'd caught Rachel watching.

'I suppose you spotted my car outside in the street.'

'Yours, without Daniel's.' Michael nodded to the passing inspector. 'Look, if you'd rather get on here–'

'No, I've finished.' To emphasize her point, Rachel rose. 'Just need to check with the police that I can go.'

'Of course.' Joe Penoyre strolled back into his office. 'No luck with our crime gallery? Well, I'm not really surprised, but it was worth a try. We are trying, Miss Falconer, but yours is an unusual case. Arson, nuisance calls, break-ins, sabotage – I'm not sure if we should be hunting one criminal or half-a-dozen.' He grinned, holding the door open for Rachel to leave.

'To answer your earlier question, we've been in touch with Interpol about Charles Elsham,' he said as she passed by him on the threshold, their heads level. 'It seems your Mr Elsham hasn't kept in touch with anyone particular in Britain, but he has been busy in Italy with, let's say, irregular contacts.'

Penoyre's hard little eyes glittered. 'So far in Parma he's wanted for corruption, tax evasion and embezzlement.'

'He's gone native,' put in Michael.

The policeman turned to include the taller man. 'Of course, where Charles Elsham is unusual is in his fleeing his adopted country. The last clear sighting of him was in Parma on 21 April. Since then, his wife claims not to know where he is. Interpol believe he's dropped out of sight somewhere in Britain, quite possibly with old friends. If he should contact you, Miss Falconer, call me.'

Smug after dropping his bombshell, Inspector Penoyre crossed into the narrow, windowless office with its ranks of grey filing cabinets. 'Tell Paul and Angwen Falconer I'll be in touch. Whatever you decide, have a good lunch.'

A Jiffybag, a rapid note, the address of Kew Gardens, long etched into Rachel's memory – sending the new samples of Aoira's healing-tree took only ten minutes at Darcombe post-office. Reassured by the postmistress that the package would be in London by Monday at the latest, Rachel handed the sealed Jiffybag across the counter, her heart thumping.

She'd have preferred to complete the analysis of the plant samples herself, but Kew was safer. She couldn't afford the luxury of personal research. If these seeds were destroyed in an arson attack, she'd never forgive herself. It was with mingled hope, wonder and regret that Rachel released Aoira's magic tree and wished it godspeed to Kew.

Outside the post office, Michael asked, 'Have you decided yet?' And, before she could answer,

'It'll be useful to find out if Elsham has any people apart from the obvious down here.'

Rachel found herself chuckling, relieved that the involved, curious Michael was back. 'About this morning–'

'Don't. I was obnoxious.'

'I was trying to find out what's going on. If Daniel's connected in any way, I need to know, and quickly. Whatever the police think, other people are at risk. Angwen and my father–'

'Rachel, I gave myself that lecture all the way through my shower, breakfast and drive to your cottage. Then, the instant I saw Daniel,' – Michael opened his hands in a rare theatrical gesture – 'Boom.'

'Why, Mike?'

'It'll take all lunch-time to explain.'

'So be it. You don't get away with it that easily.'

Semi-serious, Rachel also meant to tease, but again she sensed Michael withdrawing. She stopped him on the pavement. 'Sorry, that was the wrong thing to say in the circumstances. Shall we get on, before the Exeter carparks are utterly solid?'

'Not for motor-bikes. I'll take us there and back. Leave your car here outside a police station should make it safe from any tampering.' Michael's still, arresting face gave nothing away but his eyes widened with angry humour. 'It'll be one day when he can't catch you.'

'Okay,' said Rachel, wishing she was closer to discovering who 'he' was. 'But don't worry about the return trip. I'll catch the bus in Exeter to Topsham, spend the night with Dad and

Angwen, and get Dad to run me into Darcombe in the morning.' Kestrel House paperwork must wait. She had to know her family was safe.

'Really make him sweat, eh?' Behind the banter Michael was serious, thought Rachel, but so was she.

Turning into the shadows where Michael had parked his heavy grey bike, she suddenly stopped. 'Before we go – may I use your mobile? I'll pay for the call.'

'No, you won't.' Michael produced the mobile from under the rear seat of the Norton and handed it across. 'Tell them everything,' he said, grey eyes warm with sympathy.

Perversely, Rachel thought of the rose he had savagely tossed aside: the contrast between his behaviour then and now.

'I'd prefer to tell them face-to-face,' she said stiffly.

'You don't think Paul or Angwen might need to be warned?'

He had her there, damn him. Rachel acknowledged Michael's good sense with a frown and began to press buttons.

'Yes we're both fine,' Angwen said, in answer to Rachel's rapid enquiry. 'Paul's in the garden. Do you want him?'

'Wait!' cried Rachel, before Angwen could put the phone down. 'Listen, Angwen, I know about your phone call. Michael's told me. We have to talk. Something else has happened. Someone broke into my house this morning through the keeping-cellar and burned my South American flute – no, not the small hunting-pipe in my

194

dresser drawer, the one hanging up in the kitchen. No, I'm all right. A window was broken, but nothing else was damaged. The police are here now. They'll need to talk to you and Dad. I'd like to come down if I may—'

'And stay the night, I hope?'

This was exactly what Rachel wanted. 'Yes, please, if it's no trouble.'

'No trouble at all. Now don't you worry about us, this fellow can't be everywhere. I'll talk to Paul. You come on in your own time.'

'Thanks, Angwen.'

'You with Mike now?'

'I am. We're just leaving Darcombe police station.'

Michael stood by Rachel's shoulder and spoke into the receiver. 'And I'm taking Rachel for lunch.'

'Good for you,' Angwen called over the phone. 'Don't you hurry now. There won't be any more trouble today.'

Rachel wished she could be so confident.

Chapter 33

Michael started the bike and patted the rear seat. 'Hop on.' Rachel was checking the chin-strap of her helmet. He pitched his voice above the din of the idling engine. 'Put your left foot on this little bar. Now swing your leg over.'

With considerably less grace than Angwen, she

was on. Michael glanced over his shoulder. 'I don't take up that much room.' Sitting to attention, Rachel was as far back as the rear bar would allow. Face pale under the black helmet, she radiated strung-out energy – worrying no doubt about Paul, Angwen, Stephen Lees and Sergeant Moss.

'You can wrap your arms round.' He sensed her unease at trusting the handgrip behind her seat. He heard Rachel chuckle.

'Is that why you ride bikes, Michael? The perfect excuse to get close?'

He laughed. 'What do you think?'

'I think maybe it's why you started, but you don't need it now.'

Even as he registered that Rachel had paid him a compliment, Michael had another shock as she settled behind him, fingers closing lightly around his middle. With her long legs curved elegantly over the machine and her feet tucked onto the stirrups, Rachel was suddenly part of the bike.

'Off we go.' Pushing off with his feet, Michael sent the Norton bowling steadily down the street, out of Darcombe and into the twisting, deep lanes. Dropping into Whiddon Down and the main route to Exeter, he dismissed disappointment at not being able to resume the dig until after the weekend. Faced with such a delay at any other time, he'd have been going crazy.

Rachel made the difference. Because of her, he'd been prepared to leave the site in the care of the police and archaeologists from the National Park and English Heritage. Concern for Rachel kept him firmly in the present.

Accelerating through the green shadow of tall, fresh-leaved elms arching over the road, Michael thought about his passenger.

Even if Rachel never saw him as anything other than a casual friend, he was committed. Not because of any promises he'd made to Paul. Not because of Daniel. Oh, he was jealous – more correctly, he was envious of the relationship Daniel had enjoyed with Rachel – but he understood his own motives now. Rachel had been right in the White Hart, when she'd accused him of believing that he was better than other men. His wanting to put Daniel down was nothing more than the triumph of self-satisfaction. It was time to move on.

He wanted Rachel to be part of that future. Each time they met, Michael was more certain of it. He wanted to spend time with her. He couldn't stop this need to look out for her.

This afternoon, before he drove down to London, he was paying a visit to Exeter. Phoning round his local-history contacts after leaving Rachel's cottage for the second time, Michael had discovered that the documents he was after would be kept in the city, at the Westcountry Studies Library. The staff there had agreed to help him search out any papers connected with Rachel's rented cottage, in particular, plans or maps which showed that the cottage had a cellar. If he could find it in the records, the stalker-arsonist might have found out in the same way. If he had, someone might possibly remember a name, a face. It was worth a try.

Feeling more optimistic because he would be

doing something, Michael drew into a passing place to let an oncoming double-decker coach swing past. Waiting for a tractor behind the coach to go by, he heard the murmur, 'Blooming thing's got me.'

He twisted round, finding Rachel wrestling a long red hank of hair off a hedgerow holly. Pricked by the leaves, she stuck her fingers into her mouth. 'You'd think I'd have more sense.'

'Here, I can see where it's caught.' Waving on a hedge-hugging Merc, Michael patiently unwound the lock of hair.

'Thanks.' Rachel gave him a smile that Mavis Horton would have described as being fit to knock the spots off a jaguar. Michael kicked the Norton into life, but the image of Rachel's happy face floated before him down the lane.

Somewhere on the journey the air changed, smelling no longer of green lanes, peaty soil and cattle, but of petrol, hot metal and sullen shoppers. After parking in the underground carpark in Exeter centre, it got better, Rachel decided.

The city had changed since she'd helped an excruciatingly shy teenage Mike to buy stockings in Dingles. The view was still the same down Fore Street towards the medieval bridge, then up to the fields and open countryside beyond Haldon, but today groups of giggling French teenagers and Peruvian street musicians in their striped Andean ponchos gave the place a cosmopolitan feel. The 2000-year-old city was in festival mood. Yellow bunting rustled across the crowded pavement stalls on Sidwell Street, whilst pigeons pecked speculatively at crimson primulas in the flower-beds. Passing a bakery as the door opened, Rachel caught the warm scent of fresh bread and Chudleigh buns.

She and the adult Michael passed the front of the Dillons that had once been a cinema, Rachel marking the bookshop's multimedia display with particular interest. Raymond Trudeau, a Canadian computing expert who specialized in security, was holding a talk in Dillons that afternoon.

Since speaking to Angwen and being reassured that she and Paul were fine, Rachel thought it might be useful to look in on M. Trudeau. Keenly aware of the shortcomings of Kestrel House, she hoped to be able to pass on some cheap but useful computer security tips to Leo.

'Could Charles Elsham have been in touch with Fultons before he left Parma?' Michael was more interested in human threats. 'If he's got money trouble, there's a useful motive for scientific spying. And he'd know about Paul's research from the conference they attended.'

Thinking aloud, Michael watched a gull soaring over the rooftops towards the Cathedral. Still watching the sky, he stepped from the kerb. Rachel pulled him back before a green minibus mowed him down, stepping rapidly to one side herself to avoid an oncoming child gobbling candyfloss.

'Food first, then talk,' she said. 'Let's try to reach this café in one piece.'

'It's on past the Blue Boy.'

Michael pointed across High Street but Rachel was already striding out, snatching his arm and pulling him with her. He was a weight to haul, deliberately holding back to torment her. Laughing, strolling side by side into the less hectic, pedestrianized part of the city, Rachel found herself wishing that she and Michael were riding back together after this lunch. His black leather jacket and biker's boots, never precisely threatening, were now endearing: she knew how that long back felt against her body, just as she knew about the sprig of white heather tucked under the Norton's speedo.

They ambled past the small metal statue of the long-coated Blue Boy, Rachel rapping the metal head for luck, and continued in the direction of the cathedral, its central tower rising solid at the end of the flagged street beyond the chairs, tables and umbrellas of the French café.

'Inside or out?' Michael asked.

Spotting the huddle of wicker tables and chairs indoors, and the people filling them, Rachel was all for saying outside, from consideration for her own legs and Michael's even longer ones. 'It must be hard, having to crouch and duck everywhere in towns,' she observed as Michael opened the door and they held back to allow two young mothers with pushchairs to exit. 'Especially here, with all the low timber buildings.'

Michael chuckled. 'There are roof-beams in the Ship Inn off the cathedral that must show permanent dents from my skull. Drake and his cronies were a good head shorter than me, or you.'

They went inside, Michael stepping round the other tables and people with casual grace. As they reached the tall glass counter, Michael turned from studying the chalked-up specials for the day. 'Before we order, have we decided where we're sitting?'

Opening her mouth to say 'outside', Rachel spotted a swarm of students swooping and settling round the umbrellas, eager for coffee and *pains au chocolat*.

'Oh, Lord, history Year Ones,' groaned Michael. 'Half of that bunch know me. We'll be pestered to death.'

Rachel pointed to some black wooden stairs. 'There's upstairs. Just mind your head.'

'Right – you find us a seat and I'll order before that lot come tumbling in. What do you want?'

Rachel rapidly ordered, then clattered up the narrow wooden stairs.

There, oddly enough, the café was deserted. A copy of *Le Monde*, fixed to a wooden rod, was spread over a table. Rachel went straight to the far end of the room and settled on a high, long-legged chair at a long counter fixed under the window. She was glad the warm, sunny room was empty. She and Michael would have the place to themselves.

Staring down at passers-by, listening to smoky Parisian music playing from speakers slung high in the rafters, she heard the scrape and creak as Michael sat on the bar chair beside her. 'The waitress'll bring our order when it's ready.' He half-turned, regarding the empty chairs. 'We'll be able to talk properly up here.'

When Michael was always so still, it was difficult to say whether he was genuinely relaxed or not, thought Rachel. He looked easy enough, an arm hanging over the chair-back as he watched the stairs and her. It struck her there might never be a better time to remind him of an earlier promise.

'You said you'd explain your dislike of Daniel.'

Michael sat upright, brought his arms to rest on the counter and fixed his sights on the Thomas Cook Travel Centre opposite. He spoke without looking at her.

'I can't really explain. You know the lines, "I do not love you, Dr Fell,/But why I cannot tell"? Well, it's like that and it's mutual. Daniel doesn't like me either.'

Michael's fingers drummed the wooden counter. 'When Paul thought his research was being tampered with, I really hoped the saboteur would turn out to be Daniel. I wanted to catch him out, put him down. I wanted you and me to get him.'

After this confession he paused, then continued. 'Since you came back, you've shown me that my motives have been far from pure. I have to admit, Daniel's contacts and style annoyed me.'

'Irritated the hell out of you, more like.'

Michael chuckled at her frankness. 'Maybe. But from now on, I'm going to try to put it behind me.' He shot her a glance.

Heart quickening, Rachel found it necessary to look away. Relieved by what Michael had told her, she was still uncertain about Daniel: whether or not he could be the arsonist. Especially after what had happened this morning, at her cottage.

Footsteps on the wooden stairs. Rachel shuddered, turning with Michael to watch the waitress enter the room with their baguettes and drinks on a tray. She no longer felt hungry.

Chapter 34

'Don't know about you but I'm starving.' Michael slid the plate in front of her. 'Go on, take a bite.'

She was queasy, but to shut him up Rachel lifted her prawn baguette and nibbled at the crisp, fragrant bread. To her surprise, once that crumb was forced down, her appetite returned in a rush. She devoured the rest, relishing the sharp sauce with the prawns. Taking a long drink of her *café au lait*, she set down her cup. 'Thanks for being so frank about Daniel. It can't have been easy.'

A slight nod showed that Michael understood. He flicked the wrapped chocolate mint which came with his espresso across the table. 'I know you like them. Can we talk about Charles Elsham?'

Rachel was more than happy at the change of subject. Before she called on her father and Angwen this afternoon and Paul put his own spin on events, she needed to clarify her thoughts about Elsham's absconding to Britain. She also realized that she was looking forward to hearing Michael's ideas. She would value his judgement.

Michael continued. 'Before we do, I think I should say that I no longer consider Daniel a threat to you, Angwen, or your father. Considering he's obviously still attracted to you, I can't see him working against you.'

Rachel blushed. 'But I've turned him down, in no uncertain terms. The cottage window was shattered by Aoira's burning flute just as Daniel said, "I've finished here".' The thought was uncomfortable, but best faced up to.

'Still, how would he have signalled to an accomplice? Who'd be his accomplice?'

Rachel shrugged and couldn't resist teasing. 'Charles Elsham?'

'If you believed that, you'd have said something to Penoyre.'

Rachel licked a missed blob of sauce off her little finger. 'I suppose you could argue that some long-buried resentment has surfaced, now that Charles is wanted by the Italians. He's nothing more to lose by stalking my family and me. Dad did see Charles in Parma: that meeting might have been the trigger. Maybe the money and my father's vaccine could be a motive but no spy would betray himself by setting fires in the place he was watching. And if the arson is a threat against my father, why have no demands been made?' She traced an invisible pattern on the surface of the table. 'I suppose in the end it boils down to this. For Charles to be coming after me at this late stage doesn't match his character.'

'No. Everything fits, but it feels wrong.'

Grateful for Michael's understanding, Rachel found herself admitting, 'Just lately I've been wondering if the arsonist, or stalker, or whatever you want to call him, isn't after more than one victim. Daniel was there when the wastebin exploded. Daniel and Colin Benwick were less than a mile away when the fire bomb exploded in my office. Daniel's links to Fultons are well known. What if he's being set up in some way, as a scapegoat?'

'But by who? And why?'

'I don't know. On and off, I've had my suspicions about you.'

Michael took this in his stride. Spearing a piece of pastry, he offered the fork to Rachel. 'Want some? It's rather good.'

It would be prudish to refuse, and the gooey cake did tempt her. Rachel took the fork. 'Umm. Would you like a bite of mine?'

In answer, Michael lunged forward and gobbled the piece of apricot and chocolate off Rachel's fork.

'Idiot.' Rachel waved the fork at him.

'Use mine,' Michael said quickly. 'My lips have not touched it,' he added, hand on heart in mock solemnity.

'It's okay, Mike, I'm not afraid of catching BSE off you.' Having teased him, Rachel continued to use her own fork. She resumed their discussion between mouthfuls of apricot pastry. 'I've been reading up on stalking. Inspector Penoyre's right. What's been happening to Angwen or me hasn't the same intensity.'

Michael gave a chilly smile. 'You haven't

received hundreds of letters, presents, or phone calls. I've been reading up, too. The most common form of stalking behaviour results from stalkers being convinced that their victims are their perfect partners. But of course, for that to work, a stalker must have made himself known to the love-object.'

'Love-object: that sums it up, really.' Rachel shook her head. 'I don't know if I've been followed or not, but certainly no desperate fan of *High Country* has poured out any undying love to me.'

'And Helen's heard nothing at the television station. I rang her to ask.'

They were grown-up people, Rachel reminded herself again. It was no business of hers.

'If we can discount Daniel,' she said, 'the idea of my being stalked by a rejected partner doesn't apply. Angwen's never spoken of any one who mattered in her life before Paul, and as for Dad...' Rachel smiled. 'He met Mum at a concert in the Guildhall here in Exeter when he was twenty. Mum said he couldn't take his eyes off her.'

'Was there ever any trouble between them when they were married?'

'Mum and Dad?'

'It happens. And whether the couple remain together or not, there are always people left unhappy.'

She didn't want to pry, or cause more grief, yet something must be said. Rachel laid her hand over his wrist. 'I'm sorry. I didn't realize.'

Michael misunderstood her. His face reddened and he tore his arm free. 'Oh, it wasn't me – I

206

don't go in for affairs with married women. Not like my father: he was what people used to call a ladies' man. That's why we moved north when I was fourteen, to start again. To escape his secretary's love-letters. It was my fault we had to go. Me and my nosiness. I couldn't let things alone, I always had to know. My damn curiosity almost killed my parents' marriage.'

He stopped a moment, brooding, then started again before Rachel had chance to speak. 'Friday 13 May – I'll never forget the date. Friday the thirteenth and me leaping onto the bus to take me from the dentist's next to the bus station back to the grammar school. I'd just sprawled over the back seat on the top deck when I spotted my dad out of the rear window. He was walking with Miss Meldon along the bus stands, clearly about to go somewhere. I opened the nearest window and hollered, but Dad was too far away to hear. So I asked him again that evening, over tea, "Where were you and Miss Meldon going, Dad?"

'And then Mum hit me and she started to cry. I'd made her face it. I'd made them both face it. Then, afterwards, came the letters, the move north, the long silences.'

The angry spate of words ended. Michael crumpled his napkin into a ball and tossed it onto his half-finished cake.

'That was unforgivable,' he said. 'At a time like this, when you're in trouble–'

'I'm glad you told me,' Rachel said gently. 'I wish I'd known earlier. It was always a mystery to me, why you and your parents left so suddenly. But you shouldn't blame yourself. Surely you can see that now?'

Her hand found his and clasped it. They sat still and quiet, looking down into the street outside. A peal of bells could be heard from the cathedral. Listening, Rachel felt at peace for the first time that day.

Some time later Michael slipped his hand away from Rachel's, with a final squeeze, and stood up. 'I'm still thirsty. Fancy another coffee?'

'Hot chocolate for me, please. Angwen and Dad are great tea-o-philes: I'll be pressed into drinking several cups there.'

Michael went off downstairs and Rachel reluctantly put aside her new fragile mood of calm content to reconsider Angwen. The police seemed to be treating the theft of Angwen's mountain-bike as a separate, trivial, incident. Perhaps they were right. Otherwise, what were the connections? Angwen or herself? Which of them, in the end, was the more at risk?

Where would the next fire happen?

Chapter 35

Michael returned with their coffee and hot chocolate. When he spoke, it was as if he had read Rachel's mind.

'Instead of thinking about stalkers, maybe we should be looking at this from the arson angle. Stalkers do set fires, but usually amongst other forms of threatening behaviour, part of an escalating pattern of attack–'

'That makes me feel so much safer.'

'What I mean is, a stalker would use fire impulsively, as a ready weapon to hand. The arson attacks against you have been carefully planned–'

'I'm still not convinced I'm the main target.'

Michael took a drink. 'We'll agree to differ. But if we look at the arson from a fire investigator's point of view, the police's suspicions about you become more justified.'

Rachel swallowed her protest. 'Okay, Mr Fireman, explain.'

'I've not heard anything on the grapevine about the second fire at Kestrel House, but I think we'll have to assume that the fire investigator and forensics found evidence to prove that the fire-alarm wires had been baited with something to encourage the rats to chew through them.'

'As director, I'd have the opportunity to do the baiting. Is that why Penoyre hasn't said anything about this, do you think? So as not to warn me before he's finished compiling evidence against me?'

'Rachel, I know it's easy to be bitter–'

'It most definitely is! What about a motive? Penoyre admitted there isn't one. What about the others at Kestrel House? Are the police checking their alibis?'

'Penoyre said so.'

'Look at me, Michael! Do I match the profile of an arsonist? A loner? A protester? Do you think I get turned on by fires? Do I look the kind who wants to set fires so I can rescue others, be a hero?'

'You did rescue Stephen Lees.'

'But not Moll,' Rachel said bitterly. 'If I was that kind of arsonist, wouldn't I have made sure I could save Moll, too?'

Michael hid the smile behind his cup but she saw his eyes.

'I don't think it's funny, Michael. Would you like to be seen by Penoyre as one of life's losers, lusting for glory?'

'No, I wouldn't, and more to the point, I don't think you are. After all,' Michael added quietly, 'you're already famous.'

'Oh, yes, this wonderful TV career I'm supposed to be so obsessed with promoting that I'll actually burn my father's research station to the ground.'

'Stop being so spiky. You should be thankful for the TV.'

It was on the tip of her tongue to say, 'I suppose because of Helen', but Michael's expression made Rachel subside. Sweeping her hair off her hot neck, she muttered, 'Location fees.'

'Exactly. What financial motive have you for arson when Helen Warne's company has paid handsomely for the privilege of filming at Kestrel House? I presume the fees stave off any immediate problems?'

'They do.'

'In that case,' Michael concluded drily, 'Penoyre will have already discounted insurance cash as a motive, as he told you. And now he's talked to you properly, I think he'll have decided you're not yearning for hero status – you're too successful and too bossy. Now for the other classic reasons...'

He counted them off on his fingers. 'One, the burglar's favourite: arson to destroy evidence of criminal activity. Two, as political or social protest. Three, an unwholesome fascination with fire. Four, the teenager special – "I was bored".'

'I'm not bossy and I don't have time to be bored. The fires have all been too small to destroy much evidence and I'm the acting director, so what would I be protesting about? Wouldn't I be working to change it instead?'

'Well said.'

'Do you ever remember my playing with matches when I was a teenager, Michael?'

'Not really. That's more of a male thing.'

'So what are we left with?'

'You don't have to convince me, Rachel.' Michael leaned back in his chair. 'And I think that Penoyre will be looking seriously at the other members of staff. Apart from Edie, Muhammad and Carter, of course.'

'I'd a postcard from Muhammad yesterday.' Rachel shot a mischievous look at her companion. 'He's definitely in the clear in Bhutan, but Penoyre's other Kestrel House suspects will include you, Michael.'

'Oh, I'll admit to a fascination with fire. Or perhaps I should say, a respect for it. But I'm in the clear as much as Muhammad. Like Angwen, I don't have the chemistry. I wouldn't know how to put together that stag's head device in your office.'

'You might have bought it, had it made.' To her secret annoyance, Michael didn't rise to the tease.

'Very true.' He smiled at her, crossing long legs

one over the other. 'But that's true for everyone presently involved at Kestrel House, including Angwen. I imagine the police's best chance at uncovering our mystery arsonist is to stop him just before he's about to strike the match, or find out which of us wants to be rich, or famous, or a hero, or get some other major kick.'

'You've forgotten one motive.'

'No, I was leaving it till last, because I think it's the most important.' Michael became perfectly still, his voice cool and precise. 'I think someone at Kestrel House bears a grudge. Who and why, I don't know yet. I'm hoping the police will find out soon, otherwise it's going to get worse.'

Rachel rested her chin on her hands. 'You think grudge, I think financial gain. Dad's vaccine.'

'But if you no longer suspect Daniel and Charles Elsham, that leaves Colin Benwick and Leo Cartwright. Would they have the contacts to sell the vaccine to the right people? I've known both for longer than you, and neither strikes me as being particularly interested in the high life.'

'Okay, but what about your grudge theory? Colin Benwick wasn't delighted when I appeared on the scene, but he knows I'm only here for a year. I'm going to ask Dad and Angwen if they ever fell out with the man, if he could have felt slighted in any way, but I don't think it's going to be likely.'

'Leo Cartwright fancies you.'

'Leo fancies any reasonably attractive female between sixteen and forty. Where does that leave your grudge? Leo can't feel aggrieved about being turned down because he's only thought about asking me out.'

A smile pricked at the corners of Michael's full mouth. 'You'd turn him down, eh? Poor Leo.'

Brushing aside Michael's remark, Rachel shook her head. 'None of them match the other kinds of arsonists, either. Unless Colin and Leo are hiding some dark secrets.' She turned her blue-green eyes on Michael. 'As you say, you've known them for longer than me. From what you've seen and learned about them, is it likely?'

'None of us at Kestrel House match the usual profile of a firesetter. We're all too successful. Colin Benwick's a bit of a loner, but that hardly makes him a full-blown arsonist.'

Rachel snorted and jumped down off her chair. They were getting nowhere and she wanted to see the computer specialist at Dillons before she caught the bus to Topsham. 'It must be someone outside the institute, maybe one of our international visitors.'

'The police will be checking that angle, I imagine,' said Michael. 'And since they've said nothing, presumably they've found nothing.'

'Maybe our arsonist came in as a member of the public on one of Kestrel House's open days. Nothing else makes any sense.'

Michael also rose and dragged his jacket off the counter. 'None of it does,' he said, turning towards the stairs.

Rachel anticipated a subdued and rather awkward leave-taking in the street, but when they stepped outside the café, and in full view of the lingering students, Michael clasped her by the arms. Drawing her to him, Rachel too astonished

213

to react, he lowered his head.

'Seeing as we've just spent almost two hours in a French café...' He kissed her lightly on both cheeks, said goodbye and left.

The sun warm on her face, Rachel watched him go, waving as he pirouetted and waved. 'Pirouette' was perhaps the wrong word for so tall a man, but it matched the grace of his movements. It was a pleasure to watch him. Heartened, though no closer to any answers, Rachel walked in the opposite direction, back past the Blue Boy to her next appointment.

Chapter 36

Dillons was packed. Rachel eased her way through the crush and ran up the central stair. The talk was due to start on the first floor in five minutes.

The big blue seats ranged under the window overlooking Debenhams and the low frontages of other Sixties buildings were already taken, the rows of chairs in front were filling. She'd have to stand. That would ensure a good view of M. Trudeau: a plump, dark-haired young man perching on a swivel chair with his profile to the audience. Staring at a laptop linked to an overhead projector, Trudeau stabbed the return key. The projector screen burst into life, a cascade of violent images, of armed attack. The scene melted into large red letters: 'Crack the hackers. Firewall systems for business'.

'Thought he didn't go in for the ritzy stuff.' The speaker, gliding into place beside her, was someone Rachel felt she ought to know. The doll-like features were familiar, as was the black tasselled scarf.

Rachel smiled. 'Bethany, isn't it? I haven't seen you since last month in the White Hart. Rachel Falconer – pleased to meet you.'

Bethany nodded an acknowledgement. 'I wasn't sure you'd remember, although I recognized you – you're almost as tall as Mike Horton. How is Mike these days?'

'Fine.' Checking over the small, stiff blonde, Rachel was puzzled. Bethany wasn't easy with her, so why had she approached? She nodded at the console-tapping figure of M. Trudeau. 'You're interested in his work?'

'Not directly. Not the security applications. Some of the maths is intriguing.'

Bethany scanned the last few shuffling into their seats. 'Seems I'm the lone female systems analyst here, as usual.' She looked up at Rachel, her manner a mixture of suspicion and intimacy. 'Staying for the full talk?'

'I thought I might. Pick up a few tips for Kestrel House.'

A smile escaped Bethany. She folded her arms across her full bosom, jealously clasping her elbows.

'Did I say something wrong?'

The smaller woman chuckled. 'Trudeau's systems aren't cheap: the software runs into thousands.'

'I was thinking more of his general comments. Sometimes the most throwaway remark can prove enlightening.'

'It can to an expert.' Bethany rippled shell-pink fingernails against the raglan sleeves of her Laura Ashley jacket. 'Just so long as you don't expect Leo to help you.'

Her fist closed tightly about the ends of her scarf. 'He may have sold himself to you as a computer expert, but that young man has not the slightest idea. No use at all except in his own limited field. Excuse me, there's my friend Jancis.'

Having made her point, Bethany detached herself from Rachel and went to the top of the stairs to greet another young woman.

It was Bethany rather than M. Trudeau who hovered in Rachel's mind as she boarded the mini-bus to Topsham. The Canadian had been interesting but largely irrelevant, his ideas simply too large-scale for Kestrel House. Bethany's information was altogether sadder, but had confirmed her own suspicions. Any advanced skills Leo might have were of a seductive nature, and since his women appeared charmed, used and abandoned, stalking didn't come into it.

Paul was weeding in his garden when Rachel leaned over the low pebbledash wall and put on her best cod-Devonshire. 'They gold tulips be a proper treat, Dad.'

Her father twisted on his kneeling pad, regarding her with astonishment. 'Where's your car?'

216

'Guarding the police station at Darcombe. No, seriously, I thought it was such a lovely day I'd come by bus.' Rachel grinned. 'That way I knew you'd be obliged to invite me for tea.'

'And supper, too,' said Angwen from the doorway, wiping floury hands on an apron Rachel had once made for her. 'Have you brought your quilting?'

Startled by the question, or rather the lack of questions about this morning's fire, Rachel realized that Dad knew nothing about it. Finding out why not became a matter of urgency, but not in front of her father. Angwen wasn't naturally secretive: she must have a good reason for shielding Paul.

Going along with Angwen, she said, 'Sorry, I didn't think to bring my sewing.' She stretched an arm across the wall. 'Dad, pass that over, please.'

Angwen came out of doors, pressing Paul's shoulder to keep him kneeling. 'I wouldn't want you to crack those doddery joints, *cariad*.'

'See how she speaks to me!' Jumping to his feet to chase Angwen down the gravel path, Paul bit his lip as his right leg buckled.

Watching how he hid the injury from Angwen, Rachel was touched.

Fifty-five or twenty-five, newly-marrieds were the same. She had no heart to pierce their world. Yet Angwen had been harassed by phone and had her bike stolen. This bright, snug cottage was already under a shadow.

Angwen had removed her present from its plastic bag. 'It's nothing much,' Rachel began, but Angwen interrupted.

'Not at all, mineral water's the only drink I fancy; I've gone right off tea. Something with a bit of fizz is what I'm after.' Unconsciously, Angwen rubbed her stomach. 'I'll have some now, you know. What about you two?'

Father and daughter shook their heads – nothing would give them greater pleasure than for washed-out Angwen to drink and gain some relief from her pregnancy sickness. The instant Angwen had gone indoors, Paul said as much: 'And she will keep baking and cooking, even though the smell often turns her sick. I don't mind buying, but Angwen won't hear of it. Her mother brought her up to think that to take advantage of made-up food is a sign of moral decline.'

'You could always cook. Or take her out. The change would do you both good.'

Rachel joined her father in the small front garden, pausing on the path beside a circular stone trough filled with fresh compost and soil. Paul lifted a tuber from the deep pockets of his old tweed jacket and laid it on top of the compost. Within a breath of saying, 'Isn't a trough too shallow for lilies?' Rachel picked up the tuber instead and, taking out her penknife, trimmed a dead section from the root.

Digging in her pockets reminded Rachel of Daniel's 'gift'. The precious seeds were already winging their way to Kew, but the container he'd brought them in was hers. Guilty at having forgotten it so readily – somewhere on her bike ride into Exeter – Rachel laid the tuber on a section of freshly-turned garden soil and took out the small gold box to show her father.

The thing remained clutched in her fist when Paul fretfully jabbed his trowel into the compost of the trough and burst out, 'She does so much for my comfort, she makes me feel old. And always sweet-tempered! Instantly agreeing with any suggestion I make. Asking my opinion over everything, as if she needs my permission. Sometimes I worry that Angwen's actually, frightened of me.'

'Nonsense.' Rachel was brisk, slipping Daniel's present back into her pocket: she'd show it off another time. 'I have thought her a little in awe of you, but you seemed to enjoy that. I suppose now it's too much of a good thing. I think you're most ungrateful.' *Especially since Angwen is protecting you from news she knows will worry you.*

Paul scowled, then changed the subject. 'Anything from Joe?'

Seeing no point in telling her father of her new status as an arson suspect, Rachel shook her head. Puzzling how she might detach Angwen from her father so that she and Angwen could talk freely, Rachel was relieved when her stepmother reappeared, without apron and with a light raincoat draped over her arm.

'Paul, I've left the dough rising on the Aga top. Will it be all right if I took Rachel down to look at the estuary?'

Rachel willed that her father would agree, which he did, with a promptness she silently praised him for. Wishing them a good walk, he promised Rachel tea and Angwen mineral water on their return and returned to planting up the stone trough with every appearance of serenity.

Strolling out into the quiet street, towards Shell House with its handsome marble scallop set into the wall above the front door, Rachel tucked Angwen's arm through hers and asked her wan stepmother if she was sure she wanted to walk so far.

'You must be poorly if you've gone off your tea,' she went on. 'Usually you drain the pot, then wring out the last dregs.'

Smiling where she once would have laughed, Angwen said meekly, 'I'd like to try a circular walk Paul showed me: it's not too long.'

'You'll say if you want to turn back?'

Angwen nodded, the shadows under her listless eyes reminding Rachel of how Aoira had looked when she was first pregnant.

'I don't think I will,' Angwen added, deliberately lengthening her stride. 'We've a lot to talk about.'

Glad to hear Angwen so determined, Rachel was also alarmed. 'Has anything else happened? More peculiar phone calls?'

'No – and I don't think we shall have. We're not Rachel Falconer.'

'Is that why you've not told Dad about this morning?'

'You know why. Because the video I heard playing in the background when the man phoned me was your programme, Rachel.'

'Dad has to know. If only because Joe Penoyre will be coming to see you both again, to question you.'

'Yes, but let things lie quiet until tonight. Let him have this sunny day in peace, in his garden. You can talk to him this evening, whilst I wash up the supper things.'

Rachel stopped in the middle of the road, in view of the sea. 'Angwen? What is it?'

Angwen's dainty features, took on a faint strain of colour. 'Nothing – there's a horse coming.'

Obliged to cross to the other side of the road, Rachel ran back to Angwen's side after horse and rider had trotted by. Her stepmother was admiring an early lavender bush growing through the antique metal railings of a row of cottages.

'The scent makes me feel less sick.' She raised her head. 'I ought to buy a bottle of lavender oil. Maybe then I'll stop being so tiresomely delicate.'

'Angwen, you can't help being off-colour.'

'I wish I could have helped getting pregnant.' Angwen snorted at Rachel's stare. 'There! Now I'm another step lower than you. I promised myself that I'd not admit anything.' She flicked the arm with the coat over it at Rachel. 'You and your listening face, and that aura about you.'

Was this good, or was she off-putting? 'What do you mean?'

Angwen whipped round from lavender bush and railings. 'You know why Paul married me? Because, thanks to a faulty condom, I'm expecting. He's a new Dad at fifty-five and thrilled to bits, when he's not scared of dropping dead at its twenty-first. But where does that leave me?'

'He loves you, Angwen. He's very proud of you.'

'Is he? We're the cliché couple: boss and secretary. Except Paul's an academic, which means he's clever. Oh, why am I trying to explain to you?' Angwen flounced forward, the coat slipping looser and flapping round her heels. This time, it was Rachel who hurried to keep up.

'Angwen, please.' They were speeding along the walkway by the estuary, ignoring its tranquil beauty and the strolling families who stopped to watch the tall red-head galloping after the slim pale woman. Alarmed by Angwen's distress, Rachel did not hear the high-pitched cries of the wading birds, did not notice the yellow flowers of stonecrop bursting from the wall above the walkway.

'Please, Angwen,' she gasped, seizing on a lie, 'I've got stitch.'

Finally her companion slowed. Rachel limped convincingly to the next metal seat and sat down, head in hands.

'Sorry, I'm sure,' said Angwen stiffly. 'Usually you walk so fast.' When her companion did not stir, Angwen settled on the seat, leaning back against the sunny wall.

Silence drew on. Torn between her own feelings of protectiveness towards Angwen – especially now – and the instinct that warned her that Angwen needed to feel useful and protective herself, Rachel decided on the truth. 'I need your help,' she said, through her fingers. 'There are things I must know. Only you can tell me.'

Chapter 37

Angwen gave Rachel a questioning look. Out in this salty air she felt better, whilst Rachel's assurance that Paul loved her, although at first faintly humiliating, was on reflection reassuring. Father and daughter were close. If Rachel thought Paul was proud of her, he must be. Unless Rachel was being kind.

Frowning as the younger woman took her hands away from her face and lifted her head, Angwen thought she looked tired. Her mouth was turned down enough at the corners to be called sour.

'Why are you sitting on your hands now?'

Rachel grimaced, and, shifting, brought the offending hands onto her lap. 'I could do with a cigarette.'

'Nasty habit. Makes all your clothes smell.'

'Oh, do they?'

Angwen treasured the look of anxiety that scurried over Rachel's face, and was pleased to be in the position of telling her something. 'Not at all.' She didn't add that Rachel smelt faintly of bike oil. No need to make her more embarrassed than she was already.

Breathing in deeply, Angwen discovered that for the first time in weeks she was feeling well. Instead of feeling sick, she was anxious, but it was anxiety with a purpose. She wasn't helpless.

She had information to share.

'Colin Benwick: that's the one you want to talk about. How I know he's nothing to do with my phone call, or what's been happening to you.'

'What about you?'

'Colin, to go after the wife of the man who gave him the job of forester at Kestrel House? That wonderful arboretum? No. If you knew him, Rachel, you'd know how loyal Colin is.'

'He's certainly loyal to Daniel.'

'And to your dad! Why else do you think he made no trouble about your position as acting director? Colin has his good points, but he's forthright about the dangers of appointing women to top jobs, even for a sabbatical.'

'So far you're convincing me that Dr Benwick is a problem.'

'Can't you see it? Colin would consider any underhand moves against you as working too much like the enemy.'

Rachel's face cleared a little, her complexion warming with humour. 'Too much like a woman?'

'That's it. Think about the man, Rachel. How does Colin strike you?'

'I find him so forthright as to be tactless.' A rope of hair fell across Rachel's face as she shook her head. 'Tim Stevens was a bit the same.' She bit her lip, as though at an unpleasant memory.

'He calls me Ange-wen. Always sounds the "g". The caller who asked after my mountain-bike didn't do that.'

'Yes, but Michael told me that your caller

played a recording down the phone. The voice was disguised.'

'I heard my name distinctly, perhaps because it is my name. He said Angwen exactly as we do in North Wales. It might have been my dad. Colin couldn't have done that. Besides, there's another reason, only Paul mustn't know. It's a surprise for his birthday. A bonsai cherry. Colin's growing several. On the night I was called, Colin had dropped in to ask if I thought Paul might like one. He was on the doorstep when the phone rang. Colin wouldn't come in – said he could only stay a minute.'

'Have you told the police this?'

Angwen nodded.

'Could he have ever felt slighted by Dad? By anyone at Kestrel House?'

'Colin and Paul have always got on fine. And since Colin works in the arboretum, no one sees much of him.'

'So there's been no trouble whilst you've been at the institute?'

'Leo and Daniel have had their moments, but Colin doesn't get involved. He supports Daniel's ideas for expansion, but otherwise he's a loner, happiest in his own company. The moors suit him.' Angwen made a joke. 'You can't fall out with a patch of heather, or a magnolia tree.'

'So, Dr Benwick becomes a less likely suspect,' Rachel observed coolly – with some disappointment, Angwen felt. She watched Rachel's blue-green eyes narrow, then widen.

'Can you think of anyone who might be doing this? The phone calls? The fires? Is there anyone from your past?'

Appealed to directly, Angwen found herself at a loss. 'It makes no sense to me. The people I've known ... they've been ordinary, hard-working men and women, too busy getting on with their own lives to mess about with nuisance calls or complicated bits of arson. Normal, you know?'

She was trying to make Rachel feel easier, and Rachel was smiling and nodding, but Angwen wasn't convinced. 'Shall we go on? We ought to move. Paul will be wondering where we've got to and my dough will have collapsed.'

The two women exchanged glances, thinking of 'normal'.

'We don't have to hurry,' Rachel was saying. 'Dad won't be expecting us back yet. Look how bright it still is! May's a lovely month in Devon.'

'And in Wales. I used to smile at the tourists sloshing round Caernarfon in the wet in July when our Mays were full of sun.'

Snatching at trivial things, they slogged round the circular walk without any genuine notice of the alexanders in the lane bottom, or the lace of white stitchwort on the bank sides. Returning to the town, hurrying past the rows of fishermen's cottages, Angwen heard Rachel curse. 'Hell, I think that's Joe Penoyre's car.'

Angwen's stomach turned over. Joe would have broken the news to Paul. Paul would want to know why he hadn't been told. What could she say?, thought Angwen wretchedly. That on a beautiful day she'd decided that misery would keep? He would be furious. Worse, he would be cold. Angwen shrank from having to face the expression of distaste in his green eyes.

Confidence shredded, she scuttled ahead, ashamed of the fleeting, selfish wish that Rachel had never come back to Devon.

Chapter 38

Inspector Penoyre stepped out of Paul's cottage to meet Rachel. Face resolutely neutral, he stepped sideways to allow Angwen to pass into the house, where Paul was waiting, pacing up and down the hall.

'Dr Falconer was surprised to see me.'

'I was going to talk to him tonight.' Rachel was determined not to apologize. 'I didn't expect to see you again today.'

The inspector studied the view from the garden. Across the mud flats, over the silver sea-river channel to the green fields beyond and the distant haze of Powderham Castle. 'Dr Falconer has a very nice place. I could live here.'

He brushed the shoulders of his trim blue suit. 'I've questioned all currently available Kestrel House staff except Mrs Falconer about the fire at your cottage this morning. My men are checking alibis now and door-stepping the few houses and farms in the area. So far it seems unlikely that anyone from the institute was involved. From the timing of the attack and their statements, none of them appear to have had the opportunity. Or the motive.'

Rachel assumed he would smile then, but instead Joe Penoyre remained grave. The mild afternoon turned to ice for her.

'There's been another arson attack,' she blurted out. 'Where this time? Kestrel House? Dad's lab?' If his work had been destroyed, then she had failed. First Aoira, then her father.

Joe Penoyre turned away from the sea to look at her. 'No arson this time.' He stepped back into the shadow of the house, ducking under the low cottage lintel. 'I think Dr and Mrs Falconer should be ready for us now.'

The policeman disappeared indoors and Rachel followed, heart thumping as she anticipated more bad news. She was right behind as Joe Penoyre shepherded her father and Angwen into the study/sitting-room and onto the blue sofa. Sensing that he wouldn't start until she too was seated, Rachel slid into her father's leather armchair.

The inspector stood with his back to the mantelpiece, frowning down at a few white hairs from the hearth-rug that had impudently attached themselves to his polished black shoes. Glancing at each family member in turn, he took out a dark pocket-book but did not refer to it as he spoke.

'This morning, somewhere about the time Miss Falconer left Darcombe police station with Mr Horton, the front offside tyre of Miss Falconer's car was slashed with a heavy blade, more than likely a machete.

'No one saw who did it,' Inspector Penoyre continued. 'But until proven otherwise, we're treating

228

this attack as linked to this morning's fire, the other incidents of arson, and the nuisance calls.'

'I warned you two months ago, Joe,' said Paul. 'Back in March I was convinced my research was being sabotaged, but you didn't choose to believe me.'

Listening to her father's complaint, Rachel could only fix on one thing. 'Isn't a machete an unusual weapon for these parts?'

'Very. But it would have taken an unusually long, heavy blade of that type to cut through a tyre so quickly. And the timing of the attack is significant.' Inspector Penoyre stared at the notebook in his fist but still did not open it. 'Five minutes before you left us, Miss Falconer, your car tyres were intact. I happened to slip out of the station and saw that for myself.'

Angwen gasped. 'He must have been watching her!'

'And moved in as soon as he saw his victim leave. It's a strong possibility,' Joe Penoyre conceded.

Rachel marshalled her flying thoughts. Anger came and she welcomed it as an antidote to fear. 'Or do you think Michael or I slashed the tyre?' she flashed out. 'In which case, where would we have stashed the machete? It's far too long for the holding-seat of a motor-bike.'

Inspector Penoyre's hard little eyes widened a fraction. 'Well done, Miss Falconer. Our reasoning exactly. Which is why I'm talking to you here, now, instead of at the police station. Or, I might add, taking my wife out for a birthday lunch at Fingle Bridge.'

He did not mean it as a reprimand, but Rachel felt it as such and was ashamed. Especially when her father resumed his own agenda: 'The police must see now that we need more protection both at home and at the institute.'

'Stop being so selfish,' Angwen said sharply. 'If this had anything to do with the malaria vaccine, why haven't your car tyres been slashed? Why haven't you had the phone calls?'

Paul stared at his wife with the same degree of astonishment that he would have shown had the books in the study hurled themselves off the shelves at him. He looked stunned, then colour swam up his thin face.

Mentally applauding Angwen for finally standing up to her clever husband, Rachel was still sorry enough for her dad to want to shift the spotlight off him. 'Do you want me to return with you to Darcombe?' she asked Joe Penoyre.

'That won't be necessary, Miss Falconer. Any statements from you and your family will do on Monday. I called to let you know that from today a police car will be running past your cottage and Kestrel House at regular intervals, and that we'll be monitoring your movements most carefully.'

'Mine?' Rachel hoped she did not squeak in surprise.

'We've reached the same conclusion as Mrs Falconer. You appear to be the main target.'

'Then Rachel must stay with us,' put in Angwen firmly and, as Rachel drew in breath to protest, 'You can't be living in that lonely old cottage.'

The loss of her independence was something

Rachel would never agree to, but for now she contented herself with, 'I'm happy to stay tonight.'

'Good idea,' said Joe Penoyre. 'I have a few other suggestions, too – for all of you – about your safety.'

Paul raised his eyes from the bold geometric patterns of a sofa cushion. 'A man with a machete, after my daughter? My God.' His hand stretched across his forehead, kneading the worry lines.

Sitting beside him, Angwen squeezed his shoulder, although Rachel doubted that her father would feel that gesture of support. She too was having difficulty accepting the reality of the situation. 'Have you any idea who's behind this? What does he want?'

'The fact that there have been no demands has narrowed the field for us.' Detective Penoyre was upbeat. 'Bearing in mind your former relationship with Fultons and your warnings about the company, plus the potential commercial gains from work being done at Kestrel House, we did consider industrial espionage. So far, however, there have been no leads of that kind. As for Dr Falconer being forced into sharing his findings because of threats to his family, there hasn't been any direct suggestion of that.'

Rachel looked quickly at her father, who shook his head.

'I've had no telephone calls or letters from anyone demanding vaccine with menaces.' Paul's joke felt flat. 'But why Rachel?' he asked plaintively.

'That's what we're trying to discover.' Joe Penoyre slipped the note-pad into his pocket and strode off the rug to the window. 'And that's where your help will be invaluable.'

It was a neat appeal, Rachel thought, feeling her own attention caught and brought into sharper focus. Dad and Angwen were also game, both sitting upright on the sofa. Angwen nodded, urging the inspector to continue.

'I'd like all of you to keep a diary. Where you go, who you see, times, places. Do you all have cameras? Good. Then I'd like you to start carrying them round with you. Photograph anyone you don't recognize.

'Next, your daily routines. I'd like you to vary them, if you can. Especially you, Miss Falconer.'

Anyone else, thought Rachel, she'd be inviting to use her first name.

Penoyre was so self-possessed that even that tiny intimacy was impossible. Clearly he wanted to maintain distance. Fine by her. 'We can all work flexitime at Kestrel House,' she observed. 'But the basic journey to and from the institute will be harder to change. Dartmoor's scarcely bursting with roads. The only alternative route from my cottage is over the moor.'

She watched a flare of interest burst in the policeman's streetfighter face. 'I'll remind the men to continue their watch on walkers and horsemen. Three more things. At this point, I don't think we'd be justified in placing a tap on your phones, even with your consent, but it would be useful if you could all have your telephone numbers made ex-directory. Number two, keep an eye on your post. Leave any suspect packages exactly where they fall – don't make any attempt to move or open them. And finally, have your places checked by the fire service. You need to think about smoke alarms and fire-extinguishers in your homes, and you should carry a small extinguisher with you in your cars.'

Joe Penoyre was speaking to all of them but looking only at Rachel. 'Your car, Miss Falconer, has been taken to the police station carpark and is ready to be driven away. One of my men changed the front offside with the spare – forensics have the original, although I doubt they'll turn up anything more than what we already know.'

As Rachel thanked the inspector, Paul interrupted.

'And what, exactly, do we already know?'

Chapter 39

Michael was satisfied that he now knew how the arsonist had discovered the keeping-cellar under Rachel's cottage. The cellar was mentioned in an old history of Darcombe, a book kept on the open shelves in the Westcountry Studies Library. In the history, one of Mr Collard's ancestors, Gabriel Collard, had dug out the secret cellar under his longhouse to store contraband, then broken his back falling down the cellar steps. After that, the story ran, the cellar was 'rarely opened again'. Michael guessed that, in recent years, the cellar had been forgotten.

'Has anyone else asked to see this book in the last three months?' he asked the librarian, hoping at least to learn the sex of any enquirer. A description would be even better.

But his hopes were to be dashed. Not only had no one identifiable asked to see the history recently, or been noticed consulting it; but the book had been one of several lent to the High Moors Centre at Princetown that spring. Any number of visitors would have been able to study it on public display.

Admitting defeat, Michael felt his spirits take a farther dive when he rang Darcombe fire station to ask if there'd been any developments on the moors cottage arson case. 'Give it time, Mike,' the sub-officer told him bluntly. 'Let the police and fire investigator do their jobs.'

'Just so long as they're getting on with it,' Michael said to the dead receiver, dropping the mobile into his jacket pocket as he left the Devon records building. From personal experience, he knew how annoying – and lethal – it was to have amateurs messing around the scene, but right now he wasn't interested in ruffling egos. Resources in police and fire services were tight. He didn't want Rachel to be hurt because no one had looked into the small stuff.

Michael was aware of treading a narrow line. He wasn't a detective or a full-time fireman and couldn't begin to do their jobs. Direct inter-ference on his part would only lead to delay, confusion, contaminated evidence, spoiled interviews. And it would warn the stalker.

His own researches, Michael thought, cutting through shoppers to retrieve the Norton and be on his way to London, were an exercise in lateral thinking. The experts had to deal with the present-day stalker-arsonist. He was interested in the archaeology of it all: the deeper, buried layers.

It could be coincidence that whoever crept into Rachel's cottage happened to fix on burning the Amazonian flute and just happened to break in on an early Saturday morning when most people would be still sleeping in bed. To Michael, however, the timing of the attack was as significant as the solar alignments at Stonehenge. It had been an early morning piece of vandalism because whoever was stalking Rachel knew her habits: knew she loved mornings and would be awake. The police had to keep an open mind on suspects, but he could begin with Rachel's Rio associates, then work out from there.

Finding out more about Tim Stevens' past was as good a place as any to start. Rachel was convinced the man had left behind no relatives or friends. Although he knew that the police would have looked – or still be looking – into Stevens' family tree, Michael was intrigued. In his own work, the smallest detail was often the most telling.

That afternoon, in a break from browsing in the Westcountry Studies Library, Michael made a call to the local history library at Huddersfield, sending the staff there checking local newspapers for arson incidents near to Stevens' Almondbury home. For any mention, too, of Stevens' ethno-botanical trip to the Amazon – usually such reports were good on partners or family left behind.

An hour later, Michael phoned back. The local history library had come up with a *Huddersfield Examiner* account of Stevens' first botanical trip to the Amazon, ten years ago. The *Examiner* spoke of him as a single man, without mentioning any special girl- or boyfriend, although there was an elderly woman smiling over the fence on a photograph printed with the piece.

The picture showed Tim Stevens standing out of doors with his botanical gear strewn across the back lawn. Its caption gave the neighbour's name as Mrs Kellidrew.

A search for any reports on arsonists fire-setting in the Almondbury area from five and six years ago had drawn a blank. Trawling for such incidents was time consuming. Tactfully, the local history library staff suggested that if he wanted to investigate further, Michael could look himself.

Michael knew he could read up old *Examiners* and other newspapers whilst he was in London. First, he telephoned Mrs Kellidrew, who still lived in the same street as Stevens had done.

Posing as Mike Stevens, a distant relative interested in tracing his family tree, he reminded Mrs Kellidrew of the newspaper report, then asked if she could tell him anything about her former neighbour: 'Tim's the only botanist I've found in my family and I'd really like to know more about him. I'm hoping you can help.'

Mrs Kellidrew proved very willing to help, but

uninformative. Timothy had been quiet, polite and self-contained. He was often away, but whenever he returned there were no visitors. Timothy never entertained, or had callers.

'It's wrong to speak ill of the dead, I know, and him being one of your family, but he was always a bit odd. He wasn't much of a one for conversation, even after his jungle trips. And when he came back after his last one, he wouldn't even answer when I said "Good morning". I'd to have words with him, too, about his bonfires. He was forever burning something in the garden, even when I'd washing hung out. I told him it had to stop. Timothy got quite uppity, I'm sorry to say – said that he'd do what he liked in his own garden, and I should mind my own business. We never spoke after that.'

No wonder, thought Michael. It was strange that Rachel had never mentioned Stevens' bonfires, but she'd only known him on their field trips. As a private man, Stevens' frequent fires during the last weeks of his life could have been to destroy paperwork he didn't want anyone else to see.

'It's been good talking to you, Mrs Kellidrew. I really appreciate it.' With a few more words of thanks, Michael rang off. After an afternoon's digging, Tim Stevens still emerged as the complete loner.

Chapter 40

Michael reached London by nine, checking into a small hotel.

Ten minutes later, showered and wrapped in a hotel dressing-gown that cut off at the tops of his legs like the tunic of a principal boy, he took a pot of weak coffee from a yawning Filipino maid – who nonetheless smiled when she saw him. Her grin broadened as she left with a generous tip.

Sitting on the rock-solid bed, Michael drank coffee and planned his long weekend. The *Examiner* had given Stevens' career background. London University, then a stint at Kew before returning north to work for Fultons. So that was Monday sorted. The newspaper library at Colindale, checking for references to Stevens and Elsham, then a trip to London University. He'd start at Kew tomorrow. It would be a bonus if Elsham had also done some work for Kew, but at least someone there should remember Stevens.

'Time to get going.' Michael started for the *en suite*.

The problem always with a bike was scarcely any space for luggage. He changed underpants, socks and shirt, but made do with the jeans and biking-jacket. Catching a glimpse of himself in the room's narrow mirror as he left, Michael remained impassive. His eyes, gritty with lack of sleep, glared out of the landing shadows as he slammed the door on his reflection.

'Thug.' He ran down the creaking stairs, past the bright, empty lobby and out onto the dark street.

He'd planned to have a pint and a stroll before turning in, but found himself keeping going in a futile attempt to slow mind and body.

Playing rugby and working as a volunteer fireman he was maybe too fit. Pounding along the embankment past Cleopatra's Needle towards the Houses of Parliament and Westminster Bridge, he was the only pedestrian. Shutting out the trundling gripe of traffic, Michael mentally swept ahead. His eyes, attuned to registering ancient features of landscape, followed the river and the varied roofscapes above more modern façades.

A spry black man detached himself from a dolphin street-light farther along the broad pavement and floated over, his movements languid and casual – almost as if they were old friends, meeting every day. Was the fellow one of Kestrel House's many international visitors, or someone he'd once rescued?

Closing, Michael could see him clearly against the slick darkness of the Thames. Bareheaded, the stranger wore jeans, open-toed sandals and an elbow-length embroidered white shirt, open at the neck. A long bead and sea-shell necklace jounced against his lean frame with each springy step. Aside from a tiny rucksack, the only other thing he carried was a huge grin.

'Michael! Good to see you again!'

'Who are you?' The question was all Michael managed before his hands were seized and a smacking kiss planted on each side of his face. Close by his ear, the man whispered, 'I must have your complete attention.'

Michael stopped dead, staring at a small hand-gun aimed directly at his chest. 'Believe me, you've got it.'

The pistol dipped slightly, then motioned towards the river. 'Go down to the pier. A boat is coming to collect us.'

Michael discovered he was too astonished and too intrigued to feel fear. Any reaction would come later – if he survived. He motioned with his eyes towards the gun. 'Pointing that at someone is a highly stupid trick.'

'It saves time. Move.'

From the river below drifted the scent of oil, the sound of a swift engine, and voices. Two men, conversing in a language Michael first took to be Spanish, then realized was Portuguese.

He glanced at the man walking beside him, sensing that the stranger was uncomfortable at being scrutinized, but was permitting it, possibly as a mark of trust. In such a case, Michael felt, it was wisest to take a good look.

The stranger was black, with smooth, neat features, a grizzled short grey beard and wide sideburns. His casual clothes, suited to this warm, close evening, hung perfectly from his sinewy five-eight body. His voice was slow and melodious. Michael put his age at anywhere between fifty and sixty-five; his background anywhere between Eton and the best schools in Bangui.

'Who are you?'

The man smiled. 'All in good time, Michael.' He stepped closer to the edge of the pier. 'Let me walk you to the boat.'

Michael went ahead. The pistol knocked against his back as the stranger fell into step behind. He was talking freely now his face was hidden.

'My name is Ramon Gil. I was born in Rio, of poor parents.'

Annoyed for being so wrong in his assumptions, Michael mentally relocated the stranger to the South American subcontinent.

'Do you know what it is to be poor in the most beautiful city in the world? In Rio, the sun shines all day and everything is delicious if you have the money, because everything is for sale. That is why I fell in love with your country: free beaches. And places like these, wet and cold. I love the coldness. In Brazil everyone touches.'

Listening, Michael reflected on how easy it was to become used to having a gun jab his kidneys. Since those two on lookout from the boat pulling alongside would mow him down without thought, he put up with the discomfort.

Ramon Gil was still explaining. 'There are three ways to get rich in Rio if you are poor. Running drugs, selling women and boys, killing. I did the last, although my name has never appeared on any charge sheet.'

'I believe you. Why are you telling me?' Behind him, Michael knew Ramon Gil was smiling. He knew from the sound of his voice.

'Your parents are still alive.'

Michael slewed about. 'Leave them out of this.'

'I intend to.' English was not Ramon's first language, but he'd taken to quiet irony like a native. 'These days, I hate having to break into my retirement – ah, yes, I have retired to your beautiful country. But smaller operations – these are good. They keep my eye in, so to speak.'

Brushing past Michael, Ramon stepped onto the speedboat. 'My work has always been secret. Yours is out in the light. You attract envy. I have been contracted to kill men like you.'

'They shoot archaeologists in Brazil, do they? I'm flattered.'

'If that archaeologist finds gold, then sometimes yes.'

'Thanks for the warning, but I still don't understand the purpose of this meeting.'

'We share a mutual friend, Michael, to whom I have a huge obligation. A debt that can never be repaid – so say my wife and the *candomblé* priestess.'

Michael knew a little of *candomblé,* an Afro-Brazilian religion steeped in ritual and mysticism. Coming from a man dressed in jeans and with a pistol cradled in his fist, this was a strange confession.

'If I do not honour my debt, then I will die.'

It was as though one of the inhabitants of prehistoric Grimspound had come back to life. Ramon Gil was a fascinating mixture of the coldly rational and richly superstitious. To him, as to the Bronze Age hunter-farmers of Dartmoor, magic was as real and deadly as an arrow

– or a bullet. 'Why will you die?' Michael asked, curiosity winning over everything.

'The *candomblé* priestess commanded me to tell no one. Only the debt is important. Granting you my help will repay it.'

He wanted no help, ever, from a killer, but Ramon's gratitude might not stretch to such a blunt dismissal. 'Why do you think I need your help?'

'First things first, Michael. Get in the boat.'

Palms and temples clammy, Michael obeyed.

'The last man I let kiss me was my dad,' he remarked, when he and Ramon were on the deck of the slim speedboat, skimming downstream.

'Surprise makes men more tractable. There is always a slight delay before any reaction.' The hand-gun had disappeared. Ramon deftly took over the boat's tiny steering-wheel and nodded to the empty seat beside his.

Settling on the edge of the leather, Michael licked his lips free of the spray, his parched throat longing for a proper drink. 'Are we going to talk?'

Ramon smiled, uneven teeth the only outward sign of his deprived background. 'Is it business at once? Do I not offer you a *batida*?'

Michael understood, only because of Rachel, that he was being offered a drink, rather than an instrument of torture. Deep in his head a secret mocking voice said, 'You're enjoying this – it's as good as a fire.' Assassins had a deadly mystique and Michael discovered he was not immune.

'A drink later would be fine. You say you need some information, but until you tell me who this mutual friend is, I'm saying nothing.'

Ramon cocked a smooth grey eyebrow but continued looking straight ahead at the twin tall turrets of Tower Bridge. 'It is Rachel, of course. Rachel Falconer. I have a Gapo wife: I met Maria four years ago, on contract work in Boa Vista. When we were married, my wife told me of the whitewoman who had saved her life. Rachel inoculated Maria against measles. When Maria travelled with her brother to Boa Vista, a measles epidemic was raging through the city. Without the vaccine, Maria and Sandro would have died.'

His eyes fixed on Ramon, ignoring the passing river-bank and the anchored boats, Michael said coolly, 'Five years is a long time to repay that debt. You might be in the pay of the Rio military police, come to dispose of an inconvenient witness.'

'And you might simply be an old grammar-school acquaintance of Rachel.'

Ramon continued shaking his head. 'You also know yourself that this isn't the Rio police. If Rachel was in their way, or had annoyed them, such men would not wait five minutes, much less five years.'

'But a connection is there, maybe?' Michael's mouth twisted slightly with the distaste he couldn't quite hide. 'It could be arranged?'

'A hit contracted in Rio, to occur here? Easily. I could set the thing going myself in less than half a day. But this is not business.' Ramon's free hand briefly stroked the beads hung around his neck. 'Business is quick, finished. The police, too: they would never waste time. For a lesson, fires

244

are no good – break bones, or nothing. Burning is messy.'

'Not precise enough?' Michael was appalled at how quickly he caught on.

'Believe me, you would do it if you had to.' Ramon lowered the dark glasses slightly on his smoothly flaring nose.

Looking into the Brazilian's mild, melting eyes for the first time, Michael almost recoiled. He'd expected to see some kind of mark, a deadness, a stain on the spirit. This was an assassin with the smiling warmth of a wise old uncle. The sparkling black eyes reminded him of Rachel's.

A barge full of rubbish was left clanking in the speedboat's wake. As the stench hit him, Michael turned to the river, staring over the side. *Did they mean so little to you, your victims?* He forced himself to speak.

'Is it possible someone in the drugs trade believed that Rachel's work in the Amazon would bring them profit?'

Ramon's answer flowed back as a pulsing undertow. 'No drug baron on either side of the Atlantic is interested in non-narcotics. Again, you know this already. I think there is another issue, Michael – forgive me for not asking sooner, but I may call you that?'

Michael swallowed the answer, *Be my guest.* 'You may.'

'Then, Michael, I think you must ask yourself first what you want from me. Advice or action? I can do both, but you must decide.' Ramon changed up a gear and in a spout of icy grey water the boat leaped forward. Ramon's voice tightened a notch. 'Before you automatically go for advice and peer into my murky mind,' – a charming smile with that stiletto thrust – 'I would like to know one thing. Rachel: is she as beautiful as she looks on the TV?'

'Is that how you found her? Through the showing of the programme?'

'It's how my wife Maria came to see Rachel again. I showed a video recording of the programme to my people, and sent a tape to my *candomblé* priestess. She agreed with Maria that I owed a debt to Rachel, and that the programme was a reminder of that obligation.' Ramon flicked one of his beads. 'My wife had always wanted to thank Rachel, but she could not remember her last name. After the TV broadcast, Rachel Falconer was easy to trace. Then my people visited Kestrel House.' Ramon shot Michael a glance. 'And they found you.'

'I'm doing nothing for you. And you'd better keep away from Rachel.'

Ramon clapped Michael on the shoulder. 'Spoken like an English gentleman!' He grinned as Michael felt colour pounding into his face. 'I know what Rachel means to you – you are an easy man to trail. And your recent movements tell me everything. You are looking for the man who is stalking her.'

Suddenly, Ramon throttled back and they glided into calm waters, smooth as the group of swans bobbing by the stone ramparts of Tower Bridge. The shadow of the bridge slithered over Michael's head and shoulders and then the rising moon came out again for him.

'How do you know about that?'

'It is my business.' Ramon, peering over dark glasses at him, a dark father confessor. 'I know a great deal about Rachel Elaine Falconer.'

'Elaine.' Michael repeated Rachel's middle name. At fourteen he'd been too shy and too proud to admit how much he liked it.

'Elaine the fair, Elaine the loveable.'

Less surprised by a killer knowing Tennyson than struck by its aptness, Michael smiled. 'She's both. And a wart-charmer,' he added, simply wanting to talk about Rachel, for Ramon to be impressed. Still, assassin as confidant – not a good idea.

Michael did not expect Ramon to laugh off Rachel's bit of personal magic, but nor did he anticipate the seriousness with which his companion greeted that off-the-cuff remark.

Frowning, Ramon said, 'Brazilian witches use fire, though not as it has been employed against your woman.' Looking over his glasses, he squinted into the night. 'Is Rachel in part of an English witches' circle – a coven? Could she have fallen out with them?'

'She practises alone,' Michael replied evenly. Ramon's question had set him reconsidering Rachel's leisure pursuits. As a teenager she'd been a moor, home and family girl, but he wasn't sure of her more recent hobbies. And in England in the past – 'They used to burn witches in my country.'

'A religious zealot, perhaps?' Ramon gripped the boat wheel with both hands. 'This is more an area for a *candomblé* priestess than me. Ask me what I can answer.'

247

Deciding to take him at his word, Michael said, 'I presume you know about Paul Falconer's research?'

Ramon waved a negligent hand. 'There would not be enough money in such a nebulous area as a vaccine to excite the Mafia or my Colombian friends. For one of them to steal the research as a favour, maybe, but then Paul Falconer's work would already have been snatched, the lab destroyed.'

So far, thought Michael, Ramon had disposed of any profit or revenge conspiracy by the Mafia, drug cartels, Brazilian authorities or private deals by Charles Elsham. If he was telling the truth, the threat to Rachel should have lessened.

Michael sensed the opposite. Men like Elsham would act for motives of gain or vengeance – without that, the darker emotion of sexual obsession came into play. The area of the stalker. Yet, as Rachel and the police had already concluded, a very controlled, strange stalker.

'You're certain that Rachel is being stalked?'

'You are asking my expert opinion? Yes, she is being hunted. But not by a professional. Otherwise your woman would already be dead. Hitmen are paid to deliver.'

The idea of anyone wanting to harm Rachel was frighteningly surreal. 'I don't understand.'

Ramon shrugged. 'Me, I don't trouble with those reasons. Some psycho with no motive other than some weird internal workings – what does it matter? Would you like me to kill him?'

'How would you find him? How would you be sure?'

'Those are different questions. We return to what I asked earlier. How far are you prepared to go, Michael?'

'Maybe he'll stop.'

'No, you do not believe that. Nor should you. Would you like to hear what I think? Brazil and the past are irrelevant: five years are way too long. This is a man in a private vendetta. He is punishing your Rachel, perhaps because she has not noticed him. It will be someone she knows, who knows her and her ways – the milkman, the landlord, the tea-boy at work. Watch them. Watch if they are happy – this man will be very happy with what he is doing.'

Deep in his jacket pocket, Michael clenched the fingers of his left hand into a hard fist. 'Will it escalate?'

'This man will not stop until he has killed her.' Ramon gave a sad smile. 'So how far will you go, Michael?'

A whip of cold spray spat into Michael's face. Rachel, under sentence of death on a warm May night. And a killer coolly offering his services. Murder to stop a murder.

Michael knew he'd never ask for that, but not for any noble reasons. Quite apart from the point that he couldn't, daren't believe Ramon's story of obligation, an assassin could be bought off, could change allegiance. For Rachel, he had to be certain that the stalker would be stopped.

'How can I protect her?'

Glancing over his dark glasses, Ramon's eyes were calm. 'Ultimately, there is only one sure way–'

Michael allowed a grim smile to surface. He wasn't about to admit anything. 'In the meantime, I'd appreciate any information on stop-gap measures. Then, so far as I'm concerned, you'll have helped Rachel quite enough.'

'Then you are a fool.'

Michael shrugged. 'My choice, Ramon. Now talk to me.'

Next morning, as London bustled under an iron sky, Ramon returned Michael to the jetty opposite Cleopatra's Needle. In parting, Ramon neither shook hands nor offered any valediction but a crisp, 'Goodbye'. The moment Michael was ashore, the Brazilian streaked away, scudding the powerboat into the middle of the Thames, where it was quickly lost behind the plodding bulk of an early barge.

Relieved to be alive, yawning away the tension that had built up in him over the night, Michael began slogging towards Waterloo tube station past the solid grey lines of the Festival Hall.

Moving out of the shadow of buildings into Belvedere Road, preoccupied with what he'd learned from Ramon and an urgent need to find a toilet, it was a moment before Michael realized that the blue convertible slowly hugging the gutter was driving on the wrong side of the road.

Registering that he'd actually caught the interest of a kerbcrawler did nothing for his mood. He halted, twisted round to face the driver, his voice pleasant. 'Why don't you—'

Then he found himself staring at the brunette in the driving seat.

'Small world, Mike. I've just been making calls at London Weekend and who do I see toiling down the next street? Here, hop in before you fall over. I don't want that great big body of yours putting a ding in my car.'

It was tempting, but right now he was better alone. Five minutes of Helen's breezy 'How are things going?' and he'd finish by snarling at her. Michael's hand closed gently on the handle of the door she'd just opened for him. 'Helen, I–'

The car radio talked across him, the news announcer full of gleeful importance as she relayed the final headline. 'And in a bizarre and so far unexplained incident, Rachel Falconer, star of the television series, *The High Country*, narrowly escapes being burned alive...'

Chapter 41

Several hours before Michael's meeting with Ramon Gil, Inspector Penoyre finished his analysis.

Coiled in her father's leather armchair in the study, Rachel mentally crossed through points she no longer needed to pursue. Whatever had happened in her father's lab in March, whoever had stolen Angwen's bike, there'd been no other moves against them. Charles Elsham's Italian connections were in the cosmetics trade and the questionable fringes of accountancy – in copious telephone records, Charles had never made any calls to Fultons. Daniel's public involvement with the firm was above board.

Of the other Kestrel House regulars still in the area, Stephen Lees was officially off sick and in bed when the burning flute had crashed through Rachel's cottage window. Colin Benwick had been breakfasting alone – but had a witness, since his milkman had called him to the back door just after eight to pay his bill. Leo's alibi was a tall, auburn-haired lovely called Lucy, who'd slept over at his Tavistock flat after a 'wonderful' evening at the Northcott Theatre. Daniel of course had been there with Rachel. Michael had just left and might be considered a suspect, since he knew about the keeping-cellar and was besides a volunteer fireman, someone who might want to appear as a hero, to be taken seriously as a professional firefighter. Inspector Penoyre had smiled slyly as he floated that idea.

Refusing to rise to the bait, Rachel stretched slowly in the chair, relishing movement after being still so long. Outside the sun was shining and plants were blooming. She was tired of being indoors.

'Any ideas how the stalker knew about the cellar?'

Joe Penoyre scowled at the S-word. 'The cellar was marked on building-plans your landlord submitted last year.' The policeman's thin face unfolded into a smile. 'His application was turned down but I'm hoping we'll be more successful. The planning department are getting back to us on Monday, I hope with some names of interested parties.'

'What about that whistle-blower call?' Angwen spoke for the first time in ages. 'Outside the family, no one else knows what happened to Rachel in Brazil – except for Fultons.'

'That's where you're wrong, I'm afraid, Mrs Falconer. One of my men has been digging on the internet and unearthed several Brazilian newspaper reports that covered the shooting of the Gapo tribeswoman and her whitewoman companion, Miss Falconer.'

Rachel closed her eyes for a second. Aoira's face floated in her mind. 'Doesn't that suggest a Brazilian connection?'

'Unlikely. What's been happening to you wouldn't produce any benefits in Rio – and personal profit is the only motive over there.' Distaste wrinkled the edges of the inspector's eyes. 'My super spent some time in Brazil last year. Every official he spoke to seemed to expect a bribe.'

Rachel glanced anxiously at her father and Angwen. Dad looked faintly strung out and Angwen's breathing was shallow. They'd things to say to each other, Rachel knew. They needed to quarrel about trust, about telling each other what was going on. Angwen needed to explain to her husband why she'd delayed telling him about this morning's arson attack. They'd do better without her for an hour or two.

She looked at Inspector Penoyre. 'Are you driving back to Darcombe?' She gave her biggest smile. 'If you are, could you possibly give me a lift? There are a few bits I'd like to collect from my cottage.'

Part lie, half truth. Extra clothes, a nightdress, computer files she could read on Dad's old Elonex. The time away would give her father and Angwen a break and she could check for herself that Mr Collard and the police had left her place secure. It was time to make it much harder for the stalker, to bait the trap properly.

She talked about that to Joe Penoyre as he drove them from the salty brightness of Topsham to the burnished glow of the moor. Penoyre warned her against it but, since he couldn't stop her, Rachel only pretended to agree with him, planning to go ahead later and do what she wanted.

She recovered her car from the police station at Darcombe and drove to the cottage behind Joe Penoyre, who insisted on accompanying her home. He scrupulously searched the house and its cellar before leaving.

Inspector Penoyre also listened with Rachel to the new messages on her answering-machine – just in case. There was a request from the doctor's surgery for Rachel to get in touch. Nothing to be alarmed about, but the practice were re-doing a batch of cervical tests. Could she come in for another check?

'Something else I can do without,' remarked Rachel, irritated at the blush smudged along Penoyre's jutting cheekbones. Tense after that minor bombshell, she felt cold metal digging into her stiffened leg.

She'd forgotten Daniel's gift, again. Sighing, Rachel reached into her trouser pocket and drew out the small gold box as the answering-machine clicked on.

'Here comes the next message.' Flicking a cellar cobweb from his shoulder, Penoyre leaned forward.

'Rachel – Helen. This is a call back to your call. Where the hell are you these days? Hope there's been no more trouble at your end. Thanks for the azalea tip but this week's no use to me. The crew and I can make it up there next week, June first. That okay with you? I'm due back in the States in July, so time's pressing. Get back to me on this, Pronto.'

'Poor Helen,' murmured Rachel, absently placing the gold box on top of the answering-machine as she rewound the tape. It wasn't fair or prudent to keep Helen dangling: she'd ring her again tonight.

'Pretty little thing.' Penoyre motioned to the gold box.

'Daniel gave it to me this morning.' And she'd raged at him in return.

Sighing, she rose from the answering-machine and set her ex's expensive present on the deep stone sill of the boarded-up window. It would look better on the mantelpiece, but Aoira's flute had been set above the mantelpiece. She wasn't ready yet to see one gift replace the other.

Wishing Daniel hadn't insisted she keep it, Rachel tucked the box farther back against the sill, in the shadow of the fresh, resin-scented planking. Her landlord had fixed the window, she noted, with no sense of relief. 'I don't suppose Mr Collard has any kind of criminal record?' she asked.

'George Collard's a typical farmer. Sheep and the weather, those are his passions. You're good money to him, cash in hand.'

They continued upstairs. Joe Penoyre scanned the bedroom and tiny bathroom, raised the trapdoor on the landing to peer inside the attic. Then he escorted Rachel round the back of the cottage, to the newly cleared, highly visible cellar entrance, and explained how Mr Collard had secured the wall-door with fresh bolts. Declaring himself satisfied, the policeman went off.

Rachel scuttled back indoors, shot on the bolts and ran upstairs. Before she packed an overnight bag, she took a duster from the airing cupboard and carefully wiped away every powder-marked fingerprint. Then she brought out the old upright hoover and vacuumed up each zinc-powdered footprint.

Feeling less invaded, Rachel moved quickly to the middle of the bedroom. Flipping back the quilt, she removed a narrow box from the bed-base drawer.

Her camera equipment was sufficiently sophisticated for limited remote filming – enough at least for high speed black-and-white photographs triggered by pressure on a slim pad hidden under the rug at the bottom of the stairs. High in the shadows and with an inaudible shutter, the black Leica hidden at the top of the unlit stairwell should remain undetected. With luck, it might catch a prowler full-face.

That was the theory, as she'd explained it to Inspector Penoyre. Putting it into practice took the best part of an hour; balancing on a step-ladder at the top of the stairs the nail-biting climax. Hot and tired as she humped the ladder away, Rachel longed for a cup of tea, a shower, a cigarette and Michael's height, in no fixed order of preference.

Michael's height? Why couldn't she admit that it was the man she missed? He was in London, no doubt dashing to see Helen. And Helen was planning to return to America. How long before the lure of television cash and clout drew Michael away from Kestrel House? Away from Britain?

'Do what you can. Not what you can't.' Rachel stepped heavily across the rug and crossed the kitchen/sitting-room floor to the sink. No time for tea. A drink of water would do.

Flicking a tumble of hair back from her flushed face, Rachel grasped the cold-tap. The phone rang. She reached for the receiver before good sense reminded her to allow the answering-machine to record.

A metallic voice. *'The work, the bike, the bitch. I think it's time to get personal, Rachel. Time to suffer, then watch those you love suffer. It's coming, Rachel, the fire to burn you. You won't have to wait.'*

A ching as the contact was broken. Rachel dived for the handset. Calling 1471 brought no joy.

Watch those you love suffer. Rachel started to dial her father's number, chopped her hand down partway through. Dad and Angwen had already been warned by the police. If she spoke to them now they'd only be worried sick until she returned to Topsham. She could explain face-to-face.

'Thank God you're in London,' she said, tilting

her head up slightly.

The dungeon silence of the kitchen mocked her.

Poor Joe Penoyre wasn't going to get any of his weekend off. Rachel lifted the phone to her ear a second time.

A banshee howling of tyres and a thudding crash caused her to drop the receiver onto its cradle and dash outside.

There was nothing. No car wreck, no injured people, no scraps of metal, no oil spills, no sign of skidding. No sign of anything to prove that she'd not just imagined hearing a vehicle out of control. As Rachel sprinted out of the blue gate and over the brow of the hill to squint anxiously down the other side, sparrows placidly pecked at the roadside gravel. High in the re-established silence, a lark sang out boldly.

'What the heck's going on?' Pulling up short on the crown of the road, Rachel saw no movement in the lane or in the surrounding hedgerows. 'I'm going barmy – the stress has finally got to me–'

There was nothing. No one. Then there was fire.

Chapter 42

Instinct screamed at Rachel to run. Heat was spouting up at her, spitting over her shoulders as flames leapt from her back. There was no clear air, only the choking waste of shrivelling hair.

The vilest thing was the stink of herself catching fire. Panic flayed her mind. She was going to die.

Pitching forward, Rachel rolled over and over on the verge, beating out the flames. Her lungs felt to be roasting as each gasp drew in the stirred-up shrapnel of dust, razor-edged sparks, burning grass.

In a sulky puff of black smoke, the dancing glare was extinguished. Rachel lay on her back, sucking in air, then lurched onto her side as pain hit her. Closing then opening her eyes, she thought how strange it was that she was alone. That she could lie in a pool of grey smoke and dirt at the edge of an English lane and there was no one to stop for her, no good Samaritan.

No more assaults, either. No man stepping out from behind a hedgerow to finish the job.

Rachel shook her head from side to side, wondering if she'd lost consciousness for a second. Aware of a searing across her shoulder-blades, a dull ache in her thigh where she'd been shot in Rio and general disorientation, she made herself concentrate. If the stalker was out there, would the cottage be safe? Was he, perhaps, waiting in her bedroom?

Groaning, she made herself crawl forward. Any clues in the hedgerow – signs of trampling, bruised vegetation – must wait. She had to get herself seen to.

Tavistock hospital. Then warn the others. Should she try to walk, or continue crawling? At least she was on the right side of the road for traffic. Rachel's sooty lips twitched at the thought. She could see the blue gate now, soft blue, cool as water. Her throat was sore and parched, her hands grazed by tarmac. Her arms were shaking. All of her was shaking. Better crawl: she might not be able to keep her feet.

Cottage or car? Her mobile was in the car. The car was still locked – was it inside the garage? Fumbling on her knees with the gate latch, Rachel's face warped in concentration. Outside – she could see it. Thank God.

If he was here, if he was watching, what would he expect her to do? Phone from the house. Stagger like one of the three little pigs into her home, bar the door then go weeping for the telephone. Once she was inside, there'd be no chance of any passing farmer or walker seeing her. The cottage and its secret cellar would be her trap.

The blue gate swung closed on the backs of her heels. Rachel resisted the temptation to stop and listen. She had to behave as if the idea of anyone waiting inside her snug little cottage hadn't occurred to her. Head and shoulders lolling, she crept on. It was ludicrous, paddling along the gravel path like a baby, but her head swam. Standing was not an option. She needed to conserve energy and pain management for the getaway.

The right knee of her charred trousers snagged on the rosebush. Ripping it free with a tired hand, Rachel dragged herself to her car. If the tyres had been slashed again, she'd still need to drive it out of here, so there was no point in checking. Rachel flopped a hand over the driver's door-handle, tugged her upper body up the sun-warmed metal.

Drawing the keys from her pocket with burned fingers sent a new message of torment to her jaded brain. Treating the pain as a stimulant, Rachel fumbled the lock, levered the door open and climbed up into the seat.

Stretching the burns across her back produced a rush of pure agony. Clinging to the steering-wheel, keys swaying in the door, Rachel struggled not to slip away. The crack of a bird-scarer down in the valley acted as an alarm-clock. She tore the keys from the lock, crammed them into the ignition.

An instant before the engine fired, she thought of sabotage. Then her foot floored the clutch, her leg wallowed though the pain barrier to the accelerator and she was off, lurching at every corner, crashing the gears.

Rattling over the cattle grid at the bottom of the hill, Rachel cheered.

Driving was both habit and analgesic, and once started, easier than trying to remember the Darcombe Police phone number. Rachel puttered past a tranquil Kestrel House on the way to Tavistock, crawling at caravan pace.

Reaching Postbridge, she found herself reluctant to negotiate the narrow hump-back bridge littered with tourists gripping platefuls of take-away cream teas. Gliding to a stop alongside a pony and rider who were waiting to cross the road bridge once a coach had passed, Rachel wound down her window. Unable to manage the complex stretchings involved in leaning forward and looking up, she addressed the teenager's right boot.

'Excuse me, would you telephone 999?' How polite she was being, how middle-class. 'I've been in an accident and I'm having a bit of trouble.'

Coming to later, Rachel discovered that the pony-rider, Lauren James, had indeed dialled 999 and stayed until the ambulance arrived. Taken to Tavistock, Rachel roused herself sufficiently to tell the staff her name and to beg them not to alarm Angwen and Paul when they contacted them. Then she relaxed, waiting for the hospital painkillers to work.

The next thing she was aware of was Joe Penoyre standing with a doctor at the foot of her bed. The talk was of burns, dehydration, disorientation. Yes, she would be kept in.

Rachel slept through Saturday night and Sunday morning, unaware that she'd made the national news.

Chapter 43

'Goodbye, Helen. I'm going back, whether Rachel thinks she needs me or not.' Then, the car door still open, he was gone.

He'd stalked out of Helen's morning. By the time she'd joined her TV crew at three that Sunday afternoon at Gordano motorway services near Bristol, Michael would already be camped at Rachel's bedside in Tavis-wotsit.

'Well, Mike, I sure hope Rachel appreciates it.' Helen had been on the M4 for over an hour, driving in blinding light. She was sweaty and sour. Having heard about Rachel's condition on a news update, she wasn't too concerned. The girl was being treated free of charge, for Pete's sake.

Coming from Miami, where arson was almost a cottage industry, Helen felt that Michael's re-action was excessive.

'It's a weird kind of old friend that drives a couple of hundred miles for minor burns,' Helen observed to a passing motor-bike that she took for one single mad moment to be a grey Norton.

'Still, it's sort of nice,' Helen went on, eyes expertly sweeping for the gaps in the traffic before she bustled the blue convertible into them. 'Shows how much he can care, when he puts his mind to it. I could live with that.'

Helen drummed a fast tattoo on the steering wheel, humming along to the Vivaldi on her radio, short brown hair whipping back from her ears. She wasn't due in the States for another month. Plenty of time to refocus Mr Horton.

Smiling, Helen recalled that she always got what she wanted. A few more dates with Mike, and she'd have him, too.

Chapter 44

Lying on her stomach, Rachel saw a haggard man talking with the nurse at the ward desk. Pleasure shot through her. 'Michael! I'm so glad.'

The tall figure swung round. She saw with alarm that Michael's eyes were filling up, and flapped her free arm. 'Brought any grapes?'

A joke, intended to set him at ease. Instead, as he strode into the ward, knees cracking after being on the Norton for so long, Michael was apologizing – again. 'I heard on the radio this morning and came straight here: well, almost. Look, I'm sorry, I don't know why I didn't think...' By now he was looming, worried, at her bedside, then hastily crouching so that she did not have to twist to see him. 'Rachel–'

He stared, hypnotized, at the dressings on her back, his fair skin reddening from chest to forehead. Wishing that for once they could manage a reunion without starting off on the wrong foot, Rachel shot out her bandaged hand and shook his bent knee.

'I'm always pleased to see you, Michael. Don't you know that yet? I'm just surprised. Last time I heard, you were in London.'

Her heart was leaping because he was not. This was more than invalid gratitude, or the weakness of flesh. This was real.

Unaware of her moment of revelation, Michael sighed heavily. 'Yes, and that was a wasted trip.'

He didn't explain. Taking in the drip attached to her leg, the loose dressings, the wads of gauze and lint strapped round her hands, Michael lapsed into a brooding silence.

Again, Rachel tried to keep it light. Turning laboriously onto her side so he couldn't see the worst of the damage, she winked a blue-green eye. 'How do you like my new tan?'

The instant the words were out she hated them, their seeming flippancy flung in the face of a man who'd just driven several hundred miles non-stop to be with her. Her, not Helen. Rachel smiled, then started to cry.

'Don't, Rachel. Don't–' Michael lurched towards her, stopping abruptly as if terrified to touch.

'It's only shock,' Rachel tried to say, but the explanation was lost between her tears and Michael's mounting anger.

'He'll never do this to you again. I'll have him.'

'Michael–'

'Sssh.' Not yet ready to smile, Michael patted her pillow.

'Hug me, blast it!' Rachel wailed, breaking down completely. 'I'm hooked up to this damn drip, my back feels like flash-fry steak, my hands are trussed up in boxing gloves, I'm craving an entire box of Nicorette patches and I smell like a dog bathed in Dettol.'

'Too bad. I'm still going to kiss you.'

He swooped in. Rachel saw a grey eye wink at

her as his mouth embraced hers in exasperated tenderness.

'This is it, isn't it?' Michael whispered some time later.

'Of course – now keep kissing.'

'We'll frighten your fellow patients.'

'It'll give them something to tell their visitors.'

'Sssh, then.' Another kiss, lingering and sweet, making Rachel glad she was already horizontal.

Michael drew back, his hands releasing her face after a final caress. Comfortable on her pillow, their heads and eyes exactly level, Rachel solemnly wiped a tear from the corner of Michael's eye. He, just as seriously, smoothed away the water on her face. 'Your hair. Your lovely long hair.'

'Be thankful I'm not bald.' Rachel flicked the edges of her new collar-length hair. 'They had to cut it off.' She smirked, humour and vigour returning wonderfully quickly. *Kiss it better.* 'Rather a drastic solution for split ends.'

'Are you ever serious?'

'Frequently, Michael. Are you?'

'Let me prove it.'

'Better than chocolate mints,' said Rachel several moments later. She licked her lips, aware that Michael's kisses were a potent antismoking device. 'You're addictive,' she murmured, delighted by the rush of blood to his face. 'I never realized I could make you blush so easily.'

'It's not that kind of heat.' Michael dabbed a finger on her nose. 'As I'd be happy to demonstrate if you weren't quite as delicate as you are right now.'

'Promises, promises,' she murmured, rolling back to a more comfortable position on her stomach.

Seeing Michael's face change she wished she hadn't. She was a patient again, a victim.

'About what happened...' Michael rose stiffly and glanced about for a free chair. Seeing none, he squatted again. When his lips came close to her ear, it was not to murmur sweet nothings. 'I hope the police are taking it seriously.'

Rachel nodded, feeling the burnt skin tug painfully on the back of her neck. 'They're door-stepping all the farms. And forensics are analysing the tape from my answer machine. I had another phone call,' she explained, catching Michael's raised eyebrows. *Time to suffer, then watch those you care about suffer.* 'You must be careful, Michael. Promise me.'

'Hey, what's this?'

'You'll watch your back, won't you? I've told Dad and Angwen the same, because...' She told of the last telephone call at her cottage. 'He didn't wait long before moving against me. And I'm not sure how he did this.' She pointed. 'He must have been close. Somewhere in the hedge, perhaps, so that he could throw whatever it was, without me spotting him.'

'Have the police any ideas about what he hit you with?'

'If they have they're not saying.'

Michael shifted, going down on one knee whilst he reached into his black biker's jacket. 'I passed your cottage on the way here. Police were combing the roadside and the verges. I parked at the

267

bottom of the hill beyond the cattle grid and walked back along the fields.'

He tilted his head to match Rachel's. 'A couple of things I know a lot about as a local archaeologist are the Dartmoor soils and the animals that like to dig in those soils. And your cottage, my dear, is built on a hill that says to every rabbit in the county, "Come live in me." Of course, the warrens run down into the hill, sometimes at quite a steep angle.'

'And an object small enough to fall into a rabbit hole might roll downhill.'

'Know-all! Can't tell you anything.' Michael became serious again. 'You're right, though, dead right. Sorry, "dead's" the wrong word in the circumstances, but basically what I found in the bottom entrance of one rabbit hole in the field below your cottage was this.' He rummaged in a pocket.

'Paper and pencil?'

Michael began to draw. 'There were two and I had to leave them where they were for forensics, otherwise they might be suspecting me.'

Rachel squinted at the small spherical object, cut in half to reveal the interior. 'FIREBALL' Michael's caption read.

'Several wildlife services use these to burn off the under-storey in pine forests. It's a fire-prevention measure: lots of small blazes to prevent dead vegetation from building up and a lightning strike causing huge devastation.'

'The kind of burning for fresh growth that goes on over the North Yorkshire gorse moors?'

'And on heather moors here in Devon.'

'A fireball would explain the jab I felt between my shoulders just before the whole of my back seemed to go up in flames.' Rachel grimaced. 'I thought I was doing a Krook, from *Bleak House*. Death by spontaneous combustion.'

Michael was silent, reflecting on the dreadful horror Rachel must have experienced in those moments. Ramon Gil was right. This stalker-arsonist wouldn't stop until he'd killed his victim.

Grimly aware that time was running out, Michael wondered whether to mention Ramon Gil. Not here, in public – not without talking to Inspector Penoyre – but later perhaps, when he and Rachel could be private together.

'Oh my word,' breathed Rachel, looking behind him. 'A delegation.'

Chapter 45

Michael spun on his heels to find Inspector Penoyre, Paul and Angwen bearing down, the last two laden with flowers and brown-paper bags. Skidding on the polished floor, the Inspector put on a spurt to arrive first.

'Thanks for the tip about the rabbit warren, Mr Horton,' he said, as Michael rose. 'Very useful. Although I must say I'm rather surprised you decided to drop off, as it were, at the cottage when you knew Miss Falconer was here.'

Michael knew Penoyre was being provocative but couldn't help bridling. 'I can't help Rachel here, in the ward - I'm not a doctor. But round by the cottage I thought I could be some use.'

'Very sensible. Some would say not very romantic, and certainly not very trusting of the police–'

Rachel interrupted. 'And how long would it have taken for those fireballs to be discovered without Michael's help?'

Her fierce protectiveness disarmed Michael. He could only laugh. 'What have you got for us, Inspector?'

Lying on her stomach, Rachel smiled.

Daniel saw it all from the corridor outside. His ears, tuned to Rachel's warm voice, heard only her. Rachel, speaking to Horton as she'd once spoken to him. Rachel, looking at Horton in that lambent way which he alone had inspired, once.

The sight brought him to a dead stop, plumb in the middle of the ward entrance. A male visitor jostled past. 'Move along there, mate–'

'Piss off.' Unseeing, unaware of the rapidly approaching staff nurse, Daniel tightened his grip on the huge bouquet of freesias, crushing the stems.

Rachel had turned him down for Mike Horton. Now he not only knew it was over between them, he was glad it was over. If she could really prefer Horton to himself.'

'Who is it you wish to see?'

Daniel blinked, surprised to find the staff nurse directly in front of him.

'Nobody now.' He tossed the bouquet onto the

ward desk. 'Use these in therapy if you want. They're no good to me.'

Flicking a freesia off his Armani jacket, Daniel stalked from the ward.

Chapter 46

Rachel and the others did not see Daniel. They were listening to Penoyre.

'Last Saturday night, Charles Elsham was spotted at the Ship Inn in Exeter by one of my off-duty WPCs. We don't know yet why he's turned up in the West Country, or where he's staying, but given the sudden escalation in attacks against Miss Falconer, his appearance could be significant.'

'How is it you don't know where he is?' Michael asked.

'My WPC did follow Mr Elsham from the Ship but lost him in the late-evening traffic before we could put a trail on him. We do have the colour, make and partial registration of the car he was driving, so it shouldn't be too long before we trace him.'

'No doubt to a car-hire firm,' muttered Michael. Caught between smile and frown, Rachel shook her head at him.

'In the meantime, Miss Falconer, my men and I will be conducting interviews of your staff throughout this weekend. I'd appreciate it if we could have another trawl through the records at

Kestrel House.'

'You can start on Monday.' Rachel raised her chin, knowing that what she was about to say would alarm her family but determined to go through with it.

'I know how short-staffed you are, Inspector, but I've decided to discharge myself early. I'm going home tomorrow and plan to resume my work the day after. With these new threats against my family and close friends, I think it's the only sane course. We have to draw this man out.'

Before Penoyre could respond, Paul said, 'Rachel, it's only natural that you want to help, but this isn't the way.'

'Don't you understand? I can't do anything in hospital: I'm a sitting duck. Outside I'll be able to help, divert his attention. If he doesn't think I've suffered enough this time, he'll come back for another go.'

'And I'll be with her,' said Michael.

'With her?' Angwen burst out. 'Are you as daft as she is? Why don't you try to talk some sense into the girl?'

Michael gently touched Rachel's bandaged hands. 'Hiding away isn't for this one. If I were in her position, family under threat, I'd be doing the same.'

Rachel found her eyes filling. Of all of them, Michael was the only one who understood her need to be active.

'I really wouldn't advise you setting yourself up as any kind of bait, Miss Falconer. Police resources can't stretch—'

'What if Rachel stayed with me for a few days?

No one else knows about us – yet.' Michael grinned. 'The bush telegraph doesn't work that fast.'

'No! It's too risky for you!' Rachel was tired of obstacles between Michael and herself, but this was different.

She was overruled. 'That's fine with your father and me,' said Angwen. 'We'll be going to my parents' next week, so the police won't have to worry about us, either.'

Paul looked startled. 'My work–' He subsided as Angwen looked at him steadily. 'I suppose we owe them a visit.' He batted a greenfly off a withered bunch of flowers on the hot window-ledge.

Joe Penoyre nodded, satisfied.

Rachel heard about Daniel from the staff nurse the following morning. The nurse's excited description – 'Blonde and handsome and ever so dramatic' – fitted Daniel exactly. Much as she was sorry for causing him any new grief, she could only be relieved that her ex had finally got the message. He must have seen her and Michael together.

Michael was returning soon with some clothes for her. He was going to take her home – his home.

Rachel frowned at all the weeks when they'd misunderstood each other. Such a waste of time. Had she been wilfully blind, she couldn't have been more stupid. Then the thought of Michael loving her took her again and the delight killed all pain.

Except *that*. Rachel winced and the staff nurse said brightly, 'Sorry! Nearly done.' Though unhappy at Rachel's discharging herself, the nurse was helping: providing new dressings and advice. Perched on the edge of her bed, Rachel watched intently as the nurse started to re-dress her hands. Next time she might have to do this herself. Or ask Michael.

Smiling, she compelled her attention back to the nurse. As the nurse deftly cut, shaped and strapped a sterile dressing over her burnt thumb, Rachel deliberately switched her thoughts to the other new, and slightly alarming, development: the reappearance of Helen.

Late in the afternoon, whilst the sun was beating against the window-blinds and visitors were drifting away in search of tea, Helen had made her entrance. Swanning up to the nursing staff on the desk with the confidence of a consultant, she'd stamped herself on the place.

'Right, Sister – I am right in that, aren't I? – Sister, I need your full co-operation. We've a major news story breaking right here in your hospital. You've a patient, Rachel Falconer, who's been consistently stalked and threatened and the police have done nothing until this near-tragedy. People need to see what she's had to suffer.'

The sister murmured something Rachel couldn't catch.

Helen's pretty face drooped, but she continued without pause, 'Can I go talk with her as a visitor? Check if you need to, but we do know each other. I'm doing a film series about her work.'

Her clear voice could be heard over most of the ward. Patients glanced at Rachel, who nodded. Flicking her fingers at the cameraman to stay in the corridor, Helen sashayed in.

Unable to stop herself, Rachel twisted her head up to watch Michael. Having returned from Inspector Penoyre's latest grilling ten minutes earlier, he'd been crouched alongside her bed, quietly discussing sprinkler systems for Kestrel House. They'd been relaxed, expanded, sending little glances to each another, happily aware of the knowing looks various departing visitors had flung their way.

But at the sight and sound of Helen, Michael blushed, jumping to his feet in a rush that sent a flutter of 'get well' cards skidding off the next patient's locker onto the floor.

'So sorry,' he mumbled, scooping up the cards and replacing them carefully on the locker. Staring at his back as he worked, Rachel felt a definite tension. Clearly Helen had an effect on him.

Helen was nobody's fool. 'How's my favourite TV presenter?' she asked, brushing delicately past Michael to kiss Rachel. 'Let's survey the damage.' Eyes crackling with good humour, Helen peered over Rachel's back. 'These could be Emmy material, girl. When are you getting out of here so we can start shooting?'

Her brazen opening was met with a guffaw of laughter from Michael.

'They'll never clone me, boy.' Nicely mocking, Helen held out a hand. 'Great to see you again, Mike,' she said, nestling her dainty fingers in his lean hand. 'Where are you taking me for dinner tonight? You owe me a dinner-date.'

Guiltily aware that she'd once told Helen there was nothing between herself and Michael, Rachel looked away.

'I'm taking Rachel home with me today. I think we'll both need an early night.'

'Sure.'

Helen appeared utterly sanguine – but she didn't know how good a liar Michael was, thought Rachel, startled at Michael's easy dissembling. Not wanting to hurt Helen's feelings was admirable, but wouldn't it be better if he explained how things were between them now?

'Sure,' said Helen, in a rare repetition, 'I could do with an early night myself. The boys and I have already been out by the cottage, recording the investigation. If Rachel's okay I'd like to start filming again the day after tomorrow. This stuff is hot.'

Rachel smiled at the unconscious irony, although she sensed Michael becoming edgy. Perhaps because Helen had resumed her charm offensive. 'How about if we do lunch then, Mike? No need to be tied to Rachel's bandages. My film guys will fuss her to death. And we need to talk about your series. Several TV companies are interested, including one in the States.'

Say no! Rachel sent the frantic telepathic message, but Michael had been deftly manoeuvred into looking a neurotic, unambitious wimp if he refused Helen this time. And of course he didn't, or rather hadn't, reflected Rachel bleakly. She remembered Michael's acceptance and Helen's delighted, 'Yes!'

Returning completely to the present, the beginning of another blue, hot day, Rachel suppressed a shiver. She was vividly aware that her practical, capable view of life had let her down. Somehow, she needed to anticipate the arsonist, yet it seemed that here too she was merely waiting, passive, for the next attack.

'All finished.' The nurse smiled at Rachel, wishing she could be as pretty. But maybe not. For this anxious young woman the price of beauty was too high.

Chapter 47

The forensic team sent to recover the remains unearthed at the new dig had still not finished. Hearing on his answering-machine that all of Monday and Tuesday – when he'd been due to return to the site – were out, Michael was delighted. With no site work and no lectures or fire training drills until the end of the week, he'd be working at Kestrel House. Close to Rachel.

Research into Elsham and Stevens must wait – London and Kew were dismissed from his thoughts. Dartmoor was where the arsonist operated. The moor was where he would track him down.

And what then? murmured Ramon Gil in his head.

Tugging a checked shirt over his head, Michael restively jerked his shoulders. Forgetting to fasten the three top buttons, he grabbed his jacket and started down the creaking staircase, narrowly missing the low lintel as he stepped straight from the bottom step out through the front door of his cottage.

The Norton was parked on the gravel drive under the dining-room window, the pebbles round it swept into a series of complex spirals he'd seen on a prehistoric standing-stone in Spain. No one had disturbed the patterns.

Rolling over the gravel to the roadside, Michael didn't bother checking his watch. It was early. No dawn chorus. No roding woodcock over the copse beside his home. Dew chilled his hands through the thick gloves. He ran the bike past the stone cross and across the deserted town square of Darcombe.

He'd somewhere to go before collecting Rachel, to follow up advice he'd been given by a killer.

The milkman, the landlord, the tea-boy at work - watch them, Ramon Gil had suggested. Michael was starting with her landlord, Collard. Rachel had said the police didn't think Collard was a likely suspect, even if he did know about the old cellar. Michael was checking for himself.

After his latest interview with Inspector Penoyre at Darcombe, when he had tried – and failed – to get the Inspector as worried about Ramon Gil's appearance on the scene as he was himself, Michael felt absolutely no guilt in checking. Penoyre's thoughts were frustratingly opaque. Apart from advising him not to tell Rachel anything about Ramon Gil – 'She's under a lot of stress already, and you did tell Gil that your mutual "chat" would clear off his debt'- Penoyre had said nothing and given no promise of additional protection. When Michael had protested that Rachel had a right – and a need to know about Gil, Penoyre had remained adamant.

'I'll warn Miss Falconer to be on guard against any strangers, and that must do, Mr Horton. My people have the Photo-fit you've given us and we will catch him if he makes a move down here - which I doubt. After all, this is not a multiracial area. He will be noticed.'

'Not at Kestrel House. Foreign researchers are in and out all the time.'

Penoyre cleared his throat. 'You're going to have to trust us, Mr Horton. The doctors tell me Miss Falconer's in a fragile state. We mustn't do the stalker's work for him.'

Frustrated, Michael had let the matter drop. He'd two options. One, to win a few million on the national lottery and buy Rachel round-the-clock bodyguards. Two, to be her human shield, protect her in any way he could. He chose to stick with the second.

George Collard's farm was at Manaton, close to the big rookery behind the village. Parking near St Winifred's Church, Michael crossed the damp green with its picture-postcard row of thatched houses and strode up the lane past the neat parish hall.

As the lane became muckier with fresh cowdung he quickened his pace. He'd catch the farmer in his milking-shed and his story was prepared.

He and Collard had already met. Last summer, he'd checked a possible standing-stone row in one of Collard's hay meadows that the farmer was wanting to turn over to wheat. To the farmer's vocal relief, the 'prehistoric alignment' had turned out to be nothing more than a nineteenth-century mess of boulder-wall rubble that could be ploughed out.

Collard owed him one, thought Michael, as he pushed open the yard gate, pausing in case the dogs were free. Catching sight of the white disc of a face squinting through the open byre door, Michael resolved to push this local obligation to its limit.

'George – Mike Horton – How are you?' Slopping through the yard with the dawn chorus as his fanfare, Michael raised a hand in greeting. Seconds later he was standing hunched in the milking-shed, breath mingling with the sweet, cud-scented steam of the cows. He and George Collard pumped hands.

'Glad to see you haven't had to cull any more of your herd,' Michael said, when the farmer finally released his grip. 'How are they treating you these days? Any more daft directives?'

In local parlance, 'they' were the Department of Agriculture and Michael sent up a silent wish that Collard was not too discontented. Otherwise complaints would take most of the morning.

'No more than what I usually get from the sad old bastards.' Talking to tourists, George Collard's Devonshire accent could become impenetrable. Talking to locals, even a 'posh' like Mike Horton, the farmer stuck to using his favourite expletive.

'Win any more poetry prizes?' Michael asked, glad of his retentive memory. Until Collard introduced business with the phrase, 'What I can do for you?', the form was general topics only.

Above them the single bare light bulb flickered and Michael caught the snarled 'bastard electrics' as the shorter, stocky man strode along the milking-line. 'Get on, Twenty-two!' he bawled at one cow. Bending and chucking a dried chunk of mud at a prowling tortoiseshell kitten, the farmer said gruffly, 'Last month I had two poems in *Orbis.*'

Michael nodded, although the farmer had his broad backside to him. Impatient to get on, he heard the swallows stirring in the yard outside, saw the first streaks of colour floating through the open door.

'What can I do–?' George Collard was interrupted by an urgent rapping on the side door.

'Dad!' A rough teenage voice shouted through the wooden door. 'Forty-five's started in labour in that bottom field!'

'Leave her be to get on with it.'

'Mum told me to ask how much longer you're going to be.'

Michael watched Collard gulp in a large breath and braced himself for the explosion. It never came. Instead, the farmer twisted round and with a weary smile, motioned with a stubby thumb towards the door. 'Every day's the same. How

281

much longer? We're run off our feet here, even my boy.'

In a louder voice, the farmer called out, 'Tell your mother I'll make a start on the silage before breakfast. What can I do for you, Mike?'

'I'm here on behalf of your tenant.'

'Handsome, that one. If I were younger...' George Collard mumbled something only the cows could hear. Michael waited, listening to the gentle swish of the pumping milk, feeling the sun on his side. It was going to be another hot one today.

'Rachel was wondering if she could leave some of her old botanical stuff down in the keeping-cellar–' Michael's explanation and lie was interrupted by an enormous snarling of dogs and another anxious voice.

'Mr Collard, they potatoes shouldn't be in the ground for too much longer: they'll be getting way too big. Do you want me to start digging them up?'

A spry, weather-beaten old man had appeared in the main doorway, surrounded by three lean yapping sheepdogs.

The farmer answered without looking up. 'That would be fine, Harold. Really helpful. Now get those aniseed balls out of your pocket before my dogs go barmy.'

Harold chuckled but made no move for the pockets of his rough patched jacket. He nodded to Michael. 'Another of your young lady's admirers, is this?'

The jovial question shot a metre of ice down Michael's back. Spine pricking, he heard George

Collard say tiredly, 'That'll do, Harold. Go about your work now, else you won't be able to do Mrs Collard's bubble-and-squeak full justice.'

Trailed by whining, barking dogs, Harold ambled off across the yard, early morning sunlight lighting up his red bald-patch. Watching the old man leave, Michael cleared his throat. 'About the cottage, George. Would it be okay if Rachel put some of her spare things in that cellar, or will that interfere with anything you've left down there?'

George Collard straightened, turned. Walking forward, he leaned against one of the long shed's stone pillars to shake a gobbet of mud from his wellingtons.

'Nothing to bother with of mine in there,' he said. 'I've not used the cellar in years. In fact, as I told Inspector Penoyre last week, I'd forgotten it was there, even though the architect put it on the extension plans.'

So far so good, thought Michael. Heartened as he was by the proof that Inspector Penoyre was more than doing his job, Michael was uneasy with what George Collard's farm-hand had let fall.

'You'll be wanting to know who Harold meant.' Collard was trying to do five jobs at once but he was no fool.

'I'd like to know who my rivals are.'

A devilish smile bloomed on George's pug-like face. 'He's one of yours. That forester from Kestrel House, Colin Benwick. Came here twice in March, round lambing, asking if the cottage was let. First time I told him it was, to his new

283

boss. He went off then. A week later he was back: "Had Rachel Falconer taken the cottage yet? What was she like?" I sent him off smartly that second time: I'd got my hands full with the new lambs.'

'What did you say to him?'

'Same thing as I'll tell you. You want to meet my new tenant, go up and knock on her cottage door. She's her own woman and can speak for herself.'

'Have you mentioned this to the police?'

'Those daft bastards? We've better ways of spending our time here than passing gossip. You want to talk to Benwick about it, you ask him to his face.'

Michael stooped lower under the vaulted roof of the cow shed to step out into the yard. 'Thanks for your time, George, and the advice.' He extended his hand again. 'I'll be acting on it.'

It was past time for him to leave, and Michael did so, stalking out through the yard gate and across the green with a rapidly increasing stride. Rachel was waiting for him, and he had much to tell her. Except, of course, about Ramon Gil.

Chapter 48

The moment she spotted Michael weaving through the hospital ward, Rachel leapt to her feet.

'Ugh!' She couldn't stop the grunt escaping.

Becoming aware of a world outside pain, Rachel found Michael cupping her elbows, drawing her to him.

'I'm sure the doctors advised you to keep that healing skin limber, but you don't have to do aerobics.' His voice softened as his lips came closer. 'I'm already impressed.'

He kissed her, mouth tangy with peppermint. 'From my garden,' Michael said, when he finally raised his head. Squeezing her arm before he released it, he skidded a hand into his jacket. 'Have some?' he teased.

'Do I need a breath freshener?' Rachel teased back.

'Let's check, shall we?' Michael kissed her a second time, even more lingeringly. 'No, I don't think so. Satisfied now?'

Rachel wasn't about to admit to anything. 'Are you?'

Michael bent and put his head close by her ear. 'No.' They were close enough for Rachel to know he was telling the truth.

The rattling trolley of a hospital volunteer selling chocolates and magazines brought them back to reality. Moving with that startling speed of his, Michael seized Rachel's hand. 'Come on, there are chocolates for you at home. Amongst other things.' He swung her hand in his. 'I'm glad you're wearing a jump suit: it'll be brisk riding, even today.'

Excitement made him her Michael again, thought Rachel, nodding agreement. She guessed from the slight tilting forward of his head – Michael's 'curious' look – that he'd spent all of yesterday afternoon choosing gifts and was dying to present them. Like the peppermint, these whimsies delighted her. She'd not expected that at nearly thirty Michael would have remained so playful.

He gathered up the suitcase Angwen had brought and they started out of the ward, the volunteer steering a wide course round them when he saw how awkwardly Rachel was walking.

'Can we drop in at Kestrel House again, please?' Rachel was asking. 'I'd feel easier if I could check the place over.'

'Joe Penoyre and I have done that already. Your baby is fine. Everything's secure and as it should be. Your staff are on hand to answer police questions and workmen have started on the repairs to your office.

'On an individual basis,' Michael continued, counting off on his free fingers, 'Paul and Angwen are checking his lab before jaunting off to Wales for the rest of the week, Leo is assisting the police in their digital trawl through the Kestrel House employment records and Daniel has been helping Helen's camera crew set up in the conservatory.'

'Daniel?'

'I knew you'd be surprised.'

'You don't need to look so smug about it.'

'Do I?' Michael's expression was one of blank innocence.

'No, but if you looked as you sound...' They had stepped outside and Rachel took an appreciative breath of the fresh air. 'You hardly ever "look" anything,' she complained lightly. Before resuming her careful walking, she glanced at Michael. 'Helen's camera crew?'

Michael instantly picked up the subtext. 'Helen was with Joe and me. Said she was fascinated to watch a real country policeman at work. She asked after you – I told her you were lounging at your cottage under the pear-trees.'

'Makes sense.' Rachel wished she hadn't asked. She was surprised again at how easily Michael could lie. Would he be as glib with her as he'd been with Helen? Was he telling her everything now?

She was glad to spot the Norton in the small carpark. Leaving the hospital would surely give her back the confidence she was missing. Starting towards the bike, Rachel realized that one member of the Kestrel House staff hadn't been accounted for. 'What about Colin Benwick?'

Michael released her hand to tip the bike off its stand. His voice was suddenly flat and hard. 'Can we chat about Benwick later? I realize no one knows about us yet–'

Including Helen. The thought ran like a pistol shot through Rachel's mind.

'–but I don't think we should linger about. To be honest, I'll feel a lot easier once we're back at home.' He jerked a thumb at the bike. 'Riding this thing you'll be pretty exposed.'

The mid-morning sun did nothing to disguise the gaunt lines on his face. Rachel couldn't bear him to look so haunted. She nodded and did not ask questions as Michael produced his own dark blue winter-coat from under the rear seat and proceeded to help her into it.

'Don't you think you're being a little paranoid?' she remarked, as Michael settled in front of her.

'If I am, that's my business. Hold tight – I want to get this over as quickly as possible.'

Rachel hoped he meant only the journey.

Her feeling of being a burden increased when they reached his home. Stiffened through riding the bike, though their hectic roar across the moorland roads had taken less than twenty minutes, Rachel discovered she could hardly move. Walking the few steps into the cottage was impossible.

After opening the front door and checking round, Michael returned to find her clutching the Norton's back-rest, her face white and hands clammy. She had managed the business of sliding one leg across the seat to perch side-saddle, and had just been trying to step down.

'Oh, God.' Presenting his back to her, Michael crouched. 'Put your arms round my neck. That's it! Here we go.' Carrying Rachel piggyback, he brought her through into the cottage. 'Chair or sofa?'

'Just put me down,' Rachel gasped. 'I'd like to make sure I can still stand. Please, Michael–'

Deposited lightly onto a quarry-tiled floor, Rachel braced her knees and stood, batting away the strong, proffered arm. 'I'm not that helpless.'

She'd not meant to sound ungracious. Blushing, eyes bright, she said nothing as Michael gently wound his coat off her, hanging their jackets behind the door.

'There's wine and juice in the fridge.' He

turned to her again, his voice easy. 'Orange, pine-apple, mango.'

'Mango would be splendid, thanks.'

'Ice, I presume?'

'Yes, please.'

Watching Michael reach for a sparkling glass from the polished white unit fitted above the sink, Rachel said, 'You're a lot tidier now than you were as a teenager, Michael. This place puts mine to shame.'

'Ah, but only because of the mad cleaning session I had at four o'clock this morning. I normally let the dust layer up and my clothes get piled in heaps.'

Tutting in playful disapproval, Rachel received her juice and crunched a sliver of ice between her teeth, laughing as Michael gave an extravagant shudder. Whilst he fixed himself a drink, she glanced round, eager to learn more about him.

Thick-walled and granite-roofed, Michael's cottage was as old as the one she was renting from Mr Collard, but on a grander scale. He'd removed part of the timbered ceiling so that the main roof was far above them and the staircase rose straight from the living-area up to a sleeping-platform.

Michael had painted all the ceiling the colour of an English summer sky – a dazzling, expansive blue – and added his own photographs as contrasting studies in colour and form. Any straight walls he'd whitewashed, and here books and CDs on racks and shelves threw back richness and light in the morning sun like the glowing heart of a living flower.

Rachel saw with delight that books were everywhere. On low tables and comfortable, sturdy chairs, tucked beside the two ends of a long sofa, piled in one corner under a table.

Beside the table was an old coat rack, festooned with a pair of broken-soled boots, heavy scorch-marked navy trousers and a ragdoll wearing a tiny placard: 'Mike's First Rescue'.

'Souvenirs from my first fire kit,' Michael remarked, tossing back his juice in a single swallow. 'I promised you chocolates.'

Balanced on his outstretching fingers was a gift-wrapped box as big as a tray, with a shocking pink ribbon the size of a rhododendron blossom.

'Sorry, but I can't wait any longer. You have to open the cards first – they're your main "get well" gift.'

Two midnight-blue envelopes appeared on top of her chocolate tray. One look at Michael's flushed face persuaded Rachel to rip open the nearest as soon as possible. Inside she found a card from the Woodland Trust, promising that somewhere in England, a glade of trees would be planted in her name.

'And the other one.' Michael tapped the card on her nose as she looked up at him. Not trusting herself yet to respond, Rachel fumbled her way into the smaller envelope.

It was an acknowledgement of a second, even more generous donation to Survival, for their work with the Gapo people. Even as her eyes widened at the size of this life-saving gift, Rachel noticed from the letter that Michael had also taken out a deed of covenant option: the promise of future, regular donations.

'Money might not grow on trees but it can save quite a few.' Michael grinned at her astonishment. 'I know you already do something for those charities, but I thought rather than cut, hothouse-forced flowers, you'd appreciate–'

Rachel stood on tip-toe and kissed him full on the mouth. She felt drunk with hope and pride – renewed hope for the Gapo, pride in Michael.

Michael groaned, tossing chocolates and cards aside on the sofa, desperate to enfold her in his arms, terrified he might hurt her.

Suddenly desperate to be really close, Rachel pushed herself against his warm strong body, forgetting the glass in her hand.

'If you think that'll kill my enthusiasm you're wrong,' Michael gently plucked the glass from her strapped fingers.

Outside she could hear the sound of the wind in the trees, and faintly, the mew of a hunting buzzard. Inside, all Rachel could hear was the faint click as Michael set the glass down on the edge of the nearest bookshelf, the rasp as he unzipped the jacket of her jump suit. And her heart, racing.

He wound his arms around the tops of her thighs to tip her right off her feet. Swung up then down into a passionate kiss, Rachel saw the cottage walls spin. She rolled back her head to allow Michael to trail his lips along the stiffened tendons of her neck, closing her eyes as his fingers feathered over her face.

'Rachel?' He waited till she had reopened her eyes, his own gaze bright with concern.

'Yes,' she whispered. 'Yes!'

Arching his back, supporting her on his own body, his thighs, Michael took them both down, a swift movement perfectly balanced and executed, that had him seconds later flat on the quarry tiles and carpet, Rachel sprawled deliciously on top of him. Unbending at the knee and kicking a kitchen chair out of their way, he said, 'You've knocked the breath from me.'

'If I'm too heavy–'

Rachel tried to move but found herself trapped as Michael languorously wound a long leg round both of hers. 'I didn't mean it that way.'

'I couldn't get a bra on this morning,' Rachel began, apologetically.

Stretching up, Michael tongued her nipples through the thin cotton of her undershirt.

Rachel shuddered at the piercingly sensual touch. Injured, her back had seemed to be full of fire, but now pain was drowned in a flood of pleasure. Michael's tongue, flickering over her breasts; her eager fingers, tearing open his shirt, raking along his taut hot skin. His hands under her clothes, cupping her breasts, stroking her flanks and ribs and belly.

Their mutual need was so strong there was suddenly no time for elegant undressing. Michael could scarcely force down the zip of his jeans. Rachel was eager to help but he was more brutal, wanting only to be free. He caught her hands in one of his and kissed her again, deeply, untying her drawstring pants and dragging them down.

They made love then and there on the floor, Rachel straddling Michael, Michael supporting

Rachel. Afterwards they made it upstairs to the bed and managed to undress fully before making love again.

Lying on the sofa under the window, Rachel's forgotten chocolates melted in the sun.

Chapter 49

Rachel woke with a start. 'My test!' Tearing the sheet off her legs, she staggered out of bed, sprawling over Michael.

'What's the rush?' Michael moved to wrap his arms around her, stopping as he remembered her burns. 'What's up?'

Rachel seized the phone by the bed. 'I was booked in at the doctor's this afternoon for a repeat smear test.' Feverishly she started to stab in numbers. 'Now I'll have missed it.'

'There's no need to panic. I'm sure the doc will fit you in tomorrow.

Michael's sweet reasonableness infuriated her. 'Fine! It wasn't your mother who died of ovarian cancer. Who knows, maybe it was a mistake our making love.' She broke off to talk to her doctor's receptionist.

Waiting for her to finish, Michael rolled naked off the bed and settled on the edge of the sleeping-platform, swinging his legs over the drop. Hearing the receiver being replaced, he asked softly without looking round, 'Did you really mean that?'

He did not hear Rachel coming, but a slender warm hand was suddenly pressed against his shoulder, a gentle touch quickly withdrawn.

'I'm sorry.' And then: 'I've re-booked for tomorrow, whilst you're having lunch with Helen. I'll get a taxi to the surgery.'

As she limped slowly downstairs, Michael did not know if she was apologising for their new intimacy. Watching her move, the hurt from her burns showing in every hesitant step, he felt ashamed of his own rude health. Guilt, that he'd somehow taken advantage of Rachel whilst she was weakened, made him uneasy of her feelings towards him. Helen had said that, since Daniel, Rachel did not trust any man.

Swaying off the final step, Rachel moved carefully towards the kitchen area, passing under the hanging arch of Michael's toes. An hour ago she'd have playfully tugged his dangling feet. Now, a memory of her own burning flesh and hair superimposed itself on his face, together with a sudden resurgence of pain along her back and in her hands. The arsonist had threatened those she loved. How could she risk drawing Michael into a dangerous involvement with her when the fire-stalker was still out there?

It broke her inside to say it, but Rachel made herself sound easy. 'You know, however we are in private, we'd better cool it in public tomorrow. And not just because you're going to lunch with Helen.'

Michael dismissed her feeble joke with a narrowing of his eyes and started to tell her about Benwick.

Chapter 50

Colin Benwick skirted round the mess and noise of the workmen and camera crews at Kestrel House and escaped into the arboretum.

On Mondays, the arboretum was closed to the public. He was glad. Daniel had given him something to think about. Sure of his own bit of peace, Colin climbed through the heather gardens of the lower slopes towards the lush green of the lime avenue and its pools of bluebells.

He aimed high, at the tumbling froth of apple flowers and the scarlet and magenta explosion of the azaleas. Pausing amongst the azaleas, he turned to look back to the house, catching the glitter of Daniel's white Mazda. Cultured, aristocratic, good-looking, stylish – Daniel was everything he wasn't. Half the time he wasn't sure if he admired or envied the older man.

'You're a born follower, lad, that's your trouble.' Colin told himself. Being loyal and good at your job no longer counted for anything. He'd been loyal to Paul Falconer, who'd promptly turned round at the first bit of bother and brought in his daughter to manage the institute. As if she knew.

'Fashion gone barmy.' Where were the extra funds for the tree research and arboretum he'd been promised by Paul? By now, Daniel would have found him several juicy sponsors. So why was he hesitating to fall in with Daniel's latest plan?

A raven tumbled overhead, laboriously flapping over the topmost branches of the lime avenue. Listening to the whisper of his trees, Colin closed his eyes and tried to clear his head.

The rippling pinks and oranges of the azaleas remained blazoned in his mind's eye, a firecracker display for a rocket of a girl. He'd watched the video of her again last night with the sound off so that he wouldn't have to put up with her continuous showing off. Rachel Falconer, Miss Ethnobotanist from Brazil. Not so tough now, although that in part made her more attractive. He thought of her smiling to camera, the smile she'd bestowed on strangers but never on him. What was it with him and women?

Rachel's face vanished from his private skull view-screen. Someone was coming. Branches writhed against Colin's left arm and the strong fruity musk of commercial scent replaced the sweetness of the bluebells.

'Dr Benwick, I presume? We have met.' Helen, flushed with the climb, stuck out her hand. 'I'm hoping you can advise me where to set up to get the best angles on this wonderful May-time blossom.'

Wishing Helen Warne would take her maple-syrup voice and razor-sharp good looks else-where, Colin lumbered out of the shadows to shake hands. 'It's already going over,' he started ungraciously.

Helen Warne's stare stopped him dead in his

tracks. 'Something wrong?'

Helen wrinkled her nose. 'Only me for not noticing sooner.' She bustled forward, threading an arm through his. 'Suppose you give me a guided tour?'

Bristling, Colin plucked Helen's manicured hand off his checked shirt. 'Suppose you follow me? These paths are narrow.'

'Looks wide enough for two to me.'

Colin snorted and pushed ahead, refusing to check that the Warne woman was keeping up. She was: he could hear her chattering.

'You must come from Yorkshire, right? My mother spent some time there in a place called Bradford, working in a department store. What was its name? That's it: Brown Muffs. She was a sales assistant. Course, she didn't last more than a week. Mom was the original Sixties child, untrammelled. Went to Istanbul instead... Dr Benwick, you've dropped your wallet.'

Compelled to turn and face his tormentor, Colin received the wallet with a grudging 'Thanks.'

Their hands touched briefly, a brush that jolted Colin like an electric charge. His stocky body twitched. Something light fell from his fist and fluttered down to lie amongst the fallen azalea petals and nodding bluebells.

He snatched it up, thrusting it back into its secret place in his cracked-leather wallet. Helen Warne was transfixed, shielding her eyes as she watched a grey squirrel feeding in a glade a few paces from them.

She hadn't seen it, Colin decided. 'Shall we go

on, Miss Warne?'

'Surely. By the way, my friends call me Helen.' Powering blue eyes on him, she flashed him a big smile.

Riveted by shyness and guilty confusion, Colin remained silent.

Helen laughed, stepping closer. 'I still think there's room on this part of the path for two. I'd like you to tell me the names of these bushes.'

'All of them?'

Helen nodded, tapping her foot on the dry grass. 'Every last one.'

She really hadn't seen it. Colin gave a toothy grin, his mind registering for the first time that if he was nervous of her, Helen was also wary of him. She was in his place, and asking quite nicely to be shown around. Realizing that, Colin felt he could afford to be indulgent.

'No trouble at all, Helen.'

Chapter 51

Paul was closeted with Leo in Daniel's lab, looking over some results Leo had promised him before the Parma trip. Before she and Paul had been married, thought Angwen, tracing a fingertip along the freshly polished balustrade of the grand staircase.

Angwen wished she could leave. Paul had promised her things would be different, that he'd finish earlier and spend more time with her.

Instead, because he'd promised to spend a few days in Wales, Paul was working for as long as he ever did.

She looked at her watch: almost 9 p.m. Hungry and queasy, she'd been wandering the echoing landing and corridors for the last hour. Angwen knew that Paul would tell her cheerfully to take the car and go, but she didn't want to leave him alone. Paul seemed to have no fears for his safety, but she had plenty.

And what will you do if the arsonist attacks Paul? Be sick all over him? She wasn't as strong as Rachel, yet Rachel had been struck down.

Recalling the ugly scarlet blisters on Rachel's back – merely the edges of other wounds, hidden by dressings – Angwen's stomach turned over. She closed her eyes, repeating in Welsh what Rachel had said. Paul loved her. Her or the baby?

Deciding it was better to keep walking, Angwen swept down the broad marble stairs, moving towards the labs. It was probably too much to expect Paul and Leo to have finished, but she could check the lab again. As everyone else kept telling her, Paul was involved in life-saving research. His work had to be protected and she shouldn't really complain if he neglected his personal life for a noble cause.

Angwen paused at the door to Daniel's and Leo's lab. She could hear voices, too low to distinguish any words. She typed the security code on the next gleaming key pad and stumbled through into Paul's private universe.

Studying the glass cabinets in the centre of the long narrow room without knowing what she was looking at – much less whether the various petri dishes had been tampered with – Angwen knew she was losing confidence again. It was being drained out of her by the muggy, still heat of the building, by the torpor that lay over the moors outside, heavy as the blankets of mist she had seen round *Yr Wyddfa* as a child. 'The Tomb' – Snowdon in English. A foolish, lightweight name. The Welsh was better, more apt. The Tomb. The description fitted this place. If she thought about it at all, she could imagine fire roaring across this moorland, as it did nearly every year in swaling accidents, when farmers burned off the heather too enthusiastically. She could even bring the smell of blazing grass to mind.

Angwen turned from the final cabinet to the tiny conservatory connected to the end of the lab. Was that a phone she could hear? The ring was so faint it might be coming from somewhere else. She glanced round at the silent wall-phone, then started to walk towards Paul's mini-green house.

It wasn't imagination. She could smell burning.

Her limbs froze in shock, but her thoughts raced on. Jealous of Paul's work, of the time he lavished on it, she'd been inclined to scoff at his fears of sabotage. Rachel: younger, beautiful, a television personality, had always been the more likely target. Yet what if she'd been wrong?

'Fire!' Angwen screamed. It's *all my fault*. She heaved in despair at the connecting door.

In the next-door lab, leaning over a printout of results, Leo flicked up his head. 'Dial 999.' He tossed the printout aside, sprinting for the door.

Obeying, Paul could hear Leo outside in the corridor, bawling to anyone who might be left in the building: 'Get out, get out! Fire!'

'Fire!' The answering shout was Angwen's. As her panic-stricken voice was submerged by the racket of the fire-alarm, Paul dropped the phone receiver and ran. Angwen was in his lab.

Outside in the corridor Paul could see smoke streaming from the next door room, could hear Leo inside pleading with Angwen to leave the stuff and come with him. He could hear panic in her answer.

'Help me! We have to get these plants out – he'll never forgive me!'

Angwen appeared in the doorway, clothes streaked with soot, hair dusted with ash. She was carrying two trays of plants as though they were the most valuable things she possessed. Seeing Paul, she gasped, ducked to thrust the trays to safety on the corridor floor and whipped back inside, towards the fire. Before Paul could react, Leo had also appeared, dumped two more trays outside, and dived round for more.

'Angwen!' Inside his lab, Paul found a night-marish scene: a river of tiny leaping flames flowing over the conservatory floor. Leo bent over coughing as he snatched up computer discs and microscopes. And Angwen blundering for the seat of the blaze, her only protection a light summer-coat she was using to batter at the rising fire in the greenhouse doorway.

Leo passed him on another dash for the corridor and Paul yelled, 'Stay out now!' He chased after his wife. 'Angwen!'

He caught her as she was about to leap recklessly over a pool of fire on the greenhouse
threshold, careless of the cracking glass that
might shatter at any moment. 'Come on!'

'Save plants! Your work–' Angwen struggled
against him, her face mesmerized by the cracking
fire. She shrieked as another shelf of plantlets,
dishes, trays and tissue samples crashed to the
tiles. Paul plucked her off her feet and ran with
her into the corridor.

'I'll take her.' Still at the institute, Joe Penoyre
and his men had arrived quickly on this crime
scene. One was already leading a dazed Leo to
safety.

Paul shook his head. 'No! She's mine.' He
followed Leo and the policeman outside without
a backward look, conscious only of the figure in
his arms. 'Let's get you into some fresh air,
cariad.'

Chapter 52

Waiting in the staff carpark to catch people
coming in, Helen was in her element this
morning, loving every second. Almost every
second, perhaps, since there was the frustrating
element of luck. Last night it had been her bad
luck that she and the camera crew had missed
recording the climax of the fire in Paul's lab.

Missing Michael amongst the firemen, Helen

was told that it was Mike's week off. That was how the volunteer station at Darcombe worked: one week on call, one week off. Unless there was a really big shout.

Cutting short the fireman, Helen had collared Inspector Penoyre to line him up on camera and ask the big question. Was it arson?

Helen thought again of his answers and grinned. Penoyre was a cop all right, never telling everything he knew. Not even when Michael and Rachel turned up to view the damage and stayed on to help clear up. Not that Angwen and Rachel could be much help: one pregnant, the other injured.

Helen had concentrated on filming the half-gutted lab greenhouse, plus a few close-ups of Paul. It had been rather surprising that he hadn't looked more haggard – a large part of his research had just missed being totally barbecued. Remembering, Helen shrugged. This English reserve was so baffling.

A stern inner voice admonished her: *And what about you?* Helen coughed, embarrassed at her inability to get really pumped up over a friend's problems. Rachel was obviously still in danger – however Penoyre had slid round the question last night, the lab had got to have been fire-bombed. Helen found, though, that her strongest feeling was anticipation: a looking forward to when the arsonist was eventually unmasked. Anticipation too of the fine film she was making, a film that would stir things up, make the politicians and cops here take stalking seriously.

Raising her head, Helen thought again of the

303

camera and sound men she'd posted in the back yard of the carpark. Another staff meeting was due to start at 8.30 this morning in Michael's room, the one farthest from the grit and noise of the workmen busy in Rachel's office.

If the arsonist continued to knock out rooms at the same rate, there'd soon be nowhere left for the staff to meet. Helen twisted round on the gravel to give a thumbs-up sign to Jocasta on the upstairs landing.

Jocasta waved desperately back. Daniel Mason's Mazda, closely trailed by two black-and-whites – charmingly known as panda cars in this country – were being admitted through the security gate by Stephen Lees. And what a first day back at work he was having.

Checking the sun's position, Helen motioned the cameraman and sound recordist to a spot just off the back steps. With any luck her boys would be close enough to get everything but sufficiently tucked away so as to be missed. It was her experience that at times of stress people didn't catch on straight away that they were being filmed.

The back door of Kestrel House swung open and Rachel shouted from inside the door, 'Daniel, we're in Michael's for the meeting. If you'd like to come up as soon as you can.'

The door closed and Helen gushed out a breath in relief. Scarcely had she time to take another before Daniel swung into her sights, his head lowered, his eyes on the polished black briefcase in his hand. Helen was able to study him at leisure. The double-breasted blue suit was Hugo

Boss, worn with a Calvin Klein shirt and silk tie. Overdressed for Dartmoor, but the shimmering grey shoes were neat. Trusting her people, Helen let her eyes linger on Daniel until she heard the back door of the house open again.

Rachel had returned to hurry Daniel. Still standing within the building, she was holding the door open for him.

Interested to see if the man would quicken his smooth steps, Helen became aware that the police were spilling out of their cars. Green braces snapping lightly against his springy figure, Detective Inspector Penoyre approached Daniel in some haste.

'Mr Mason, I'd like you to come with me to Darcombe police station to answer some questions.'

Daniel stopped and spun about. 'Now? I've an important meeting.' He spoke as though he was to chair and control it.

Penoyre's hard little eyes glittered. 'If you would just step into the car, Mr Mason.' Intent on Daniel, the policeman's eyes suddenly flashed at Helen, letting her know he was aware of her. Whether Rachel was also aware, Helen couldn't say – Daniel certainly wasn't interested in anybody but the inspector.

'What's going on? Can't it wait?'

Wagging a finger to a uniformed constable, Penoyre stepped closer to Daniel. 'We've recovered your mobile from the seat of last night's arson attack, Mr Mason. I'd like you to tell me how it got there.'

Daniel's stunned face was a wonderful picture,

and he and the darker, wiry Penoyre made a marvellous scene, thought Helen. She clenched her fingers into fists. 'I knew something was going down here!'

It got better. Rachel came outside, frowning at the camera but fixing on her colleague. 'Daniel?'

'That's impossible! I don't know the code to Paul's lab. None of us know each other's key pad numbers.'

'We should continue this at the station,' said Joe Penoyre. A constable had opened the back door of one of the panda cars.

Staring at Rachel, Daniel made no move.

'Mr Mason?'

Silently Rachel turned away, limping back inside. Only when she had gone would Daniel allow himself to be put inside the car.

Hustling the crew indoors and upstairs, Helen was guiltily glad that Rachel was injured. Invisible except for the dressings on her hands, the burns slowed her down. She wasn't able to catch Rachel on the landing for a reaction shot, but her people were ready when Rachel opened the meeting.

Sitting on a lab stool, Rachel broke the news of Daniel's departure to the rest of the staff clustered on high-back chairs round Michael's desk.

'I'm afraid Daniel won't be joining us. He's been taken to Darcombe police station.'

'By "taken" do you mean arrested?' demanded Colin Benwick.

Rachel shook her head. 'I don't know.'

She seemed dazed, thought Helen, checking that the lights were showing up the shadows under Rachel's eyes. As she did so, Michael shot Rachel a look over the top of his computer and asked, 'Did Joe Penoyre give any reason why he wanted to talk to Daniel?'

Gently prodded, Rachel appeared to recollect. 'He said that Daniel's mobile had been found at the seat of the fire. The police appear to think that very ... suggestive.'

'Why?' growled Benwick.

The question was not directed at him, but Michael answered. 'Fires can be started by a telephone call. The arsonist can ring in from anywhere, even abroad, and start a pre-set sequence with a rigged phone that creates an electrical contact, in turn creating a spark, in turn lighting a fuse or detonator. Mobiles are small, easily hidden–'

'Not in my lab,' cut in Paul stiffly. 'I check everywhere daily.'

'Daniel would have been able to work out your routine,' said Michael.

'So might any of us,' said Leo. 'Do you think perhaps Daniel's phone was stolen from him, perhaps to incriminate him?'

'But why?' said Colin Benwick again, glaring at Rachel.

'If I knew that, Dr Benwick, I'd be talking to the police right now.' With a visible effort, Rachel took the meeting in hand. 'Speculating on events is unfair to Daniel. I'd like to remind everyone that Inspector Penoyre and his team are the professionals. None of what we discuss here today should be broadcast outside this room.'

Ouch! thought Helen, acknowledging Rachel's warning with a nod. From the corner of her eye she saw Colin Benwick bridle then relax, folding his heavy arms across his chest. He wouldn't be so easy when she'd finished with him, but that treat was for later. Just before lunch with Michael. This was truly going to be a great week.

Chapter 53

The meeting lasted two hours. Staggered by events, Colin found himself as dazed at the end as at the start. Daniel, taken away by the police. Rachel, still in charge of Kestrel House. Paul, glibly announcing that his work was still on course.

Frowning, Colin recalled what Paul had said at that point: 'It'll take a little longer than I first projected. I could say that the fire has actually sorted out my real priorities.' Smiling at Angwen when he'd said that, Paul had made it glaringly obvious that she now took first place above his research.

Their simple-minded pleasure in each other was cringe-making, thought Colin, although not as embarrassing as Helen Warne's outrageous flirting with Michael Horton. Winks, nods, smiles: the instant the group broke up and filming stopped, she started and never let up. Michael himself appeared flattered and indulgent, but then he liked women. Less sure of himself, Colin was disconcerted when Helen made a pass at him.

He was slipping out of the door at the end of the meeting, congratulating himself on not staring at Rachel's strapped fingers or the back of her baggy shirt. A hand closed on his round the doorknob. Twisting round, Colin found Helen Warne's blue eyes sparkling up at him.

'Hi, again. I think you'll want this to update your wallet.' She pressed a dark Polaroid against his free hand. 'Careful, the print's still developing. You're off to Rachel's crystal palace, right? See you there.'

Alarmed by her mention of Rachel, Colin hurried downstairs, piling through the rear entrance of the main conservatory. Snatching his pruners from a baggy cotton trouser pocket, Colin stared at them. What work had he planned to do in here? The photograph fluttered to the floor.

'You do keep dropping your pictures, Doctor Benwick. Is that a Freudian slip?'

Helen had rejoined him. Stopping alongside, she held out the fully developed Polaroid. 'Take it. That's right! I know you want to.'

'You don't know anything. She doesn't want me.'

'And don't you loathe that independence.'

The gloating voice was too much. In another second the Polaroid was a crumpled ball in his fist. 'Do you run after anything in trousers?'

'What low self-esteem! But you're wrong, Colin. I like a challenge.'

'Keep after Horton and Cartwright, then. Though I'll be surprised if either of those stay keen for more than two weeks.'

'What about you? How long have you been faithful to Rachel? How long have you had that little coloured picture in your wallet, Colin?'

Colin jutted his black beard at her. 'So you did see it in the arboretum.'

'Rachel's picture? Yes, I did. What I'm wondering, Colin, is what the police will make of it. If I tell them.' After a moment's silence, Helen lifted an arm and pointed. 'Those blue flowers were grown from seeds that Rachel brought back with her from Amazonia. Does her past excite you?'

Colin grunted in bitter amusement. 'What do you want?'

'First up, for you to answer my question.'

Colin relaxed his fingers on the crumpled ball. Later, perhaps, he'd be able to erase the creases from Rachel's face. 'It's schoolboy stuff, really.'

'You're too old for that, Colin. But there is something about her height and strength, isn't there? Kind of maternal.' Helen shook his arm. 'Only kidding. You don't have to flinch.'

'Shut up.'

'I've great instincts for a good story. Prove my instincts right, Colin, and I won't make that call to the police.'

'Don't think you can blackmail me, woman.'

Helen looked round. 'Is there a seat any place in this birdcage? I'd like you to listen, Colin. Listen carefully. I've got a proposition for you.'

Chapter 54

Michael took Helen to lunch at the Two Bridges Hotel. Her film crew took themselves off downstairs to the west wing, lunching in the stately comfort of the common room whilst midday heat sweated the landscape. Outdoor filming would resume at six – better light.

Leo, Jocasta, Paul and Angwen had decided to walk the half-mile to the Warren House Inn for a pub lunch. Hearing them in the marble hall, Rachel caught them exchanging travellers' tales – Parma, Provence, Geneva – in a web of relaxed banter.

They'd wanted Rachel to go with them. The policeman on duty at Kestrel House had been equally encouraging. 'One of our WPCs is going to the Warren House to keep an eye on that lot, so you'll be quite safe.'

'I know.' Smiling genuine gratitude, Rachel had still refused. It wasn't that she didn't feel like company. It wasn't that she didn't feel safe. It was not – most definitely not – because Helen was, according to her own crew, 'Giving Mike Horton the full treatment.'

It was she, thought Rachel, who had suggested that any public relationship between Michael and herself be put on hold until the stalker threat was over. *Time to suffer, then watch those you love suffer* She couldn't stand the idea of Michael being hurt. Better that no one knew how she felt about him.

'And I trust him,' Rachel said aloud, regretting even so that she'd seen Helen leave clutching Michael's spare helmet to her bosom, or heard Helen exclaiming, in her persuasively breathy voice, 'When I get you over to the Anasazi settlements in Colorado and Utah, Mike, then you'll see some serious prehistory.' Returning to the States in July, Helen made no secret of her delight at going home.

Rachel hoped that Helen would continue to feel that way. She liked Helen, and didn't want her hurt. That was the most vital thing – that no one be hurt. Including Daniel.

Daniel was the reason Rachel had chosen to remain behind. While the institute was quiet and the police, fire investigator and camera crew were eating in the common room, she was going to ring Inspector Penoyre. Was Daniel under arrest or not?

Aware that she was being discreet, Rachel wondered if she was also being furtive. Daniel was a member of her staff, she was responsible for him, but that explanation wouldn't satisfy Michael if he had any inkling of how concerned she was. And he would be right, thought Rachel, refusing to look at her reflection in the tall sash-window as she wandered along the landing. Daniel's new involvement with the police had stirred old feelings: he'd been her first lover and had shown himself still willing. She remembered him in Rio after the shooting, slogging through the humidity and crowds to grapple with intransigent officials for her sake. Now he needed her help she wouldn't cast him off.

'It's wrong.' She teetered on the top step of the grand staircase as a ribbon of pain scrambled over her back, a bodily reminder not to push her luck. But she was determined to go on. If the police were happy with the situation and with Daniel as their main suspect, Rachel was not.

Daniel was an intelligent, well-educated man. Had he set last night's fire at Kestrel House, he'd have bought a prepaid phone-and-calls package, its number untraceable, not used his own mobile as part of the detonator. It was too stupid. Even Leo, bedazzled by the new, exotic Jocasta, had put his finger on the logical explanation. Daniel had been set up by someone. Why?

Gripping the balustrade, Rachel began her careful downward negotiation of the steps, glad that her police 'minder' had slipped to the Gents. With no one waiting, she could move at her own pace. Walking wasn't too bad, but the stairs called for uncomfortable stretching movements. Thankful it was no worse, Rachel recalled her sense of achievement when she'd climbed to her first-floor office a few moments ago to check on the repairs.

They were coming along. The best of it was that the hideous stag's head had gone for good. Putting her head round the door and seeing the brilliant white paint, Rachel had whistled in appreciation. If she could only find some funds from somewhere to install sprinklers on the upper floor.

'Need any help?' Stephen Lees, a little less

tanned and strapping than when she'd first met him, was hovering by the stairs.

Rachel grinned ruefully. 'A helping hand with the front door would be useful.' She forced herself to hurry, passing the caretaker on the threshold as he held the door open for her. 'How's Meg?'

Stephen's gritty, weather-beaten face glowed. 'Chewing everything in reach. Including a pair of my brogues.'

Rachel laughed with him, then walked slowly into the dazzling midday.

Shielding her eyes with a bandaged hand, she made for the heather – the rough moorland stuff she'd run through and played in since childhood. She needed to have her arguments ready for Joe Penoyre, and to decide whether to approach the media. With Helen's crew on hand, Rachel knew she could make a direct, visual protest at Daniel's treatment.

She also knew videotape could be edited creatively. The reputation of her staff might be tarnished, or destroyed. Involving Helen any further might be dangerous – and not only for her people at Kestrel House. If the stalker was to learn that Helen was a friend of hers...

Rachel quickened her steps, ignoring the jagging ache across her shoulders and the heavy drumbeat of the policeman's feet as he jogged into the fresh air to trail after her. Strange how she hurt now, whereas in her love-making with Michael she'd known nothing but pleasure. Pleasure given and received, deep in the centre of herself, the centre she still distrusted.

Walking onto the road and crossing Statts Bridge, Rachel paused to stare down at the dusty bottom of a dry stream-bed. She was aware of being passive again, even with regard to her health. Her GP had repeated her smear test that morning: she was waiting for the results.

'You're not your mother,' Michael had told her, but Rachel knew she'd remain uneasy until the all-clear. She'd been stupid in dumping her ridiculous fears on Michael. Most men had a horror of illness, particularly "women's problems". Besides, Michael had more important things to concern him.

Flicking a pebble over the bridge into a burnt-off – swaled – patch of heather, Rachel continued on her way.

Stepping from tarmac onto springy grass, she crouched. Across her line of sight a ghostly cranefly swayed down invisible currents of air, a befuddled creature of dusk and morning, out at midday. The smell of lightly boiled tar mingled in her nostrils with the desiccated scent of baking moorland. In the haze the grey-green swathes of heather swam to and fro.

Too quiet. Rachel's instinct prickled against it, her head buzzing as though there was thunder in the air. She'd not felt this tense since Rio, where a killer could come at you with an open smile.

Rio and Daniel, Daniel and Penoyre. The police appeared satisfied that Daniel might be the arsonist. Rachel read it in the relaxed body stance of those set to 'guard' her. The policeman who was following her now was ten metres back, kicking a pebble along the edge of the road.

To spare him from plunging into the coarse mats of heather, Rachel turned to retrace her steps, pointing back to Kestrel House so that her shadow would know. Sweating, with a sun-reddened neck, the bulky young constable was only too glad to return to shade.

Irritated at having her independence curtailed, Rachel also felt pity. She tried to hurry, her mind quickening faster than her stumbling feet.

She'd been stupid in not anticipating the timing of the strike against her father's lab. After the arsonist-stalker's last phone call, Rachel felt she should have been ready.

Forget guilt, she told herself. Paul's work was still intact. Whoever had fired his lab hadn't been trying to stop him. That ruled out Fultons or any other commercial rivals.

Perhaps it was simply that she was being too soft, that she didn't want to admit that her colleagues at work, people she saw almost every day, could wish her or her family so much harm.

Had it been softness that had prevented her from confronting Colin Benwick today? Or the insidious awareness of the moving film and cameras, recording everything? Ducking gingerly under the security barrier at the gatehouse, Rachel knew she had no answer. Yet the thought nagged at her: why had Dr Benwick been interested in *when* she was taking farmer Collard's cottage? And why had his guarded respect for her changed to sullen hostility?

It was time to find out, Rachel decided. She'd a few traps of her own in mind. Once those were put in place, she'd be a stalker herself.

First she had to lose her police escort. Or rather, keep him out of Colin Benwick's range of vision. She wanted to face down the forester in his natural habitat, where he'd feel comfortable and probably be bluntly indiscreet, particularly if she made him angry.

The trees would give her sweltering 'shadow' some cover. She'd be able to ask him to hang back in the shade whilst she had a word with Dr Benwick – a loud word, for the constable's benefit.

Rachel stopped on the drive. 'I need to talk to Dr Benwick in the arboretum. We can walk up through the cherry trees – it'll be cool under there.' She smiled, feeling the same kind of indulgence for the fair-skinned, moon-faced constable as she did towards young Leo.

The young policeman nodded although, turning to begin the steady climb along the grass avenue, Rachel thought she heard a sigh. She had no choice. She sensed that Colin Benwick, stiff and shy in company, would never admit anything in a crowd. Once she'd hidden her escort behind a convenient pine or maple, though, things might get interesting.

Chewing her lip as she leaned forward to attack the slope, Rachel felt the cool fingers of cypress shadow touching her raw neck. It would be down-right idiotic, she admitted, to go looking in the quiet, private glades of the arboretum without having help at hand. In a straight tussle, Rachel knew she would fight as hard and as dirty as she needed to, but her fists were strapped and

Colin Benwick was as solid as an oak. Not as fast as Michael, but if he landed a blow she'd know it.

The Japanese cherries had dropped their white and pink flowers three weeks ago and the English bird cherry was already in bloom. Inhaling the sweet scent of the cherry's long flower spikes, Rachel caught the splintering and cracking sounds she'd been listening for: Dr Benwick, busy clearing and tidying dead branches.

She couldn't see him yet, which suited her. Invisible to Benwick as he was to her, Rachel stopped and waited for the young policeman. As she waited, she thought over the danger these arson attacks posed to visitors. Inspector Penoyre had advised her not to cancel the July symposium. That might suit the arsonist, indeed might be his intention, and the institute couldn't afford the loss of revenue. Nor could she keep the visiting overseas researchers away. Most would be coming in June, but some groups had arrived today, after a morning session and lunch at Exeter University, and were already settling in – walking the grounds and corridors between sessions in the library, labs or glasshouse.

All had supplied personal details and photographs for the records. So far as she knew, the only academics still to arrive in May were two archaeologists from Colombia. Michael had the details of their visit and had provided her, the police and the other permanent staff with photographs of the two women. They weren't arriving until next week and perhaps by then the arson threat would be over.

Comforting herself with this idea, Rachel

smiled as the young constable finally caught up, breathing easily now that he was out of the sun. Rachel tipped her chin in the direction of the fern terrace. 'Colin's working just above us. Would you mind waiting here, please? I'll only be a few moments.'

Giving the constable no time to protest, she limped off the path, weaving as rapidly as she could through the fading bluebells and lily of the valley, stepping carefully over the unfurling fronds of bracken. The trees above the fern terrace shielded her from sight and her light boots made scarcely a sound on the vegetation and hard-packed earth. Walking sideways, it was easy climbing even in her present state.

At the top of the terrace Rachel briefly touched the trailing white blossoms of the nearest false acacia in gratitude. Ducking under the trees, she moved forward again, keenly aware that the young policeman would soon be losing sight of her in the fresh foliage. She'd be able to shout to him, though, and he'd be able to hear her conversation with Colin Benwick, once she stopped Benwick's wood cutting.

At the rim of her left eye, she spotted a flicker of activity. A bird or a squirrel, rooting in the undergrowth. Rachel nodded with satisfaction. The last thing she wanted was for one of the international visitors to interrupt her meeting with Benwick. Concentrating on the chunky figure slowly emerging through the leaves into full view, she drew in a deep breath. She couldn't delay this meeting with the forester. Her escort would come looking.

A second flash of movement, in the same place as before. Rachel whipped aside, towards the trembling branch, and the hand reaching out from behind failed to connect with her arm.

Small, stockily built, the man grinned up at her, a shaft of light playing on his broad cheekbones and flattish nose. He had Aoira's round dark eyes, and he wore the same kind of western clothes: floppy T-shirt and baggy shorts. A baseball cap, turned backwards, sat jauntily on a spreading crown of straight black hair.

Still grinning, the man put a finger to his own lips, then pointed back towards Kestrel House. He wanted her to go back there.

'Who are you?' whispered Rachel in the Gapo language.

He answered in the same tongue, 'I am Eusebio. Second cousin of Carlos the shaman, who once had a sister called Aoira. We need to speak to you, Rachel.'

'We?'

'My boss.'

'There are two of you? You just walked in with today's other visitors?'

Eusebio ignored her questions as too obvious to answer. Pressing an envelope into Rachel's clammy hand, he darted away, falling blossom sticking to the brim of his baseball cap. Another instant and he was gone.

Heart drumming, she tore open the envelope and read the printed note. 'Be in the women's toilets in the main building in twenty minutes.'

Colin Benwick would have to wait.

Chapter 55

Rachel did not tell the police. Once they were involved, any information would be lost to her. Penoyre was good, but she knew the Gapo. It was a risk but, if her plan worked, not a stupid one.

She dropped the constable off at her father's lab, with the white lie that she'd be changing her burns dressings in the loo. Then she paid a rapid visit to the main conservatory.

Seventeen minutes after reading the note she was crouching on top of a lowered toilet seat, feet drawn up so that she was invisible to anyone entering. The door to her cubicle was wide open, whilst the door of the toilet closest to the window was shut. Rachel had locked it from inside, wriggling painfully back under the narrow gap between the two cubicle partitions.

If her plan worked, she'd have the advantage of surprise. She glanced at the object gripped in her hand between gloved fingers. The disposable gloves, snatched from Dad's lab, fitted snugly over her dressings.

A women's toilet block, smelling strongly of fake lemon – not the place she would have chosen to make a stand. What was Eusebio's mysterious boss doing in Devon? How did he find her? What did he want?

The outer door swung inwards. Rachel's guts made a downward dive. She stared at the floor-tiles and shadows. People sense when a pair of eyes are trained on them.

The stranger moved decisively towards the locked door, clearly no innocent visitor. Rachel sprang.

The adrenalin hit in her veins was so massive that she felt no pain, and the stranger's reaction seemed pathetically slow. The blade was jabbed against the black man's throat before he'd half-turned.

'It is a long time since I was threatened with a penknife,' came a slow, cultured voice.

Speaking in English, the stranger reminded Rachel uncannily of Daniel. She turned the penknife slightly against the obsidian column of his neck, allowing him to feel the sticky resin plastered over the knife's tip.

'Curare. One small cut, and you'll be paralysed, then dead.'

'Ah, the "flying death". You learnt fast amongst the Gapo. I did not think to check if you grew the vine in your magnificent glasshouse.' Astonishingly, a smile lifted the corners of the man's mouth.

Unimpressed, Rachel checked him over. No weapon she could see, but his olive-green trousers and light jacket would hide a pistol. She'd have to knock him out to be sure of her escape. Or cut him.

She dared not let the stranger move. They'd have to talk as they were, backed uncomfortably against the toilet partition wall with the door creaking softly as it ground to a stop on its hinges.

Rachel tightened her grip on the penknife.

'Why are you here?'

'As the bearer of good news.' He swallowed, the only sign so far of stress. 'You will know officially in a few days, but I assumed you would wish to know at once. Kew have tested the seeds the Gapo sent you. Kew are very excited. They predict great things, many cures. And the Gapo forest will have its reprieve: the seeds are more valuable than oil, or gold.'

He paused. 'This is not what you wanted?'

'It may be. But the Gapo have been tricked before.'

'Believe me, this is no joke. Kew will be calling you tomorrow – letters have already been sent to people in Brazil. It is real.'

To stifle feelings of relief came easily. This news should have come five years ago in Rio. Her hand was becoming tired. She needed to be quick. 'Are the Gapo the only reason you came?'

'You know that isn't so, Rachel.' He smiled as he said her name, even though he must feel the knife nibbling lightly against his skin.

Could he have come specifically to kill her? Rachel felt sweat break out over her back. 'You have the advantage. I don't know your name. Nor your business.'

· 'Forgive me. I am Ramon Gil. Before you ask, I will say that what I do is not important to you, except that when I make it my business to find out about someone, I am very thorough. You were not hard to trace. Rachel. You are too visible and you have too many friends. No,' – Ramon Gil swallowed again – 'I have not threatened any of your people. But there are few western women who have lived amongst the Gapo. It is through them and Kew that I made the final connection. I have obligations with the tribe.'

Under the crisp moss-green shirt, Rachel spotted a dark shadow circling Ramon Gil's throat. Using her free hand, she touched part of the shadow, feeling rings of tiny beads, part of a longer necklace.

'I wear the beads in honour of my god,' said Ramon Gil.

'You are *candomblé?*'

'I am of the faith.'

'And your obligations to the Gapo? How far do they stretch?'

'My heart is Gapo. My woman comes from the people.'

A trickle of sweat ran down Rachel's spine. Her arm was going numb. She decided to test the Brazilian's story. 'If you have a Gapo wife, then we are family,' she said. 'Aoira adopted me as her kinswoman.'

She felt Ramon Gil relax slightly. Chancing more, Rachel withdrew the knife a fraction. 'You are obligated to me, Ramon Gil, through Aoira and the powers of her healing-tree that will save the Gapo land.'

Slowly, Ramon Gil turned his head. Full face for the first time, he and Rachel stared at each other, Rachel assessing, Ramon Gil patient and still.

Gil spoke first. 'There is more to it still, Rachel, and you may be certain that I have already accepted my obligation. That is the reason I am here.'

'And your Gapo companion.' Deftly, she pressed back the knife. 'Any more friends of yours I should know about?'

'Two men slipping unobserved into such a place is easy. More and we should certainly be spotted.' Ramon Gil kept a dark pleading eye on her. 'My people did drop in here on open days, when the groups of African scientists came calling. Most whitemen can't tell the difference between Africans and black South Americans. But today, Rachel, it is only Eusebio and myself. I have come because I have information on your problem.'

Rachel heard the sound of a banging door, the clatter of footsteps. The film crew were moving downstairs and the others returning from lunch. Jocasta might come in here. Her policeman might decide to wander along from Paul's lab to check on her. Reaching a decision, Rachel lowered her arm. 'Okay, tell what you know. Quickly!'

A soft chuckle escaped Gil. 'Should we not talk somewhere else? More private?'

The voices along the corridor were getting louder. Rachel shuddered as she recognized Michael's laughter, followed instantaneously by Helen's gleeful shout: 'So right!' They must have had a good lunch, she thought.

'Phone me,' she said harshly. 'Kestrel House is in the book.'

Ramon Gil stepped back, flicking a paper towel from a pile in the window-ledge to wipe the deadly traces of curare from his neck. 'Another time, as they say.'

Rachel backed to the door of the ladies' room and, without taking her eyes off Ramon Gil, opened it a crack. The group containing Michael and Helen had wandered on down the corridor to the common room. She could hear the emptiness of the upper floor, like a slow and heavy breath.

She closed the door. 'Leave now, while no one is looking, and take Aoira's second cousin with you. Go! Before someone is hurt–'

Slipping through the door, Ramon Gil paused to remark conversationally, 'You can ask Michael about my debt to you. Remember me to him, please. You can also tell him that I will pay my obligations in full, whether he wants it or not.'

He was gone. Suddenly Rachel had a desperate need to use the lavatory. Her penknife clattered to the tiles as she scrabbled for the lock on her cubicle door. She managed to drag her jump suit and panties down, raise the toilet seat and get in position before her legs and bladder gave way.

Were the Gapo truly safe? She couldn't be sure. Ramon Gil's final message had centred her thoughts on Michael. How did Michael know someone like Ramon Gil? Why, in their long conversations, in their intimate moments, had he never mentioned Brazilian connections?

What else had Michael not told her?

Chapter 56

Cleaning her penknife at one of the grey basins, Rachel heard the outer door open. Watching in the chipped bevel-edged mirror, she tensed as Helen rushed in. To her relief, Helen was too absorbed in her own concerns to notice the knife or that she was wearing plastic gloves.

Helen slammed the door of the cubicle where Rachel had ambushed Ramon Gil, and a moment later started the flush and her 'pitch' simultaneously.

'Rachel, we must get some footage of you in the conservatory. We're stymied today for anything else, and my boys are getting restless. Besides, it just isn't economic to have the crew standing around.'

Helen was in full spate. Rachel let her flow, dumping the plastic gloves in the sanitary disposal unit and slipping her glinting knife into her jump suit trouser-pocket. By the time Helen was vigorously washing her hands, Rachel was ready to go.

'That sounds fine to me,' she said as Helen finally fell silent. 'The glasshouse will be impressive at this time of day.' Rachel paused on the threshold. 'Do you know where Michael is?'

'He said something about having a word with the fire investigator at your father's lab.' Helen raised clear blue eyes to the mirror. 'Takes his

volunteer duties seriously: I approve of that.'
Helen puckered her lips and took a lipstick from
her purse. 'This shade isn't too scarlet? I'd ask
Mike, but you know how men are with loud
colours.'

'It's great,' Rachel said evenly. 'I'll see you in
the conservatory in twenty minutes. I need to
make a phone call.'

She left before the weak tears swam up into her
eyes. Despising them, Rachel set off for the lab,
praying that Michael would be there.

At the sight of him standing in the corridor
beside the fire blackened lab door, Rachel felt her
resolve melting. It would be so easy to lean on
that tall, agile figure, except she wasn't sure now
how strong Michael was inside. Had she let
Michael's appearance, like Daniel's, influence
her judgement? Only one way to find out.

She moved carefully past her police minder, the
fire investigator, Leo and Jocasta. The visiting
researchers were still gathering in the common
room and the film crew were nowhere, but there
were enough interested parties for her to speak
softly.

Rachel discovered that she was shy of tackling
Michael, reluctant to confront him so soon after
their intimacy had been established. Perhaps it
had been a mistake to move in with him.

Michael had seen her. He stepped closer,
shielding her from onlookers. 'How are you?' He
lightly touched a finger to her flushed chin.

Considering what he'd kept secret from her, the
private gesture was too much. 'Fine! How was
your lunch with Helen?' Jocasta and Leo turned

to watch, suspending their murmured conversation. Struggling to keep her temper, Rachel lowered her voice. 'Did you see Ramon Gil leaving?'

Michael's grey eyes widened, but he gave no other sign. Rachel hated him in that moment for his control. 'Couldn't you even try to deny you know who I'm talking about?'

'Gil was here today?'

'The monolith speaks! Yes, Michael, and he gave me to understand that you know each other.'

Michael broke in urgently. 'Keep your voice down.'

'That you'd even discussed me with him.'

'Rachel, that's not how it was.'

'I'm not interested, Michael. But you'd better be there when I phone Inspector Penoyre and fill him in on our mutual acquaintance.'

'Will you be quiet?'

The cutting menace in Michael's voice silenced everyone. Staring up into his gunmetal eyes, Rachel swung round on her heel.

Helen and the film crew had arrived, of course. Perfect timing. Rachel snatched at the first excuse that rushed to mind. 'Need to check the plants in the glasshouse are moist enough – camera lights and heat are fearful at drying things out.'

Helen nodded, as eager as Rachel to allow her friend a moment alone. 'No need to hurry. I've a few more shots here first.'

No one was looking at Michael until Rachel began to walk away, limping in her haste. She heard him clear his throat, then came running footsteps and a warm hand embraced her wrist.

'We have to talk.'

Rachel shook her head and pulled free. Once inside the conservatory she'd no longer have to listen to him, because she wouldn't be able to hear.

'Let me help.'

'Let her go, Mike,' Helen said sharply.

Rachel thought she heard Leo say something to the same effect. Then the fire investigator called Michael's name and she made her escape.

Entering the glasshouse, Rachel realized that neither Paul nor Angwen had been amongst the tight little group who'd seen Michael snap at her.

'I sincerely hope you're not in here, Dad. I really don't feel like supporting your paranoia right now.'

The sounds faded quickly in the crowded jungle interior. Today the temperatures outside were in the nineties. The panes of the glass roof, brushed with their thin white coat of shading, gave the conservatory the muted, dusty splendour of an antique jewel.

Rachel looked up at a misty, opaque shadow hanging from the exact centre of the slender metal roof-beams. She blinked and the ghost of Polly Brewer, the jilted kitchen-maid, turned into a spider's web, huge, gross and comfortingly mundane.

Clearly she wasn't yet desperate enough for Polly to appear, Rachel thought, wiping away a tear of stress. She walked farther into the conservatory. Crossing cool dark bands of shade, then sparkling pools of sunlight, she checked on the sprinklers and hose-pipes. Her excuse to Helen had been a partial truth: television lights were drying. But her main reason was privacy for the telephone call she was about to make.

Carefully lifting her penknife from her jump suit trousers, Rachel dug deeper and brought out her mobile phone. Inhaling, she began to dial the Darcombe police station number to tell Penoyre everything about Ramon Gil.

There was a scent - a smell. Something was very wrong. Rachel cut the connection.

Striding over a rank of seed trays and scrambling under a cycad, she scowled at the stink of herbicide, a kind banned at Kestrel House. Lifting a long palm frond she choked, fumes causing water to stream from her eyes. Fumes and shock - the blue skyflowers she'd brought back with her as seed from the Amazon were dead. She found a plant tag plunged into the remains with the epitaph: *'Rachel Falconer Memorial. No flowers by request.'*

'Got you!'

'Rachel!' Michael crashed through the back door of the glasshouse. The young policeman was with him.

No time for explanations. Whirling to her feet, flinching at the nerve-tangle protest in her burned shoulders and neck, Rachel ran towards the front door, away from Michael, from the police, from Helen. This was no time to be captured on film: she was doing the hunting. A single idea seared her mind, the key to the mystery.

Daniel couldn't have poisoned her Amazonian flowers – the herbicide was too fast-acting. But someone else at Kestrel House had done it, had left that message, had been too clever. Did he think she'd forgotten Tim Stevens' final instructions? She had been at his funeral. No flowers by request.

The police had taken the employment records and a computer to the upstairs common room. One check of the records, Rachel thought, then she would understand everything.

The front door of the glasshouse shimmered as she slammed it behind her. Pounding over the gravel drive and up the main entrance steps, she skidded on the marble floor as she hit the grand staircase. As she'd hoped, this part of the institute was deserted, although a loud belch issued from the formal meeting-room above. The police must still be working in there, trawling through records without realizing their full significance.

Her phone was ringing. Stopping on the lower part of the stair, Rachel opened the receiver. 'Yes?'

'Rachel! The baby.'

'Where are you, Angwen? Where's Dad?'

'Rachel! The baby.' The same cry, the same tone, repeated.

Footsteps sounding on the stairs behind her. Then, as she turned, a clenched fist speeding straight at her face.

Chapter 57

For the first time since I set the whole long plan in motion, Ms Falconer has surprised me. After that deliciously heart-rending phone call from Angwen, I fully anticipated seeing Rachel haring to give the mother-to-be comfort and support. Instead, what do I find? Questions! Where the emotion? Where the dash to help?

After what Tim had told me about Aoira, I can't believe how cold Rachel is. Attacking her conscience is clearly of no use; hence my more direct approach. In fact it was fortunate I happened to slip away for a call of nature, otherwise I would have missed her on the staircase.

And what on earth was she doing there? I'd planned for her to receive Angwen's call in the conservatory: the old legend of Polly Brewer appealed to me. Although if Rachel sees anyone before she dies, it ought to be Tim.

After the hours I spent splicing together sound-tape, I do feel rather aggrieved with Rachel's lack-lustre reaction, but disappointment does have its compensation. I'd intended to slip away later, once the full conflagration started, but by leaving now – with Rachel stowed safely in my car boot – I know I shall be in at the kill from the start.

Chapter 58

Had he been alone, Michael would have heard Rachel leaving the conservatory, but with the constable breathing down his back he didn't realize that she'd gone. 'Where are you, Rachel? We must talk!'

'You're not helping.' The constable, playing second conscience under his right ear. Michael would have flattened him, if there'd been time.

'For fuck's sake, Rachel! Let me explain!' The glass walls of the conservatory rang around him like tableware tapped with a finger, a mocking sound of normality. But after Ramon Gil, nothing was normal.

Michael was horrified that Gil had become part of the Dartmoor scene. He'd unleashed an ageing contract killer. His fear for Rachel was absolute.

And he'd snapped at her. Appalled by her news, angry at her suppositions against him – above all, desperate that she not speak of the lethal Ramon Gil in front of the camera crew, who wouldn't care less what Gil's reaction to Rachel might be after they'd broadcast his name round the planet – he had wanted her to be silent. Now she was.

'Rachel, please.' A jogging of his elbow made him whip round. The constable paled – Michael had no idea why, but he wasn't looking in a mirror.

Then Helen's voice. 'Any luck, Mike?' Walking rapidly but without breaking into a sweat, Helen had entered the glasshouse at the head of her camera team. Taking silence as an answer, she said easily, 'Probably slipped out for something. We'll start setting up. Jocasta! Get yourself over here.'

Her casually professional attitude struck Michael as a revelation. Cheerfully directing her people into position, Helen had no qualms, no doubts. She worked in celluloid, yet the world she inhabited was of diamond, hard-edged. He'd fretted through his lunch with her, wondering how to tell Helen gently that he wouldn't be joining her in the States. Now he saw it wasn't necessary. Helen had already moved on.

She winked. 'Go find Rachel then, you dumb oaf. Settle it.' Swinging round in a kingfisher dash of colour, she began shouting at the technicians.

The young constable beside Michael was talking into his radio, asking the uniforms upstairs to look for Miss Falconer.

Distracted, Michael did not wait but set off striding along the path, head veering left and right as he scanned between ferns and creepers. He spotted the poisoned blue flowers almost at once, and the print made by Rachel's trainers where she'd crouched to examine the macabre message.

'What?' The constable ducked past to see for himself.

'What's up?' Helen was bearing down, face alight.

Leaving the policeman to explain and keep the film crew off the forensics, Michael followed Rachel's trail. A single bright red hair, drifting down from the serrated edge of a glossy long green leaf, showed where she'd cut across to rejoin the main path closer to the front door.

Avoiding the way she'd taken, Michael ran round on the path, emerging seconds later into the brilliance of a summer's afternoon. Squinting out the glaring sunlight, Michael focused on the gravel, a wave of pebbles spilled against the glinting marble steps. Rachel had been running there. His heart ached when he thought of her denying pain in her struggle for speed.

The gravel marks were too inconclusive for him to hope that no one had been chasing her. Sprinting, Michael shouted again, 'Rachel!' Bounding up the steps to the main entrance, Michael smashed through the doors and cannoned into Colin Benwick.

'What the hell's wrong with you?' Colin grumbled, as they disengaged from a solid tangle of arms and chests, 'Almost flattened me.'

'Sod you, Benwick. Where's Rachel?'

'No call for that. I haven't seen her since this morning.'

'What about Leo?'

Colin Benwick jutted his beard. 'What about him?'

Michael almost threw Benwick back out through the double doors. Only a policeman's call from upstairs – 'No sign here' – kept him on the manageable side of anger. Benwick might have lingered around Rachel's cottage, but that didn't make him the stalker.

Michael forced himself to cool down. 'Where's the Manchester Casanova? Have you seen him in the last half hour?'

Either Colin Benwick enjoyed dicing with danger or he hadn't the wit to take a good look at Michael's narrowed eyes. 'Leo, from Manchester? I know his accent's faint but surely even someone from Devon can spot the difference between Yorkshire and Lancashire.'

A large hand clamped down on Benwick's shoulder. 'You tell me where he's from then,' Michael suggested.

'Leo's from Huddersfield way. Me, I'm a Bradford man.'

Huddersfield, where Tim Stevens had once lived. 'And do you know where he is right now?' he asked, ignoring the policeman jogging down the staircase.

Colin Benwick shook his shaggy head. 'What's this about?'

Close to the bottom of the stairs, the policeman had halted and squatted, peering at one marble step. As his companion WPC reached the top of the stairs, the officer raised his head to her.

'Fresh blood.'

Chapter 59

Colin stared at the crimson splash. He'd read that marble absorbed certain fluids – that stair might always be stained with Rachel's blood.

Shock overwhelmed him. He stumbled back and twisted round, leaving the field to Michael Horton and the police. For no clear reason he could conceive of, Colin felt compelled to announce to the world what had happened. He blundered into the conservatory. Helen looked up from her clipboard. 'Hi, Colin. Got an answer for me?'

Her question was an irrelevance, but she'd keep hounding. It was quicker to agree than have her start on at him again. 'I'll do it. Everything we talked about. Helen, there's something...'

His voice seized up. He croaked. 'Rachel's vanished. She's bleeding–'

Helen jabbed the clipboard back at Jocasta. 'You, you and you,' she pointed to the nimblest of her crew – 'go find out what's happening. Stay sharp but keep out of the way. Jocasta, you go with them. Jump to it!'

Colin leaned against a cycad, his head swimming.

'Deep breaths, Dr Benwick.' Helen was still there. She wound a surprisingly strong arm around him, bracing him against her hipbone. 'Come on, Colin, don't faint on me. It'll be all right. Rachel's a smart one – she can take care of herself.'

Colin blinked and the path stopped wavering in front of his eyes. 'Why are you being so nice to me now?'

'Even media moguls have their human moments, and I'm only a producer. Don't you worry. The police and Mike will surely find her.' Helen squeezed Colin's waist. Then she gave him an old-fashioned look. 'You're a fan. Do you know already where she is? What's the deal?'

Inspector Penoyre reappeared at the foot of the stairs. He was incensed.

'Whatever interesting evidence you might have discovered here, however hard you were searching for Miss Falconer, Dr Benwick shouldn't have been allowed just to wander off,' he snarled at the three uniformed figures clustered sheepishly on the staircase. 'Two of you get on and find him. And while you're at it, get that camera crew in here for questioning. This is an investigation, not an audition for *The Bill*.'

The inspector dismissed them with a savage jerk of his head.

'Inspector Penoyre.' Michael moved at once to intercept.

'In a moment.' Sweating in shirt-sleeves, Joe Penoyre distractedly fiddled with one of his green braces.

'This is vital information–'

'I said in a minute, Mr Horton.'

In his years as a volunteer fireman Michael had never admonished a bystander with the 'Let us

339

do our job' line, but now he understood vividly why people ran back into burning buildings, tried to get to a crime scene ahead of the police. Experts simply took over and those most involved – lovers, husbands, mothers – were dumped on the sidelines.

Talking sharply to the remaining WPC, Penoyre wasn't ready to deal with him yet. Frustrated, Michael swore, ignored Penoyre's scowl and ran up the steps to the landing window.

There was no one out there but police and police cars - what else had he expected? Michael mentally divided the landscape into sections as though for an archaeological dig, intently scanning each section to the horizon. Somewhere out there were two men he had to track down before they hurt Rachel.

Michael still didn't know the answer to Ramon Gil's taunting question, 'How far will you go?', but he knew that soon he'd have to make a decision. Right now, he was going to make Penoyre listen to him about Leo Cartwright's birthplace, Leo's possible connection with Tim Stevens and the sudden appearance of a Brazilian contract killer.

From the corner of his office a phone began to trill. Without checking with Penoyre or the WPC, Michael started along the landing to answer it.

Even before he reached the office door, he knew the sound was coming from the wrong corner for his desk phone. He had his bleeper with him. The mobile – it was in his biker's jacket, hung on the coathook behind the door that morning. He belted out the release code on the door-pad next to his office, yanked the wooden door open and dragged the jacket off its hanger. Another second and the mobile was in his fist, the call taken.

'I have a pistol trained directly at Rachel. Unless you do exactly as I tell you, Michael, I will shoot her.'

Suddenly, the world slowed as adrenalin mainlined through his body. Anger, concern, fear were all switched off, to be replaced by swift calculation, speeding thoughts, working the odds.

'Where are you, Ramon?' Reaching to his desk for a marker pen and scribbling 'FIRE-STALKER?' on the door, Michael opened it to its widest extent. He didn't want the police blundering in.

'I know where Rachel is. Think about it.'

Michael already had, and about the likelihood of the Brazilian squeezing the trigger. Listening intently, trying to pick out background noises, he worked hard at keeping his voice gentle. 'I'd like to talk to Rachel, please.'

'That is not possible.'

'Ramon.' The name alone was a reproach, but to be clear Michael added in a tone of utmost reason, 'You know you owe a debt to Rachel. You also know we cannot proceed unless I can speak to her.'

A sudden, terrifying silence, then Rachel. *'Michael?'*

Her voice was replaced immediately by that of her keeper. *'You have heard her.'*

'What would you like me to do for you, Ramon?'

'Come out to the arboretum alone. We'll take it from

341

there.' The phone crackled with static tension. *'I give you ten minutes.'*

Don't argue, Michael warned himself. Don't ask him to prove any part of what he's saying. Keep it friendly. 'Too tight, Ramon. The inspector's just appeared and wants all the Kestrel House staff and visiting researchers brought together. If I'm to slip away without being seen you'll have to give me more time. Forty minutes.'

Michael held his breath whilst Ramon Gil considered. If he could negotiate, persuade Gil that neither he nor Rachel were any kind of threat, there would be a way through this. The first span in the bridge between them was made of time.

Ramon Gil chuckled softly. *'Twenty.'*

Michael made a silent fist in triumph. 'It's a deal.' He fixed the place with absolute precision: for Rachel he could afford no mistakes. 'I'll see you and Rachel by the water pond in the arboretum in twenty minutes.'

'Agreed.' Ramon Gil cut the connection.

'That's it then.' Michael saw the moving shadow on the landing and called, 'You'd better come in, Inspector.'

Within twenty minutes it was impossible for Joe Penoyre to summon a trained negotiator or send to Darcombe for a wire for Michael to wear. The location chosen as the meeting also presented problems – the pond was in an open area of the arboretum.

'I realize it seems a crazy place to suggest, but I had to think of somewhere that was obvious as being what it was,' Michael rapidly explained. 'In an arboretum, I could have told Gil to meet me under the lime avenue and he might have gone to the rowan walk by mistake.'

'Whereas a pond is a pond,' said Joe Penoyre.

'Exactly. And because I'll be able to see whether he's got Rachel with him. There's cover about fifty metres back. Plane trees and elms. Your people should be able to watch from there. If they're careful.'

Joe Penoyre nodded a grim acknowledgement. He rapped the open door with his fist, over the scrawled 'FIRE-STALKER?'. 'I could stop you going out there, Mike. It might be a hoax.'

Michael pushed past him on the threshold. 'And I might get Rachel back.' He stepped closer to Penoyre. 'Don't get in my way.'

Joe Penoyre stared, obviously trying to decide whether the trouble involved in arresting him was worth it, thought Michael. 'You need me,' he said, in the same gentle way he'd spoken to the contract killer. 'I know the institute inside and out: glass-house and arboretum. With my help, I can get your people within a safe range to do whatever you think possible against a very dangerous man. You've no guns, have you? Well, without me you simply won't get close enough to make any difference to Gil's plans. And please,' – Michael's grey eyes flashed with harsh irony – 'no heroics.'

'If he has a hostage we'll certainly do exactly as this Brazilian asks until we can get negotiators out here.' It was Penoyre who now pushed past Michael, fingers punching numbers into his mobile.

Chapter 60

The young WPC, her face rigid yet flaming, met them at the top of the staircase.

'Yes?' Joe Penoyre barked.

'Sir, Mr and Mrs Falconer have just returned from the Warren House Inn – sir, they don't know yet about their daughter. I took them to the conservatory and asked them to wait there, away from that lot.' She jerked her chin towards the miscellaneous crowd gathered in the lobby.

'Good. Now, go back and tell Mr and Mrs Falconer that I'll be along as soon as I can.' Loosening collar and tie, Joe Penoyre took another look at the group. Jostling and grumbling in audible whispers about wasted time, nannying police and the safety of equipment left in the glasshouse, the film crew stared back sullenly. The scientists watched with interest.

'When are we going to find out what's going on?' bawled a technician.

'When can we get back to our work?'

'Why are we cooped up in here, anyway?' shouted Jocasta.

The inspector held up both hands in an 'I don't know' gesture but did not enter any discussion. Instead he asked Michael from the corner of his mouth, 'Is there a back way out?'

Turning to lead the way, Michael felt no relief that it was Penoyre who'd have to break the news about Rachel to Paul and Angwen. He'd twenty minutes to kill – *wrong word*. In his heightened state, each second had stretched to seem longer than a minute, but he knew the coming meeting would be final. He'd less than half an hour to work out how to save Rachel from Ramon Gil.

What was the Brazilian's true part in all this? Was he a late involvement, or had Gil been in at the very start, with Paul Falconer's ruined research? Surely there could be no doubt now that Paul had been right. Someone had sabotaged his work as a ploy to lure Rachel to Kestrel House.

Was it likely to have been Ramon Gil? It would have been much easier for someone inside the institute. Someone with strange little secrets. But who, and why?

Michael sensed a lightening in the shadows behind them. Spinning round to confront the new threat, he saw the front double doors flung back, sunlight lasering into the lobby. Sprinting to the landing window, he mouthed the word which Helen, bursting back indoors from the drive, shouted: 'Fire!'

Chapter 61

Joe Penoyre was shouting orders. Helen was talking to her crew, gesturing with rapid hand movements. On the landing, making the 999 call, Michael caught odd phrases: 'Don't bother with the smoke – go for the flames... It's a war zone

345

out there: get what you can but stay out of trouble... Remember atmosphere: keep that tape running!'

Michael finished the call and tore downstairs, catching Helen before she shot back out through the main doorway.

'It's not safe.' He gripped so she couldn't stir. 'Are you listening, Helen? Fire like this can flow at thirty feet a second – don't tell me you can outrun it!'

'We'll stay behind the road, Mike.'

'And it could jump the road. Listen to me!'

His mobile and bleeper sounded together. Switching off the bleeper – the Darcombe lads would learn soon enough that he'd a ringside seat at this incident – Michael answered the phone.

'*Remember our appointment, Michael.*'

'Did you set fire to the moor, Ramon?'

'*No. Fire is too unpredictable. You have fifteen minutes.*'

'Who's Ramon?' Helen asked.

Glancing over heads, Michael spotted Penoyre closing fast. 'He'll tell you,' and to Penoyre, 'I'm going, Joe.' It seemed right – quicker – to use the man's first name.

'I'm coming too. The others know what to do till back-up and your brigade get here.'

'Inspector–' That was Helen.

'What about Paul and Angwen? They don't know–'

'They'll have to wait, Mike. I haven't the bodies here to observe the niceties. We have to check that all today's researchers are in the lobby. Can't have people wandering about at a time like this.'

346

'Inspector–'

'Talk to my WPC, Miss.' Joe Penoyre followed after Michael.

Michael took the back way out of Kestrel House. He could smell the fire but not see it. He faced Joe Penoyre in the carpark. 'Once we're out of here, we'll make our way behind that stand of Scots pine and slip into the arboretum from there. We'll need to crawl till I've got you to where I can leave you to go on safely by yourself, okay?'

The two men slipped behind the Scots pine. The younger, shorter trees gave bushy cover and they could move fast. Reaching the cherry avenue, Michael went down on his stomach and elbowed forward, head down. He crawled several metres on a carpet of cherry blossom.

Joe was still behind him and Michael waited for the smaller man's breathing to steady before whispering. 'From here on we'll have to separate. You keep crawling between the pines and through that fern section till you come to a row of apple-trees. From there if you look due west you'll see the pond; you should be able to hear, too. I'll double back to the start of the grass avenue and come striding along past you – that way Gil should think I'm on my way to him alone. Good luck!'

'Same to you, Mike. Be careful out there.'

Snaking across the cherry blossom, petals and twigs sticking up his nose and clinging to his hair, Michael crawled to the cypress tree that marked the entrance to the grass avenue. Crouching, he roughly brushed himself off, then ran forward,

347

hitting the grass avenue at his top speed.

Michael liked to run, and that afternoon, forcing his pumping legs up the steep slope, he hurtled forward at his limit. Rachel drew him on, pulled him forward. Time was running out for her.

Past bright green limes, through elm leaves, then finally, the placid glitter of water. Michael pelted off the track into the darkness of trees again. Dismissing the froth of leaves and fluffy seeds of an old coppiced willow as too obvious a screen, Michael forced himself to endure uncertainty a few moments longer whilst he cut round to the pond from the east side. He'd approach the meeting place publicly, but wanted to see first if there was any sign of Rachel or Gil. The tactic should also give Joe time to be in position.

He looked, but the bluebells remained un-trampled for as far as he could see and the open space around the pond was empty. Lustrous as a bleeding cut, a scarlet damselfly darted past his ear. The only sounds were connected with fire: closing sirens, the rumble of heavy moving engines, the distant crackle of burning heather. A taste of soot kissed his lip.

Michael shifted forward, scalp tightening as he straightened then strode straight out into the light.

'Michael.'

He turned. A red laser-sight winked. Ramon Gil was waiting behind the shield of a plane tree, a rifle braced against the tree's lowest branch. Coming by the elms, Michael had passed him, neither man aware of the other.

'Where's Rachel?'

'I hope you will see her soon, Michael, but I regret she has never been with me.' Without shifting his grip on the trigger, the Brazilian held up the small tape-recorder clutched in his other hand. He pressed it, and Rachel's voice, distorting at full volume, asked, *'Michael?'*

'Scanned and recorded from your telephone.' Ramon Gil smiled, showing his crooked teeth.

'You bastard!'

Ramon Gil dropped the recorder and slapped the rifle barrel in warning. 'It was necessary that you believed I had Rachel. How else would I have ever got you away from your comrades in the fire-brigade? Or that policeman whom my Gapo friend has just overcome? Only a gentle blow to the head, Eusebio?'

'Si, Senhor.' A stocky figure emerged from the bluebells.

'English, Eusebio.'

'He sleeps in white flowers.' Eusebio flicked the peak of his baseball cap at Michael in greeting. 'You are Rachel's man.'

'You and your boss would do well to remember it.'

Eusebio laughed, turning the baseball cap backwards on his smooth black hair.

Michael glared at Ramon Gil. 'If we don't move soon, we're all going to roast. I need to carry Joe to safety.'

'Once we are on our way to free Rachel, you can call whoever you want. We must move. I put an electronic tracker on Rachel – quite a feat, I assure you, considering the position she had me in.' Ramon Gil chuckled at the private memory, whilst Michael, eaten with curiosity, curbed questions. Until Rachel was safe, everything must wait.

Ramon Gil lifted the rifle barrel away from the crook of the tree, turning towards the rising clouds of smoke. 'We shall go now and find her. You will have the satisfaction of disposing of the man who has been stalking your woman. Come!'

Chapter 62

Her head was splitting, her nose and jaw felt pulped. Someone had cleaned the blood off her face and throat.

Rachel was in no hurry to open her eyes. If the man who had kidnapped her thought she was still unconscious, it might give her an advantage.

Kidnapped. Angwen and Dad were in some kind of trouble, certainly needing help, and she was kidnapped. Rachel almost groaned aloud, her limbs trembling and clammy, her mind bawling, *why me?*

A slight rubbing sound saved her. Alert, she locked on to the outside world and was herself again: the compassionate, capable young woman who'd come to unlock the mystery of Kestrel House. If Angwen could phone her, she could phone for help. The emergency services would have reached her stepmother and father by now:

they were in the best of hands.

Even if she could be there, Rachel forced herself to admit that she could do nothing practical for them. Her skills lay in other areas. Take the threat over Kestrel House. She had solved the 'who' but not the 'why'. If she couldn't escape at once, it would be fascinating to find out more.

The two alternate plans: escape and discovery, calmed her. If she could be active she was no longer a victim. If she could survive she wouldn't be a victim. And if she could learn why, she would face down her nemesis. The insights gained here might give her the chance to commute the guilt of Aoira, Rio and Tim Stevens into forgiveness. Forgiveness of self, of Fultons and of the sad creature who'd brought her to this place.

This place. Rachel listened for clues. Indoors, certainly: no throb of insects or birdsong. No cars – she must be in a place far from a road, or at least a main road. Only her breathing lay on the silence. So far she was alone, but he could be watching through a window or a camcorder viewfinder.

Rachel allowed her chin to droop so that her lips opened. She smelt the air: musty, warm, still. Snaking her tongue quickly between her teeth, she tasted dust. A bachelor pad, she thought irreverently. Sunlight scorched her left elbow but otherwise there was shade. A curtained room.

Her skin was stuck to the varnish on a wooden carver. Her forearms rested along the curved chair arms and were tied by a smooth cord Rachel assumed to be a washing-line. The cord was trussed around her legs and feet. It was this she'd heard make the slight friction sound when she'd tensed to scream. He must be nervous of her strength. Or did he plan to torture her?

Stopping herself sliding over the edge of panic, Rachel concentrated.

She was naked – even the hospital dressings had gone. Thrust against the hard back of the carver, her burns and blisters had burst open. Her bare feet brushed carpet, thick shag-pile. She was in somebody's bedroom. Not her own - her Leica would bring no results. But it was not needed now.

Still hearing nothing, she decided it was time to chance more. She opened her eyes a fraction.

The shag-pile carpet turned out to be a brightly patterned Indian rug. Rachel recalled seeing it once before, in photographs Daniel had shown her of his parents' county home. He must have brought the thing with him when he moved to Dartmoor.

She'd been brought to Daniel's. Where did he live now? She stared at the Indian rug. An address from Daniel's c.v. filtered into her consciousness.

Daniel had a cottage near Bellever forest: Smith Hill, off Higher Cherrybrook Bridge. The cottage was on its own, detached by several fields and pine plantation from the nearest hamlet, Postbridge. Off any regular walking-route, it was unlikely that anyone would pass close to the place.

Was that why she hadn't been gagged? Yet sound carried a long way on the moor. She might make herself heard to walkers on Bellever Tor, or to day-trippers strolling along the forest walks of the plantation.

Maybe that wasn't important to him. Maybe he'd an escape route planned.

Rachel opened her eyes wider, taking in the dimensions of the room. She was in Daniel's bedroom. Her chair and the Indian rug were on top of his king-size bed. The single window was close to her left, shrouded by a heavy curtain.

Tucked under the rug and spilling down over the bed were piles of Daniel's clothes and shoes. An easy-chair and five dining-chairs were buttressed against the divan, all wound about with sheets and towels, padded coathangers, empty shoeboxes and official documents.

The entire contents of the room had been removed from the gaping open drawers of the built-in wardrobe and arranged with her about the bed. She was a guy, sitting on an unlit bonfire.

A groan of disbelief fell from her lips. Bracing her legs against the chair, Rachel strained against her bonds. Risking that her captor would discover she was awake, Rachel tilted her head, looking for any kind of recording or listening device hung from the bare low ceiling.

There was nothing. Breathing out in relief, Rachel glanced here and there for any object she could use to loosen or cut her bonds. She might be able to rock the carver off the bed, smash it against the cottage walls or bedroom floor, but only if she was certain she was alone. That there was no one downstairs, no one listening at the bedroom door.

Rachel caught the distant wail of sirens. Surely that couldn't be an ambulance for Dad and Angwen; it wouldn't take so long, would it? And was it only her febrile imagination that made her think she could smell smoke?

Seeing nothing in the room she could use to sever the white washing-line spun around her limbs, Rachel gave up discretion and struggled violently.

Then she heard it, a tread on the bottom step. Someone mounting the stairs quietly, but not interested in catching her unawares. He was talking.

'Scanners and tape recorders are wonderful things, Rachel, you can fake all kinds of messages. Did you like Angwen's call? I thought it was rather good myself, and it did do its job of distracting you, at least sufficient for me to land a knockout punch. I suppose you'll be asking how dear old Dad and understanding Stepmum are doing, so I'm going to save you the bother. They're disgustingly healthy, sipping cider and staring deeply into each other's eyes in the Warren House. Least they were when I left them. But now it's us, Rachel. You and me and our unfinished business.'

The bedroom door opened, and Rachel's eyes were closed, hair lolling over her face. She knew that the backlit figure would be too slim to fill the doorway, as Michael would have done. Michael. She was so sorry she'd parted from him the way she had, on a stupid argument.

The rasp of a match being lit ignited an updraught of terror, blasting away coherent sense or plan. She'd never know why, never see her family again. Never have the chance to tell Michael she loved him.

Rachel did not stir.

'You can stop pretending. I'm not coming any closer.'

Rachel did not move. She smelt burnt phosphorus as the match was blown out. Heard the muttered, 'Must have clocked her harder than I thought.' Felt the mattress sag as another body climbed onto the bed.

He leaned over her, and Rachel learned all she had to know. He was unarmed, and he had her penknife fastened to his belt: she felt it swing against her hip as a faintly sweaty hand was pushed under her left breast.

Now he was touching her, feeling her living body, and the penknife was a nail-tip away from her stretching fingers. Her arm straining as she reached desperately for the release clip, Rachel knew she had to keep him close.

She fluttered open her eyes, a groggy half-smile lifting the corners of her mouth. 'Are you Tim's adopted son?'

His wide dark eyes bored into hers, his suddenly stilled hand rather than his blankly handsome face revealing that her question had caught him by surprise. 'I suppose Charles Elsham is staying with you? Or did he call on you unexpectedly? Was that why you decided to accelerate your arson campaign?'

Leo laughed. Recovering, he deliberately fondled her nipple with his thumb. 'You think you're very quick, don't you Rachel? But you weren't fast enough on the uptake to pin me down till I was ready. But you're partly right: Charlie's the only one who knows about me and Tim, and Charlie's in a flap these days. Had him camped on my living room floor until he realized he'd outstayed his welcome and moved on. Would you believe he's flitting round the country getting his head together, calling in on his old mates? Worried me sick when I first saw him looming on the doorstep, especially since Bethany was with me. Fortunately she was asleep when he came by the first time. I sent him away and sent Bethany packing.'

His thumb ran over the curve of her breast and continued teasingly along her flank. Rachel was careful not to tense or smile. The hanging penknife was almost within reach, but only if Leo stayed leaning over her.

'The girls were a good cover.' The fingers and thumb of her right hand brushed the clip holding the penknife to Leo's belt – had he felt the touch? 'I suppose they gave you alibis.'

'Oh, yes, especially Lucy – she was a real star. Covered me completely for that time I came calling at your cottage, even though she was fast asleep at the time. Well, she would be, seeing I'd fixed her my special mulled wine laced with sleeping-pills the night before. Never heard me move. Never felt me slide back into bed. Did feel me inside her later though: we had some fun then. Made Lucy's statement to the police even more convincing.' Leo smiled.

Rachel looked at him. She'd seen the white needlecords and blue-checked Gucci shirt before. 'You dressed like Daniel so any stray fibres would be taken as his.'

Leo laughed delightedly. 'Of course! And I wore a blond wig – natural hair – in case anyone ever saw me. Sadly, being Dartmoor, where witnesses are thin on the ground, no one did. Not even you at your cottage when I came up through the cellar – aren't local history books wonderful, by the way? Two American girls and I read all about your cellar at the High Moors Centre. Gave me a wonderful way in and out – I really expected more of a chase from you, Rachel. But then I suppose you were blubbing over your lost rainforest memento. And I was down those cellar steps, over the moor and far away before Daniel stirred himself. Even had time to scuff my footprints. Cut back to the road below the cattle grid and down the fields to Darcombe.'

'Where you'd left your car.'

'Hardly! My Audi is too well known to be left in the open. But Lucy's house is in Darcombe and her house has a garage. I drove my car there, hid it in her garage, paid my little visit to you, then drove Lucy's car back to my place. She never noticed a thing, not even the extra miles on the clock.

'So you see, Rachel,' Leo concluded glibly, 'my girls give great all-round alibis. And I really do like my girls. There's something about female skin, about discovering a new girl's secret pleasures.' His thumb had reached her stomach. A smile lit his pleasant face. 'Pretty things,' he murmured.

They meant nothing to him, thought Rachel.

Far from being an open, friendly young man, Leo was a loner. The endless parade of conquests disguised his self-sufficiency, his reluctance to share his life with others.

'Bethany was sad you'd stopped seeing her,' she remarked, subtly flattering. She had the penknife clip open, waiting for Leo to speak before she risked taking the knife away. As one of his 'girls', Rachel knew, had always known, that he found her attractive. Now she could only hope that his physical response to her was stronger than his need to see her punished ... for his stepfather, Tim Stevens? Was Tim his stepfather?

'Little Bethany.' Leo chuckled, slim fingers vibrating lightly against Rachel's stomach. 'She was pissed off when I chucked her. Do you know her final insult? That I was a computer moron. But I was too bright for you, wasn't I? Both with the fake voice recordings and with your father's feeble lab security.'

'You spoiled his research in March by breaking into his personal lab computer,' Rachel said, her confidence increasing as she closed her own knife tightly into her fist. She had got it away from him, and he didn't realize. She had to keep him occupied, keep him talking. Those sirens she'd heard could be for her, a rescue party. Perhaps with Michael at their head.

Quickly, Rachel buried that idea. 'You covered your tracks by purging files. So simple: you could tamper with vital things like temperature and moisture without setting a foot inside the place. No wonder the security video recordings showed nothing.'

'The police did check your father's computer, but I knew what they would look for. My last move – the mobile in Paul's lab – was even easier. Just as he'd done before, Paul put his new access code on his computer: a little reminder he could print off and pop into his wallet, I suppose. I lifted it from the computer file and, hey presto!, keyed my way in. The video cameras were easy to ignore: they were fixed, so I just worked out of their range. Must have driven the police bonkers.'

'You were out of their league.' Rachel hoped she sounded sufficiently impressed. 'And that day when you came to help me in Dad's lab. You were always just tentative enough on the key-board: nothing too slow or too showy. I never suspected.' Rachel licked her bone-dry lips. 'I suppose Angwen never caught on, either? The mountain-bike and phone call?'

'One of the beauties of my working at Kestrel House has been the easy opportunities to record all of you. Every last member of the staff is on my tapedeck at home. A few added bits of static or crackle can provide tension where the speaking voice doesn't. But my first call to Angwen was easy – I copied the idea of the weird speaking voice from that old suspense film: you know, the one where Doris Day goes manic. Angwen rather reminds me of Doris – a dark-haired version. And it was one of my mum's favourite films.'

The reference to 'my mum' tripped an alarm siren in Rachel's aching head. Allowing her head to loll forward and slurring the words as though more groggy than she actually was, she said, 'I lost my mum, too. Cancer.'

A hiss of indrawn breath, Leo's sensitive features becoming more pinched and fine-drawn, showed Rachel that she'd hit the mark. 'It happened to you, too, Leo. I'm so sorry.'

'She passed away six years ago.' The words broke from Leo with the force of a dam-burst. 'She struggled with cancer for years, but clung on until I was over sixteen and the authorities couldn't touch me. My mum knew I would have hated going in a home, hated it!'

Colour flushed over Leo's taut cheekbones, visible even in the gloom of Daniel's bedroom. Abruptly he withdrew his hand from her. Rachel's heart began to pound in horrible anticipation. It was coming: the reason why he'd stalked her.

'But you still have your father, Rachel. I have no one. Not any more. Not since Tim took an overdose of antidepressants. I was at college when it happened, and sick with pneumonia. The doctors wouldn't let me move, and besides I was too ill, even to attend the funeral. Whilst you were walking behind Tim's coffin, I was sweating in a poxy college bed in a poxy hall of residence in Manchester.'

Manchester was where Leo had claimed he was from, Rachel recalled. 'I always thought you came from Manchester,' she said, shying away from talking more about Tim Stevens. Where was that rescue she had hoped for? Rachel caught a distant sound, the clanging of a fire-engine siren.

The smell of smoke she thought she had imagined was becoming more distinct. Fearfully, she glanced at Leo, but he hadn't noticed anything. *Keep him talking, keep him full of himself.* 'You even called me "chuck" to throw me off the scent.'

'Manchester is where I was born, certainly – that's what's on my documents. But it was really my mum's parents' home: we were only there on sufferance. It served as a base though, when the snoops came round – the social-worker types checking that my home education was adequate, that sort of thing. When the old folks died, my mum rented it out to students. We made a bit of money that way.'

'So where did you live?' Rachel asked, the need to know, to understand, stronger in that moment than prudence or self-preservation.

'Why, with Tim, of course.'

Leo picked one of Rachel's red hairs off his checked T-shirt. That was one reason Leo looked strange to her, thought Rachel irrelevantly: quite apart from his eerie habit of dressing like Daniel when he committed his acts of nuisance and arson, she missed the spectacularly spotted lab-coat. What also disturbed her was his obvious lack of concern at leaving fibres or fingerprints. Did he no longer care if he was caught? Or did Leo believe, as many car thieves did, that fire removed all forensic traces?

She swallowed hastily, suddenly taking in what Leo had just said. 'You lived with Tim Stevens? At his house?' Surely what Leo was suggesting was impossible. A neighbour would have known; the connection would have been spotted at once by the police, by Michael and herself.

361

'No! Silly girl.' Leo patted her bruised cheek. The mattress sagged again as he straightened, playfully touching the ceiling rose with a hand. 'My mum and I never stayed in that dreadful little terrace house in Huddersfield.' He steadied Rachel's slightly tilting chair with a slim leg, tracing the ornate patterns on the Indian rug with a trainer.

'My mum thought the street common, and she was right. Tim admitted that his neighbours were dreadful. No, we lived on the Pennines, on the moors between Huddersfield and Manchester. My mum bought an old farmhouse and we did it up. We were completely independent: oil tank, cess-pit, generator. And every winter utterly cut off. It was wonderful.'

Leo stepped back and the mattress sagged violently again, flicking Rachel's chair into a drunken see-saw. This time he didn't bother to stop her chair rocking. His eyes were glassy.

'My mum knew I was different, sensitive. She didn't make me play with other children, let me hide whenever the farmer came by – which wasn't often, I can tell you! Mum didn't encourage visitors, said they caused too much mess and disruption. Even when Tim was allowed to stay, we would go through the house afterwards, spring cleaning. My mum taught me fire was clean, although really it was Tim – did you know I used to call him Dad? He wanted to adopt me, make it official. He and my mum had an understanding. Mum said that was enough. Tim understood: he was a private man, with no family he was interested in acknowledging. He loved to come to us on the moor, live in our silence. He tried to teach me about plants and I did learn – enough to be able to pick up more detail later, before I sabotaged your father's work. But I wasn't really interested. Plants were dirty, full of horrid insects. So he showed me fire instead.'

Leo was off the bed now, staring up at her with the look of a convert on his face. Rachel recalled what Michael had learned from Tim Stevens' neighbour: Tim's own fascination with fire, revealed in his manic burning spree before he died. Had he been cleansing his life then? Respecting the obsessive secrecy of Leo's mother? *I used to call him Dad.*

Rachel felt sweat break out on her again. She had to get Leo back on the bed, stop him staring at the clothes piled as kindling round the mattress.

'It must have been hard for you, Leo. Losing your father so soon after your mother. Being unable to pay your last respects.'

Leo shrugged. 'Funerals are nothing. I went to my mum's, although she didn't want anyone there. Said the living should get on with living. She made Tim promise he wouldn't come. I heard about Tim's cremation from Charlie Elsham: he phoned me whilst I was sweating in bed in Manchester. Told me you'd come but that you hadn't cried.'

'Tim was a fine man, Leo. I miss him.'

'Not half so much as I do.' Leo's dark eyes were black with tears. He let them fall without wiping them away, a silent tribute to grief.

'I started to plan then.' Leo gulped, then went

363

on. 'A way to bring you and Daniel to justice. To make you suffer as my dad suffered before he died.'

'Daniel?'

'After you blew the whistle in Rio, Daniel left Tim and Charlie to cope alone. He saved his own skin, like you. But he didn't know about me. He didn't know Tim had left a son to avenge him.'

'You wanted Daniel to be blamed for the arson attacks. That's why we're here, at his home.'

Leo glanced down at his waist, frowning. Had he missed her penknife from his belt? No, he was working his hand into a pocket, bringing out the matches again.

'I'd planned it so that he would be charged with your murder. The attack on the road by your cottage – I'd no alibi for that, but I knew the forensics would show strands from blond hair and fibres from designer clothes when the police finally scoured the bushes where I'd hidden. I thought that would keep the police off my back and I was right. The police have disappointed me, though. I'd expected Daniel to be arrested before my sleight-of-hand with his mobile. I suppose he always had wonderful alibis – and of course his county connections would make a plod like Joe Penoyre wary.

'It was all a long-term plan, a long-term thing. My mum said all good things come to those who wait. Tim taught me how to wait – I'd waited for him long enough, when he went off on those botanical trips. So after he died – because of you, Rachel – I went to work at Kestrel House. It was always you I was after. Daniel coming to work there was a bonus. He made no secret of your joint past, although I knew it already. But your history together gave me a perfect finish: Daniel was going to be my mop-up man. While the police were busy with him, I'd make my getaway.'

'And Daniel was there at the first fire, wasn't he?' *Keep talking, Leo.*

'Oh, yes, the wastebin fire. A rapid swap of metal bins and stashing yours in the Gents – in, out with a pass key, whilst you were checking your father's lab. The beauty of working with Daniel was that I was right below you. Even in that house I could hear you moving about and slip upstairs to the Gents and your office whilst you were occupied.'

Leo sniggered. 'I was going to provide an interesting trigger, but then I heard Lorna waddling back and thought I'd better make myself scarce in the Gents again. And then you beat me to it, setting the whole thing going with your cigarette.' He wagged a finger. 'That was very naughty of you, Rachel, but rather fun. You really thought it was your fault – that did make me laugh!'

Registering that Michael had been right about the wastebin fire – that had Leo not been interrupted, it would have been much worse – Rachel said aloud, 'But you must have had pass keys for the second fire.'

'The blazing stag's head.' Leo nodded. 'And the rat bait on the alarm wires. A double midnight escapade with a dopy Lucy as my alibi again. I was rather proud of that.'

His voice trailed off. Hearing Stephen Lees'

attempted murder and Moll's death dismissed as a caper, Rachel forced herself to ask, 'Was that intended for me, Leo?'

'Only indirectly, Rachel. I knew by then how disgustingly sentimental you were over the dog.'

Thoughtfully, Leo struck a match, watched it flare, blew it out. 'I did wonder whether to dispose of Paul and Angwen, but then I thought they should suffer as I have. They can blub over your charred remains. And Daniel – I know he's with the police now, but he'll still be under suspicion. Penoyre will never quite be sure if Daniel hired someone to do it. And if Daniel does walk free – well, he'll have lost his moorland home.' Leo's voice hardened. 'As I did.'

'Your mother didn't leave you the cottage?' Rachel asked, quickly. Anything to keep him talking. The smell of smoke was constant now. What was going on out there? She could see nothing in this closed, curtained room.

'I didn't want it, I sold it.' Leo said petulantly. 'Tim had given me money: he was generous to Mum and me. That gave me the working capital I needed for my American trips.'

He grinned, a smile that, even in the stuffy airless bedroom, chilled Rachel. 'You can buy anything in America, transport it in hand luggage. That's where I got hold of the "ping-pong" balls I used to burn you up – did you like my recording of the car crash? I loved the way you hared out of your cottage. And nobody saw anything; it was nothing but a stroll for me from Darcombe. Give me wide open spaces. I'm flying out to America when I've tidied up here, starting a clean new life.'

He shook his dark head wonderingly.

'When I first spoiled Paul's work to get him to turn to his high-profile daughter for support, I wasn't sure if I could carry it through. The day you were appointed as acting director, I didn't know whether to cheer or throw up. You know the thing that really set me going, Rachel? That stupid television programme, *The High Country*. You were so high and mighty: you acted as if you had it all. I decided then you had to go. You're a frivolous, worthless person. Red-heads are cheap, that's what my mum said. If you could see yourself, untidy, uncombed, blood on your common little face. I had to wash it off before I put you up there.'

Rachel made herself smile, kept her voice comfortable. Leo was working himself up, and needed no help from her. 'Must have been hard for you to wear that grubby lab-coat, Leo. Must have taken a lot of self-discipline. I was completely taken in.'

'You and everyone else. But it was difficult. And when Charlie appeared, that was difficult, too. Almost threw me off balance.'

Panicked him into early action, Rachel translated in her own mind. The return of Charles Elsham, the only man who knew of Leo's close ties to Tim Stevens, had provided the final impetus and justification for Leo to escalate his arson and stalking campaign.

'But I used the time well,' Leo was saying, 'Charlie made me accelerate my activities, but I stayed sharp. No one saw me in Darcombe when

367

I slashed your car tyre: I could watch the police station from Sharon's and pick a time when no one was about.'

'Sharon?'

Leo laughed. 'Another of my girls, Rachel – keep up! After the police had come and gone at my place I left Lucy making lunch whilst I went out for some wine. I told Lucy I was going to the other end of Tavistock, but drove on to Darcombe. Sharon had given me her key whilst she was away on holiday in Greece – I'd arranged to look after her place. Of course, Sharon didn't know why I was so keen to oblige, but her house gives a grandstand view of the High Street and police station. I was able to leave Tim's old machete there too, use it, pop it in Sharon's attic, nip back to Tavistock and buy my wine plus glamorous gift for Lucy.

'Yes, I stayed sharp,' Leo repeated. 'Tim's wisdom helped me there, his knowledge of fire. Until Tim started coming to our cottage we'd never bothered with bonfire night. My mum liked a good garden fire, but it was Tim who showed me the joy of a real big blaze – with the guy on top, of course.'

Leo struck another match and let it burn. 'Kestrel House is being immolated this afternoon, right about now, in fact. A few well-placed incendiaries and timing devices and this long spell of dry weather. Very easy. I doubt if the place will be gutted, but it'll keep the police and firemen busy – Michael Horton included. I know Michael's touchingly concerned with his fellow watch-members. I expected the police to suspect him too. You know, the eager volunteer, lusting for glory.'

He flicked the burning match at the mattress, laughing as Rachel flinched. 'We won't be disturbed here. Not till I'm long gone and you're long dead. You do have something in common with Mum. Know what?'

Instinct prompted, and she trusted what it told her. There was no time for anything else. 'We're both wart-charmers.'

'Witches, Rachel.' Leo wagged a reproving finger. 'Daniel would groan on about your Brazilian exploits, but I'd guessed already. It's an old country superstition that witches have red hair, and in your case it's true.'

'And your mother?' Rachel broke in, seeing Leo poised to strike another match. The last had gone out in a puff of twirling smoke.

Leo scowled. 'I told you. My mum thought red hair common.' Lighting the match, he plucked one of Daniel's shirts from the bed and began to scorch the pristine collar. 'My mum was a white witch. Her fear was water, but she told me most witches hated fire.'

The shirt collar had begun to smoulder and vent tiny leaping flames. Leo watched, utterly absorbed. 'I checked you for witch marks when I stripped you off. That strawberry mole by your temple was enough, though I was disappointed you didn't have more. I was planning to stick pins in them.'

He'd gone beyond reason. If she begged, it might only inspire his cruelty. She heard the whoosh as Daniel's best shirt crackled into flames, felt the heat beating up her body in stultifying waves.

'This is going to get very messy, Leo,' she warned, attacking the one point she hoped would tempt him to leave the room. 'Fire may be clean but burning flesh isn't.'

'Oh, you needn't worry, Rachel, you'll be gone long before that. And so will I. This mattress gives off toxic fumes as it burns – at least it will now. I've covered it with a wonderful chemical whose name I won't bore you with. You'll be overcome in about five minutes and dead in ten. By then of course your witch's funeral pyre will really be going. I'd intended a grand outdoor burning at the stake, but as a stop-gap this is quite acceptable and nicely private. You'll die alone. I think Tim would have been pleased with the justice of that.'

Leo dropped the burning shirt on the foot of the bed and backed from the room, closing the door after himself. Rachel heard him running downstairs and knew he'd not lied. She had less than five minutes.

Screaming would bring no rescuers in time: it would only hasten her end, drawing in more of the lethal cocktail of smog, toxic fumes and fire. Holding her breath, Rachel began to sway on her chair. Any risk of falling badly whilst strapped to the carver was a better chance than remaining fixed on top of this poisonous bed. She rocked fiercely, away from the side where the fire was catching, closing her eyes against the glare of the rising flames.

Her seat heeled over then crashed off the bed

against the wall, scraping her right shoulder and arm down Daniel's trendy burgundy paintwork. Part of the washing-line bound round her legs and feet hooked round another chair, tightening the cords further and flaying her thighs. The burns on her back were pools of molten agony – but the right-hand carver arm had splintered.

Rachel forced her battered right arm to jerk upwards, squirming within the little space of the washing-line. Seconds later she heard another satisfying crack and the carver arm came loose from the body of the chair.

Now she was able to slacken her bonds, clenching and working her arm and shoulder muscles against them till she had enough leeway to be able to stretch across with her right hand to take the penknife from the white-knuckled fingers of her left.

The blade was sharp enough to saw through the plastic-coated washing-line, but she was starting to have trouble breathing. Thick clouds of fumes, rolling like marsh gas, had begun seeping from beneath the Indian rug. The room was heating rapidly, fire running amok through the shirts and clothes and settling to gnaw at the chairs and mattress. Ten minutes, this place would be an inferno and she would have choked to death.

One end of the line was severed. Rachel began unwinding it, fingers groping as smoke scorched her eyes. Her ploy of pretending she was weaker than she was had in the end been of little use: it wasn't Leo she had to fight but the heavy, lethal black fumes.

Her left arm was out. She was free of the chair. Black smoke poured up to the roof. Legs still bound, right arm still enmeshed in the line and the splintered chair arm, Rachel dragged herself towards the door.

At first she thought the pounding was her heart, about to burst under the stress. Or maybe Leo, returning for a final gloat. Rasping and coughing, she head-butted the door, knowing if she stopped now she'd never move again: the fumes would have her.

She couldn't force the door. She heard the dull scrape of a chair leg. Leo had made sure, jamming a chair under the door knob. Gasping, Rachel rolled onto her back, which strangely wasn't hurting quite so much as before. The window was too far away, and double-glazed. She had nothing to throw through it, and hadn't the breath any more.

Flopping over onto her front, Rachel sucked the air from the bottom of the door. It wasn't whether she would live or die: breathing something more than that stinking cindery fug was all that mattered.

Something crashed – inside the room or out, Rachel couldn't tell, but she felt the door give. One final effort and the clean fresh air of the landing was hers. She slithered forward, clearing the threshold. Behind her Daniel's bedroom exploded, spouting fumes and flame.

Michael was calling her. Strong arms were pulling her further along the landing. Rachel forced air into her protesting lungs. 'No others!' she gasped.

Chapter 63

After that things got hazy. As she came round, Rachel found herself out of the burning wreck of the cottage. Michael had carried her down one field and across the Cherry Brook stream. She was lying in recovery position on fresh damp grass, wet cloths draped over her.

Trying to brace her body on her elbow, she felt a hand touch her shoulder, heard Michael's voice: 'You're safe. Help's coming.' A pair of grey eyes smiled at her as Michael brought his face level.

'How you find me?' she croaked.

'Ramon Gil slipped a tiny tracking bug into the pocket of your jump suit top. Luckily for everyone, you never felt it and Leo never spotted it.'

Rachel imagined the furtive, gleeful haste with which Leo must have peeled off her clothes. Her skin crawling, she shivered.

'Sssh.' Michael cradled her least injured hand in his, running his fingertips lightly over her nails. 'Such narrow little fingernails,' he murmured.

'Mike, I want to know–'

'Where Gil and Eusebio and Leo have gone to? I honestly don't know. In spite of what Ramon thinks about my revenging myself, I left him and his mate to go after Leo. All I'm concerned with is right here.'

'Saving lives,' whispered Rachel.

'Yes, but it's more than that with you.' Michael gave her hand a light, exasperated squeeze. 'Lie still.'

'And keep quiet?'

'Yes.'

'Kestrel–'

'Crews are already there and working. They'll get the moor under control, and faster now that it's raining.'

She felt it, then, cool and soft against her eyelids. The drought had broken. Rachel lay quiet, enjoying the soft mist breaking on her face and hair, listening to the distant grumble and spit of the burning cottage and the welcome peal of an approaching siren.

Chapter 64

Two weeks later Rachel had lunch with Helen at a favourite restaurant in Topsham. It was a farewell lunch before Helen returned to London, then America.

Rachel was almost as glad as she was sorry. There was a constraint between them now. She and Helen remained friends, but their association had cooled. They'd still be working together when Helen returned from the States, but each had more pressing commitments.

Driving them to Topsham, Helen came briskly to the point. 'Mike made it pretty clear the day of the moors fire that he wasn't interested in me or in visiting the States – nicely, but for keeps. So when are you two going to stop hedging and make the announcement? I expect to be maid of honour, only don't make me wear frills. Or sashes.'

'Helen!' Rachel protested. 'Michael's been snowed under with work these last few days. The dig's started again, he's teaching at the university, he's got the two Colombian researchers at Kestrel House and he's been on fire-watch and training drills. I've been run off my feet. Edie Fleming wants to show off her new son when she returns next week from Nigeria, academics and visitors are flooding in this month, there's the symposium in July to prepare for and we're interviewing in less than two weeks for replacements for Leo and Daniel.'

Helen dropped into low gear as they followed local traffic in the June sun towards a tiny roundabout. 'I imagine you're glad there still is a Kestrel House,' she said, peering ahead. The moorland fire had been brought under control before it could touch the surrounding walls.

'We were very lucky.'

'Leo would say he had miscalculated.' Helen continued to probe. 'Colin told me this morning that he still hasn't been found. That doesn't worry you?'

Rachel unconsciously scratched the strawberry mole on her left temple. Thinking of her own plan and the secret weapon she now carried, she said, 'I'm not going to hide from him. He's already tried his last grand vengeance and failed. I can't see him coming back. Nor does the inspector.'

Ramon Gil, of whom Helen knew nothing except for a name which she'd fortunately forgotten, had also disappeared, along with Eusebio. Rachel's police protection had been scaled down.

Helen changed the subject. 'Kestrel House won't be the same without Daniel Plewes-Mason.'

Released by the police, Daniel had tendered his resignation whilst Rachel was still in hospital. Taking leave due to him, he had already gone. His 'revenge' had been businesslike: Daniel was going to work for Fultons again, although not in Brazil. The Gapo tribe, flexing the strength that Kew and Aoira's healing tree had given them, had insisted that the pharmaceutical giant have no stake in their part of Amazonia.

The Gapo had invited Rachel to return – there'd be no more difficulty with an entry visa for a young woman described as 'saviour of a noble native people' by the *Journal do Brasil*. Deeply moved by the offer, Rachel had not yet responded, although she knew she must soon.

Silent whilst Helen nonchalantly took the last space in the tiny carpark close to the bowling-green, Rachel was confounded when Helen observed, 'Life's been pretty hectic for you, especially with the media love-bombing of the last week. But I noticed you weren't too busy to move out of Mike's.'

'It was an understood thing. Michael knows I value my independence.'

'Sure,' Helen said. Rachel closed off further discussion by slipping on a pair of sunglasses and a huge floppy sunhat.

In the restaurant, flicking off Rachel's sunhat for her and plomping it down on the green table-cloth, Helen said, 'Well, here we are. Just about in one piece.'

Conscious of their new awkwardness, Rachel smiled and said, 'As this is a glad-to-be-alive lunch, I'll treat us to some champagne. Or would you prefer sparkling wine?'

'Oh, bubbly for me.'

'Maybe we should drink it from the pianist's shoes.'

'No thanks!'

A small pause whilst she and Helen glanced over the menus, broken by Helen suddenly leaning forward across their circular table. 'Has Colin told you he'll be wanting a leave of absence?'

Rachel shook her head. 'What's going on with you two?' she asked mischievously. It was well known by now that Colin and Helen spent most of their free time together.

'It's not the way you think, Rachel,' Helen said, nettled. 'Colin's got no chance with me personally, but he'll be wonderful in front of camera. At Discovery and PBS they really lap up your serious English types with beards. He'll be a great gimmick for my natural history work.'

'He's going to be working for you in America?'

'Sure. What Colin doesn't know about trees is no odds to anyone.'

The champagne had arrived. Rachel took a sip whilst she considered this news. Learning of Colin Benwick's interest in her, which appeared as much grounded in dislike as in attraction, she'd first considered him a threat, then had lately dismissed him as another obsessed loner. Yet it had been Colin who had helped the police and fire crew find Joe Penoyre, following Michael's tip-off. Given no time, Michael had only had the chance to say 'Inspector Penoyre's unconscious in the arboretum,' before Gil had cut the mobile connection. Without Colin's knowledge, it would have taken much longer to find Joe Penoyre and bring him out to safety.

Rachel could respect Dr Benwick for that, although watching Helen raising her champagne flute in self-congratulation, she wondered how Colin and Helen would hit it off in America.

Draining her glass and recklessly pouring, Rachel said, 'So how did all this happen? Did Colin have any idea of jetting to the States before you approached him?'

'Far from it. He was brutally resistant.' Helen wrinkled her nose whilst fiddling with her napkin. 'But I've always enjoyed a challenge. And I made him an offer he couldn't refuse.' She held out her glass for a top-up.

A waitress appeared, order pad in hand. Across the small room, other diners gossiped happily whilst the pianist conjured a Gershwin medley from the keys. Keen to hear more from Helen, Rachel picked the first thing on the menu and waited impatiently for Helen to choose her main course. 'How on earth did you persuade him? Come on, Helen, I'm dying to know.'

'Pure charm.' Helen gave her glass a bright little ping with her fork. Her blue eyes gleamed. 'This summer I may go to work on Colin a bit.

Close to, that beard of his is really rather cute. Mind you, the accent will fox them in the States. They'll probably think he's Australian.'

Rachel laughed and raised her glass, wondering whether Colin Benwick knew what he was letting himself in for.

Chapter 65

'I don't like it,' Michael said.

He was with Inspector Penoyre, snatching a midday drink in the beer garden of the Darcombe Arms – the same inn where a few months earlier he and Helen had spent a pleasant evening together. Although only a season had passed since then, it seemed years ago, a distant, pleasing memory with no regrets. He'd made his choice. Whatever Rachel decided in the end, even if it was 'no', Michael knew there was no other for him.

But Rachel had withdrawn, shutting him out. Leaving hospital, she'd plunged into her work and filming – ironically she saw more of Helen now than he ever had, even when seeing Helen had been a bonus to him. Rachel asked no questions, not even about Ramon Gil.

Attempting to break through, Michael had explained how he'd been shanghaied by the Brazilian in London. His terse account, given whilst Rachel was in hospital for the second time, had not gone well.

Appalled by her injuries – though assured by the nurses and by Rachel herself that they looked worse than they were – Michael had been wrung out with a mixture of pity and anger. Afraid to tire her, to trouble her, to explode into fury himself, he'd been taciturn and stiff.

Rachel had coolly accepted his apology for snapping at her on the day of the moor fire. 'I do understand, Michael, how frantic you must have been. Hearing me blathering on about a contract killer who'd threatened murder if any of us so much as breathed his name.'

Perfectly reasonable. If Rachel had yelled at him, had smacked him one, Michael felt he could have borne it more easily. He missed her essential spikiness, her quirkiness. She never teased him now.

Leo, Gil and Eusebio had not yet been picked up by the police. Was that the reason? Michael could only hope so, but the knowledge that she might be withdrawing from him because she cared, because she didn't want him hurt, made it hard to fill his frenzied, empty days.

Rachel didn't know, but he kept watch now every night by her cottage, including those nights when he was on call.

'Michael?' Joe Penoyre reached across the wooden table and shook him by the shoulder. 'Not sleeping too well these days?'

Michael ground a knuckle into his aching eyes. 'I've had better nights. Please go on about Leo Cartwright.'

'We're doing everything we can, but resources are tight. That's why I've decided to withdraw the police presence from Kestrel House and Miss Falconer.'

'That'll tempt Leo to have another go at her. He's already proved how determined he is by planning a hate campaign for five years before actually starting it going.'

Joe Penoyre's thin lips tightened. He lifted his pint and drank deeply. Setting the glass down, he said, 'What do you suggest, Mike? Miss Falconer clearly feels uncomfortable with us around.'

'Better you than Leo or Ramon Gil.' Michael drained his cider and rose to his feet. 'Don't worry about a return drink, Joe, I ought to be getting back to the institute. I'm teaching in an hour or so.'

'Wait, Mike.' Joe Penoyre stopped him. 'I did ask you here for another reason. I've some good news. I just left a telephone message at Kestrel House with Paul and Angwen and a message on Miss Falconer's new answer-phone there.'

Michael resumed his bench seat. 'I thought those two were setting off to Wales this morning.'

'They are, but you know Paul. Angwen says she's used to his stopping off at the lab for a last look round by now; she expects and accepts it. And to be fair, Paul has a lot to take care of these days.'

'Umm.' In his own mind, Michael reluctantly conceded that Paul Falconer's dream of an effective vaccine for malaria had grown closer in the last few days. In spite of the fire at his lab, Paul's core research had been undamaged. Now news had come through that an American research institute had successfully reproduced

Paul's results following the same procedures. Once he and Angwen had returned from their Wales holiday, Paul was going to announce his findings at the symposium in July.

'Aren't you pleased for him? Angwen told me that his vaccine could save millions.'

'Of course I am.' Michael slid his empty glass along the wooden table from hand to hand. Yes, Paul deserved his triumph. Yes, he was pleased. But Ramon Gil and Leo Cartwright were still at large.

'My news might make you more enthusiastic. Exeter police contacted me thirty minutes ago. They've taken Charles Elsham into custody.'

'That's more like it!' Michael bounded to his feet, nodding at Joe Penoyre's rapidly diminishing half of bitter. 'Let me get you another.'

'No thanks, you're not the only one who ought to be moving.'

Michael set down the cider glass and held out his hand. 'Thanks, Joe. I appreciate your telling me.' They shook hands and parted.

Several hours later, Michael was preparing for a long night in the open near Rachel's cottage. He strode over the quarry tiles of his small kitchen area, impatient for the kettle to boil. For the last few nights he'd taken two flasks of black coffee with him, although he'd still dozed sometimes beside his camouflaged bike.

'Must be barking mad,' Michael muttered in self-disgust. Was this simply a method of putting off the day when he'd approach Rachel again to ask her out?

'She could ask me.' Alone in the cottage, Michael talked to himself, glowering at the slowly bubbling kettle. Rachel could ask him out, but so far she hadn't.

Knowing about the Gapo's request that Rachel return to Brazil didn't make Michael any happier. He knew she would be tempted: bright, ambitious, committed – how could she not be? And if she returned to the Amazon after her year as acting director, she'd surely be out of Leo's reach.

'Why can't the police find him and Gil?' Staring out of the kitchen window with hot eyes, Michael had no answers. Leo's Audi had been found abandoned close to Cherry Brook Bridge. Had he escaped Ramon Gil and the police on foot, on horseback or in another car? Dartmoor had its wild places, but police had scoured the likely ones. A search of nearby farmsteads, barns and hamlets had produced nothing, although local farmers and the local people were on their guard.

Someone must have taken Leo in. One of the sillier girls of his harem, Michael decided grimly, flicking off the electric kettle at the mains as it finally boiled. As for Ramon Gil and his sidekick, Michael knew the Brazilian would have made contingency plans. As a contract killer who had survived into retirement, Gil must be used to lying low.

'Bunch of scumbags,' Michael said aloud, filling the first flask. A rich swirling scent of coffee drifted into his nostrils, followed by a faint scent of new-mown hay.

Spinning round on the kitchen flags, Michael was facing the door as it opened wider.

'Finally I get you at home.' Leo walked in with the evening and motioned with a thumb towards the gravel path behind him. 'Now if you'd like to call off your dogs, we can work this out.'

Glancing outside, Michael caught the lengthening shadows of Ramon Gil and Eusebio. The Brazilian was in a grey lounge suit, slightly spattered at the ankles with fresh mud but otherwise immaculate. He had a pistol aimed at Leo's back.

'Ramon,' said Michael, with a calm he didn't feel. 'That isn't necessary.'

Ramon answered, 'Forgive me, but we were not fast enough in picking up the trail of this beast. Still, if he has beaten us here, now he is at bay.'

Leo sucked in an audible breath. Like Ramon Gil, his jeans and white shirt were pristine, his straight dark hair freshly showered. The only clue that he'd been involved in any kind of flight were his broken-down trainers. And the shining, joyous look in his slim tanned face. He looked like a man on the verge of a mystic experience, thought Michael.

Without turning, Leo drummed the metal object he had braced tightly in both hands. 'Would you mind explaining why it wouldn't be a good idea if anyone shoots me in the back?'

Leo's voice quickened, rising at the end, and Michael lost no time in answering. 'Ramon, that metal cylinder he has strapped to his shoulders is a part of a home-made flame-thrower.' It was pointed directly at him.

'Runs on a mix of diesel and petrol.' Leo grinned and joggled the narrow rifle-style barrel. 'Good, isn't it? Inspired and adapted from the gear foresters use to burn off desert scrub in southern California. Throws a ribbon of fire over twenty metres a time. So basically Michael, if I go, so will you and your dark little pals.'

'Nice idea, Leo. An instant fireball.'

Leo laughed. 'I like that, Michael. But then I've always liked you. Pity really that I'm going to have to use this toy on you, but after I'd heard about Rachel's latest escape I decided it was time for a change in tactics. After all, when Tim killed himself, I had to live with the knowledge that my love wasn't enough to save him. Now Rachel can learn to live with that same lesson.'

'No she won't,' said Rachel.

Leo staggered and crumpled without a cry. Michael kicked the trigger away from his limp fingers and straightened to find Rachel staring at him.

'Are you all right?' she asked.

Michael nodded, indicating the prone Leo with his eyes. 'What did you do to him?'

Rachel held out a tiny wooden pipe, no bigger than a descant recorder. 'I shot him with one of my old darts. I only had three, so I'm glad I could get in close. He'll wake up in an hour or so: the poison's only meant to stun fish.'

She turned to Ramon Gil and the Gapo. 'Will you leave this matter with us now? You've more than fulfilled any debt.'

Smiling as if Rachel was a particularly

promising pupil of his, Ramon Gil slipped on the safety catch of his pistol. 'We shall be delighted. Goodbye, Rachel ... Michael.'

First he was only a shadow, then a soft clinking of pebbles, then nothing. Eusebio had also vanished.

Another moment passed, then Michael heard Rachel drawing in a deep breath. 'I'm sorry, Michael. I was watching your house whenever I could. I wondered if Leo might try something on. There's never been a police guard here.'

'You were watching my place? But I was camped by yours! Every night for the last two weeks.'

'I know.' Rachel blushed. 'I did know,' she said shame-facedly, 'but I thought you'd be safer hidden amongst the roses than in your bedroom at home.' Her fiery blush deepened. 'He does seem to have a thing about bedrooms,' she murmured, pointing the tiny hunting-pipe at the crumpled, sleeping figure.

Staggered, Michael did not know what to say.

Rachel cleared her throat. 'I suppose we'd better call Joe Penoyre. Although it's tempting—'

'Looks harmless, doesn't he?' said Michael, conscious that Rachel was offering him a choice, and wanting to make the right choice. 'Like a young boy. Did you hear what he said about his love not being enough to save Tim?'

A tear ran down Rachel's cheek. 'I heard.'

She'd beaten the stalker, seen off Ramon Gil and most likely saved his life, thought Michael, and yet in that moment she looked utterly defenceless. Firmly stepping over their unconscious enemy, Michael took Rachel gently in his arms.

'Love you,' he said.

'Mmm,' said Rachel. 'Better tie him up.'

Chapter 66

Another week passed. Helen and Colin prepared for their trip to the States. Paul and Angwen remained on holiday in Wales – a well-deserved vacation, thought Rachel. She was tremendously proud of her father, and of Angwen for giving him a life outside Kestrel House. They were well suited, and, recalling how she had waved them off, Rachel hugged herself, delighted at their happiness. Sure of Paul now, Angwen had at last also thrown off her morning sickness and taken on the full bloom of pregnancy. Nut-brown skin, hair shining like black silk, Angwen was truly beautiful. She had a sexy stepmother, Rachel decided, laughing softly as she thought of her father's bulging eyes.

Sitting at her desk in her newly decorated office – minus the stag's head – Rachel shook herself out of her reverie and tried to concentrate on the application forms in front of her. It was late: the institute was quiet, and everyone but Stephen Lees had gone home. He'd just popped his head round her door to ask if she wanted anything and to show off the leggy, growing Meg.

'Do what you can, and stop meandering,'

Rachel told herself. She should be over the moon. Her father's vaccine was closer than ever to being realized. She'd achieved her other goal of protecting the Gapo's forest homelands. Her family were safe from persecution. Michael was safe. She had nothing more to fear from any stalker. With Paul's achievement, funding had been raised well beyond the needs of field-testing and the future of Kestrel House was now assured. And that morning, the Darcombe surgery had phoned: her new smear was normal.

So why wasn't she dancing round her freshly painted office?

Footsteps on the main stairway, a longed-for moment.

'May I come in?'

'Be my guest.'

When Joseph Penoyre strolled into her office, Rachel furtively wiped the treacherous tears of disappointment from her eyes. She was, in her mother's phrase, 'a real watering-can' these days. Maybe it was to do with shock. Squeezing her fingernails into her palms, Rachel rose to greet her visitor. 'Good to see you again.' She smiled to disguise her watery vision.

'And you.' Joe Penoyre beamed back. He had a new blue suit on, new blue braces. He looked energized, thought Rachel, moving away from her desk to settle the policeman on one of a trio of large new comfortable chairs.

When Penoyre sank into the nearest, stretching out and crossing his sinewy legs, Rachel bit back the mischievous, 'Why are you so pleased with yourself?' Sticking to convention, she lifted the warming cafetière off its stand. 'Coffee?'

'No thanks, this is only a flying visit.' Joseph Penoyre uncrossed his legs and sat up. 'Charles Elsham has been extradited to Italy. And Leo Cartwright is in a remand centre up north. I wouldn't be surprised if he pleads guilty, you know. After trial it's likely he'll spend a considerable amount of time anyway in a secure psychiatric unit.'

Rachel nodded, thinking of the flirtatious young man in the spectacularly spotted lab-coat. 'At least there he'll receive some treatment.' She looked Joe Penoyre straight in the eye. 'Leo didn't fit any of the textbook examples of an arsonist, did he? Wrong age, no obvious motive, no lingering by the fires, no witnesses.'

Penoyre pursed his lips. 'We were thrown rather by the phone calls and his different MOs, too, but there were clues in his background. Now we know Leo's genuine past, as much of it as we'll ever learn.

'He was certainly a ladies' man. He spent the last few days and weeks before and after the Kestrel House fire comfortably holed up with the owner of a riding-school centre. That's how he moved on the moor when he fled from Daniel's house – on horseback. We'd already questioned the owner and her stable girls early in the course of the investigation, and later, after Leo went missing, but none of the stable hands knew of Leo's advent and the woman herself was completely besotted. Gave him any alibi he wanted. Remains convinced of his innocence.'

Listening, Rachel said sadly, 'Women were

Leo's great shield. He fooled all of us. And with Daniel and Charles Elsham always looking so much likelier suspects–' She stopped. 'Sorry, I know it was difficult. I'm really relieved and grateful that you've caught him.'

She wondered if he was going to ask the question that burned behind his hard little eyes. Had she found it hard to give Leo up to the law?

There was a small silence. The inspector glanced at his watch. 'I'd best be off, Miss Falconer.'

Rachel nodded, relieved Penoyre had not asked. Walking with him out of her office and down the stairs, she said, 'Now you've finished here, could you bring yourself to call me Rachel? Surely you've been formal long enough.'

'You're right.' Pausing on the steps, Joe Penoyre held out a hand. 'Goodbye, Rachel. And good luck.'

'The same, Joe.'

After he'd gone, Kestrel House seemed worse than deserted, it oppressed Rachel as an alien presence. She did not want to remain in it for another instant. What had she to stay for? Michael had told her he loved her, but still he had not come.

Their quarrel on the day of the moor fire, her earlier jealousy of Helen: these silly differences no longer mattered. What did it matter these days who made the move, so long as it was made? Yet each time in his presence Rachel found herself paralysed by shyness – or was it a perverse pride? The thing she cleaved to was that if Michael had saved her, she had saved him. They were quits.

Scowling at her reflection in the double doors, Rachel let herself out of Kestrel House and went in search of Stephen Lees.

Ten minutes later, on the beautiful, lonely drive to her cottage, her eyes kept straying towards her mobile phone. Rachel kept her hands tight on the steering-wheel. She didn't want to whine. She didn't want Michael's pity.

The thunder of a motor-bike behind had Rachel joyously glancing in her rear-view mirror, but it wasn't the grey Norton. Willing her heart-beat to subside, Rachel stolidly faced front as the biker buzzed past into the twilight.

She rumbled over the cattle grid, nursed the diesel up the steep, twisting hill and at last tipped over the rise.

Her cottage was ahead, and a full summer moon and the evening star. Accelerating duti-fully, although her spirits felt dim, blotted out in spite of this deep ultramarine sky and golden moon, Rachel cleared the farmstead's beech hedge.

Astonishment widened her eyes.

She backed the car off the road, stalled the engine in front of the ancient garage and scrambled from the driver's seat. Dashing past the dark cottage, Rachel ran into the blazing orchard.

Everywhere she looked, there were lights. Coloured lights, twinkling fairy lights, lanterns, torches. Hung from branches, wound round twigs, nestled in tree-forks, the orchard shone out a thousand welcomes that drew her in as surely as the blundering moths. And on the orchard floor, drifts of white and red roses, spelling out the words, 'Stay here with me.'

'Oh, lover!' The West Country epithet rose naturally to her lips.

'Should I take that as a yes?'

Rachel started as Michael came out of the blue shadows. He'd been sitting on the orchard wall, waiting. Now he advanced, dressed in green cords and mallard jumper. His best clothes.

Seeing him finally here where she wanted him, Rachel felt her feelings expanding again, opening and deepening as instinct and reason combined to say this was it.

'Shouldn't you be wearing a suit?'

'Later.' Michael swept her right off her feet, carrying Rachel into the arching lighted bower of the pear-trees. Suddenly he stopped, fawn eye-brows bent together in a frown. 'That was a yes?'

'Absolutely.' Rachel raised her mouth to his as Michael lowered his head, kissing her with a passionate intensity that left no doubts of his feelings.

'Michael, listen – no, wait, I have to say this.' Rachel managed to turn her head slightly away. 'After we made love that first time, I wondered if it was because you'd felt sorry for me, my being injured–'

'Daft creature!'

Rachel gave him a look of affectionate appraisal. Michael still needed some work done on him, she thought, and someone had to do it.

The publishers hope that this book has given you enjoyable reading. Large Print Books are especially designed to be as easy to see and hold as possible. If you wish a complete list of our books please ask at your local library or write directly to:

Magna Large Print Books
Magna House, Long Preston,
Skipton, North Yorkshire.
BD23 4ND

This Large Print Book for the partially sighted, who cannot read normal print, is published under the auspices of

THE ULVERSCROFT FOUNDATION

Other MAGNA Titles
In Large Print